DEEP CONTROL

MIKE SEARES

Vinci Books

vinci-books.com

Published by Vinci Books Ltd in 2025

1

Copyright © Mike Seares 2021

The author has asserted their moral right to be identified as the author of this work in accordance with the Copyright, Designs and Patents Act 1988. This work is a work of fiction. Names, characters, places and incidents are the product of the author's imagination or are used fictitiously. Any resemblance to actual persons, living or dead, places and incidents is entirely coincidental.

All rights reserved. No part of this publication may be copied, reproduced, distributed, stored in any retrieval system, or transmitted in any form or by any means, including photocopying, recording, or other electronic or mechanical methods, nor used as a source for any form of machine learning including AI datasets, without the prior written permission of the publisher.

The publisher and the author have made every effort to obtain permissions for any third party material used in this book and to comply with copyright law. Any queries in this respect should be brought to the attention of the publisher and any omissions will be corrected in future editions.

A CIP catalogue record for this book is available from the British Library.

Paperback ISBN: 9781036704018

Printed and bound in Great Britain by Clays Ltd, Elcograf S.p.A.

By Mike Seares

The John McCready Thriller Series

Deep Steal
Deep Impact
Deep Hostage
Deep Control

Chapter One

One month ago

The nine-inch rat scuttled along the narrow tunnel sniffing the air as it went. It was trying to search out something to eat. Dark gray in color, it had long white whiskers that stuck out from either side of its nose, allowing it to feel its environment, even when it was pitch-black.

Several hours earlier it had found a quiet place to hide up and rest. But its ever-vigilant senses had alerted it to possible danger, springing it awake, ready for any threat to its well-being and safety.

The rat was well used to the concept of fight or flight, and while its usual response was flight, it had no problem, when cornered, in fighting to the death if necessary, though for obvious reasons it hadn't found the need to do so yet.

However, when it had been woken, there had seemed to be no immediate threat. It was merely noise that was the disturbance. There had been a clanging and banging coming from about ten feet from where it had been hiding.

It had carefully moved forward from the dark corner and watched through the slatted metal ceiling a few inches above its head as a number of men maneuvered a large object on a cradle-like trolley into the area beyond its hiding place. The object was about thirty feet long and cylindrical in shape, and partially hidden by the thick metal bars of the cradle. It was being pushed by a small vehicle and it looked like it was heavy. Not that the rat would have noticed, but on the side was a symbol. It was black and yellow and similar to how you might imagine a whirling propeller to look. Immediately above it was the Chinese word for CAUTION, and immediately below, the one for DANGER.

After the men had positioned it in the middle of the space, the vehicle had disappeared. The men had then grabbed a series of wide webbing straps and secured the object to the floor.

They had then left.

About five minutes after they'd gone one of them had returned and headed straight toward where the rat was hiding. He had been carrying a small metal box with wires protruding from both sides. He'd approached the dark corner and reached down to a section of the floor. He'd then pulled it up, revealing a large compartment beneath.

The rat had wanted to run, but the smell of something the man had been eating overpowered any fear it had. As the man had worked in the compartment he'd placed a half-eaten burger in a wrapper on the floor. The rat had wanted to grab the food, but it was too close to the man. Too risky. The man had his arms in the compartment and was using some sort of tool. He worked away for several minutes. As he did so, he kept glancing around nervously.

Clearly, he wasn't meant to be there either.

Finally, he was finished. He had peered down into the compartment to make a last check.

At this, the rat had scuttled away, not wanting to be caught. It had stopped a few feet down the dark tunnel and looked back.

A second later and the top of the compartment had been closed with a bang, causing the rat to scurry further along the space beneath the floor.

After about twenty minutes there had been another loud noise. At first there had been a mechanical boom, as though something was closing, then later, a high-pitched whine that grew louder and louder. The rat had scurried deeper into the crevices and hidden in fear of this new danger. It had stayed there for quite some time, even managing to sleep.

But when it had awoken, it was still hungry.

So now, with renewed confidence, it was heading back along the underfloor space to where the man had been working, and from where there was the lingering smell of food.

Once the rat reached the compartment, it looked around. From all sides there was a steady drone and vibration, but it was more concerned about finding something to eat. The burger was gone, but some sauce and bits of meat had fallen into the compartment in the space beneath the floor.

The rat squeezed through a hole in the back and found the food. What was left of the meat was wedged behind some wires leading from the box the man had put in place. The wires led off either side and disappeared into other parts of the surrounding structure. On the front of the box was a screen. The rat had no interest in this, but if it had, it would have seen four numbers displayed on a digital display.

The first was a zero. This was followed by an eight. There were then two dots aligned vertically. The last two numbers were three and six. Every minute, the right-hand number reduced by one. Above the screen were two lights.

One had the word TRANSMIT next to it. The light was on and glowing red.

One had the word ARMED next to it. The light was on and glowing red.

The rat ignored the display and grabbed the wires with its front feet. The meat from the burger was behind the wires. It would be difficult to get to.

Fifty feet from the rat the captain of the Boeing 767 banked the massive machine round to follow the air corridor to the west of Thailand and on over the Bay of Bengal.

The two-man crew were members of the Chinese military and their mission was of the utmost secrecy. Even the aircraft being used was decked out to look innocuous and unremarkable. There were windows down the sides, but all the seats had been removed to allow the interior to be filled with cargo. The outside was white, with no markings, and a loading ramp had been added at the rear. But this flight was carrying only one thing; a very special item that was the property of the Chinese government.

The captain checked the systems and then settled in for the rest of the flight to South Africa, their final destination.

They had originated from an air base in the Guangxi region in southern China. The flight had no digital identifiers or beacons of any kind and would be blind to all tracking software used by people across the globe to follow aircraft as they sped through the skies.

The plane, for all intents and purposes, did not exist.

The rat was becoming ever more desperate. It could smell the food and it was driving it mad. But the wires were in the way. It reckoned if it could just get through them it could reach the meat lying on the other side.

It moved forward and opened its mouth, revealing two long razor-sharp incisors.

Rats had been known to gnaw through concrete to get to where they wanted to go, so the flimsy plastic coating of the wires was no trouble at all. Even the wire itself was made fast work of.

It bit through the final red wire in a cluster at the bottom and then cautiously moved forward for its prize—the morsels of meat behind.

It was completely oblivious to the screen on the box.

If it had looked, it would have seen that when it bit through the final wire, the numbers started changing rapidly. What had previously been a slow, predictable reduction of digits every minute now became a rapid torrent of falling numbers, heading in only one direction—00:00.

The numbers on the left were now at ZERO.

The two numbers on the right were counting down fast.

A second later and the right-hand number reached ZERO. There was a beep, a moment of silence, and then a large BANG.

The explosion took out the box and the cables and wires surrounding it.

The cables that led off into the plane were completely severed. Also, at the top of the box, the now cracked light with the word TRANSMIT next to it was no longer glowing.

The rat was hurled back by the blast, knocked unconscious with the impact on the far side of the compartment.

After a few minutes it came to. When it worked out

where it was, it stared briefly at the remains of the box and then scuttled away as fast as it could.

There had to be easier ways of finding food.

In the cockpit, Captain Zhao and the co-pilot heard the explosion. It was not loud, muffled by the noise from the aircraft and the depths of the hold from where it originated, but there was a sudden judder to the airframe and the captain's instinct told him something wasn't right. He exchanged a glance with the co-pilot. He was about to stand to go and investigate when there was a violent dip in the plane's attitude. He looked back at the controls and instruments and his face filled with shock and horror.

All the screens were blank.

And the aircraft had gone into a dive.

The reason for this was soon apparent. The quiet in the cabin indicated the two engines had shut down. The plane was now gliding steeply and was on a one-way ticket to the waiting water below.

Zhao leaned back in his seat and tightened the double harness over his shoulders. He gripped the controls and pulled back on the U-shaped yoke. The plane started to respond, but you could only do so much with an airliner-sized aircraft with no engines.

The co-pilot grabbed the radio, but when he tried to send a distress call he didn't even get static.

It was also dead.

And because of the secrecy of the flight, no one knew where they were and that they were in trouble.

They were on their own.

Zhao glanced out of the windows. The night was clear

and the weather fine. There were stars across the sky. The bright gleam of the moon cast a pale glow over everything. At least they would be able to see where they were going. The forecast had been good, so the sea would be flat when they eventually reached it, which by current reckoning would not be long. They were losing altitude at around a thousand feet per minute. He knew from his training that at their current cruising altitude of 29,000 feet they could glide for around a hundred miles. What he didn't know was their exact position. And while under normal circumstances he would have turned and headed for shore, there was no way he was going to try to bring the aircraft down in this condition on land, and definitely not with the cargo it was carrying. Any attempt to do so, even if they survived, would be met with brutal punishment, possibly even death, from his superiors. No, he'd just have to try and put her down in the water and see what options they had if they were still alive.

Zhao was trying to work out their location when the moonlight revealed the glassy water below. It was the perfect night to attempt a landing, but there were no guarantees as to the outcome.

He nodded at the co-pilot. Both of them steeled themselves for what they knew would be the most terrifying few minutes of their lives.

The huge aircraft dropped ever lower.

Out of the corner of his eye the captain noticed a large cargo ship about a thousand feet below them, but then it was gone and his focus was back on the rapidly approaching water ahead.

It came closer and closer and then he braced himself.

At the last moment, he pulled back on the yoke, aiming

to pull the plane up at an acute angle and stall the airframe in the hope it would flop back onto the water.

It almost worked.

The plane rose up in the air but then rolled to one side. The port wing hit first, flinging the 767 round, almost ripping the engine from the wing. The nose smashed into the water. The pilots were thrown forward hard, the G-forces knocking them unconscious, but the seatbelts saving them from being hurled through the windows.

The plane spun horizontally, throwing a massive plume of spray high into the air and an impact wave off toward the horizon.

It then settled in the water.

A minute later all was quiet.

But beneath the waterline damage had been done to the belly of the beast. A section midway down the plane had been torn open. Water thundered in, slowly rising up through the compartments and spilling over through holes and cracks in the superstructure caused by the crash.

When Captain Zhao came to, water was seeping under the cockpit door. He glanced around in a daze, trying to remember what had happened. It came back to him all too quickly as the water sloshed around his ankles. He undid his straps and looked over at the co-pilot. He was still in his seat, but it was clear he was dead—it looked like the whiplash from the impact had broken his neck. He stood up and crossed over to make sure. He raised the co-pilot's head and checked for a pulse, but it was no good. He laid his head gently back down and then looked around the cockpit for the emergency equipment. He knew there was a raft in the cargo bay, but basic supplies like food and water, a knife, flashlight and flares were kept in a locker at the rear of the cockpit. He crossed over to it and pulled the door open. He grabbed the pack and hoisted it onto his shoulders. He then took a last glance around in case there was anything else that could be of use.

There was nothing.

The water was now halfway to his knees. He could feel the angle of the aircraft starting to shift. He didn't have long.

He moved to the door and grabbed the handle.

He turned it and pulled.

And nothing happened.

He yanked it as hard as he could, but it was no good. It was stuck fast. The impact must have twisted the frame.

He started sweating. His heart rate was thumping. He dropped the backpack and tried again, putting all his strength into opening the door. It was quite literally the door to the rest of his life.

The water was up past his knees now, the plane tipping even more. It was at forty-five degrees. He didn't have long.

He reached for the handle, put one foot against the bulkhead at the side, and pulled for all he was worth.

But it was no good.

The water was now above his chest. He was about to make one last effort when the fuselage jerked alarmingly. Out of the window, the captain could see the black of the night sky and the myriad of stars, and he knew he was not long for this Earth. He said a quick prayer, and a brief, final message to his wife and daughter they would never hear, and then the waters closed around him, sealing his fate forever.

The plane slipped almost silently below the calm waters of the Bay of Bengal.

There was barely a ripple as the nose was fittingly the last to disappear. There were a few spouts of gas that had been trapped in the fuselage, which were expelled like the breaths of impatient whales, but then she was gone.

For around a minute there was nothing to see across the surface, but then one by one a number of objects started to appear. Somehow they had become dislodged from the sinking plane and their buoyancy had brought them up.

One of the objects was a large wooden box of food supplies that had been in the galley. It broke through the surface and bobbed innocently in the vast expanse of water.

A couple of minutes later there appeared to be movement from within. The box wobbled. A broken splinter of wood was pushed to one side, and the inquisitive nose of a rat appeared. It sniffed the salty air and then ran out of the box and onto the top. It looked around. There was nothing to see in any direction. It paused for a moment, adjusting to the new world it now found itself in, but then it ran back inside. It wasn't particularly worried, the pile of biscuits and crackers it had found would be more than enough to keep it going for quite some time.

Deep below the rat, the plane headed into the depths. It sank fast, coming to rest on a sandy seabed at a depth of seven hundred and fifty feet. It had miraculously remained largely intact. One of the wings landed first, pulled down by the weight of the dislodged engine, but then the airframe folded itself down onto the bottom, sending up a wave of silt into the surrounding water.

A couple of other objects managed to break free from their watery grave and make their way up to the surface. But one object that very definitely didn't move was the cargo in the rear of the plane. It remained secured to the floor, sitting there, dormant, its massive power unable to be unleashed so long as it was held captive.

For the safety of the world, it would be better if it was never found.

Chapter Two

Today

John McCready cast an imposing figure as he leaned against the glass surround of the pool area of a spectacular house built high in the Hollywood Hills overlooking the city of Los Angeles. He was barefoot and dressed in a casual light blue cotton shirt and tan knee-length shorts as he soaked up the rays from the early afternoon sun.

Normally, his relaxed, easy-going demeanor would have shown a man at ease with the world. But right now his piercing blue eyes stared out over the city with a concerned, worried intensity that implied a state of mind that was far from calm and relaxed.

The house belonged to someone he loved dearly and, in fact, had come within seconds of asking to marry, when he'd been stopped in his tracks by the greatest shock he'd ever received in his life.

As he gazed out over the city, he tried to take stock of

what had happened over the previous few weeks, which, for some, would have been enough for any lifetime.

Put simply, he'd nearly died on multiple occasions after traveling halfway round the world to save the woman he loved and whose house he was now standing in.

Her name was Clare Kowalski.

In doing so, he'd ended up helping to thwart a terrorist operation that could have resulted in a nuclear war between East and West that would have killed millions.

He thought that would have been enough for one week, but now, seven days on, and just as he was starting to heal and recuperate, there had been the phone call.

Phone calls can change your life—for both good and for bad. They could be the bearer of tragic news, such as the death of a loved one, or the joyous tidings of a new baby, or of securing a job—but this one, this one was different.

When he'd been eighteen, off discovering the world for the first time, he'd met a girl in Peru. Her name was Carlita. She had captured his heart in a way no one else ever had. And while Clare was now the woman he wanted to spend the rest of his life with, at eighteen, your first love was something that could never be repeated, never replicated. At that age you were full of hopes and dreams and the fairytale of living happily ever after. As you grew older, you realized things were not always quite that simple, but for McCready, back then, it was real. On top of which, she'd saved his life. He owed her in a way it would be hard to describe. But events had not turned out how he had imagined. Her father had not been happy with the way Carlita and McCready were becoming so close. He'd asked McCready to leave. It had pained him to go, but out of respect, he'd honored her father's wishes. When he'd left the small mountain village he'd been distraught. The feeling had only grown when he'd found something Carlita had made for him and hidden in his backpack before he'd left—a poncho with colored stripes representing the two of them intertwined together... forever. When he'd returned home, he'd written to her every week for six months. He'd never received a reply. But he never forgot her. How could he? The poncho had hung on the wall of every house he'd owned since, including the one he'd built over a number of years on the west coast of Scotland. Barely a day had gone by when he hadn't thought of her in some way.

And now, after twenty-five years, she'd called out of the blue.

But it wasn't just any call.

Clare had answered the phone, and what she'd told him had filled him with dread. There had been shouting and screaming, what had sounded like gunfire and loud blasts... and in the middle of it all, the desperate, terrified voice of a woman asking for John and saying her name was Carlita.

And then the line had cut out.

He had tried to call back but it was dead.

His mind had been in turmoil ever since.

What he had done, though, was place the small velvet box he'd been about to present to Clare back in a drawer in the bedroom until he could work out what to do. But there was one thing he knew for certain: it wouldn't stay there forever.

He was still gazing out over the city when he felt a hand softly touch his shoulder.

He turned and smiled down at the beautiful green eyes that gazed up at him.

"Hi," he said.

"Hi," said Clare.

As he looked into her face he realized there was

nowhere else he would rather be. But there were things that had to be done, a debt that had to be repaid. He just wasn't sure how he was going to explain everything to her, or if she would even understand.

"Do you want to talk about it?" she asked gently.

McCready paused and then nodded slowly.

"Yeah, there're some things I need to explain."

She reached up and kissed him on the lips. She then led him back into the house through the large sliding glass panes. As they opened, Max, Clare's one-year-old retriever, shot out, barking at the indignation of being cut off from his human playthings. She opened her arms, fully expecting him to leap up, like he usually did, but instead, he raced straight past her and jumped into McCready's arms. Clare looked at him and shook her head.

"Traitor!"

But she was smiling.

They crossed over to one of the wide, comfy sofas in the modern open-plan living space. She fetched a couple of glasses of orange juice from the fridge and then sat down next to McCready. She looked straight into his eyes.

"So, who is she, John? Who is Carlita?"

McCready looked at her and took a deep breath…

…and told her the story.

As he spoke, Clare watched him with feeling and emotion. She could see how much Carlita meant to him. She almost lived the heartbreak he must have felt when he told her how he'd had to leave. It must have been so hard. She'd seen the poncho when she'd visited him in Scotland at the beginning of the year but had never known its significance.

When he'd finished, he looked suitably drained. She looked at him with affection and understanding.

"What will you do?"

"I don't know what I can do from here. I need to know where she is and what's happened to her. She wouldn't have called after all this time if it wasn't serious."

"So how can you find her? I mean, her phone's dead. I can't see any other way of tracking her down."

McCready thought for a minute. He took a sip of juice. He then seemed to focus on something.

"There might be a way. There's a guy I know," he said.

She looked at him and could see he was becoming more determined by the minute.

He stood quickly, now completely absorbed with what he had to do.

He walked over and grabbed his phone, searched through the SPEED DIAL numbers, and clicked on one. The phone rang four times before being answered.

"Hello, John. Nice to hear from you," said a voice over the phone. It was friendly but the tone was guarded.

McCready gritted his teeth. He would have to tread carefully.

Martin Steel worked for the British government. He was responsible at the highest level for security issues in the United Kingdom. If there was any threat to the nation Steel was the one who had to deal with it. McCready had first encountered him when he had been involved in putting McCready's former boss, Malcolm Mercer, behind bars for fraud, theft and numerous other crimes. He had subsequently been coerced by Steel into an operation in the Western Pacific that had resulted in them coming to an understanding that was not quite built on trust, but more on convenience, with the hint of veiled threats, but it seemed to work. More importantly, if anyone could find Carlita, it would be Martin Steel.

"I need a favor," said McCready. It was always best to get straight to the point with Steel.

There was a pause.

"I thought that was my line."

McCready said nothing.

"Okay, what can I do for you?" said Steel. The tone was now even more guarded.

McCready explained about the call, what Carlita meant to him, and how serious it must be for her to try to contact him.

"So, let me get this straight," said Steel. "You want me to use the resources of the British government to track down some ex-girlfriend you knew twenty-five years ago and haven't heard from since."

"Pretty much sums it up," said McCready.

He could hear a heavy sigh down the phone, but Steel hadn't hung up. It took a couple of moments but then he replied.

"Okay, let me look into it. I know you wouldn't be asking if it wasn't important. And as much as I hate to admit it, we're in the Americans' good books because of your actions in LA. Well done, John, you have my respect."

"Thank you," said McCready, surprised at the compliment.

"I can't promise anything," said Steel, "but I'll have a talk to the guys at GCHQ, see if we can't come up with something."

"Thank you, Martin, truly. You don't know what this means to me."

"Right, but it also puts you in the category of owing me one, which is really where I like you to be."

McCready grinned. "Fair enough… You okay, you sound a bit stressed?"

"Oh, the usual. There's been a bit of a ruckus with the Russians. They seem to have lost some rather nasty inventory. Also, there's some chatter coming out of China that I can't get a handle on—don't have quite the same intel there, if you know what I mean." McCready knew exactly what he meant; it was what the whole Pacific incident had been about. "Still, keeps me off the streets… Okay, I'll get back to you when I have something."

And with that he hung up, not waiting for a reply.

When McCready put the phone down he felt a whole lot better. Not knowing what had happened to Carlita was bad enough. Feeling helpless and unable to do anything was even worse. Now, though, the mere fact that Steel had said he would help made McCready feel like a massive weight had been lifted from his shoulders. If there was anything he knew about the man, it was that he would do what he said he would do, and it would always be to the best of his ability—something that was more often than not better than anyone else's best ability. He actually found he was smiling when he walked back into the living room and put his arms around Clare, who was playing with Max on the sofa.

She turned to him.

"Hey, you look better. Your friend able to help?" she said.

McCready grinned wryly at the use of the word 'friend.'

"I wouldn't quite call Martin Steel a 'friend' but he is a man I can trust and he does know how to get things done. He said he'd look into it and get back. All I can do now is wait."

They were eating dinner out on the terrace that evening when the phone rang.

They'd spent the afternoon just being with each other—fooling around, being silly, having fun and playing with Max. He must have thought he'd died and gone to heaven. He'd never had so much attention.

It was the first time McCready had been able to unwind in a long time. Even when he'd been in Scotland before the recent incident in LA, he knew something had been missing. He had to admit, though, his encounter with Brandy Carmine, the world's biggest movie star, a few weeks earlier, had been a welcome distraction, but her name was *persona non grata* in the house and he didn't want to upset the beautiful tranquility he seemed to have reached with Clare. Even the issue with Carlita, after he'd got over the shock, he was sure would turn out to be nothing. Maybe Clare had misheard the name, or it was a wrong number. And at the end of the day, what could Martin Steel actually find out? Even with the resources at his disposal it was hardly likely he'd be able to discover what had happened to her. She could be anywhere in the world.

So when the phone rang, he took a long sip of the rather pleasant Chardonnay they'd almost demolished, and crossed back inside the house to pick up the handset.

He spoke for ten minutes.

As she watched from outside, Clare could see McCready's body language change. It started out relaxed and casual, but then became more upright—more tense. Occasionally, he would be animated, as though he didn't believe something, but then he'd brush his hand through his hair, as if in exasperation.

She had a very bad feeling about this.

When McCready came back outside, his face was serious. The smiles and irreverence of earlier were gone. He sat down in front of her and looked straight into her eyes.

A cold breeze blew in off the hills, but neither of them felt it.

"Okay, how bad?" asked Clare.

"I don't know," said McCready. "He wants me to go to London." He glanced at her.

She looked shocked.

"But you can't. You're only just starting to heal. You're here with me now, John. You can't go away."

McCready just looked at her, his expression torn.

"He told me he'd tracked down the location from where the call had been made. He wouldn't tell me where it was or if he knew what had happened to her, only that she was in trouble and her life was in danger. He gave no further details, other than to say he couldn't speak over the phone and it was serious enough for me to fly to London. He also added that things were way more complicated than he'd originally thought they'd be."

"But he can't just expect you to drop everything and… and…" She was almost becoming desperate.

McCready looked at her and smiled. He took her hands in his and spoke gently.

"It was me who contacted him, remember? I asked for his help. He wouldn't be doing this if it wasn't for me. And for Martin Steel to say something is serious, you better believe that it is. This guy doesn't mess around."

He looked at her.

"I have to go."

Clare stood up, tears welling in her eyes. She looked out over the skyline of the city to the ocean beyond, to where the sun was just starting to dip below the line of the horizon. A second later she turned to him.

"How can this happen now? We've only just found each other again." Her eyes were pleading. "And you're not fit to go anywhere. You nearly died. I can't lose you again, John. I don't know what I'd do."

He stood up and wrapped his arms tight around her, holding her close.

"It'll be alright. I'll be careful. And if Steel is involved, he has access to the best intel, the best people in the business. It's all going to be fine."

"But why do you have to go?"

He looked at her with a simple expression.

"Because I have to. Because she saved my life. Because I owe her, and because I need to know she's okay. Surely you can understand that? I came for you, didn't I?"

And she knew, in that moment, he had to go. Nothing would stand in the way of McCready's desire to do the right thing, and if that involved someone he cared about, or had loved, then there was no way she could ever stop him. And if she dug deep into her heart of hearts, there was no way she would ever want to stop him—it was why she loved him so much.

"When do you have to leave?"

"First thing in the morning." He noticed a tear in her eye. "Hey, don't worry. I'll be back before you know it."

She clung close to his body, wondering if it would be the last night they would ever have together.

Chapter Three

The Congress Center Basel was the largest conference facility in Switzerland. Located in the heart of Europe, it held international events from across the world, but today there was a particular buzz about the place. A series of TED talks were to be given for the first time, and on the schedule was someone everyone wanted to hear speak.

The TED series of lectures had started in 1984. Created as a platform to disseminate current thinking in the world of technology, entertainment and design, the talks had gone from strength to strength. They represented an accessible resource that delved into topical, sometimes controversial, and future-looking aspects of the world we live in. They took place across the globe and were readily available online for free for those wishing to seek them out. Speakers were limited to eighteen minutes to get their points across, so there was no time for waffle or padding—just wall-to-wall facts and ideas. They were held in high regard around the world. And you knew, if you attended, watched or listened to one, you were in for a scintillating eighteen minutes.

Previous notable speakers had included: Sir Richard Branson, Bill Gates, Madeleine Albright and James Cameron.

Today's lineup included: Dexter Talbot, an engineer who claimed to have invented a fuel system that could power vehicles with zero emissions and rivaled batteries and hydrogen; Erica Shultz, a documentary filmmaker who was attempting to cross the Atlantic Ocean on the seabed with a newly designed submersible; Professor Stanley Fisher, a particle physicist who was claiming that electrons couldn't just exist in two places at the same time, but millions—he was clearly after another grant. And then there was the big-ticket item, the one everyone had come to see—Victor Solano, the world's richest man. He would have created a sensation whatever the subject of his talk, but the title had merely added fuel to the fire—*Change is Inevitable - Eighteen Minutes to Fix the World*. As a result, the event was being held in Hall 4.1 on the first floor, which could hold three thousand people.

It was sold out.

To say that Solano was successful was a bit like saying the universe was quite large. Constantly vying for the top spot with the electric car guy and the online shopping guy, and way eclipsing the Windows guy, Solano cut a dashing figure. He was fifty-five years old and known as somewhat of a recluse. The occasional magazine article he allowed to be published had stylish photographs that showed a tall, fit, well-tanned man who seemed at ease with his place in the world. His face showed the rugged affability of a South American heritage, but with the presence and intelligence of a man of the world. He had dark gray eyes above an elegant, slightly rounded nose. His cheeks were lean, and his lips, while thin, bordered a mouth that could smile with incredible warmth. He wasn't known to socialize much, and people said his close friends could be counted on the fingers of one hand, and as far as women were concerned, he kept his private life private. In his earlier years he'd been seen on vacation on a number of secluded holiday islands with a string of beautiful partners, but he'd never been married, though there was a rumor he'd had a close relationship for some time, but no one had ever been able to pin down with whom.

One thing was for sure, though, he hadn't reached the position he was in by being a saint. Those who had ever expressed a knowledge of how he worked would say he could be brutal in his decision-making, to the point of being cruel. He knew what he wanted and would do whatever it took to achieve it, a hangover from the times he'd lived on the streets in the favelas of Rio de Janeiro as a child. There, it was dog eat dog, where, quite literally, only the fittest survived. That time had taught him much—to be able to use what you had at your disposal, and more importantly, how to assess any situation you were in to come out on top —which sometimes meant losing one day to fight another. Also, to work out who you could trust, and to surround yourself with an inner circle who were completely loyal. And the one thing Solano had been very good at was judging character and choosing wisely. It had taken him from being one of the poorest in the world to the richest in the world.

Much of his fortune had been made on the stock market, but he'd had to be in a position to take advantage of that, and that could only have come from having the necessary finance available. This had been accumulated through risky, but brilliant, investments in start-up companies that had gone on to take on the world. And many of the decisions around these companies had come from the brilliance of one man, and it wasn't Solano.

When he'd been in his thirties, he'd come across a young man, twenty years old, who'd been imprisoned in Sao Paulo in Brazil. He'd heard about him, as the word on the street was that he had special gifts. These gifts actually turned out to be a highly analytical mind that could calculate amazing things and determine outcomes in situations that always seemed to come true. There was nothing magical about it, it was just that he had a brain that functioned differently to most people—on a higher level. And while he could often seem distant or aloof, that was just the way he was. Underneath, there was more going on than you could ever have imagined—think Stephen Hawking.

Solano had seen an opportunity.

The man was in prison because he'd made some powerful people look incompetent and corrupt, and in Brazil that could mean you were likely looking at a reduced lifespan. Solano had used his contacts to break him out of prison. The escape had been front page news. The corrupt local police searched for many months but never found him, and they never would. Once he was safe, Solano had said he would give him a new identity and future if he came to work for him. He had readily agreed and had been reborn with a new face and a new name. He had chosen Juliano Mendes. When asked about the choice, he had simply said it had personal significance for him, but he would elaborate no further.

Mendes had gone to work for Solano, and Solano had never looked back.

With the knowledge and perception Mendes brought to Solano's operations, they were only headed in one direction. But aside from the obvious success, there was one overriding factor that had influenced Solano's decision to wholeheartedly embrace Mendes—he brought something with him that was far more precious than all the money in the world, something Solano would have killed for. It bound him to Mendes in a way he would never reveal to anyone.

It was all part of the enigma that was Victor Solano.

On the stage, Professor Fisher was just finishing up his presentation. Although he'd kept it within the allotted eighteen minutes there seemed to be a certain restlessness among the audience. It could have been down to the content of his talk, or, more likely, the thousands in the crowd who were waiting in anticipation for the next speaker.

In the wings, Solano stood with his eyes closed, taking a moment before he walked out onto the stage. He was dressed in his usual attire: jeans and black roll-neck jumper, a fashion cue he'd taken from someone he greatly admired —and there weren't many of them—the late, great Steve Jobs. Just go out there, keep it simple, don't distract, say amazing things, and change the world.

That was exactly what he intended to do.

He opened his eyes and glanced at Mendes, who was standing next to him. Mendes handed him a small plastic bottle. Solano took it, unscrewed the top and dropped a couple of round white pills into his hand. In the background he could hear the presenter starting to announce the next presentation. There was a buzz from the audience. Someone started banging the floor with their feet. Within a minute the action had been taken up around the hall. The whole building was shaking. He threw the pills into the back of his throat and took a swig of water from the glass offered by Mendes. He returned the small bottle to him just as the presenter announced his name with a flourish. It was followed by whoops and cheers. And without another word, Victor Solano walked out onto the stage to thunderous applause.

He had eighteen minutes to change the world.

The roar from the crowd reached new heights.

One of the hallmarks of the TED talks is that they were minimalistic. No great sets. No fancy props. Just the speaker and a stage.

Solano was no different.

The stage was all black, matching his roll-neck. There was a large screen behind him, suspended from the ceiling, so even at the back they could see him as he prowled the area below. He'd also asked for a single spotlight to follow him. As the lights dimmed, the shaft of light was all that could be seen.

As the lights faded, so did the noise. The air was thick with anticipation. Everyone was waiting to hear what he would say—what his words would mean for the world.

Solano walked to the middle of the stage with his head bowed. When he reached the center he turned to the audience and looked up. He glanced around, calm and serene, and with supreme confidence.

Then he spoke.

"Ladies and gentlemen, we find ourselves at a crossroads in our history. At a time when the human species has to make a decision as to the path it will take for the future. Our ancestors first appeared on the Earth between five and seven million years ago, but it is only now that we hold our destiny, our very existence, in our hands.

"But the world has to act now, and that's not a politician's 'now,' it's a realist's, a scientist's 'now,' and it means today—not tomorrow. It means that when you leave this hall, when you go home, you, your friends, and everyone else on this planet has to act. To not act TODAY will mean the end of the human race as we know it."

There was a buzz from the audience as murmured comment spread like wildfire.

Solano continued.

"Human beings have always thought they were special, have always thought they were different—the chosen ones. But at one point they also thought the world was flat. We have to wake up and realize that, however special we might think we are, there is no one to stop us walking off a cliff into the history books—except ourselves. The shameful thing is we know what we have to do but the politics of nations will not allow the necessary action to be taken to make this happen.

"On top of that, we have a number of influential people proposing we leave this planet and start anew on another... Really? Let's take a look at that. The idea of interplanetary travel is appealing. We've all seen the films, the TV shows over the years, but the reality is very different. Even if we can develop the technology to do so, it's another case of *should we do it just because we can?* Remember the dinosaur guy?"

There were a few laughs from around the hall.

"I'm all for pushing the boundaries of technology. The thrill of adventure. The challenge of the unknown, and let that happen in the pursuit of knowledge. But the spin of 'we're going to have to have another planet as one day this one will die and the human species has to endure' is probably one of the dumbest statements ever uttered with regard to where we are today."

There were some gasps from the crowd at this.

"They're right about one thing—the planet is going to

die, from a human perspective, but it's going to happen way before we have the ability to go anywhere else.

"Think about it. What are our options? We don't have the technology to travel to other star systems where there may well be planets that could sustain a level of lifestyle people would be willing to accept. All we have is Mars. A rock over thirty million miles away at its closest orbit. Have you seen the photographs and video from there? I bet if you didn't know where it was you'd say it was somewhere on Earth. And in a way, you'd be right, Mars is like Earth. In fact, there are scientists who will tell you that at one time it was *very* much like Earth, with rivers and oceans… and maybe life of some kind—but it isn't today.

"Again, think about it. Would you go and live in the desert on Earth? Would that environment, and that alone, be enough for your whole life? I think the answer is no. And then take that environment and change the temperature. Even in summer, at the equator, nighttime temperatures can drop to minus a hundred degrees Fahrenheit. Then take away all the air to breathe. You couldn't go outside without a spacesuit. You'd probably have to live permanently underground because of the radiation hitting the planet due to the lack of atmosphere. And even if you did manage to survive, there would be no realistic way you could ever visit Earth as your body would have adapted to Martian gravity. So, there you are, stuck living out your life either indoors or underground beneath a desert. Appealing, huh?

"So, the attraction of Mars, I suspect, is rapidly fading. But that's it. There is nowhere else we could reach that we could inhabit. Scientists are desperate to look to the stars to find a perfect planet to colonize. But what they seem to forget is we already found one. We're living on it. The only problem with the Earth is there are people on it. We've screwed it up. The only likely reason we might have to leave one day is because WE, no one else, WE have made it uninhabitable for humankind.

"So what's the answer?"

He walked to the front of the stage and looked down directly into the first few rows of the audience. He saw rapturous faces, hanging on his every word.

"Well, there is a way."

He looked up, all the way to the back.

"The world needs to stop the path it is on right now and change direction, or it's over. It's as simple as that. Fossil fuel production must stop. The world's population must change to a plant-based diet. Only one child per family should be allowed until the population is under control. All future development of weapons and their deployment must end. The senseless eternal race for economic growth must cease. The nations of the world must come together in one effort, one goal, as one entity, to act to save the life of the planet. And we will be doing it for selfish reasons—something humans are very good at. For our own survival, not the planet's. If we're gone, and that will happen very quickly if these actions aren't taken, then the planet will, in time, move to rid itself of our presence. Sure, the grotesque carcasses of our cities and infrastructure will take many years to break down, but nature will eventually return to equilibrium and life will continue as though we were never here. The planet was around for millions of years before we intruded on it—it'll be around for millions more after we're gone."

When he finished, he paused, as though taking in the words himself, and then looked up at the audience.

"That's the reality, folks. That's what we're facing."

He walked slowly over to the side of the stage.

"So, how can this be achieved? There's really only one way. Those who have the capability, those who have the vision, those who have the courage to live in the real world, have to put every resource, bring every political pressure to bear, to make this planet ours and create a sustainable environment for millennia to come. Because right now, we have maybe fifty years, if we're lucky, before society starts to break down due to lack of food and water, and unbearable living conditions in much of the populated parts of the world. All caused by climate change and the subsequent sea level rise, extreme weather events, and population expansion."

There was total silence in the auditorium. You could barely even hear people breathing.

"So, instead of reaching for the stars, let's make THIS our home, because if we don't, we'll have nowhere else to go. Nowhere else to live. Let's develop technology that'll allow us to live in deserts, in ice-covered regions, in the mountains—even on and under the water, and live there with comfort and style. Why look elsewhere, when we already have perfection?"

He paused in the middle of the stage and looked out.

There was immediate cheering and shouting.

He raised his hand.

The noise quietened.

"Unfortunately, what needs to be done will not be done. The governments of the world do not have the political stomach to work together to bring in the laws and regulations required to do what is necessary." He paused. "I am therefore going to make it my mission, my legacy, to bring about a situation where they have no choice but to comply. Where they have to resolve the problems facing them, because if they don't, they'll face the downfall of civilization."

Again there was silence, punctuated by a few gasps.

"One of the problems is that these issues take time to reveal themselves. It's like a slow-motion car crash. It doesn't seem so bad at slow speed, until you get to the end when the outcome is the same. But what if we speeded things up? What if there was no time left, except the time it took to solve the problem only by everyone working together because they had no other choice? Then… maybe then, something might be done."

He paused again.

"I will have more to say on this in due course, but for now, the governments of the world need to act. They have one month to start cooperating, to start moving forward. They know what the solutions are. They know where I am. They know how to get in touch, and those who have had dealings with me know I am not bluffing. I need to be taken at my word."

He again stopped and looked at the audience.

"Thank you for your attention."

He bowed slightly and started to walk off stage, the stab of the spotlight following his every step.

It was the normal protocol that no questions were allowed at TED talks, but what Solano had said was so profound, so alarming, the tension in the room was palpable. Everyone had a question; it was just a matter of who would go first.

He was halfway to the side of the stage when someone finally found the confidence. She stood up from ten rows back, close to the center aisle. Even without a microphone, her voice carried clearly across the room.

"If they don't comply, what will you do?"

There was a collective intake of breath from three thousand people.

On the stage, Solano paused. He looked at the floor for a full ten seconds and then turned to look straight at the audience. You could have heard a pin drop. Everyone was holding their breath.

Solano's face was deadly serious. It left no room for interpretation.

And then, almost in a whisper, but amplified by the microphone and sound system, he said three words that gave no answers but put the world on notice.

"Wait and see."

Chapter Four

The flight from Los Angeles had been long, and despite everything on his mind McCready had slept fairly well. There had been some turbulence over the mid-Atlantic that had jolted him awake, but other than that he felt rested when the in-flight service provided him with a far from adequate breakfast at seven-thirty in the morning, UK time. He finished it off quickly, had a second cup of coffee and then an hour to think about what lay ahead before landing at Heathrow.

He had no idea what Martin Steel would have to say when he saw him. But whatever it was, it couldn't be good. He had to brace himself for any outcome. At least it didn't sound as though Carlita was dead, though the fact Steel had said her life was in danger didn't bode well. It made McCready more anxious than ever to find out what was going on. The one thing he did know, was there was no way he was going to jeopardize his relationship with Clare again. He'd done that once, and never again. If he did eventually see Carlita after all these years, he had no idea how he would feel, but he could see no scenario where she would be a threat to what he and Clare had finally found together.

Going through customs was surprisingly fast. There were no holdups. He had to wait around five minutes for a cab, but then the drive along the M4 to Central London had been smooth. The traffic was heavy but kept moving. He always enjoyed the trip on the elevated section of road, before dropping down just past Hammersmith and then the slower drive through Knightsbridge and past the southern side of Hyde Park.

In all, it took fifty-five minutes before the cab pulled up outside the impressive black gates of Downing Street in Whitehall.

Once two Metropolitan police officers, armed to the teeth, had confirmed he was no threat, he was let through the imposing steel barrier. He walked the hundred yards to the front door that opened as he arrived. He was then led up to a first-floor drawing room and told that Martin Steel would be with him shortly. He'd been there once before, after the incident in the Pacific, and had been amazed at how large the interior was, given the narrow frontage the world saw on television.

Ten minutes later Steel walked through the door. He was dressed casually, as was his style, with smart slacks and an open shirt. He carried a bundle of folders with him. He extended his hand and smiled at McCready.

"John, nice to see you again. Sorry to keep you. Flight okay?"

"Yes, thanks. Not bad. At least I got some sleep."

"That's good. I think you might need it." McCready looked at him with a questioning expression. "All in good time. I expect you'd like to get straight to it."

McCready nodded.

"Okay, follow me. Coffee?"

"Sure."

Steel indicated the way and led McCready to an elevator at the rear of the building. They descended two floors to a basement level. When the doors opened they walked down a narrow corridor to a room at the end. Steel walked in and held the door for McCready.

Inside was what could best be described as a mini-ops center. It was like a small theater. There were four rows of plush, banked seating facing a screen on the far wall. In front of the seats, at the lowest level, was a line of computer displays. There were two swivel chairs in front of these.

"Have a seat," said Steel.

McCready found a seat in the middle of the second tier and sat down. Steel walked to the front of the room and switched on some equipment. The screen came alight with a government screensaver. He pressed an intercom and asked for two coffees to be brought in. He then opened a laptop and clicked on a file. The computer wirelessly connected to the projection system and the desktop was mirrored on the wall. Steel noticed McCready glancing around.

"It's a control room for strategic ops. Allows the PM to watch any operations we have going on without leaving the building," said Steel.

A couple of minutes later a man entered with two coffees. He passed them to McCready and Steel. They took a sip. When he had gone, Steel turned to McCready.

"Okay, John. I'll give you some background first and then we can look at the current situation."

He picked up one of the folders he'd been carrying and opened it at the first page.

"Right, name, Carlita Fuentes. Born in Arequipa, Peru.

Parents, Diego and Maria. One brother, Fernando, eight years younger than her."

As Steel talked, it transported McCready back in time to the few short months he'd spent with the family, and to his surprise, he found there was a sudden ache in his heart he hadn't thought he would feel.

"There's not a lot on her early life," continued Steel. "Why would there be? But we pick up information when she's nineteen. It appears she became involved with a radical environmental group called Planet Survive. They're at the extreme end of things. Into direct action. Way beyond Greenpeace... way beyond Sea Shepherd. They take the law into their own hands and are not afraid who gets in the way. It appears she was a highly active member of the organization." He turned a page. "At one point she was linked to a Rafael Cortez, who was also part of the group. Possibly high up in the leadership."

"You say, 'was,'" interrupted McCready.

"Yes, he was killed in an operation to stop an oil pipeline being constructed in the Arctic."

Again, McCready found his thoughts flying back in time. He could see how she might have gone down that route. She'd been so passionate about animals, nature and the environment when he'd been with her. It also brought back memories of his own mother, who'd been killed by Japanese whalers when she'd been volunteering with the Sea Shepherd organization and had been run down in a RIB by the Japanese ship.

"Which brings us to where we are now," said Steel.

He looked up at McCready.

"This is going to be hard, John."

McCready leaned forward, waiting to hear what Steel

had to say. Steel clicked a key on the laptop and an image appeared on the screen on the wall.

"She was involved in a direct-action operation at a facility in North Africa. The company was into heavy metals and the illegal dumping of toxic materials into the Med. She and her group broke into the complex and damaged equipment and infrastructure. What I'm going to show you is CCTV footage taken two days ago."

Steel clicked another key and the image on the screen started moving. The camera was clearly mounted high up on a pole overlooking a compound. There was a desert backdrop, but in the foreground there appeared to be a series of large circular chemical tanks with pipework connecting them together. It was at night and the image was grainy, but you could make out what was going on.

As he watched, four figures appeared from the bottom of the screen. It looked like they were running covertly, keeping low. They all wore backpacks. They ran over to various parts of the facility and then knelt down and seemed to be doing something at their specific locations. A minute later some security lights must have come on as the whole area was flooded with light. The figures all looked round in surprise. A jeep raced in from the top of the frame. Two armed men jumped out. They ran alongside one of the tanks. When they saw one of the figures, they opened fire without hesitation. Next, the other figures ran from their hiding places. One of them ran directly under the camera. Before the figure, which looked like a woman, though it was hard to tell, reached the camera, there were two large explosions from behind. The woman was thrown to the ground. She then picked herself up and pulled something out of her backpack. She looked behind her and then raised what was clearly a phone to her ear. At that point there was another large explosion. Bullets ripped toward the woman. She ducked to her right and the light of the explosion lit up her face. Steel hit a key and froze the video.

"We think that is Carlita Fuentes."

McCready was riveted to the screen. The image wasn't clear, but it was enough to cause the ache in his chest to get worse. He hadn't seen her for twenty-five years. Her hair was cut short, no longer the flowing curls that had stretched halfway down her back, and she was wearing dark clothing. But he could see in the way her jaw jutted defiantly and the glint of light that showed the fire in her eyes that, yes, he was indeed looking at Carlita. He had to take several deep breaths. He hadn't realized he would be affected like this.

Steel was watching him closely.

"So, I can assume from your increased breathing rate, that's her?"

McCready nodded slowly, unable to take his eyes off the screen.

"That must be when she called," said McCready. "There was the sound of explosions and gunfire in the background." He was still staring at her.

"Okay," said Steel. "Good, we've established it's her. But I'm afraid it gets worse."

McCready glanced at him.

Steel pressed a couple of keys and the video changed to another location. This time it was clearer. It was still nighttime, but he was looking at a shot of a marina on a coastline that was illuminated by high arc lights.

"It would appear she was caught by the local police after she escaped from the facility. In fact, it's lucky she wasn't shot by the company's security guards given the way they behaved in the last clip. She was taken to a police station—we're in Algeria by the way—where there's a single image of her in a cell. However, the disturbing part comes up now."

McCready looked at him.

"The company that owns the facility, Tranter Chemicals, based out of Illinois, seem to have done some sort of deal, because the police appear to have handed her back over to them, which is not a good sign. Throw a few shekels their way and they'll do anything, it appears."

"What would the company want her for?" asked McCready.

"That's what we don't know," said Steel. "There's some earlier video of someone we think is her inside the company offices accessing one of their computers. It's possible she found some information they didn't want to get out, but that's all just speculation."

He clicked a key and the video at the marina played out. McCready watched as a car drove up to one of the pontoons, moored to which was one of the largest superyachts he'd ever seen. A man climbed out of the car. He glanced around furtively, checking no one was watching. When he was sure all was clear, he signaled to another man who also climbed out of the car. They both then walked around to the trunk, opened it and pulled out an elongated package wrapped tightly in black plastic, around five feet long. To many, it might have looked like a rolled-up carpet, but there was just enough shape to the package for McCready to know it was no carpet. He also saw it move slightly. He felt the hairs on the back of his neck stand on end. His fists started to tighten. The men then quickly walked down to the yacht, climbed on board and disappeared inside.

Steel clicked off the video and turned to McCready.

"She sailed later that night. She's called the *Freedom Seas* and is currently moored just off Monaco. It took a lot of work, but by a convoluted trail, her ownership appears to trace back to Tranter Chemicals. I say 'appears' because there are some anomalies in the data that we're looking into, but it would be logical. They clearly want to find out something from her away from the scene of the crime, so to speak."

"Or they could be just going to dump her at sea to get rid of the body," said McCready.

"I don't think so. If you looked carefully, she was still alive. If they were going to dump her, they'd have killed her already. No, this is something else."

McCready sat back in his seat. He felt completely drained, but also completely overwhelmed at what Steel had managed to find out. He turned to him.

"How the hell did you…?"

"That's what we do," said Steel matter-of-factly. "The question is, what do *you* want to do?" McCready stared at the floor for a moment. "The British government can't get involved in this, John. Clearly crimes have been committed… on both sides."

At this, McCready looked at him sharply.

"She was trying to blow up the facility," said Steel, his eyebrows slightly raised. But then, after a moment, he added. "But the situation does interest me." He looked cryptically at McCready.

McCready sat up straighter. He was all attention.

"What does that mean?"

Steel glanced at him, as though deciding something. He then walked across the floor, thinking. Eventually he stopped.

"Okay, this is the best I can do. There is some chatter out there that Tranter Chemicals is involved in something that would garner our interest. At the moment there's nothing solid enough to warrant a full-blown operation from our end… But, if you decide to do something on your own, we could possibly supply some form of support—equipment, communications, that sort of thing, on the condition you bring anything you find to me. How far that support would extend would depend on what you would plan to do." He looked at McCready. "How does that sound?"

McCready looked at him. He didn't quite know what he'd expected as he'd had no idea what he was dealing with, but Steel's support meant everything, and while he wouldn't exactly be able to call in a special forces operation or the marines, sometimes he was better off working with those he knew in a small select team.

"I don't know what to say."

"Nothing required. Work something out and get back to me."

McCready stood up and walked over to Steel and shook his hand.

"Thank you," said McCready.

"But John, there are limits to what I can do."

"Then I guess we're going to find out what they are," said McCready with a grin.

Steel looked at him dubiously.

McCready left the building feeling somewhat happier than when he had entered.

Once he was outside, he turned left onto Whitehall and then headed up to Trafalgar Square. He remembered sitting on a bench there some months previously, but it was under totally different circumstances. This time, he was all focus.

He had to work out what he needed and how he was going to get to Carlita. He also knew he didn't have much time. While they may need her alive to question her, if they didn't get the answers they wanted, she could very well then be dumped at sea. In fact, that may already have happened. He shuddered at the thought.

He pulled out his phone, hit a SPEED DIAL number and waited for it to be answered. When it was, he smiled. He knew the response he was going to get.

"Hi, Craig," said McCready. "We need to have chat."

Chapter Five

Doctor Rudi Gerber stepped out of the cab and breathed in the fresh Swiss mountain air. It was a fine day, hardly a cloud in the sky, but there was a strong wind. It was also cold and stimulating. He buttoned up his long Burberry cashmere coat and headed in the direction of the cable car station carrying a black leather briefcase.

Gerber was in his early sixties. He was a cancer consultant and ran a world-renowned clinic in Bern. It was usually non-stop appointments, but today he had a day off—well, he was working, but he looked upon the day as a field trip. As well as running the clinic, he was also Victor Solano's personal physician, and when Solano called, he answered. He'd known the man for over twenty years and considered him a close friend.

He'd arrived at the small local airfield by private jet and would usually have had the pleasure of a helicopter ride up to his patient's stunning Alpine home, but the helipad was closed due to finishing up some repair work so he would just have to settle for the thirty-minute cable car ride, which was fine by him. The views were spectacular and it would give him time to go over his notes and thoughts on Solano's condition. He had said he'd had to up the dose of Oxycodone to minimize the pain. He would have to check on that. The pills could become addictive, but given Solano's condition, that might unfortunately not be a long-term problem.

Gerber walked up the steps to the base station of the cable car. It was situated on the outskirts of a picturesque village not far from the Matterhorn. And while the cable car was open to the public, it provided access to a private transit system at the top that led to Solano's home. He never really liked that part of the journey. It involved taking a train made up of three smallish pods that traveled through a tunnel not much wider than the pods themselves. He suffered from claustrophobia, and although it was only a ten-minute ride, things could always break down. He'd actually had nightmares at the thought of being stuck in one.

Solano's residence was built two-thirds of the way up a vertical cliff face. It was a miracle of engineering and must have one of the best mountain views of any home on the planet. The Swiss government had given permission to build there on condition he fund an observatory on the top of the mountain. This was used for astronomical research, as well as being a functioning weather station for meteorologists and climatologists.

Gerber made his way into the foyer of the cable car station and over to the ticket office. A pleasant young lady was sitting behind the counter. She looked up and smiled in a Swiss, business-like way. He showed his ID, which was registered as a VIP guest of Victor Solano.

"Good morning, Herr Doktor. Welcome. The car is ready for your trip. You can board immediately."

Gerber nodded and thanked her. She then stood and escorted him down a short passageway to the boarding station. While the cable car was used by the public, one of Solano's conditions had been that if he had personal guests, they would have exclusive use of the cars and others would have to wait. It had caused issues on some occasions, but that was just the way it was. When you were the richest man in the world, it had its perks.

Gerber walked through a door at the end of the passage and found the car waiting. The boarding station was like a spotlessly clean garage. The suspension cables were hidden from sight through a groove in the ceiling. The whole space was sealed against the elements in case the weather was bad outside. In front of the car were two doors that would slide open once he was safely inside.

"Would you like a coffee or anything for the trip, sir?" asked the assistant.

"No, thank you. I'm fine," said Gerber.

She saw him inside the car. When he was sitting down, she made sure the door was securely closed. She then lifted a walkie-talkie and spoke briefly.

A moment later the doors at the front of the station slid to one side revealing a green Alpine pasture beyond. The car rocked and swayed slightly as it ran onto the cables. It then moved smoothly forward and up into the air.

There was a slight judder as the wheels clattered over the first pylon, but then it was upward with a fast, steady glide that seemed effortless and whisper quiet.

There were seats at one end, and all around, large windows gave a panoramic view of the Swiss countryside. There was a grab rail round the side in case it got a little windy, as it could on occasion.

Gerber opened his briefcase. He took out a sheaf of

papers and glanced through Solano's medical records and the prescription regime he'd brought with him. But after ten minutes the pull of the view was too great. He stood up, walked to the front of the car, and looked out.

They had just passed over a large lake and were coming up to a second pylon at the top of a thousand-foot cliff. It was situated on the summit of a low Alp—at least it was low compared to the surrounding mountains. To the side was a steep snow slope with a massive vertical drop to the lake below. The level part of the Alp was a few hundred feet across before the ground steepened to head up to the top of the mountain. The snow glistened in the morning sunlight as they climbed ever higher. He could hear the tinkling of cow bells coming from somewhere below.

But it was now that the most spectacular part of the trip started. Once the car had cleared the pylon, it veered steeply upward toward its final destination, three thousand feet up the vertical wall of the mountain ahead.

Gerber looked down. While he might have an aversion to claustrophobic places, he had no problem with heights, which was a good thing. Below him the ground dropped steeply away into the valley. It was awe-inspiring. He looked out, further along the valley, to one of the ski resorts. There were numerous skiers and snowboarders out enjoying the slopes. He could see their ant-like figures way below as they whooshed and shushed over the snow.

He turned back to look ahead.

In front of him was a solid vertical wall. He still couldn't believe anyone had been able to construct a home up here, but Solano liked his privacy and he could afford whatever it took. What it had taken, was two years of construction, the engineering minds of several great architects, and a cost of over two hundred million dollars.

As he looked up, he could make out the sleek outline of the residence. It was around eighty feet in width and protruded ten feet out from the cliff face. There was nothing above and below but sheer rock. The top and bottom were made of curved steel, which was separated by a continuous glass frontage, eight feet high. In the middle, an open-air balcony protruded out over the void below. The building, if you could call it that, then extended a hundred feet back into the rock over two levels.

Gerber watched as they climbed higher.

He could now see the upper station, some way above and off to the right of Solano's home. Although he felt safe and cocooned where he was, the winds whistled through the cables causing the car to sway slightly.

As the car approached the upper station, it started to slow. It eased itself into the docking area and came to a stop. When it was secure, the door slid to one side and Gerber walked out onto the hard surround. He knew where he was going and made his way out into the main atrium. While the public turned to the right at this point, Gerber headed left toward a short corridor that led to the transit system. It was blocked off by a red rope strung between two gold-covered bollards. On the wall to one side were the words PRIVATE and NO ACCESS in numerous languages.

He glanced up at the camera above and then walked past the rope and down the passage.

At the end was a door. He opened it and walked through. The area was small. To the left was an office for a security guard, to the right, the transit system. The three connected pods were sitting there waiting for him.

The guard had known he was coming and welcomed him.

Deep Control

The door to the first pod opened automatically. Gerber walked inside. He sat down and put his briefcase on the seat beside him. The door then swiftly closed and the pods moved off with a smooth electric hum.

While Gerber didn't like the tunnels, he did marvel at the ingenuity of the engineering that had put the system in place.

As he sat back in his seat, the pod moved briskly forward. A few seconds later and the rock opened up on his left. Panes of reinforced glass made up the side of the tunnel, giving a breathtaking view across the valley. Immediately below, the mountain dropped vertically away. He always liked to look down at this point. As he did, he smiled, happy he was safe within the confines of the pod. But the view only lasted a couple of minutes before they were back in a tunnel.

As they progressed, the angle of the track started to change, steepening in a downward direction. As far as the pod was concerned it made no difference. It rotated on its axis, a bit like the capsules on the London Eye. The angle then steepened further until they were descending vertically like an elevator. After five minutes the reverse happened and the pods returned to a horizontal position and drew into a small station at the rear of Solano's home deep in the mountain.

The doors slid smoothly to one side. Gerber grabbed his briefcase, glad they'd arrived without incident, and walked out onto the small platform.

When he looked up, Victor Solano was there to greet him.

"Rudi, good to see you again. Thank you for coming."

They shook hands.

"Of course, Victor. I always love it up here, and we have things to discuss."

"We do indeed."

Solano led Gerber into an airlock. This allowed the air in the main part of the residence to be kept purified and temperature controlled.

When they emerged through the second door they were on the upper level. This was where Solano had a large office dubbed 'the control room,' from which he ran all his businesses. The kitchen, bedrooms and other utility rooms were also on this level. Gerber followed Solano around a gallery that looked out over the floor below.

They descended an elegant, curved staircase and made their way along what was colloquially known as Main Street, an open thoroughfare, twenty feet wide, that led to the front of the home and gave the place a feeling of space and grandeur. It was from here you accessed all the other areas. They passed a gym and spa on one side, while on the other, behind a glass wall, was an ornate swimming pool, complete with rock surround and waterfall.

And everywhere it was quiet.

There was the faint, far-off thrum of an air-conditioning system, but it was barely audible. The walls were a light pastel color and the thick pile carpet deadened any sound. It was a place of extreme calm.

When they reached the front, it always took Gerber's breath away.

To the left, at one end, was a formal dining area with a large oblong glass table with seating for ten. Behind this was a bar with a wide selection of drinks. The area in the middle, at the head of Main Street, led out through double-sealed glass doors to the balcony beyond. To the right were a series of seating areas. One was made up of comfortable leather chairs arranged around a circular sunken fireplace —another, a set of deep sofas around a low glass table, all with spectacular, unobstructed views across the valley.

Solano walked over to the sofas.

"Would you like a drink, Rudi?" he asked.

"Thank, you," said Gerber. "Bourbon would be nice."

Solano crossed over to the bar and poured a whiskey. He also opened a small fridge and pulled out a beer. He poured it into a glass and then returned to the sofas. He gave the whiskey to Gerber and was about to sit down when the doctor placed his glass on the table, still standing.

"Victor, could you please show it to me again? You know I can't resist when I come up here."

Solano paused. A smile crossed his face. He placed his drink on the table and turned to Gerber.

"Okay, Rudi, just because it's you."

He slapped Gerber on the back and they walked back along Main Street to the rear of the residence deep in the rock.

When they reached the far end they stopped at a brushed steel door the size of a double garage.

Solano walked up to a pad at the side. He typed in a code and placed his palm on a reader. When the system identified him, there was a beep, and then the sound of an electric motor as the door slid smoothly back into the rock.

Beyond the door was a darkened room. Solano walked in and flicked on four strategically placed spotlights. Their powerful beams illuminated something in the middle. Gerber knew what he was going to see, but it was a thrill every time. While many rich people had priceless art treasures hidden away from the rest of the world, Solano had something quite different.

The floor, ceiling and walls were all spotlessly white. But

it was what was sitting in the middle of the space on a raised turntable that was the focus of attention.

It was a car, but not just any car.

It was the most famous car in the world.

Solano flicked another switch and the turntable started to turn.

Gerber watched in awe as the silver machine moved around.

It had been in profile when they'd walked in, but as the grille came into view, he could see the winged badge of Aston Martin on the end of the long, low bonnet. Below the grille was the number plate BMT 216A, which could rotate. Either side were the indicator lights, which hid two machine guns. As the DB5 turned further, Gerber could see the rear wheel hubs that could extend as tire slashers, and then finally, at the back, he knew a thick slab of metal could rise up from the trunk to act as a bulletproof shield for the rear window.

When the car had completed its rotation, it came to a stop facing them. Many would think this might be one of the twenty-five replicas Aston Martin had built at a cost of over three million dollars to any prospective buyer.

But no—this was the real thing.

It was the original car used in the James Bond film *Goldfinger*—chassis number DP/216/1 that had disappeared off the face of the Earth from a hangar at Boca Raton Airport in Florida in 1997.

How it had come into Solano's possession and how he had got it up there, Gerber had no idea, and he wasn't going to ask. He also wasn't going to tell.

"Want to sit in her?" asked Solano, jolting Gerber out of his trance.

He didn't even need to answer, the look on his face said it all.

Solano moved round to the driver's door and pulled it open. Gerber climbed reverentially inside. Even the smell of leather was still present. He looked over the instrument panel, the concealed compartment to the rear of the gearstick between the two seats where all the gadgets were operated from, and the hidden screen that followed a tracking device. He then took hold of the wheel. He pushed the pedals and worked the gearshift. He glanced down at the ignition. The key was there. He looked at Solano, who nodded with a smile.

Gerber turned the key.

The engine sprang to life with a throaty roar. He revved it a couple of times, sending a tingle up his spine as the noise from the exhaust reverberated through the car. It was muffled somewhat by a pipe that had been attached at the rear to draw the gases away, but even so, it made the hairs on the back of his neck stand on end.

He was about to push one of the buttons in the center console when Solano laid a hand on his shoulder. When Gerber looked up, Solano shook his head with a smile.

"I wouldn't."

Gerber looked confused.

"Why, you haven't gone and…?"

Solano raised his eyebrows.

"For real?" said Gerber. "But why, you can't use them?"

"Just because I can, Rudi. Just because I can," said Solano with a smile.

Gerber shook his head with wonder.

After a couple of minutes he turned off the ignition and climbed out. Solano shut the door and the two men shared a moment.

Gerber knew Solano came in here on occasion and sat in the car with the engine running just to get away from the world. It wasn't over any childhood fantasy of being a certain character—it was the fact that he, and he alone, owned it and could take pleasure from it whenever he wished. Something no one else in the world could do.

As far as Gerber knew, the DB5 was the second most precious possession in Solano's life.

A couple of minutes later he was back in the real world. The car had been shut away and they'd walked back to the front and that amazing view. They were now sitting on the sofas. Gerber took a brief sip of whiskey and turned to Solano.

"So, Victor, how can I help you?"

Over the next twenty minutes Solano explained how he had been feeling. The fact was, he needed more painkillers for the worsening of his condition—which was an advanced progression of stomach cancer that had spread to various other organs and was, unfortunately, inoperable. Gerber listened attentively and prescribed a number of options. At the end, he leaned back into the deep cushions with a sigh and looked straight at Solano.

"I've been going over the results of the tests you had last month and checking the daily data you send me from your watch." He took a deep breath. "I'm not sure how long you have, Victor, but I think you need to think about getting your affairs in order. It could be weeks, more likely months, certainly not years."

He looked at him seriously.

Solano looked at Gerber for a few moments and then stared out across the valley. He then stood and walked over to the glass. It was the perfect place to contemplate life and death.

After a minute he turned to Gerber.

"Thank you for being so honest, Rudi. I know we've discussed this before, and I've been preparing myself, but it's still sobering when it's there in black and white." Gerber nodded gravely. "But I'm ready. I just have one last thing to do. Something I feel will be a fitting epitaph."

Gerber watched him closely. Solano had always been calm, but now, facing what was ahead, he had to marvel at his composure.

"That's very pragmatic, Victor, but I'm not sure you have that much time to achieve any more in your life."

Solano smiled.

"I think there is time for one more thing. I have been preparing it for a while. All the pieces are falling into place. There are just a couple to go, and then I'll be ready."

Gerber looked intrigued.

"Would it have anything to do with your talk in Basel the other day? That caused quite a stir."

Solano looked at him seriously.

"Yes, it did, didn't it?" He smiled ruefully. "And yes, you are right, it has something to do with that." He paused. "We are at a crossroads, Rudi. There are things that have to be done that only someone in my position is able to do. If anything, my medical condition makes it an easier decision. But I can see things clearly now. When you don't have to plan for the rest of your life, it frees up a lot of thought."

Gerber nodded sagely. He then stood and walked over to the window to join his friend. He stood there in awe. In the distance it looked like the weather was turning. Black clouds were rolling in over the jagged, saw-tooth peaks on the horizon.

There was a storm coming.

"In that case, Victor," he said, still staring out across the mountains, "I wish you very good luck."

Chapter Six

Craig Richards was fifty-six years old. He'd been married three times and could never seem to hold down a relationship for some reason. It was probably something to do with his commitment to work at the expense of all else, and the focus he had for it, but he was also pretty set in his ways, and any partner was likely to have to fit into his way of doing things, or not at all. Given that, he was a caring and generous person, so all his friends hoped he would eventually meet *the one*. He had a gruff, but kind, demeanor and a craggy, avuncular face that was starting to show its age. He still had most of his hair, which was usually kept short, and there was a tinge of gray around the edges, which, if asked, he would say had come from hanging around McCready for too long.

But he wouldn't have it any other way.

The two had met when Richards had been an engineer working on the rigs in the North Sea. At the time, McCready had been a fairly inexperienced commercial diver cutting his teeth in the dangerous world of saturation diving.

They had immediately hit it off.

When Richards had decided to set up his own company, Ocean Oil Ltd near Aberdeen, McCready had been one of the original investors. The company had recently been rebranded as Ocean Tech, and they now specialized in the design and development of underwater technology for the scientific and military communities. They used their skills, experience and imagination to produce some seriously high-end kit that was both functional and ground-breaking in many ways. A prime example of this now sat battered and bruised in the main construction building after a recent adventure in Los Angeles. It was called Skyline and was an advanced prototype delivery system that could transport a small cargo, or human being, anywhere on the planet. And given its recent excursion, Richards was more than happy to say the prototype could move on to full production, having just been through what was effectively the most brutal test drive it was ever going to get. In fact, he'd been surprised to actually see it again as McCready had left it in the middle of a freeway in Los Angeles. But a few days previously it had been delivered to them courtesy of a grateful United States government, who had McCready and the hardware to thank for avoiding a global catastrophe.

And while the US had returned the machinery, he hadn't expected to see McCready for quite some time. He had nearly been killed in the operation, and Richards had thought he'd take some well-earned rest with Clare in Los Angeles. So when he'd received the call from him earlier, saying he was in the UK and they needed to have a chat, it didn't bode well. All he could do was take a deep breath and see what his closest friend had to say. He trusted him with his life, and while he would always say there were limits to how far he would go to help McCready achieve his aims, past experience would prove that statement to not be entirely correct.

He glanced out of the window of the design studio on the first floor of the large water tank facility at Ocean Tech and saw McCready climb out of a cab and walk toward the building. He sighed deeply and stood to welcome his friend.

A couple of minutes later McCready entered the studio. When he saw Richards he gave him a somewhat guilty grin, and then walked over and the two embraced fondly.

"What the hell are you doing back here?" said Richards. "Thought we wouldn't see you for weeks, if ever."

"Yeah, well, it's a long story," said McCready.

"It usually is. I guess you'd better come in and tell me all about it," said Richards, heading for the small conference room next to the studio.

Once inside, and with coffees made, they sat down and faced each other.

Richards could tell it was serious. There was a certain strain around McCready's eyes. He could normally function through all sorts of stress and usually come up with the right course of action, but right now it almost seemed as though he was lost—not sure what to do. Rather than push him, he let him tell it in his own time, in his own way.

McCready took a large gulp of coffee and let the liquid warm him up. He then leaned back in the chair and looked directly at Richards.

"You remember a few weeks ago... blimey, it seems like years... when we were on the deck at the back of the house and Sarah had been round, and after she'd gone we'd chatted about women and any we'd had regrets over?"

Richards remembered it well. He and Sarah,

McCready's sister-in-law, had been sitting on the deck of McCready's house in the remote bay on the west coast of Scotland. After a great meal, Sarah had had to take her little one-year-old girl, Shauna, home. Once she'd gone, the two of them had moved onto the whiskeys and reminisced into the night. It could have been predicted the subject, at some point, would have turned to women.

"You showed me pictures of that Ukrainian dancer..." said McCready, at which Richards groaned, "...and I told you the story of Carlita." Richards nodded. When McCready had told him the story it had been no contest. He had nearly even had tears in his eyes.

"Well," said McCready, "I had a call from her a couple of days ago... She's in trouble, Craig. Like life and death trouble."

McCready let that hang for a moment.

Richards started having a very bad feeling inside. When McCready said someone he cared about was in trouble, it never ended well. He felt a knot tightening in his stomach.

"Okay," he said slowly. "What sort of trouble are we talking about?"

"The sort where Martin Steel is getting nervous."

The pain in Richards' stomach grew even worse.

McCready then relayed what Steel had told him in London. While he was speaking, Richards listened attentively, staring at the table. When McCready had finished, Richards continued to stare at the table. He had to think of what to say before they went down the inevitable path. He also knew he wouldn't be able to stop McCready doing anything to help Carlita. She clearly meant a great deal to him, and it seemed there were many unanswered questions between them, even after all these years. The only question for now was how far could he go in helping him, and how much of the company and its assets could he reasonably allow McCready to use. The fact that Steel had said McCready could draw upon him for support meant that he took the situation seriously—which meant it was serious.

"Okay, so what do you want to do?"

"What, no pushback? No, 'why are you doing this?'"

"Well, for a start, you haven't said what you actually want to do yet, and secondly, I've learned to save my breath until it's really necessary."

McCready smiled and relaxed a little.

"You know, for once I don't have a clue."

Richards stared at him. It was the first time McCready hadn't spurted out some harebrained scheme of how to save the day that would result in them being thrown headfirst onto an uncontrollable train that was potentially heading for disaster. For him to have no idea was, on one level, a relief— it meant any plan they came up with might be within the realms of sanity—but it was also concerning. Maybe his friend really had been through too much in the last few weeks.

"Well that's a first," said Richards.

McCready was silent.

"Okay, let's take it slowly and work from what we know." He paused. "You say she was last seen being bundled aboard a motor cruiser in Algeria, which as far as we know is now in Monaco." McCready nodded. "But we don't know if she's still alive?"

"That's what Steel said. He seems to think the company that owns the yacht—though he was a bit vague about that —want to know if she's acquired certain information, and it's so important, they can't kill her until they clarify it."

Richards thought for a few moments.

"But we've no way of knowing if they managed to get

the information, so they could have got it halfway across the Med and dumped her en route?"

McCready's face hardened.

"Hey, we have to go through all the scenarios, John."

McCready relented. "Yeah, okay, it's a possibility. But if we assume that, we may as well not even bother."

"Okay," said Richards, "so we assume she's still on the boat and still alive."

"Yes... but she could be in a bad way, so anything we come up with has to take that into account."

Richards glanced at him. He was about to say he hadn't actually agreed to do anything yet, and that this was just spitballing, but he didn't want to get into the inevitable long-drawn-out argument. That would come later, and anyway, John looked pretty tired and stressed for all that right now.

"Well, the first thing we need is intel on the ground. We have to know if she's alive, what condition she's in, and where, specifically, she's being held, then we can work out if it's feasible to get her out."

"It's feasible," said McCready, emphatically.

"You don't even know where she is or what opposition you'll face."

"It's feasible," McCready repeated. His expression said that for Richards to disagree would mean stress levels were going to soon be off the charts.

"Okay, it's feasible," said Richards, shaking his head.

McCready started to wake up to the idea, as though his brain had suddenly clicked into gear and the tiredness was being pushed aside.

"So, we go down to Monaco and watch the boat. I could do an underwater survey, maybe plant a bug—I'm sure Steel will have something I can use—and then we can plan an assault to get her off."

"Hang on a minute. You can't just go in there guns blazing, so to speak. It's Europe, for god's sake. You don't want a diplomatic incident. And, as you say, Steel is not officially involved, so he clearly won't want to pick up the pieces if it all goes south."

"Yeah, I know, which is why we have to be the ones to go on board."

"But what if they're armed? We can't use weapons, John."

McCready looked at him before continuing.

"Okay, fair enough, but there are other ways. I could take a minisub and get her out underwater. They'd never see me coming… never see me leave."

Richards looked at him.

"We haven't got anything right now. The XB4 is out on trials and there's nothing here ready to go."

"You said that about Skyline."

"There's nothing here ready to go, John."

"Okay. Can't you try and see if you can get the XB4 back for a few days. This has to be done now, Craig. I have to leave today, tomorrow at the latest. I've no idea how much time we have."

Richards sighed.

"Okay, I'll see what I can do."

The XB4, which stood for X-Boat, generation 4, was a two-man submersible that could travel at thirty knots underwater and fifty on the surface. It would be the perfect vehicle for this sort of operation, but it was currently under trials with the Ministry of Defense. And they were sometimes prickly about changing schedules or contracts. There was a second machine, but it was still in pieces in the construction building and there was no way to get it ready in time.

"Okay," said Richards, "the best I can do is contact the MOD and see what they're prepared to do. Why don't you go out there and get a lay of the land. Take Eugene. I'll get in touch when I have anything." At least this would get McCready off his back for a while and Eugene Porter was good to have in the field. He was an expert with explosives and all things mechanical, so could be a great asset to whatever transpired.

McCready thought it over. He looked up.

"Okay, sounds like a plan. But stay in touch and let me know when you can get down there with the kit."

"Will do," said Richards, and then silently to himself, *here we go again.*

Chapter Seven

Holmes Summit was the highest peak of the Shackleton Range of mountains in Antarctica and rose to a height of just over six thousand feet. The mountains stretched for a hundred miles in the north-western region of the continent, and lay between the Slessor and Recovery glaciers.

As Doctor Nyah Hawthorn climbed up onto the summit and stared out at the view, she smiled broadly. She could see snow and ice in all directions. Looking one way, there was the interior of the coldest place on Earth, while the other eventually led down to the Weddell Sea that bordered the Ronne Ice Shelf.

There was just something so pristine about the planet's last untouched continent.

T. E. Lawrence had commented on his love of the desert because it was so 'clean'—well, it couldn't get much 'cleaner' than this. She could relate. Admittedly, there were a large number of countries that had a presence down there, but with strict rules and guidelines in place, there couldn't be the grotesque development and rape of resources that happened elsewhere in the world.

Her current research centered on seismic activity in the region, and where might be the best location to place sensors to detect any tremors and movement of the Earth.

A crackly voice came over the walkie-talkie she had strapped to her chest, distracting her from the view.

"Okay, when you've finished the sightseeing, can we get some science done here, please," said her colleague, Josh Murphy.

She grinned, lifted her snow goggles onto her forehead, and reached down to pick up the mike. She gripped it in thick thermal gloves and pressed the TALK button.

"Hey, some of us want to enjoy our time at the bottom of the world, you know," she said. "All work and no play… blahdy-blah! Coming down now."

She replaced the mike, grabbed hold of her ice axe and then turned to head down the steep two-hundred-foot snow slope to where Murphy was setting up the equipment.

Nyah was twenty-nine years old and based out of the Halley VI Research Station.

She had always loved the outdoors. She had been drawn to it, but it had come out of a troubled childhood.

Her father, who was English, had suffered from severe depression for many years, much of which had been hidden from her. She had been a precocious kid and had been sent to boarding school at the age of six, as her mother, who was Jamaican, had been unable to cope with looking after her as well as her father.

Being by far the youngest boarder at the all-girl school, and being of mixed race, she was excluded from many of the cliques that developed between the other girls. She found, more and more, that she was ostracized. She became withdrawn, introverted, having to accept her own company as the norm. It made her feel as though she was somehow different to other people, that she wasn't a whole person—there was something missing.

To escape from this, she threw herself into her schoolwork and found that she loved science. It opened up a whole new world for her to explore—one that didn't need the company of others, and one she could escape to anytime she pleased.

When she needed life outside the classroom, she turned to the mountains.

The school was located in one of the most beautiful parts of England—the Lake District in Cumbria. This was where she developed her love for the outdoors and wild spaces—particularly in winter when there was snow on the ground and the air was crisp and clear. It had a certain isolation, desolation—how she felt about herself.

She spent much of her time hiking and walking, and she learned to rock climb.

Once, when she was fourteen, she had been on a school camping trip in the mountains when the weather had rapidly deteriorated with high winds and thick snow. As was her want, she had fallen behind from the group—something her teachers had come to expect, but with the urgency over the weather, she'd been forgotten and had become separated as the blizzard closed in.

The panic that had followed had resulted in a mountain rescue team scouring the hills for two days on foot, supported by a helicopter in the air. Nyah, meanwhile, had been oblivious to the drama. She had calmly built herself a snow hole in a thick drift and sat it out until the weather had cleared. She had been found walking happily down to a main road to hitch a lift back to the school, none the worse for wear.

They'd kept a closer eye on her after that.

As time went on, she had been accepted by the University of Bristol to study Earth Sciences. She had been in her last year when her father committed suicide. She just managed to get through her final exams and gave up a research placement to care for her mother, who was devastated by the loss.

Everything else was of little concern.

But there was only so much she could do.

She had to watch as her mother slowly lost the will to live, and over the coming months faded into someone Nyah hardly recognized. She did what she could, but to no avail. Her mother passed away from an illness not long after.

Nyah had been distraught.

She now had no real direction. Nowhere to go. No rock to cling on to.

She had tried a few relationships, but none of them had worked out. Either she had terrible taste in men, or men just weren't worth it. A couple of times when she thought it might have gone somewhere, she'd discovered her boyfriends had been cheating on her.

At her lowest point she had considered taking her own life—what did she have to live for?

But then, out of the blue, an old friend from college had sent her an ad for the position of science technician with the British Antarctic Survey.

It was one of those pivotal moments that could change a life in an instant by arriving at the perfect time.

She had leapt at the opportunity. After all, if she wanted

to run away from the world and hide, where better than the last unexplored continent at the bottom of it.

And now, in the barren wastelands of Antarctica she had found her calling—her place in the world, if you will—and that she belonged somewhere, and it was as far away from the rest of it as it was possible to get.

She also found she could relate to the people down there. While many were dedicated scientists, pushing the boundaries of knowledge and discovery, there were also those who didn't fit in in the world above and were seeking an escape, just like her.

She had a new family and she'd never been happier—at least she had convinced herself of that.

Over the years she had taken a PhD and progressed from technician to full-blown scientist, running projects of her own, which had, today, brought her to the slopes of Holmes Summit.

When she reached Murphy he'd just unpacked the first of two crates.

The equipment was made up of a series of sensors that had a new generation of sensitivity and accuracy when it came to detecting tremors and predicting possible future quakes.

She enjoyed working with Murphy. He was a twenty-five-year-old Irishman with a wicked sense of humor, and someone who never took anything too seriously, except for his work. He could seem to determine problems and their solutions quicker than anyone she knew and she always enjoyed spending time with him. She also thought he had a crush on her, but the banter between them meant it wouldn't be a problem. She'd told him on many occasions, and in no uncertain terms, that he wasn't her type. He'd replied that she was clearly delusional and they'd left it at that. It didn't help matters that, despite her deep-rooted mistrust of men, she was somewhat attracted to their American helicopter pilot, Matt Bowman, who was due there any minute, and who Murphy ribbed mercilessly.

She helped him carry the sensor package over to an area of snow clear of any rock. They buried it to a depth of four feet to ensure it was protected from the fiercest gales that could blow across the region, making sure the transmitter aerial was poking out, clear of any obstructions.

Once it was secure, they did a systems check. When they were satisfied it was working and online, and could be monitored from back at Halley, she turned to Murphy.

"All set?"

"All set," he replied. "Guess you can call in that Yank Neanderthal to pick us up."

She grinned and hit him playfully on the shoulder.

"You can always walk back."

He glanced at her. "No way. He needs me to explain what all the instruments do. Without that he'd be flying round in circles all day."

She hit him again and grabbed the mike for the walkie-talkie.

"Okay, Air Two, this is Shackleton ground team, ready for pick up."

There were a few seconds of static, then a crackly reply.

"Roger, Shackleton, Air Two en route. Ten minutes, out."

Nyah glanced at Murphy. "Come on, let's check the landing site's clear."

As they were so far up the side of the mountain, there was nowhere for the helicopter to land on flat ground. What they had to do was clear a six-foot-square area that was level, so the chopper could get the front of the skids down horizontally, while the rest of the machine was effectively still hovering with the blades inches from the slope above. It required great skill but was something the pilots had to do on a regular basis to support the research teams in the field.

Nyah and Murphy made it down fifty feet lower to where the chopper had dropped them off. The increasing wind had blown snow over the makeshift pad. They used foldable shovels from their packs to widen the site and ensure it was level. By the time they'd finished they could see the little red speck approaching in the distance.

They sat down in the snow and waited for it to arrive.

As the chopper approached, it flew close by to check the winds and the landing site. After it swung round it came straight in toward the slope and effortlessly dropped the front of the skids down onto the cleared area. The noise was deafening, and they needed goggles to protect them from the flying snow and shivers of ice that were flung into the air by the screaming rotors. But a minute later Nyah and Murphy had thrown their packs into the back and jumped in. When Nyah was secure inside, she slammed the door shut and tapped Bowman on the shoulder to indicate they were ready. She then pulled on her comms headset as the helicopter lifted up and reversed away from the slope before spinning round and heading off over the pristine white landscape.

Nyah always loved the flights down here, at least when the conditions were good. There were obvious limits, when flying was prohibited for safety reasons. If you crashed in bad weather there was no quick support to help you out, but on days like today, with uninterrupted sunshine and blue skies, there was nowhere else on Earth she would rather be. It was the barren emptiness of it all, somehow made to appear virginal by the blanket of white that covered the landscape.

Antarctica held ninety percent of the world's ice, which in turn wrapped up seventy percent of the world's fresh water. Much of the current research was to determine how fast the ice was shrinking. What they'd found had been alarming. If it all disappeared it would raise sea levels by not far off two hundred feet, which in turn would submerge many of the world's great cities and render miles of coastline uninhabitable. It was a crisis that was coming, however much people might want to brush it under the carpet. Sometimes she thought humanity was like a bunch of lemmings heading toward the proverbial cliff. Even with an advance party at the cliff's edge telling everyone where they were headed, it seemed to make no difference, the mindless lemmings just kept on going—right over the edge.

She felt sad there was no way out of this, but some things were just not possible to stop—even if it meant the end of society and the human race as most people knew it.

As she gazed out of the window her attention was drawn to a small black shape way off in the distance. It was heading in toward the center of the continent. It was clearly a helicopter, but whose?

"Hey, Matt, you know who that is over there, where they're headed?"

Bowman looked out to the right of the cockpit. He watched the aircraft as it headed further away from them. It was black, not the bright red of the British and many of the other choppers operating in the region. It also looked like there was some sort of large drum suspended beneath it.

"No idea... And I don't know who uses black helicopters down here. The flight plans for the day didn't say anyone would be out there. Might be worth checking when we get back. We don't want anyone left without support if they go down."

"Roger that. I'll check it out when we're home."

Murphy mimed someone whining away with his mouth and head movements. Nyah elbowed him in the side, but she was grinning.

Chapter Eight

"Bloody hell, guv!" said Eugene Porter as he walked into the ten thousand dollar a week apartment on the waterfront in Monaco. "This is amazing!"

McCready and Porter had flown down to Nice in the South of France earlier in the day with a couple of large cases of equipment. They'd rented a Toyota Land Cruiser and driven along the spectacular French coastline to the Principality of Monaco, less than ten miles to the east, and a similar distance from the Italian border. The weather was fine and the holiday-like atmosphere of the region seeped into both of them, though for McCready it was no holiday.

Monaco was situated on the glistening shores of the Mediterranean. It was one of those places that, if it didn't exist, a writer or filmmaker would have made it up. Most famous for having a royal family that at one time had included Princess Grace, formerly Grace Kelly, and the world's most glamorous Formula One race, it was also home to more billionaires in its under one square mile area than anywhere else on Earth.

In fact, it was such a desirable place to live, primarily due to the lack of income tax, that they were running out of land to build on. As a result, new multi-billion-dollar developments were being constructed on land reclaimed from the sea. The resultant apartments and villas were some of the most expensive real estate in the world.

It was to one of these that Porter and McCready had arrived half an hour earlier. The penthouse apartment was situated in a new block just to the east of the main harbor. The tenth-floor position allowed an unhindered view of the harbor and beyond along the coast. It was one of those cases where Martin Steel had a friend... McCready had left it at that. The only instruction was not to trash the place.

Porter walked into the main open-plan living area from the entrance hall and stopped dead in the center of the room. He'd never seen such an opulent space. Designer furniture was attractively arranged throughout, while distinctive artwork hung on the walls and marble tiles covered the floor. At the far end, a wide glass frontage, bordered by two Greek-style pillars, opened onto a terrace that ran the full width of the apartment.

He crossed over, pulled back one of the large glass sliding panels, and walked outside.

In front of him was the sparkling water of the Mediterranean. To his right he could see the harbor filled with numerous superyachts, and beyond, the sprawling buildings and apartments that made up the bulk of the sovereign city state. Rising above them in the center were the battlements of the magnificent Prince's Palace of Monaco that had originally been built in 1191 as a Genoese fortress but was now home to the royal family.

He turned round and looked at McCready, who had

dropped his bag on the floor and was checking over some paperwork.

"Any chance we could stay here all summer, guv?" said Porter.

McCready looked up. He put the papers down on an elegant sideboard below a large mirror and then joined Porter out on the terrace. He breathed in the warm air and looked around. Despite everything, he had to smile. It was an incredible location.

"Afraid not. We have a week. Make the most of it," he said.

They both looked out over the cramped buildings and streets of the tiny principality.

"Hard to believe they have cars racing round here at nearly two hundred miles per hour," said McCready.

Porter looked at him skeptically.

"Bloody boring if you ask me. All they do is go round in circles. And here it's a parade—one behind the other," said Porter.

McCready grinned, but he had to concede the last point.

"Yeah, but think of all the technology, the strategy. I mean, they can change the wheels in one point nine."

"One point nine minutes to change a wheel," spluttered Porter. "Can get mine done faster at Kwik Fit!"

"Er… one point nine *seconds* to change all *four* wheels," said McCready.

Porter looked at him, not sure if he was having him on.

McCready nodded.

Porter looked out across the bay. "Yeah, okay, that's pretty tidy."

McCready grinned.

Porter walked back inside to go and find his room and unpack. McCready followed him in and explored the rest of the apartment.

Half an hour later, he'd changed into a short-sleeved shirt and cut-off jeans. He grabbed a beer from the fridge and walked back out onto the terrace.

He had been looking out to sea and taking in the view for about five minutes when he noticed a water-skier weaving a slalom wake behind a fast-moving boat. The wake grew ever wider as the skier jumped the rolling water, left and right, before swerving to miss a large white RIB that cut across her path. The ski-boat driver and the attractive girl in a bikini in the back shouted and threw derogatory hand signals at the two men in the RIB, but they ignored them.

McCready walked quickly into the apartment. He grabbed a pair of binoculars from his backpack and then went back outside and focused in on the boat.

Both the men were dressed in black. There was a certain military style to their clothing. They looked fit and strong—possibly bodyguards of some sort. Given the value of the boats in the marina and at anchor in the bay, and some of their owners, that wasn't a surprise. As he looked closer, though, he could see an automatic weapon in the bottom of the boat. He moved up and zoomed out, checking the predicted path the boat was taking. It was headed straight for a large superyacht moored about a quarter of a mile from the harbor. As McCready focused in on the name at the rear, a chill went up his spine.

Freedom Seas.

He now had time to look her over more closely, and in more detail, than he had on the video Steel had shown him.

The binoculars also had a record capability. He pressed down on the small red button that sent the images to a microSD card in the glasses.

She was definitely a spectacular boat—in fact, 'ship' might be a more appropriate term. She was over four hundred feet in length, with five decks, including the bridge. At the rear was a large open area with steps down to the water to aide entry and exit for swimming. On the deck above, an oval swimming pool stretched almost the full width of the ship. There was a helipad two decks above the pool, as well as one at the bow. There was currently a small executive chopper on the pad at the bow, its rotors whirling. Someone had either just arrived or was just leaving. Above the bridge were a number of large radar domes and tall communications aerials. There was no doubt she had all the technical gizmos and toys to take her across any ocean on the planet.

As he watched, the RIB approached the cruiser. It drove up close to the side of the hull and he saw one of the men lift a walkie-talkie. A minute later, a section, just above the waterline, swung open to reveal a large space beyond. Two metal arms extended out over the water from the cavernous interior. McCready watched, fascinated, as the boat was winched up out of the water and drawn back inside. Ten minutes later the section had swung back into place. It was as though the RIB had been swallowed whole by the larger vessel.

Despite the heat of the day McCready shivered as he realized Carlita may very well be on board somewhere. In fact, he prayed she was, because if she wasn't, he dreaded to think where she might be—the bottom of the blue water that stretched to the horizon being the most likely.

He watched for a minute longer. He was about to return

inside when he saw a figure walk toward the helicopter at the front of the yacht. He put the glasses back to his eyes but missed the figure before it had disappeared inside behind blacked-out windows. He carried on recording as the chopper lifted off the deck and headed toward shore. A minute later it was above Monaco and then disappeared over the hills beyond.

He walked back inside the apartment and grabbed the large bag that contained the equipment he'd been given by Steel. The gear was on loan from the special forces and had no markings that could be traced back to the British government.

He pulled out a throat comms system that would allow him to talk to Porter. There was also a laser mike that could detect conversations behind any window you fired it at, up to a mile distant.

He grabbed the laser mike and a tripod from another case and walked back out onto the terrace. The sun was still quite high, but it was starting its long arc down to the horizon. He set up the tripod and attached the mike. It had a rifle-like grip and telescopic sights that allowed pinpoint accuracy. The received audio could be played back by a secure Bluetooth connection to a pair of AirPods he'd placed in his ears.

Once the mike was on the tripod he swung the barrel round until it was pointing at the *Freedom Seas*. He looked through the sights and moved it until the crosshairs were on one of the side windows of the bridge. He squeezed the trigger and locked the invisible laser in position. Immediately he could hear what was going on inside. He adjusted the gain and volume and used a filter to remove some interference that was likely coming from electronic equipment on the boat. He then stepped to one side and leaned on the rail surrounding the terrace to concentrate on the conversation he could hear.

Initially there was nothing much of interest—just the usual daily ship-related talk. The captain was discussing maintenance schedules and refueling. Apparently they were okay for the next trip. But then there was a heated exchange between the captain and someone he clearly disliked. They were speaking in French, which McCready couldn't understand, except the odd word he'd remembered from lessons at school many years ago. While he couldn't be sure, it sounded like the newcomer, a man, was discussing a woman, and that there would be 'finality' tonight. The captain then flicked back to English and spoke to another person, instructing them to prepare the vessel for departure later that evening.

It didn't look good.

He moved the position of the mike and targeted the laser at a lower cabin window two decks below the bridge.

He went from window to window. There was nothing from the first three, but when he reached the fourth, his veins turned to ice water.

He could hear a faint noise over the AirPods.

It was a low groaning.

It was the sound of a woman.

She was clearly in pain. A moment later a door was opened and shut, then footsteps moved across the room. They stopped. A man's voice spoke. It was direct and left no room for misunderstanding.

"We leave tonight. You either tell us what we want to know, or you will suffer even more. Is that clear?"

The woman groaned.

"Go to hell!" she managed.

There was the sound of a slap and then a cry. It was followed by footsteps and the slamming of a door.

McCready pulled the pods out of his ears and sat down on one of the recliners on the terrace. He stared out at the yacht moored a mere quarter of a mile away and realized he had heard Carlita's voice for the first time in twenty-five years. He felt a pain grow deep in his heart, but it was soon replaced by growing anger and the thought of what he was going to do to the people holding her captive.

He jumped up and walked back inside. Porter was still in his room.

He pulled a laptop out of his case. Once it was fired up he opened a file containing the specs and layout of the *Freedom Seas*. He looked through them carefully. He would need to know every inch of her if any plan to rescue Carlita was going to succeed.

After he'd gone over the schematics in his mind, he grabbed his phone and hit a speed dial number. It rang four times and was answered.

McCready didn't waste any time.

"Craig, how you doing on the XB4?"

"And hello to you too," said Richards.

"She's on the boat, Craig. Carlita's on the boat. It looks like they're going to kill her tonight if they don't get the information. I have to go in. There's no more time."

There was a pause on the line. "There's no way we can get the kit by then. The MOD have her way out on a vessel doing sea trials. But I can come down anyway to help if you want."

McCready thought for a moment.

"Did Steel come through with the transport?"

"Yeah, there's a Chinook sitting on the back lot. It's

unmarked and he said there's no crew, except a doctor we can take along to treat her if she's in a bad way."

"She'll be in a bad way."

"Okay, Charlie can pilot. She couldn't wait to get in the cockpit. Says she has such fun with you and helicopters."

"She did, did she?"

"Yeah."

"Okay, stay in touch with Eugene. If I have to leave before you get here, just play it by ear. We'll have to make this up as we go along."

"Nothing new then?"

Despite everything, McCready grinned. "Guess not."

And with that he clicked off the phone. He was glad Craig was coming down. And Charlie flying the chopper would be a great asset. She hadn't been working with them for long but she was one of the best pilots he'd ever seen. Her skills had saved his life in California several weeks before. She was also Richards' niece and had some sort of relationship with Porter, though no one seemed to know quite what that was.

"Eugene, how are you doing?" McCready shouted to the rear of the apartment.

A couple of moments later Porter emerged from his room. He was wearing a loud Hawaiian shirt and long Bermuda Shorts. He had a pair of garish bright yellow sandals on his feet. McCready just stared at him.

"Jesus!" said McCready.

"What?"

"It's Monaco, not bloody Benidorm!"

"Top kit," said Porter. "Show the locals how to dress!"

McCready shook his head.

"Okay, guv. We got a plan?"

An hour later they were ready. The sun was starting to go down and Monaco's vibrant nightlife would soon be switching into high gear. Their first task was to find a boat, and as they didn't have one, that meant stealing one. McCready had assumed they'd be able to use the XB4, so he hadn't planned for needing any other craft. But now, with time of the essence, there was nothing else for it.

They made their way out of the apartment and round to the back. When the block had been built, the complex had incorporated a small marina where residents could moor their boats without the need to use the main harbor in town.

McCready looked around. He carried a dive bag containing a thin wetsuit, mask, fins and weight belt. He wasn't sure how he was going to get aboard the *Freedom Seas* but he was sure it would involve some form of excursion into the water.

There were about fifteen boats floating next to the pontoons in the marina. No one was paying them any particular attention.

A small sailing yacht, with the sails down, motored in and moored up. After the occupants had jumped ashore, the couple, arm in arm, wandered up toward the apartment block entrance.

When they'd gone, McCready and Porter walked down onto the pontoon. At the far end was a large speedboat. It was black, had a streamlined hull, and twin Mercury SeaPro 500hp engines on the back. It would be more than capable for what they had in mind.

McCready had actually been surprised when Porter had volunteered to come with him, knowing they were likely to be going out on the sea. Porter had an unhealthy fear of water as he couldn't swim, but apparently he'd been taking lessons since nearly drowning in the River Thames a year previously—and now he said he loved it. Whether that was false bravado, McCready wasn't sure, but he'd keep the faith until proven otherwise. Also, Porter had the uncanny ability of making things go bang in spectacular ways, as well as being adept with all things mechanical. So, as they walked toward the small powerboat at the end of the pontoon, McCready had no doubt whatsoever that within a few minutes they'd be heading out of the marina—keys or no keys.

Five minutes later Porter had worked his magic. McCready jumped on board, checked over the controls, and then grabbed the wheel. Once Porter had untied them, McCready put her into gear and started to ease away from the pontoon. They didn't want to attract any undue attention. For all he knew, the owner could be watching as they maneuvered out from the mooring and would be rushing down to alert the authorities. But he couldn't worry about that now.

He turned the boat around and then headed slowly away from shore and out to sea. Once clear of the navigation channel, he glanced at Porter, who was gripping the side rail—maybe all that fear hadn't gone after all. He then pushed the twin throttles forward. The boat leaped ahead like an eager racehorse, and as the sun slipped below the horizon and the light faded on another day, McCready felt his adrenaline surge as he prepared himself for the fight he knew was coming.

As the boat sped out of the marina, a pair of binoculars followed its progress. They were held by one of two men who were sitting on the balcony of a nearby apartment close to the main harbor, and which gave them a clear view over McCready's block. They'd been there all day and watched McCready on the terrace and the subsequent action in the marina.

As they tracked the boat heading out to sea, the second of the two lifted a walkie-talkie and spoke briefly into it.

Chapter Nine

As McCready headed out over the water he wished he was there under different circumstances. He'd never been to Monaco before and the atmosphere and sheer vibe of the place seemed intoxicating, even though he'd only had time to see it from the fringes.

As the hull of the boat crackled over the calm water, the sound of laughter and music wafted on the breeze from onshore bars and restaurants and the large yachts that were moored in the bay.

But he had to put all that out of mind.

Up ahead was his mission.

He focused on the rapidly approaching outline of the *Freedom Seas*. Somehow he had to work out how he was going to extract Carlita from the depths of the ship and the hell she must be enduring. It didn't help that every minute that passed could be more pain and agony for her. For all he knew, she could already be dead. It spurred him on.

Five minutes later they were two hundred yards from the rear of the superyacht. McCready knocked the throttles down and the boat glided off the plane and came to a smooth stop in the water. He grabbed a pair of binoculars and scanned the hull for any crew who might be on duty.

It was hardly difficult to see. The boat was lit up like a Christmas tree. Lights were blazing on all the decks and glowing from the windows along her side. The upper decks had wide glass panoramic panels, while those lower down were more porthole size. He figured this was the crew area, but it was also from where he had heard the exchange between Carlita and the man who had threatened her.

He passed the wheel over to Porter and then quickly slipped into his wetsuit. They'd discussed the plan earlier. They would surveil the boat in a wide circle, hopefully unobserved. If McCready could see an easy entry point he would go for that. Porter would then stay back a safe distance, blending into the night, and when McCready had Carlita, he would call him in to pick them up. Then it was just a matter of hightailing it out of there. McCready had no idea how long it would take Craig to get down. The last message he'd received from him was that they were over central France but with no definite ETA.

McCready was well aware the best-laid plans could go sideways, so the instruction to Porter, if things went wrong, or if they lost comms, was for him to head back to shore and contact Richards to plan the next move. The *Freedom Seas* could be tracked by GPS, so even if she departed with McCready on board, the helicopter should be able to find them.

But all that was in the future.

What he needed to do now was work out the best way to get on board.

Back at the apartment he'd looked over the entire yacht through the binoculars, searching for weak spots, any areas that might be less visible. The one that had stuck out was the rear swim deck. While in daytime this was the most open area, at night, it was low down and would be largely hidden from the decks above, which were layered back at an angle. Someone would have to be specifically looking there to see anyone. And he had the element of surprise. The crew wouldn't be checking for someone trying to get onto the ship. Once there, though, he'd have to be careful as he moved about. If he was spotted, there were only so many places you could go, even on a boat of this size.

With his wetsuit zipped up, he grabbed a dive knife from the bag and attached it to his calf. He then slipped the weight belt around his waist. While McCready was fit and lean, and his body was pretty much neutrally buoyant in the water, he was wearing the suit, which would require a small amount of weight to counteract its buoyancy and allow him to stay underwater without expending energy.

He then pulled on his Mares Plana Avanti fins and grabbed his black Oceanic Shadow mask with snorkel attached. He spat in the mask and rinsed it in the cool Mediterranean water to ensure it didn't mist up. He checked the throat mike comms were secure around his neck and then turned to Porter.

"Okay, let's do one final circle. If all's clear I'll head for the rear. Once I'm in the water, stand off and cut the engine. It's pretty calm and still tonight. If they hear a constant motor noise from one location they might come and investigate."

"Sure thing, guv."

Porter pushed the throttle gently forward. The speedboat moved off slowly to circle the yacht, a couple of hundred yards clear.

As McCready checked her over, everything seemed

Deep Control

quiet. There was no overt activity. They clearly weren't expecting anything out of the ordinary.

Once they'd completed a full circle and were back at the stern, McCready indicated for Porter to stop. He pulled the mask onto his face, nodded at Porter, and then slipped quietly into the cool, dark water.

He immediately set off at a slow but steady pace toward the yacht. With the water this calm and it being a clear, moonlit night, any disturbance to the surface would be able to be seen from a reasonable distance—there were no waves to hide his presence. Another reason for the weight belt—it would keep his legs down so the fins wouldn't splash the surface. He swam with his hands at his side, creating as smooth a profile as possible.

He had made it about halfway when all those best-laid plans went south.

He watched as two of the crew walked down onto the deck just above the swim platform. The area had seating with thick comfy cushions set back in a wide semicircle with a table in the middle looking out over the water. It was normally used for relaxing and watching the swimmers at the rear. Both of the crew had beers in their hands. They were clearly taking some time out from their duties. They sat down in the deep cushions and leaned back, completely relaxed.

It looked like they'd be there for some time.

McCready looked around for options. This had been his primary access point.

He had to think.

He looked along the side of the vessel and then glanced back at Porter. It might work, but it would leave him with serious problems for an exit strategy later—but if he never made it on board that was all academic.

He pressed the throat mike and spoke quickly and quietly.

"Eugene, the rear platform's no go. I want you to make a nuisance of yourself. Speed around close to the yacht. Circle it. Run in. Turn at the last second. That sort of thing. Be visible. I need them to come after you."

"You sure, guv?" came the crackly reply. "But if I'm gone, how will you get off?"

"I'll worry about that later. Now go!"

A second later McCready watched as Porter gunned the engine and accelerated toward the *Freedom Seas*.

He drove in a fast circle close to the yacht. When he was halfway down the port side he turned sharply, sending a wave crashing against the larger vessel. It didn't do much, but all he needed was to attract attention. He then repeated the action on the starboard side.

He was turning round, ready for another run, when a number of the crew came out on deck to see what was going on. The two at the rear, however, stayed where they were. One of them took a walkie-talkie out of his pocket and spoke into it. He was clearly off-shift and it wasn't his problem. Someone on one of the upper decks crossed to a spotlight and flicked it on. McCready noticed he had a weapon slung over his shoulder. For the moment it wasn't held aggressively—but it did show intent. The strong beam of light flooded the water at the side of the ship. It followed Porter as the small boat raced around. That was good. The light would make everywhere else appear darker, giving McCready more cover, but Plan A wasn't working—the two guys were still at the rear. A minute later and Plan B looked like it might work. It was what McCready had been waiting for, and he always loved a Plan B.

From the side of the ship came a low humming, as

though an electric motor was working hard. A second later and the large panel that housed the tender started to swing open. McCready watched as the boat slid out on mechanical arms. When it had been lowered into the water, two crew members, both armed, jumped in and sped after Porter. All eyes would be on them as McCready swam fast for the open side of the yacht. It wouldn't close until the boat came back, but there could still be someone inside. He'd have to be careful.

When he reached the hull just below the open panel, he listened for anyone. He couldn't see in, but it seemed quiet. It was likely most of the crew were higher up on the decks watching what was going on. A couple of ropes had slipped over the side and down to the water. McCready checked both of them, selected one, and then cautiously pulled himself up until he could peer over the lip into the space beyond. It was well lit. The gantry for the boat was still extended over the water. But there was no one there.

He quickly pulled himself up and over the side and then removed his mask, snorkel and fins and hid them in a corner in case he could get back this way and needed them later. He then made his way over to the door that led to the interior of the yacht.

From the plans, he knew he was on the second lowest deck. Much of this level was taken up with equipment and storage, and then there was a deck below just above the waterline where he knew Carlita had been imprisoned. He made his way toward the steps that would lead below.

He had reached the last one when he heard talking. Two people were heading his way. He darted back up to the deck above and hid behind some fire-fighting equipment at the side of the corridor. A man and woman came up the steps. They were conversing in French and seemed preoccupied with something. They never even looked in his direction. Once they had gone he headed back down.

The lower deck consisted of a number of narrow corridors with regularly spaced doorways on each side. No doubt the crew's quarters as well as more storage rooms. He crossed to the other side, where he knew Carlita was being held.

He turned a corner into a new corridor.

It ran for about twenty feet and then stopped at a dead end. All the doors were closed, except for one. He could hear talking from within. He made his way carefully up to the door. As he reached it, he heard a loud slap and a cry. He gritted his teeth. He could feel his fists clenching—but he had to stay calm. To run in now might mean he would never leave. The alarm would be sounded and he'd have the whole crew on top of him, trapping him in the bowels of the ship.

He had to think this through.

"For the last time," said a voice with a heavy French accent, "where are the files you stole?"

"I don't have them." The voice was weak and full of pain, but McCready knew beyond any doubt it was Carlita.

He took a deep breath.

"We have no more time. We're leaving within the hour. When we are ten miles offshore you will be thrown over the side. Depending on if you tell us what we need to know, that will determine how much pain you have to endure in the last hours of your life. I will be back in five minutes for your decision."

McCready heard the sound of a hand hitting a face. There was no cry this time, merely the sound of something heavy hitting the floor and then silence.

He was about to rush into the cabin when he heard a noise behind him.

"Oi, who are you?"

McCready turned. A large man stood in the corridor. His aggressive stance indicated things were about to turn bad.

Then the man from the cabin walked out.

McCready turned to face him. The odds weren't good. He had to decide. He charged at the first man, knocking him to the floor.

McCready ran straight over him as the man from the cabin gave chase, shouting for help. Soon the whole crew would know of the intruder.

He'd just made everything that much more difficult.

He dashed back to the steps that led to the upper deck. Once at the top he could hear more shouts. He raced down a corridor that ran the length of the yacht. He was heading toward the bow. As he ran, a man emerged from a side corridor brandishing a gun. Without stopping, McCready smashed into him, knocking him over. The man hit his head as he fell and went out like a light.

McCready ran on.

There was the sound of pounding feet from the corridor ahead. He ducked into a small room and listened as they ran past. He gave it a second and then emerged, checking each direction. He then ran further forward.

He was now almost at the bow.

He heard a shout from behind. It looked like the men had turned around. They caught a glimpse of him as he disappeared round a corner and chased down the corridor after him. He jinked through a number of passages in different directions. He must surely be close to the bow by now. Suddenly, there were voices from ahead, coming his way.

He was trapped.

He saw a large hinged panel to his right. He lifted it and squeezed inside. A second later, feet pounded the floor from both directions. There was a heated exchange of words he couldn't understand, and then the voices disappeared in opposite directions.

He let out a breath and looked around.

He was right at the front of the yacht. The steep angle of the floor of the compartment showed he was in the bow itself. The room was full of ropes and mooring equipment. It was also the storage area for the chains of the twin anchors he'd seen when watching from afar. He leaned back against a large coil of rope and took a deep breath. It was a good place to hole up, but what the hell did he do now? They knew he was on board, and Carlita only had an hour before they sailed to get rid of her at sea, having no doubt suffered greatly in the meantime.

He leaned back and tried to think, but a moment later, he realized the timetable had been changed.

The engines, way back in the depths of the hull, started up. There was a loud, throaty rumble as the turbines kicked in before settling down to a steady background thrum.

They were setting sail.

The mission, now, was beyond impossible.

Chapter Ten

After McCready had told him to make a nuisance of himself, Porter intended to do just that. It was something he was very good at. And while he'd had a love/hate relationship with boats over the years, he was starting to enjoy the experience. He also tended not to hold back with anything he did, so once McCready was clear and close to the yacht, he pulled himself into the driver's seat and gripped the wheel, determined to cause as much chaos as possible.

His first action was to circle the yacht as fast as he could. This would create a wash that would slam into the sides and should get their attention. As he was coming round for the second time, he saw some men rush out onto the top deck and watch what he was doing. They shouted at him, waving their arms at him to leave—*yeah right!*

As he turned the boat around, he could see one of the men brandishing a gun. He aimed at Porter but seemed reluctant to fire—it was probably the risk of attracting attention. But what he did see was the large side panel of the ship open up and a fast boat being lowered into the water. And although there was now a spotlight shining down on him, he could also make out the small figure of McCready close to the open side of the yacht. He waited until the boat was in the water and then raced in and launched a wave over the two men who were now in the boat.

Once they had the engine started, they chased after him.

Porter checked to see that McCready had climbed into the ship through the open panel and then high-tailed it back toward Monaco.

He was about halfway, and starting to pass the other large mega-yachts moored in the bay, when he looked back. The boat was no longer chasing him. It was sitting a hundred yards away. The driver and second occupant were watching him, making sure he didn't return. A minute later they turned around and drove off, heading back to the *Freedom Seas*.

Porter chuckled to himself and then headed for the marina. He pulled up to the pontoon in the same spot they'd taken the boat from. He checked all was secure and then jumped out and tied it up. Hopefully no one would even notice it had been gone for an hour or so—that was, unless they checked the fuel tank.

He climbed up the steps from the pontoon onto the concrete surround. A family, dressed up to the nines, made their way along the walkway, heading for a restaurant at the end of the block. He checked he had the keys for the apartment and then made his way under the canopy that led to the entrance. He had almost reached the door, and was still in the shadow of the building, when he heard a noise behind him. He turned in time to see a large baseball bat crash down on the top of his head.

Everything went black.

He never even felt the impact as he hit the ground.

Porter had no idea how long he'd been out, and when he came to, he had a splitting headache. He tried to stretch out, but when he moved his body, not only did it hurt like hell, but after extending his legs a few inches they came up fast against something solid. Couple that with the loud engine noise and continued motion of his environment, and he surmised he was in the trunk of a car.

He winced again at the throb from his head, but then he had to focus.

He had to get out of there.

Right now there was no one to back up McCready. It also crossed his mind there was every possibility that whoever had thrown him in the trunk might actually not want him to survive when they opened it—all the more reason for not being there when they did.

He turned over slowly and tried to see if there was anything he could use to help free himself. His hands were bound with thick gaffer tape behind his back that would be hard to remove, but there were often objects in the trunks of cars that might help with such a task—tools, for example.

He reached out with his fingers. He couldn't move them far from his back, but he managed to slowly shuffle around the cramped space feeling for whatever was there. It was pretty dim but some illumination came from the rear light cluster.

As his fingers scrambled around, they made their way over something in the corner that had wedged itself between the layer of carpet and the left-hand side of the car. He moved to grab it. When he did, he found he had hold of a medium length screwdriver. He maneuvered it into a position where he could draw the tip over the gaffer tape.

Ten minutes later he'd split the tape enough for the power of his arms to wrench the rest of it apart. Once his hands were free, he pulled them round to the front and took a deep breath. The car was still driving at speed. As it negotiated the curves of the road the centrifugal force pushed him from side to side. He'd thought boats were bad enough, but much more of this and he'd be throwing up.

He turned so he could try and see the release mechanism for the trunk lid. He couldn't see it properly, but as he ran his fingers over it, the metal spoke to him as if it had been as clear as day.

He positioned the screwdriver within the clamp and pushed up.

Nothing happened.

He tried from a couple of different angles.

Still nothing.

He thought for a moment and then felt carefully around the side of the locking mechanism fixture plate.

A minute later he smiled.

Five minutes later he had the screws from the mechanism undone and had pulled it free from the body of the car. He then gently lifted the lid a couple of inches and peered out the back.

Outside it was dark. There was the spill of red light from the rear lights, which was enhanced every so often when they braked approaching a bend. Every now and then the high beams of other vehicles shot past, illuminating the road further behind the car.

It looked like they were on the coast road from Monaco, and from the position of the sea, they were heading east toward Italy. As he didn't know how long he'd been unconscious he couldn't tell whether they had already crossed the border, but that would have been risky in case there were checks. Explaining someone tied up in the trunk wouldn't have been easy, so he had to assume they were still in France. Either way, he didn't really want to hang around. He wasn't sure if he could get out without the occupants knowing, but there was only one way to find out.

He took a deep breath, braced himself, and then lifted the trunk lid far enough for him to crawl out. It was unlikely he'd be seen in the rear-view mirror due to the darkness. He waited until the car slowed slightly at a corner and then eased himself out and dropped onto the road.

He landed hard, the impact knocking the wind out of him. His body bounced on the tarmac and rolled over into the oncoming lane.

He was just getting his breath back, and about to try and stand, when the high beams of a fast-moving car sped round the corner coming straight for him. It was going so fast there was only going to be one outcome.

It was going to hit him.

He shut his eyes.

There was a sudden dramatic change in engine noise and the oncoming lights slowed to a stop in what should have been a mechanically impossible period of time.

When Porter opened his eyes, he found he was staring at the front grille of a silver Mercedes-AMG Project One, two inches from his face.

He rolled slightly to his right, away from the car.

He heard a door open and someone climb out and run round to the front. He felt a strong arm grab hold of him and start to lift him up. When he was upright, he turned to stare into the face of a well-dressed black man in his mid-to-late thirties. He was looking at him with a concerned but calm expression. How he had managed to stop, Porter had no idea—he must have the reflexes of a cat.

"You okay?" the man asked.

Porter looked at him, his eyes trying to focus.

"Yeah, thanks… You're English," he said, noting the accent.

"So are you," said the man.

"Yeah," Porter still wasn't quite all there and looked around him. He suddenly heard the screech of tires somewhere in the darkness.

"Can I give you a lift?" asked the man.

Porter could hear the revving of an engine further up the road, and the sound of a car doing a three-point turn.

"Yeah, brilliant idea. Let's go!"

Porter moved quickly to the side of the car and tried to open the door, but he couldn't find the handle. He glanced in confusion at the driver. He just looked at him with an inscrutable expression and pressed a button on his side of the car. Immediately Porter's door swung vertically upward.

When he was inside, sitting in a deep leather sports seat, he glanced around.

"Nice ride."

"Do you want to go to a hospital? You look pretty banged up there."

Porter suddenly concentrated as his situation swam back into sharp focus.

"Monaco. I need to get to Monaco—on the front."

"Cool," said the man, "that's where I live. I'll take it easy, don't want to throw you around too much."

Porter glanced behind them. He could see headlights approaching fast.

"Er, no, I think you'd better drive fast. Like really fast. And like right now!"

The man looked at Porter strangely, but a second later, as the sound of a gunshot echoed through the night and his wing mirror disintegrated, his expression turned to shock. He glanced at Porter.

"Who the hell *are* you?"

"Not now. You can drive, can't you?"

The man looked at him for a second.

"Oh yeah, I can drive."

He floored the accelerator, flicking the gear change paddles on the steering column in quick succession. The car took off like a rocket ship heading for the stars.

Porter glanced in his side mirror. He heard another shot but it missed its mark. The lights behind were fading fast.

The car took the corners on rails. When Porter glanced at the speedometer it was showing a hundred and eighty kilometers per hour. He glanced at the man next to him. He was totally focused on the road ahead but was also totally calm, like he was out for a Sunday afternoon drive.

Porter thought it best not to disturb him. Ahead, they were approaching a long curve in the road. There was a minibus in the way. The man slowed the Mercedes, pulling up close behind the minibus as they went round the corner. A second later there was a shot from behind. This one hit the bodywork somewhere at the back. The driver made a quick decision—did some more fancy work with the paddles, and the car took off again.

Porter grabbed the side of his seat as if his life depended on it. Ahead, a truck was bearing down on them fast. It flared its lights. There had to be a collision…

…but there wasn't.

They were past it in less than two seconds, before the truck driver could even let go of the headlight flasher.

In the distance, Porter could see the lights of Monaco.

A couple of minutes later and they were approaching the built-up area of town. They headed down through the narrow streets and pulled up outside the stylish Casino de Monte-Carlo in the Place du Casino.

The car came to a halt. The driver turned to him.

"You sure you're okay? I could always call an ambulance."

But now Porter was back in Monaco, he was focused on what he had to do. He turned to the driver.

"Thanks, mate. Appreciate it. But I'm fine."

"Hey, who were those guys, and why were they shooting at you?"

"Long story. Maybe another time. Thanks again."

Porter looked at the door, still not sure how to open it. He glanced at the driver. The man flicked a switch and the door rose up. Porter climbed stiffly out and then leaned back in.

"Not bad driving. Gear shifts could maybe have been a bit smoother, but under the circumstances, and it is quite a high-powered car, bit of practice and you could be really good."

And with that he was gone.

The driver just stared after him. He then climbed out to survey the damage.

A valet ran up a few seconds later. The driver glanced at him and threw him the keys.

"Take care of her, Mario, had enough prangs for one night."

"Sure thing, sir. Same time as before?"

He thought for a moment.

"Nah. I might leave it all night—think I need a couple of drinks."

When Porter made it back to the apartment he checked nothing had been disturbed. The security seemed to be good enough, as everything was there. He needed to find out how McCready was getting on, but his throat mike had been removed when he'd been kidnapped.

But that didn't mean he couldn't keep an eye on things.

He walked out onto the terrace with a pair of binoculars and scanned across the bay, looking for the *Freedom Seas*.

But she was nowhere to be seen.

He looked again, thinking he'd maybe got her position wrong, but she was definitely not there.

"Shit!"

He ran back inside, grabbed his phone, and called Richards to check where they were.

They were over southern France and wouldn't be long. He told them in no uncertain terms to hurry up—the yacht was gone. He received an equally blunt reply that they were going as fast as they could… oh, and Charlie says, "Hello."

He grinned, but a tight knot was beginning to form deep inside.

Where the hell was the boat?

Chapter Eleven

McCready had been holed up in the bow storage locker for half an hour. He could feel the movement of the hull beneath him, and although the sea was calm, being at the bow ensured a gentle rise and fall as the vessel plowed through the water.

But the time was coming when he had to act.

He couldn't leave it any longer. If he did, there might not be anyone left to save. It could even be too late already.

He was about to make a move when he heard voices. A man and a woman, presumably members of the crew, were right outside the locker. As he listened, he could hear them speaking in French. He could only catch the odd word, but it sounded like they were more than just good friends. It also sounded like they weren't going anywhere anytime soon.

That was all he needed.

He checked around the locker again. He had tried to contact Porter earlier to make sure he'd made it back to shore okay, but all he had got was static. That wasn't good.

It meant something could have happened to him. It also meant he was on his own.

There was very little light in the space, but enough seeped beneath the panel for him to make out the numerous ropes and chains. He could also see a hatch above. It was about three foot square and would be on the front deck close to the bow to allow access to the equipment below. As there was no real way he could leave through the way he'd come in right now, he would have to risk it up on deck.

He stood slowly, careful not to make any noise that might be heard by the two outside, though it seemed they were so wrapped up in each other, little would distract them.

He felt around the hatch. Normally, it would be opened from the outside, but there might be a way to open it from within. After a couple of minutes, he found a small catch at one side. He pulled it, and four lugs disengaged, allowing the hatch to be cleanly lifted out. He gently pushed up the end closest to the main part of the boat, stood on a coil of rope and peered out through the inch-high gap. From here he had a commanding view of the yacht sweeping back beyond him. There were some lights coming from the large windows on the upper decks, but the bridge above was dark, ensuring the captain and anyone present maintained their night vision. Although he was at the front, directly in line of sight of anyone looking out of the bridge, the bow was so far away and in darkness, it was unlikely anyone would see him emerge from the hatch, but to then make his way over the deck and back inside, he would be a sitting duck.

He had to think of something else.

He looked around the locker again. There was now more light as he held the hatch open slightly. As he scanned the coils of rope and chains, a plan came to him. It was high-risk, but right now high-risk was all he had.

He thought back to when he'd seen the yacht from the apartment, and also the specs he'd poured over on the way down to Monaco. She was over four hundred feet long and had two propellers at the stern. There was a large rudder in the center and a space of about ten feet between the props.

He looked at the rope coils. Some of them were brand new. He checked the labels and read off their respective lengths. One was fifty feet, another a hundred feet, but then he found a couple that were two hundred feet. He pulled the coils over and undid the thin straps holding them tight. He then undid the ends and tied three of them together, giving a total of four hundred and fifty feet. Next, he looked around the compartment and found a small foldable grapnel anchor that was likely a spare for the tenders. He pulled out the four short arms and screwed the locking collar in place so the arms were now spread out and secure. He then found a short length of chain. He attached one end to the anchor and the other to the rope.

He unwound about twenty feet of rope and tied the free end to a secure bulkhead in the locker. He then made sure, as best he could, the rest of the rope was in a neat coil and would not become snagged or twisted as it paid out. That could result in him having a very bad day.

He took the anchor in his hand and prepared for what he knew would be one of the most dangerous things he'd ever done in his life. He'd have to move fast. Once the plan was in action, any hesitation, any doubt, and he'd be dead.

He started a series of deep controlled breaths to saturate his lungs and tissues with oxygen.

Once he was happy, he took a final deep breath, and

with the anchor in one hand, he pushed the hatch up slightly and slid it to one side.

He climbed out as fast as he could onto the deck and then leapt forward to dive headfirst over the bow into the water below.

He made sure he dived out as far as possible. The boat was doing about twenty knots, and as soon as he hit the water he would be smashed back against the bow below the surface. He hoped the weight around his waist and the small anchor and chain in his hand would help with that.

He hit the water hard, and while the additional weight did help, he was hurled back with force, smashing into the hull, knocking the wind out of him. He had to hang on to the rope and anchor for all he was worth as he was bashed and battered against the hull, all the time being dragged back toward the churning propellers at the stern. Above, the pounding roar of the engine could be heard through the hull, mere feet away.

And then, a few seconds later, he was approaching the whirling death of the propellers.

The flow of water dragged him to one side. He had to make it back to the middle, but he was on a ride he couldn't control. Then the boat turned slightly and the flow swept him back. He shot between the two props.

He only had a split second to react.

He thrust the anchor and chain at the port-side propeller. It missed, but the suction pulled the rope into the spinning prop shaft, winding it up and pulling the anchor and chain in with it. As soon as that happened the propeller jammed fast. There was a whining and groaning and then a loud bang from inside the hull, and the propeller shut down. The other screw was still turning, though, and McCready had to grip hard onto the loop of rope that hadn't been wound round the propeller to stop from being sucked into the other one.

The boat was still traveling through the water at pace. It was all he could do to hold on as he was dragged behind. His calculation had been right, though. He was about twenty feet to the rear of the stern of the boat. He had to pull himself to the swim platform before anyone arrived, or else his whole plan would have been in vain.

The yacht was slowing.

It took him thirty seconds to make it to the platform. He lifted his head carefully above the surface and took in much-needed gasps of air, trying to stay as quiet as possible. The two men had long since gone from the rear deck, but he could see a heated discussion in progress on the bridge, which now had all the lights on. The engines had finally been shut down while they tried to work out what had happened.

McCready pulled himself onto the platform and made his way up to the deck above. He hid under a tender that was suspended from a small crane on a cradle at the side of the yacht, while a member of the crew ran past. He was going to have to have a way off the ship if all went to plan. He looked at the controls for the tender above him. They seemed simple enough. He undid the lines securing the boat and swung it slowly toward the side of the ship, but not far enough to draw attention.

Now came the tricky part.

He ran to the nearest door. It took him into the large, plush dining area. There was no one there. He walked quickly over to a stairwell he knew would take him down several decks to where he needed to be.

Once he was at the bottom he made his way along a corridor. At one point he had to duck into a cabin to avoid someone coming the other way. But then it was on toward the cabin where Carlita was being held.

He made it to the end of the corridor. He could hear voices from within, all male. They were not aggressive, or questioning. They seemed to be calm and going about their business. It didn't look good. He ran quietly along to the door, undid his weight belt and held it securely in one hand. He then sprang through into the cabin.

There were two men in the room. But what was more worrying was that Carlita was lying face down on the floor, unmoving, her face bloodied from frequent blows. Her arms had been cut with a knife and blood oozed out of long gashes onto the floor.

McCready's heart caught in his chest. He hesitated for a moment.

It was enough for the first of the men to lunge at him.

McCready reacted quickly. His blood was up. Live or die. Nothing else mattered.

He swung the belt. One of the lead weights hit the man on the jaw, shattering the bone and knocking him backward into the second man. They fell over in a heap, the first one lying unconscious on top of the second. The second man struggled, trying to move the hulk of his colleague off him, but before he could, McCready had moved forward and kicked him as hard as he could in the head. He was instantly out.

He moved quickly over to Carlita and knelt down next to her. He rolled her over and saw her bloodied and bruised face. Now he was this close to her, all the memories and thoughts came flooding back, but he had to force himself to go on. He checked her pulse. It was there. Her chest was rising and falling. He spoke urgently to her but there was no response. They must have drugged her with something. This was going to make everything that much more difficult. He picked her up carefully and laid her over his shoulder. She was as light as a feather.

He walked out into the corridor and made his way back to the stairwell. At one point two men ran past, but McCready hid in the shadows of the stairs. He moved quickly up to the top and out into the dining area. He was ten feet from the exit when there was a shout from behind. He didn't even bother to look back, but instead, he ran outside and over to the tender hanging from the small crane.

He laid Carlita down in the boat and swung the craft out over the water. He then hit the release handle that disengaged the brake on the supporting cable. At the same time, he jumped in. The boat dropped thirty feet to the water below with a hard splash, still attached by the cable. McCready started the engine with the keys that were in the ignition. He then knocked it into gear, unclipped the crane cable, and accelerated sharply away from the side of the yacht. He could hear shouts from above as they sped into the night.

He powered the boat directly away from the side of the ship. They were now several miles offshore and he had no idea which way land was.

He pushed the throat mike.

"Eugene, are you there?"

There was only static.

He repeated the call—but nothing.

Shit!

Right then he heard a loud crack and a whistling sound. He looked back to see a flare streak high into the air. It exploded like a firework on New Year's Eve, but this was a parachute flare that hung in the sky illuminating the dark sea below. The boat was now clearly visible, a small speck in the vast expanse of water. But what was more alarming was the sight of two fast boats heading after him from the stationary yacht.

There was nowhere to hide.

There was nowhere to go.

There was no escape.

Chapter Twelve

Charlie Menzies checked the radar plot in the middle of the dashboard of the Chinook helicopter that was speeding south at its top speed of just under two hundred miles per hour. She was twenty-eight years old, and her distinctive long red hair was currently restrained by the comms headset she wore. She glanced up as Craig Richards entered the cockpit.

"How long?" asked a nervous Richards.

They'd received a call from Porter explaining what had happened to him and that he hadn't been able to get in touch with McCready. All he knew was that the yacht had sailed. Richards had said they were tracking its transponder on radar and would head straight out to see what they could do.

"About twenty minutes," said Charlie. "The weather's good so no headwinds. With the sea this calm, though, they could be making good progress. According to the plot, they're heading straight out into the Med. They're already ten miles offshore."

"Okay, we need to be there soon as."

"Doing the best I can, boss... Uncle Craig!" said Charlie with a grin.

Richards smiled, patted her on the back, and then walked through into the main cargo area. When Steel had given them the use of the aircraft he'd said there could be no trace back to the UK government. If anything happened it should be described as belonging to Ocean Tech and it was their responsibility. He had, though, allowed a medic to go along with them as McCready had been concerned about the condition Carlita would be in if he was able to get her off the boat. Richards had wished he'd been able to bring the XB4, as that would have given them more options, but sometimes you just had to react to the situation on the ground—or water—and clearly McCready had had no choice other than to go when he did. He just hoped they'd get there in time to render any assistance they could. At the end of the day, it wasn't like they had a whole assault team they could storm the ship with. But he knew McCready was resourceful, so he'd deal with whatever scenario presented itself when they got there.

McCready was thankful the sea was calm. He was at full throttle, trying to evade the chasing boats, and he was concerned about Carlita. She was still unconscious. He'd managed to wedge a lifejacket under her head to protect it, but even with the calm water the bow lifted now and then over a swell and thumped down harder than he would have liked. The flare had almost died but the boats behind had powerful searchlights that lit up the water, giving them a pinpoint position as to where he was.

He wondered how much fuel he had left. He had no

idea how long Craig and Charlie would be, and as he couldn't reach Porter on the comms, there was no way to contact them. It also looked like he wouldn't be able to outrun the boats over a long period of time. His only option was to stay within range of the *Freedom Seas* so the Chinook would be able to home in on it. With that in mind he took the boat in a wide arc to circle round and head back toward the yacht, while at the same time ensuring he kept a manageable distance from his pursuers.

They were still a hundred yards behind when he stared back and saw one of the men lift a weapon. It looked like an automatic. Seconds later there was the staccato rapid-fire noise of a gun. McCready kept his head down and stayed on course for the yacht. The gunfire continued, but either they were terrible shots, or else at the edge of their range, as nothing hit the boat.

He was closing on the lights of the *Freedom Seas* when he saw another light. It was far brighter and seemed to be coming from the top of the yacht. In fact, it seemed as though it was on a tall mast, which he didn't remember the ship having. A moment later, though, his heart started beating faster as he realized they might actually be going to make it.

The light soared ever higher, and with it the roar of the twin Honeywell turboshaft engines of a Chinook. The helicopter swept over the yacht and then arced round. It looked like it was working out who was who and where everyone was.

As his friends were there, McCready headed away from the *Freedom Seas*, giving no one on board the chance to fire at the helicopter.

He was now in open water. The two chase boats were still a way behind, but closing. He was about to look up at the helicopter and wave them over when there was a stuttering noise from the engine. He glanced at it. The stuttering continued.

A moment later it died.

McCready ran to the back and picked up the fuel can. Empty.

The last time this had happened to him he'd had a spare to change over to, but this time there was none.

He glanced at the approaching boats. They were seconds away.

He then looked up for the Chinook. It was banking round in a tight turn to run in toward him.

He waved frantically.

There was nothing else he could do.

The boats were almost on him, but then he saw the Chinook run in low over the water. It was approaching from the side, aiming for the rapidly closing gap between McCready and the chasing boats.

The boats were fifty feet away when the Chinook flared up almost vertically mere feet from them. The downwash from the twin rotors flipped the boats over, sending their occupants flying into the water.

The helicopter then leveled out and came in to hover close to McCready. He glanced up and could see Charlie grinning at him from the cockpit. He waved an acknowledgment, but then focused on the rear of the helicopter. The loading ramp was lowering and the chopper started reversing toward him. It dropped down until it was touching the surface. When it was ten feet away the ramp was lowered into the water.

McCready moved to the front of the boat and threw a line to Richards, who was standing at the rear, water sloshing around his feet. Richards caught the line and pulled the boat to him. A moment later and McCready had lifted Carlita off the floor and stepped out onto the ramp. He moved quickly up inside the helicopter and laid her gently on a bench seat near the forward bulkhead. He could hear the whine of the hydraulics as the tail ramp was raised, and then felt himself rising as the Chinook lifted high into the air out of range of any gunfire from below. A couple of minutes later and all was calm, though not quiet—the Chinook was not renowned for its soundproofing.

McCready looked around. Richards walked over, along with another man.

"John, this is Lieutenant Paul Graves. He's a doctor Martin Steel sent along."

"Paul, John McCready. Thanks for coming," said McCready. They shook hands. "She's in a pretty bad way. They knocked her around, cut her—God knows what else. Also, I think she's been drugged. I haven't been able to speak to her."

"Thanks," said Graves. He wasted no more time on pleasantries; instead, he pulled a medical case over and started working on Carlita.

Richards winced when he saw her face. Now was the first time McCready had been able to relax since climbing on board the *Freedom Seas*. He was starting to come down off the adrenaline high and suddenly felt extremely tired. He had to sit down.

He crossed over to the other side of the cargo bay and watched Graves go to work. Richards sat next to him.

"You okay?"

"Just about, thanks. But have you seen what they've done to her?" he said, the anger rising. "I barely got there in time, Craig. Another few minutes and…" He let the words tail off.

Richards' expression had hardened since he'd seen Carlita.

"Well, done, mate. As always, you saved the day."

"Maybe," said McCready. "And thanks for showing up. Didn't need the XB4 after all. Don't know why you kept going on about it!"

Richards smiled. It broke the tension.

McCready rested for a few minutes but then stood and crossed over to where Graves was working on Carlita. He'd bandaged the cuts on her arm and was taking her blood pressure. There were a couple of syringes lying on a makeshift table close by.

"How is she?" asked McCready.

Graves looked up.

"She's taken some knocks. I don't think there's anything broken, but she's going to be sore for a while, and these bruises on her face will take time to go." McCready could again feel the anger growing. Someone was going to pay for this. "She's been drugged with something. I'm not sure what, but her blood pressure is okay for now, so I don't think it's anything life-threatening. Once I've finished a couple more checks, taken a blood sample, I'll give her a shot to stabilize her. Then the best thing is to let the drugs wear off in their own time and for her to sleep. She's going to need a lot of rest and support. I'd recommend her going to hospital as soon as we get back."

"No!" said McCready, emphatically.

Graves and Richards both looked at him.

"So long as you're sure there's nothing life-threatening, I want her at my place. If she goes to hospital, Steel or one of his departments is going to want to talk to her, and I don't want that right now. She's been through enough. She needs peace and quiet, not questions and interrogation."

McCready's expression was uncompromising.

"Mr. Steel may have something to say about that," said Graves.

"Let me worry about him. I don't want anything happening to her now that I'm not aware of."

Graves shrugged good-naturedly. "Okay, your call."

McCready walked away from them. Richards followed.

"He's going to want to talk to her," said Richards.

"I know, but it's just for a few days. Let me find out what's going on. She'll be frightened, disoriented, and she did contact me, remember? At least I can be someone she feels safe with."

"Okay, fair enough… Now you'd better go say hello to Charlie. You know how she just loves saving your ass!"

Chapter Thirteen

The one thing Dr. Nyah Hawthorn wanted most when she arrived back at Halley was a large mug of hot chocolate.

During the flight, the heater had packed up in the helicopter, and while their clothing—four layers, starting with thermal underwear all the way up to the latest in Gore-Tex waterproof jacket and salopettes—did the job pretty well, a nice hot mug of Cocoa to warm the insides would hugely increase the comfort factor.

Before she could get a fix of her one indulgence, though, she had to check in. Any excursions out on the ice had to be logged in and out to ensure a record of her return to base was entered into the system.

She signed the electronic form with her access code and then made her way to her quarters.

The Halley VI Research Station was an amazing piece of engineering. It was built on the Brunt Ice Shelf in the Weddell Sea and consisted of eight connected modules, each sitting on ski-fitted hydraulic legs. These could be individually raised, depending on snowfall, and also allowed the modules to be detached and relocated to a new location, should the station ever be at risk from a chasm opening up in the ice—something that had happened during the 2016/17 Antarctic summer. If it hadn't been moved it would have been in danger of finding itself on the world's largest iceberg, floating off into the Southern Ocean—something that was preferable to avoid.

All the modules were painted blue, except for the larger central one that was red. This housed the eating and social areas, while the others provided accommodation, research labs, offices, equipment stores, etc.

Nyah's room was like a cabin on a ship. One side was taken up with two bunk beds, while on the other there was a desktop that ran the full length, with shelves above and drawers below. At the end of the room was a tall window, a bit like an elongated porthole. The space was small and cramped but it was her home away from home during her stay. She had a number of photos pinned on a corkboard above the desktop where she kept her laptop.

She tore off her outer two layers and then made her way through to the cafeteria in the central module, shouting friendly banter at the other members of the base as she passed.

Once she'd fixed her drink, she sipped the glorious liquid, feeling it slip luxuriously down her throat.

She sat for a few minutes, looking out over the ice through one of the large triangular windows as she went over the day's work in her mind. Her research was progressing well and she loved the thrill of discovering new data and the implications it had for life in Antarctica and, indeed, the rest of the planet as well sometimes.

Outside, a couple of helicopters arrived and departed, taking scientists to and from their field trips—which reminded her about the black helicopter they'd seen heading into the interior on the way back from the mountains.

She finished up her hot chocolate and made her way through to the air operations center. It was located in a small room in the command module between the central and accommodation modules, and was set up like a mini air traffic control. It covered a quarter of Antarctica, linking in with the bases of other nationalities that were spread across the continent—ultimately forming a network that provided total coverage of the land mass.

She walked into the room.

There was a bank of displays along one wall, above which were large maps of Antarctica. One of the displays showed a constant weather chart with real-time satellite information. It was essential to know when storms were moving in—something that could happen at short notice and disrupt planned expeditions out into the field.

A woman in her mid-forties was sitting at a chair in front of the displays.

"Hi, Hannah," said Nyah, cheerily.

Hannah McAlpine turned round. She had short brown hair and a friendly face. She smiled at Nyah.

"You back so soon? Thought you'd be out all day."

"Nah, managed to get the sensors in place in record time. Also, there were clear skies so we had no delays."

"Glad you did, we've some weather coming in from the west." She pointed at the display above her. Nyah looked at the front that was moving in.

"Will it be bad?"

"Looks like it at the moment, but the forecast is variable. Could turn away, or else head in and cover everything—snow, gales, you name it."

"Great!"

"So you might have some downtime coming up."

"That would be nice." Nyah paused, looking at the display that showed the aircraft tracks in real time.

"Hey, Hannah, would you know who was heading into the interior about an hour ago, flying in from the Filchner Ice Shelf?"

Hannah glanced at her.

"Er, not sure. Any reason?"

"Well, when we were on our way back, we saw a black helicopter way over, heading deep inside. Never seen it before. Just wondering if we had some newbies down here."

Hannah looked puzzled for a moment.

"Don't think so. There are no black helicopters I'm aware off. Most people go for yellow, orange or red—stands out more. Let me take a look."

She brought up a recorded display from the previous few hours. A log was kept of all flights in and around the area for data recording, but also in case of emergency or if an aircraft's transponder went down.

She played it back, fast-forwarding until she had the correct time relating to Nyah's information. She hit the play button. The view covered the area Nyah had been talking about. A few seconds into playback they both saw a small dot appear at one side of the map and move steadily across to the other. It seemed to be hugging a mountain range.

"That's funny, its identifier isn't working," said Hannah.

"That unusual?" asked Nyah.

"Yes. They're supposed to be checked before they go out. Maybe it's some new outfit, but we're supposed to be kept informed of anyone operating down here."

They both watched the track. A minute later it stopped moving.

"What's wrong with it?" asked Nyah.

"Nothing. They must have landed."

Nyah looked more closely at the position, then looked somewhat puzzled.

"There shouldn't be anyone working out there. It's really dangerous in that region."

"Couldn't they just be checking conditions? Monitoring movement of the ice?"

"Could be," said Nyah, "but I'm not aware of any projects scheduled."

Hannah fast-forwarded the replay. The blip of the helicopter was stationary for about an hour. It then moved to a location on a nearby mountain range about a mile from the original position. It stayed there for a further half hour before again moving and eventually disappearing off the screen.

"Hmmm," said Hannah, "that's strange."

"Can you give me a readout of the locations where they stopped?" said Nyah. "We're headed past there on the next trip. Might check it out, see what they were up to."

"Will do," said Hannah.

Chapter Fourteen

When the Chinook had arrived back at Ocean Tech after picking up Porter from the roof of the apartment block in Monaco, McCready had spoken to Graves. He'd agreed, from a medical point of view, that McCready could take Carlita home, though he had said he would have to make a full report of her condition to Steel. On the flight, he'd managed to carry out several blood tests with a mobile kit, and all seemed to be okay. She had been given a sedative while on the yacht, but it would likely wear off within a few hours, and there should be no negative aftereffects. Otherwise, she just needed rest and care, something McCready had said he was more than capable of giving her.

McCready had spoken to Richards and told him not to say anything to Steel if he rang—he'd contact him when he had Carlita safely at his house. Richards had agreed, but said to call if he needed anything. McCready had then carried Carlita over to his Range Rover, which had been parked up at Ocean Tech since he'd left for Los Angeles several weeks before. He'd put her in the front passenger seat and secured the seatbelt, reclining the seat so her head wouldn't loll forward and she'd be more comfortable.

He'd then driven all the way across Scotland to his home on the west coast.

The house was situated in a wild bay at the end of a half-mile dirt track—secluded and quiet. On the way, he'd dropped in at Sarah's, his sister-in-law, to ask if he could borrow some clothes for Carlita as they were about the same size. She would need something to wear and there was nothing at McCready's place. Sarah had been intrigued by the whole situation and happily gave him a selection for Carlita. After half an hour of McCready fussing over his one-year-old niece, he'd climbed back in the car and made it home. He'd also stopped off at a local supermarket and picked up some food and provisions.

When he arrived home, the house was cold. He quickly turned on the heating and carried Carlita up to one of the first-floor guest bedrooms. It had a large double bed and a spectacular view across the bay. He made sure she was tucked in and comfortable. He could still hardly believe she was actually there. He could see the essence of the girl he had known in the woman who was sleeping before him. The years had clearly hardened her physically, but there was still the look of the person from all those years ago. He was almost scared for her to wake up—to find out about her life and why she had contacted him. He loved the memory just as it was.

He took a last look at her and then made his way downstairs.

He crossed over to the oak bar opposite the kitchen and poured himself a brandy. He then walked through to the lower split-level area of the living room, where the wide thirty feet of window panels looked out over the bay. The weather appeared to be turning. Some mist was blowing in off the sea. He looked at the view for a few minutes, just relieved to be home. He then walked over to the sofa and slumped into the deep cushions. He leaned back and closed his eyes.

He hadn't realized just how tired he was. Since the call from Carlita in LA, he'd barely slept, and when he had, it had been fitfully. The worry and concern had been constant. The time in Monaco had taken away some of the stress as he had to concentrate on the physical aspects of what he was doing, but now he was coming down from the physical and emotional highs. On top of that, he was still recovering from his exploits in Los Angeles, and it was all catching up with him. He'd barely taken a sip of the brandy and placed the glass down on the table when he was fast asleep.

When he awoke, it was dark. He rubbed the sleep from his eyes and glanced around the room. The lights had come on on their timers and the room was illuminated with a warm, comforting glow. He stood stiffly and walked over to close the drapes across the full-width windows. He then checked the time. He realized he hadn't called Clare since he'd told her he'd arrived safely in the UK from the States. She'd probably be worried sick. He crossed over to a phone on a side table and rang her number. It was answered on the third ring.

"John! Are you okay?" He could hear the stress in her voice.

"Yeah, I'm fine," he said wearily.

"You sound terrible."

"That bad, huh?" he said with a weak smile.

"So, what happened?"

He recounted everything that had gone on in Monaco, leaving out some of the more dodgy moments, like the excursion under the yacht. He finished by telling her that Carlita was sound asleep upstairs at the house, but he hadn't been able to speak to her yet. When he finished there was silence over the phone for a moment.

"So, she's there, with you?" asked Clare cautiously.

"Yeah. Look, don't worry. I haven't seen her in twenty-five years. It is a bit weird, but we're different people now, Clare. I love you, remember."

"Yeah, well, you better had," she said, with a slightly lighter tone. "So what will you do now?"

"I have to find out why she called. From what Steel said, she's been involved in some environmental group that have seriously upset certain people. She could still be in danger. But more crucially, why did she call *me*? I still can't figure that out. She must have made hundreds of contacts over the years, so why me?"

"Good question," said Clare, the wariness back in her voice.

Just then McCready heard a groan from upstairs.

"Look, I have to go. I think she's waking up."

"John?"

"Yes."

"I do love you."

"I love you too. Got to go."

And with that he put down the phone.

He stared at it for a moment and then stood up to make his way upstairs. As he left the room, he glanced at the poncho hanging on the wall—the one Carlita had given him all those years ago. He tried to fight it, but a deep yearning grew inside him.

He took a deep breath and climbed the stairs.

He made his way quietly up to her room, pushed open the door and stared at the figure lying on the bed. She was on her front with her arms splayed casually either side and the sheets halfway down her back. As he watched, she turned over and groaned slightly, as though a small pain had encroached on her being. A minute later her eyes struggled open. She looked tired, but nowhere near as bad as when McCready had found her. Much of her face had been cleaned up and the bruising wasn't as bad as he'd thought it would be. Also, Graves had bandaged the cuts on her arm with clean white bandages.

As she woke, she noticed her arm and looked down at it. The room was dark. McCready could see her feel the bandages, testing them. She winced slightly, clearly confused. She looked around the room. Eventually her gaze fell on the figure at the door. She gasped and pulled the sheets tighter up to her neck.

"It's John," McCready said simply.

He moved slowly into the room but remained close to the door, not wanting to scare her.

She just looked at him. He could see fear, and then confusion, on her face.

He took a step nearer. Some moonlight fell over his features. She sat up slightly, trying to see him more clearly. He moved closer, until he was right next to the bed.

Then he sat down slowly.

She looked into his eyes, and as she did, he could see the recognition dawn on her. Her eyes filled with tears, and the look of astonishment and sheer love that filled them made McCready go weak at the knees. She didn't say anything but reached up to wrap her arms around him and bury her head in his shoulder. She clung to him for several minutes.

He could feel her body as it was racked with convulsions, and he could hear her sobbing quietly. She clung tighter. He put his arms around her and held her close, keeping her safe, showing nothing could harm her now.

After five minutes she relaxed her grip and drew slowly back, but only as far as she needed to stare into his eyes again, disbelief on her face.

"John," she said, eventually. "My John. Is it really you?"

But he couldn't reply—couldn't speak. The emotion had overtaken him, and for a moment he felt himself transported back in time to when the positions had been reversed and he'd woken up in her parents' home. She had been looking down at him with such care and tenderness, dabbing his forehead with a damp cloth, and telling him he was safe while he was with her. He almost wanted to cry, but he couldn't. Everything was different now. It was a different time. They were different people. But how different? Did people really change that much?

"How do you feel?" he asked eventually.

She continued to stare at him, but there was now a hint of relief, as though her mind had given her the okay to relax—that she knew she was safe.

Eventually she managed a smile.

"I am better *now*," she said, looking up into his eyes.

"Are you sure? You've been through quite an ordeal."

Her face darkened for a moment, as though the horrors were coming back, but it was only for a moment. She winced as she moved her body and some pain somewhere made its presence felt.

"How did you find me? How did you save me?"

"We have time for that later." He paused. "Why did you call? After all these years. I've thought about you so many times."

At this, there was a slight look of confusion, as though she didn't understand something, but it was only there for a moment. Then she suddenly looked serious.

"It's a long story. But it's an important one. Something terrible is going to happen. You must help me."

"Anything," he said slowly, not knowing quite what she meant.

"I don't know if you will say that when you know." She looked out of the window for a moment, her face clearly focusing on thoughts far away. Then she turned to him and smiled weakly. "Could I have something to eat? I'm starving."

"Of course. Look, if you feel up to it, have a shower. A friend of mine has lent you some clothes. They're in the case by the table. Take your time. Come down when you're ready and I'll make some breakfast." He smiled at her.

She reached up and kissed him on the cheek.

"I am so happy you are here, my John."

McCready stood and walked for the door. He glanced back to see her smiling at him before he made his way downstairs.

Forty-five minutes later, McCready was standing in the main living room looking out across the bay when he heard a gasp from behind. He turned to see Carlita. She was dressed in a pair of Sarah's jeans and a clean sky-blue sweatshirt. She was standing at the top of the couple of steps that led down to the lower level, staring at the end wall of the room—the one with the poncho on it.

As he looked at her, he could see confusion cross her face again, but this time tears welled in her eyes. It was as though she didn't know what to do, how to react. After a minute she turned to look at him, and he almost saw an expression of fear and despair. He crossed over to her. She continued to stare.

"You kept it… after all these years," she said, incredulously.

He looked at her. "Of course I did. You were everything to me."

Again, she looked at him as though he were a stranger. She walked slowly down the couple of steps and over to the wall. She reached up to feel the material, touching it to make sure it was real. She then ran her hand along the wavy colored lines she'd sewn in twenty-five years earlier. She then closed her eyes, took a deep breath and turned to McCready.

"John, I never knew."

"Of course, how could you? We were a world apart."

He didn't feel it appropriate to go into all the letters he'd written that he'd never had replies to. She seemed to be in a state of confusion. It looked like everything that had happened was too much of a shock to her and she was having trouble taking it all in. Maybe they'd done more damage on the yacht than he'd thought.

He gently took her arm. "Come and have some breakfast."

He led her up to the dining table and poured her a coffee. There was toast and fruit and cereal. He offered to make her some bacon and eggs, but she said she was fine.

He watched as she ate quickly. It must have been a while since she'd had any food. There were so many questions he wanted to ask, but given how she'd reacted so far, he thought she needed time to come to terms with everything that was happening to her. There was plenty of time, but he was concerned about her comments that something bad was going to happen.

After breakfast they walked down to the beach. Some of the mist had blown away and the waves lapped gently on the sand. He could see her starting to come back to life as the wind blew through her hair and she breathed in the fresh sea air.

As they walked, they told each other about their lives.

He listened with interest at the life she had led.

As she spoke, it became obvious it had clearly been hard at times. She told him of the blazing rows with her father after McCready had left. He couldn't help feeling guilty, but what could he have done? She then told him how she had been drawn to the environmental lobbies and organizations. He knew how much she loved nature and animals, and it seemed a logical route for her to follow. The groups, though, had been radical, and become ever more so over time. He cringed when she mentioned some of the actions she'd participated in that crossed the line between breaking the law and helping a cause. As he watched, her expression seemed to glaze over at times, as though she'd gone to a place from which there was no return. It was like she was trying to justify her life with something to make it matter—to mean something. He suddenly found himself feeling sorry for her, desperately wanting to protect her from whatever had drawn her into this world. He knew deep down the spark for this had been ignited when he'd left. How could he now tell her it had been because of her father—that he'd written to her every week for six months?

He couldn't.

When she finished, he put his arm around her. They walked further along the beach to the rocks at the end. He told her about what had happened after she'd tried to call him. About Martin Steel, about seeing the CCTV footage of her and about how he had gone to Monaco to rescue her. As he spoke she listened intently. He could see the emotion building inside. He was about to tell her more when they reached the rocks and noticed movement around the waterline. Large kelp fronds slapped against the shore with the gentle swell, and just beyond, an otter poked her head above the surface. McCready pointed her out and told Carlita her name, Mira. He then recounted the story of Mira and her pups—that her mate had died, and when one of the pups had been killed he'd taken retribution against the people who had done it.

After he finished, she reached up and kissed him on the lips. It was sudden and passionate and McCready found he was responding before he knew it. They had been in the embrace for several seconds before he slowly drew back, pushing her gently away.

"I… I can't," he said.

She looked at him imploringly.

He had to step back and take a few breaths. He led her over to some grass at the side of the rocks and sat down. He looked at her seriously and then told her about Clare—everything they had been through together and what she meant to him.

When he finished she just looked at him, and in that moment he could tell he had lost her, or at least, whatever there might have been between them. It almost seemed as though she became hardened with the revelation—as though she was no longer the girl he had known who had loved him unconditionally. It was sad. It was overwhelming, but it was reality, and he knew it was for the best. And beyond that, what could she have expected after all this time?

She looked out to sea for several minutes. When she turned back to him, she smiled, but her expression held a sad, faraway look.

"John, of course there would be someone else. How could I have been so stupid to think otherwise? You are a wonderful man. I should have known. Part of me didn't want to contact you because I knew my heart would be broken. But I had to. When I tell you why, you will understand."

"I'm sorry. I'm so sorry." There was real pain in his eyes, but life sometimes sent you these curved balls. You just had to deal with them when they came out of the blue.

"So what's so important you had to find me?"

She looked at him intently for a few seconds.

"Let's go back to the house."

And with that, she stood up and led McCready back up the hill.

Chapter Fifteen

Ten minutes later they were back at the house and sitting on the sofa in the living room.

After composing herself, Carlita turned to face him, her demeanor now serious. McCready had not seen her this focused in the time she'd been there. He knew she was going to tell him something profound.

She took a deep breath and started.

"What I am about to tell you may affect the rest of your life."

She had his complete attention.

"When you saw the footage of me in Algeria—when I tried to call you—my group had come into possession of information that was too terrible to ignore." McCready watched her intently. "We had been monitoring a company for a while. It was clear they were abusing environmental regulations in many of their plants across the world, but what we found was they were trying to acquire something that could take out one of their competitor's operations completely. Not only that, it's apparently powerful enough to destroy a whole city. I don't know what it is, or how they plan to use it, but just the thought of this is beyond imagining. We were trying to find its location and prevent them from using it."

McCready felt he had stopped breathing. She looked at him, checking the impact she was having.

"So, did you find out where it is?" asked McCready, barely able to comprehend the magnitude of what she was saying.

"Yes," she said, simply. "We know where it is—sort of." He looked at her curiously but let her continue. "It's why they wanted to kill me. Why they wanted to know what I knew and if I had told anyone." After a pause she continued. "It's on a plane at the bottom of the sea. The plane was sabotaged. The company somehow tried to bring it down in shallow water close to South Africa, but something went wrong. Instead, it came down in the Bay of Bengal. I have the approximate area where it might be."

"Won't the owners, whoever they are, be looking for it?" said McCready, trying to focus on what he was hearing.

"Yes, but it appears the radio was inoperative and the plane couldn't be officially tracked. The only information that's known is that it went down a month ago at an approximate location."

"So if this company you're watching has the location, why haven't they retrieved it?"

"It's only approximate and the whole area is very deep. They don't have the equipment or expertise. It's not as though they can just contract a salvage company—anyone they hired would want to know what the job was and what they were searching for. When they found out, they'd drop it immediately."

Deep Control

McCready was starting to build up a picture of the situation.

"So, what is it you want from me?" he asked carefully. But he was pretty sure he knew where this was going.

She looked at him desperately.

"I want you to go and get it, John. I've been following your life…" He glanced at her. She looked embarrassed for a moment, almost ashamed of the admission. "I know what you do. I know how good you are. That you have the equipment. This is something you could do, John. We have to get it before the company works out a way to find it. They can't be allowed to get hold of this thing."

McCready could see her passion—how serious she was. He looked out across the bay for a moment, and then came to a decision.

"There's this guy, the one who gave me the information about you. If I tell him, he'll know what to do. This is a security matter. It sounds like whatever this thing is, it's some sort of weapon. Many lives could be at stake. He has a lot of pull. Access to equipment, military personnel. Things I have no control over."

She looked at him, and where he thought he would see relief and thanks, all he saw was panic.

"John, no. You can't tell anyone. It's not possible."

"Why not?"

"Because my brother's life is at stake."

McCready sat up with a jolt. It had been her brother, Fernando, who had brought them together. He remembered the fierceness with which Carlita had protected him when he'd been attacked by bullies in the street in Peru before McCready had come to their rescue.

"They threatened me with his life if I told anyone. They

said, whatever I told them, if someone went down to the wreck after I was gone, he would be killed."

"So what happens if we go after it?" said McCready.

Carlita looked heartbroken for a moment. A tear came into her eye.

"I do not know. Maybe they will not find out. It is a big ocean out there. Maybe they were bluffing. I don't know, but I do know if your friend gets involved with the military and governments, they will somehow find out. They have people highly placed in organizations. These things cannot be kept quiet. But still I do not know. I cannot risk his life—but then there are the lives of others if I do nothing."

She looked up at him. The tears were flowing freely now.

"John, I do not know what to do."

He held her close to him and stroked her head soothingly.

"Shhhhh. It's okay. We'll sort something out. I promise."

She cried in his arms for several minutes, and then after the tears had dried, she looked up at him. She looked straight into his eyes. There was nowhere for him to hide.

"I love you, John. I know what you said earlier. I know you have someone, but we were soulmates once. I love you. I always have. I always will."

And McCready found himself tearing apart inside.

How he could help, he didn't know, but he knew one thing, he'd do whatever he could—whatever the cost. She'd been right, he was going to be affected by this for the rest of his life. They may be different people now, but the stakes had just been raised and he was involved whether he liked it or not. He would try to protect her and her brother, but he also wanted to make sure this weapon, whatever it was, was found and stopped from falling into the wrong hands.

And it would have to be without the help or knowledge of Mr. Martin Steel.

Chapter Sixteen

Nyah ran into her quarters at Halley and grabbed her Canon EOS R6 with 24–105mm lens. The bad weather had not reached them yet and all looked good for a productive day out on the ice.

She'd been held up by a call to her best friend from 'the world above' that she only managed about once every few weeks. As usual, her friend was worried about her and wanted to know if she was warm enough. She had to smile. Friends would be friends and she loved her to bits, but Nyah was twenty-nine years old and thought she'd earned the right to make the correct decision as to how much thermal underwear to put on!

She made her way down the main corridor and out through the airlock system they had to keep out the extreme weather that could surround the habitat. Outside, it was a chilly -4°F. She zipped up her outer jacket and pulled on her gloves. She could see the rotors starting to turn on the chopper out on the pad. She ran over and tapped on the cockpit glass with a grin. Inside, Bowman shook his head and smiled. She jumped in the back and Murphy gave her a quizzical frown.

"So, missy, when you're quite ready, we've work to do!"

Nyah grinned and punched him again. This was getting to be a regular occurrence. Murphy had already complained he was black and blue from her blows and would soon have to go on sick leave.

She slammed the door to, strapped herself in, and put on her headset.

"All ready, Matt, let's go!"

And with that, Bowman pulled back on the controls and eased the machine up into the air.

Nyah watched as the base receded below them. She could make out other scientists preparing for a day out on the ice. Some had already left. There were three expeditions she knew of. One that was close by was on skidoos—she could see the small bike-like vehicles racing out over the white expanse. A second was using snowcats and was already a mile from the base, while a third was taking small Zodiacs out into the Weddell Sea to monitor phytoplankton samples underwater. She shivered at the thought of diving down there and subconsciously zipped her jacket even tighter.

Their task today was to position more instruments—this time on a glacier fifty miles inland. They were carrying an array of equipment, from vibration sensors to a Geiger counter to pick up any of the Earth's background radiation.

As they headed off, she brought out her camera. It was a perfect day for photographs. She also wanted to document anything they found at the location of the black helicopter she'd obtained from Hannah.

She watched the endless white disappear into the distance. It was amazing to think that in places the ice was nearly 16,000 feet deep, and within it was a wealth of information that could provide a window to the past. It acted as a repository for atmospheric records stretching back over millennia that were trapped in cores that teams had drilled over many years.

Up ahead she could see a range of mountains in the distance. She pulled out an iPad and clicked on a map that was enabled with GPS information. She had preprogrammed the locations of the black helicopter and brought up the details on the screen. It also showed their current position. As she oriented the map in relation to the view outside, the location the helicopter had spent the most time at appeared about a mile out from the upcoming mountain range.

She squeezed the mike button.

"Hey, Matt, can we drop off for a few minutes up ahead?"

"Er, why do we need to do that?"

Murphy also looked at her curiously.

"You know that chopper we saw the other day—the black one with no markings?"

"Yeah."

"Well I checked it out with Hannah. It's apparently made a number of flights, but none of them were logged, and it had no electronic identifier. It flew this route and stopped off near here. Would be interesting to see what they were up to."

There was a pause.

"We're on quite a tight schedule before the weather closes in. You sure you have time?"

Nyah glanced at Murphy, who was giving her a *not again*

look, but she knew he would go along with her. She looked at him with cow-like eyes. He nodded, then shook his head at his own weakness. She grinned.

"Yeah, we've got time," said Nyah.

"Okay, it's your dime," said Bowman from the front. "Just send me the coordinates."

Nyah tapped the iPad a couple of times and the coordinates showed up on a screen on Bowman's instrument panel in the cockpit. A moment later she felt the helicopter bank steeply over and drop altitude heading for a spot in the middle of the glacier.

Five minutes later they were on the ground and the blades had stopped turning. They all jumped down onto the ice. For now, the weather was calm, but the wind was starting to increase and trails of spindrift were blowing across the surface like wraiths searching for a home.

Nyah looked around. There didn't seem to be anything immediately obvious where they were. Any marks left from the other helicopter would have been erased by falling overnight snow. But there had to be something. They had spent over an hour at this spot—what had they been doing?

They fanned out in different directions, searching for something—anything.

They spent the next twenty minutes looking.

As they did, they failed to see a glint of light reflecting off something on a ledge on the side of one of the mountains a mile distant. It bounced off the lens of a compact video camera in a waterproof housing secured to the rock face. At the rear of the camera was a small aerial. The images were being transmitted to a separate location.

Someone, somewhere, was watching their every move.

"Over here," shouted Murphy.

Nyah and Bowman glanced up. They walked over to where Murphy was staring down at the ice. When they reached him, they looked at where he was indicating.

"There's been some sort of disturbance here," he said, brushing away a layer of snow. "It's not obvious, but there might be something deeper. Difficult to tell. It could be nothing, but there's nothing else around here."

Nyah looked at the ice. It definitely appeared as though someone had been there, but for what reason? It was in the middle of nowhere. There was no evidence of any scientific equipment or monitoring devices of any kind. It could be someone had tried to set something up but then decided to go elsewhere. She pulled out her camera and took some pictures of the ice as well as the surrounding mountains and the location.

Bowman checked his watch.

"We should be going, guys, if you want to get your work done and make it back to base before dark."

Nyah looked at the time and glanced around. There was nothing else they could do there.

"Okay, thanks for indulging me, Matt. Let's get going," said Nyah.

"Yeah, thanks for indulging, Matt," said Murphy sarcastically. "You're a real good indulger!"

Bowman looked like he might hit him and glanced at Nyah. She rolled her eyes and looked daggers at Murphy.

"What?" said Murphy, innocently.

They climbed back into the chopper. A minute later Bowman pulled on the collective, lifting them into the air.

Deep Control

But unnoticed by any of them, an instrument deep in the crate of equipment in the back of the helicopter had started recording readings that should not have been present on the Antarctic continent.

Chapter Seventeen

As McCready drove up to Ocean Tech, the sky was overcast and a brisk wind was starting to pick up.

The drive over had been one of contemplation. They had spoken little. Carlita still seemed tired following her ordeal, and McCready thought there must be so much turmoil going on inside her it was almost like she was a lost animal with no home. All he could do was provide a safe place for her to be right now, though her feelings for him made him deeply conflicted. And although he knew he couldn't go down that path, the longer he stayed in her presence, the more he found himself thinking back to the time in Peru when they'd discussed changing the world together. Now it looked like they were going to have a chance, but not in a way either of them could ever have imagined.

He indicated left and pulled the Range Rover in through the main gates. A quick wave at the security guard and he drove over and parked next to the large water tank building.

They climbed out and walked up the exterior steps to

the first-floor design studio. When they entered, Richards was talking to one of the engineers at a work station. He looked up and crossed over to greet them. He nodded at McCready and then stretched out his hand to Carlita.

"How are you feeling? I'm Craig by the way."

Carlita smiled and took his hand.

"Much better, thanks. I hear you helped to rescue me and John in Monaco. Thank you so much."

"Ah, it was nothing," said Richards with a grin. "At least by John's standards." McCready rolled his eyes. "Come on in, I'll get you both a coffee."

They walked into the conference room and sat down. Once Richards had made the drinks he sat and faced them.

"John tells me there's something you need to locate underwater. Something pretty dangerous by all accounts."

Carlita shot a look at McCready, who nodded, indicating it was okay to tell Craig all about it. She took a breath.

"All I know is there is this company that is planning to acquire something, maybe a weapon of some sort, that could cause untold devastation to the environment and potentially kill thousands if it was used."

"Any idea what they're going to do with it?" asked Richards.

"No, but with the effort they've gone to to get hold of it, they definitely plan to use it."

Richards thought for a minute.

"And you've no idea if it's a bomb, some kind of chemical pollutant… anything?" he asked.

Carlita shook her head. "I'm sorry."

He looked at McCready.

"And you say you can't call Steel?"

McCready glanced at Carlita and then back to

Richards. "No. There are reasons, but we need to keep this to ourselves for now."

Richards looked at him dubiously.

"Okaaay. So what about location? What sort of depth are we talking?"

"Do you have a map? I can show you," said Carlita.

Richards opened a laptop on the desk that was connected to a projector. He clicked some keys and a map of the world appeared on a screen on the wall behind him.

Carlita stood up and walked over to it.

"Can you enlarge this area, here?"

Richards zoomed in on the computer. The Bay of Bengal, surrounded by India to the west, Bangladesh to the north and Myanmar to the east, filled the screen.

Carlita walked closer. She drew a circle with her finger.

"I think it's somewhere around here."

Richards looked at the screen. The area she had indicated was about a hundred miles in diameter and about sixty miles out from the Indian coast. He did a quick calculation.

"That's nearly eight thousand square miles. That's a hell of a lot of sea to search. No way of pinning it down any more?"

Carlita looked apologetic.

"That was all we could find," she said. "There was a device on the plane that transmitted a location to the people who planted it. However, when it exploded, the tracking capability stopped. I can give you the position of the tracker when contact was lost. The plane could have disintegrated there, or if there wasn't extensive damage, it could have traveled some distance before hitting the water—that's why the area is so large. If it helps, from the information we have, the plan was to disable the plane, forcing it down, rather than blowing it out of the sky."

Richards thought for a minute.

"Okay, give me everything you have and I'll see if we can come up with a more accurate position. We'll need to get it as precise as possible to determine the approximate depth. It can range from a few hundred feet to thousands out there. Depending on which, it creates a whole different approach with regard to personnel and equipment."

"That's why we still have time," she said. "The company will find it hard to get anyone to help them."

"But if that's the case, maybe the owners, whoever they are, will reclaim it. They presumably want it back. Surely the best outcome would be to just let them find it and then this other company can't get hold of it."

A flick of fear crossed Carlita's face.

"We cannot take the risk. We cannot let that happen." She looked desperately at McCready.

Richards looked at McCready, a skeptical look on his face.

"Your call, John. You think we can do this?"

McCready glanced at Carlita and then Richards. "We have to try."

"So who owns this thing anyway?" asked Richards. "If we go, are we likely to have any problem with them?"

Carlita was hesitant for a moment. "I don't know. We couldn't find out."

Richards looked at her but let it pass.

"Okay, let's get some lunch," he said with a smile.

They ordered some takeaway food, consisting of sandwiches, chips and sodas. After they'd eaten, Carlita said she wanted to get some air. McCready explained the layout of the site and that if she went out the rear of the building she'd find a large back lot and the sea just beyond.

When she left, Richards turned to McCready with a questioning expression.

"So, what do you think? This really isn't something we should get involved in, John."

McCready thought for a moment before speaking.

"We have to try, Craig. If what she says is true, and why wouldn't it be, there could be hundreds, maybe thousands of lives at stake."

"But what if the owners come looking for it? From the sound of it, it's military, so we're talking about a state here, not some tech company. We could end up clashing with them, and they won't be happy. It is their property, after all. Maybe we should just step away."

McCready took a deep breath before continuing.

"For one thing, it appears they don't have the data Carlita has—so they would be searching a far larger area. You know what underwater searches are like. Look at MH370. They had all the kit and some of the brightest minds on the planet looking for years and they never found her. We may get lucky, and if there's the slightest chance of stopping these guys getting hold of it, I say it's worth a shot. Also, I've never been out there before—might be fun."

Richards shook his head. He then looked at McCready seriously.

"You sure you're doing this for the right reasons? I saw the way she looks at you. She's got you round her little finger. You haven't seen her for twenty-five years. Don't go and throw away everything you have with Clare over a teenage fantasy and a wall decoration."

"It's not that," said McCready emphatically. "I want to

help, that's all." But even to himself he didn't sound that convinced.

Richards sighed.

"Okay, I'll take a look at what she has, see if we can narrow the area, but whatever the depth, we're going to need at least a couple of side-scan AUVs, a serious ROV, and, depending on depth, and if we can't salvage it remotely, some sat gear—which all requires a ship. And if it's really deep, we'll need a sub, but there's no way we can get one ready in the timeframe." He paused. "And we'd better give Logan a call. He's happy diving to those depths. I assume you're not too rusty?"

"Count me in. And thanks, Craig. We're doing the right thing," said McCready.

"Yeah, right! Of course we are."

After Richards and McCready had agreed on a way forward, McCready rang Martin Steel and explained that although Carlita was safe, she needed time to recuperate before she'd be strong enough to be questioned by anyone. Also, she hadn't told him anything he thought would be of any use to Steel. He again thanked him for his help and said he'd call as soon as he felt she was up to it. Steel had sighed and said he didn't completely believe him, but to stay in touch. He had added that he'd be very disappointed if McCready wasn't telling him the truth. McCready had hung up, feeling somewhat guilty, and walked down to the ground floor and out the back of the building to go and find Carlita.

He found her walking along the side of the dry dock that was used as a confined-water test tank. It was currently full of water and millpond flat, in contrast to the waves in the sea beyond that were being whipped up by the brisk wind.

"Hi," he said.

She turned and smiled, but he could see she was anxious. There was a certain intensity to her expression as she spoke to him.

"John, we have to do this. I am not sure your friend Craig understands how serious it is."

He smiled and put a calming hand on her shoulder.

"Don't worry about Craig, he's just trying to be cautious and think things through. I can usually persuade him to do the right thing in the end. You just have to give him time. I trust him with my life and he's had my back more times than I'd care to mention."

This seemed to put her more at ease. She relaxed and linked her arm around his waist, pulling him close. He let it happen—how could be not?

They made their way down the side of the dock until they reached the end. There was a big wooden barrier that sealed off the estuary beyond. They walked along the edge of the water for a while feeling the freshness of the sea air blow over them.

Eventually they stopped and watched the water for a few minutes before Carlita looked up at McCready.

"John, what's going to happen to us?"

He looked down at her.

"I don't know. Let's sort one thing out at a time, shall we?"

Chapter Eighteen

The United Nations was formed in 1945 to try to bring countries together after the Second World War. At its inception there were fifty-one members—today there were a hundred and ninety-three. The aim was to ensure a melting pot of discussion that could iron out any pressing problems throughout the world and hopefully somehow resolve issues before they reached a point of no return and nations went to war with each other.

Unfortunately, that was not how it had worked out. With the world becoming ever more polarized and nationalism on the rise, it was doubtful any agreement on major global matters would ever be reached again. And when it came to the UN Security Council, things were even worse. For agreement to be reached, it required all five permanent members—China, France, Russia, the United States and the United Kingdom—not to use their veto. The problem with that was that recently some of the members were those in breach of international agreements and laws and were the ones that needed reining in. Of course, they were never going to allow that to happen, so either a stalemate ensued or nothing was ever put to a vote as the outcome would be a forgone conclusion and not in a positive way.

It was into this cauldron of stagnation that the UN was meeting for a vital environmental conference. It was held at the organization's impressive headquarters in New York and would deal with many of the issues raised over recent years, looking specifically at the best ways forward for countries to take that would allow them to meet the targets of the Paris Accords—the world's only real hope for a possible way out of the growing crisis.

Unfortunately, for many scientists, the little that had been achieved—and most of that had been mere words—had not gone far enough. This had resulted in heated arguments and disagreements between nations that continued to call themselves 'developing.' They argued, not unreasonably, that they needed to maintain carbon emissions in order to increase their standard of living to bring them in line with everyone else, given that many of the other nations had plundered the planet since the industrial revolution, and so now it was their turn. While this was a completely rational argument, it didn't take into account the state the world found itself in. If action wasn't taken, disaster was the only outcome—for everyone. The only right thing to do was for the richer nations, who had taken advantage of the world's resources for so long, to contribute and compensate the smaller, developing nations to even things up and create a more level playing field. Unfortunately, every nation wanted the most for itself. It was an intractable problem that was unlikely ever to be resolved.

What was going to add spice to the mix this time was that the assembly was to be addressed by Victor Solano. The recent speech he'd made in Basel had raised quite a few eyebrows, though most of the leaders put it down to mere grandstanding—that he was just trying to garner attention for some new product or initiative he was planning to launch.

None of them could have been prepared for what they were about to hear.

Alejandro Gonzalez, the United Nations Secretary-General stood up from his chair at the podium of the main assembly room. The tall gold-colored wall stretched up behind his head, with the iconic UN logo of maple leaves surrounding a map of the world halfway up. It was an impressive backdrop. In front of him, the members filled the hall in rows of seats that fanned out and curved around at the sides.

Gonzalez was in his mid-sixties. He had dedicated his entire adult life to helping serve the world and try to bring peace where there was war, provide food where there was famine, and reason where there was discord, but the task that faced him now was beyond what any Secretary-General had faced before. No agreement had been reached on many of the pressing issues, and he had a feeling that in the next few minutes things were only going to get a whole lot worse.

As he looked out over the multitude of nations that had sent their representatives to the meeting, he hoped some of them would be able to see it in their hearts that they were all part of the same world—one world—and one that needed their cooperation and agreement if it was to survive.

The general hubbub that had followed the previous speaker slowly died as people noticed Gonzalez standing at the podium.

He raised his hand to ensure complete silence. When he had their attention, he took a deep breath and started to speak.

"Ladies and gentlemen, thank you for your often frank and passionate speeches. We have heard many opinions from many corners of the Earth today, and although there has been no mandate for a clear way forward, I hope you will return to your countries and think carefully as to how you proceed from here on. We are faced with an escalating crisis that will not go away. It will not be contained or defeated by our differences, but only by our understanding that we are really all just one nation—the human nation, and totally dependent on each other for the survival of our planet.

"So finally, to close our gathering"—as he said this, two large screens above and to either side of him lit up with the face of Victor Solano against the dramatic backdrop of the mountains of Switzerland. There was a murmuring from the assembled delegates—"we are joined by someone who is known to you all. Victor Solano has made his presence felt on the world stage over many years. And while he has no official capacity here today, he has requested he be allowed to speak as he has something of the utmost importance to say to us."

Gonzalez turned to look up at the screens.

"Mr. Solano, the floor is yours."

Solano stared out from his position high above the delegates. He looked out of the screen with an expression of extreme confidence, but one that was deadly serious.

"Thank you, Mr. Secretary-General for letting me address you all today. I promise I will not take up any more time than is necessary to instill in you the gravity of the situation we—you—face. I have listened to your speeches, some of them impassioned, some of them not so, but one thing is clear—there is still no true comprehension of the problem. There is no seriousness to your words—no understanding of the stark reality and timescale of the threat." Again, there were murmurings throughout the hall, only this time there was a certain hostility to them. "Many of you may have heard my recent talk in Basel. What I said there was to put the world on notice—to try to wake you up to the certainty of the situation we face. I mentioned there would be something coming that would show the world a glimpse of its future. I even gave anyone the opportunity to approach me. To talk to me about what to do. Sadly, it is often the governments who are unable to see clearly—are unable to make the right decisions for their people, because governments have a built-in self-interest toward their own preservation of power. That is why I am here today, to explain to you that that power is about to be taken away."

This time there were more than murmurings. There were shouts of indignation. Gonzalez had to stand and raise his hand before the noise quietened.

On the screen, Solano didn't show any anger. His expression was one more of sad acceptance and confirmation of what he already knew. As he turned back to look at the assembled members, his face was totally calm, but it had hardened. And when he spoke, the assembled group was left in no doubt as to how seriously he expected to be taken.

"The climate disaster facing you will be demonstrated in two stages. The first will be just that, a demonstration, to show you what will happen in time when the sea levels rise, when the situation is so out of control you will not be able to stop it even if you wanted to. In fact, we have already reached that point. Even if all the measures required to halt climate change were taken today you would not stop the rise in sea level. That has been secured by the absorption of heat within the oceans that has taken place over many years and will continue to raise temperatures, melting the ice sheets for centuries to come. That has already happened—that horse has bolted. Sea level rise of many meters is an absolute.

"When my demonstration has been delivered, I suspect many of you will wish to act to do something about it. Those of you in low-lying countries will have the most to lose in the short term, but as the effect of turmoil in those countries overflows, refugees and social unrest will spread to all corners of the Earth. All of you will feel the effects. All of you will be impacted."

He paused.

"The second part of the demonstration is…" he paused again, "…not so much a demonstration, more a deliverance of reality, only accelerated."

He looked around at the assembled group. There was now no murmuring, no shouts of outrage. He could see they were listening to his every word.

"The problem is that you all think the consequences of climate change will not happen in your lifetime, let alone your administrations, therefore why should you risk political backlash, lose your jobs over something that may not happen for many years, possibly even decades into the future? Well I'm here to tell you that if you still do not listen after the demonstration, I will be compressing those decades into the space of a few months, maybe a year."

There was complete silence in the hall. Incredulous gasps could be heard from a few of the members. Most of them just glanced at the person next to them. There were no words to say.

"I will let you think on that for a while. But as you do, you need to plan ahead. It seems the only way to get you to work together is for you to have no choice but to work together if you want to survive. So that is what I am going to give you—no choice." He again looked around at everyone. "Be under no illusion. I am deadly serious in this matter... And should you think if I do this I will have everything to lose, you would be wrong. I'm dying of cancer. I have maybe six months to live. I have nothing to lose."

And with that the screen went blank.

For a moment there was stunned silence in the chamber —shock written across many of the faces. But then there was uproar. Members stood and looked around. Some shouted at others. Everyone was talking about what they had just heard. They were incredulous. They labeled Solano's words an outrage, but above all, they didn't believe him. What he had threatened was impossible.

From the stage at the front of the hall Gonzalez looked out at the discourse and outrage flowing across the room. He didn't try to stop it. It would have been in vain. But what he did have was a deep, creeping unease. How could Solano threaten such a thing if he couldn't back up his claims—if he couldn't call their bluff?

As he looked around the room, a sad reality came to him.

It looked like Solano's bluff was going to be called—and that frightened him more than anything he had experienced in his entire life.

Chapter Nineteen

The bow of the rig support vessel *Ocean Challenger* carved its way through the calm waters of the Bay of Bengal. They were two days out from the port of Chennai on the east coast of India and the ship was making good time in the benign conditions.

Ocean Challenger was just under three hundred feet in length. She had a high, stubby bridge painted white, which set it off against the dark blue of her hull. Above and forward of the bridge was a small round helipad, and at the rear, a long, open deck that was usually used for carrying pipe, and other drilling-related equipment. At the stern, a massive A-frame towered over the vessel that was used to raise and lower items into the water, while a small crane was situated halfway along the port side.

The ship was not normally used for diving operations, but she was all Richards had been able to secure at short notice. As it was, it had taken a week of harried phone conversations and calling in favors to pull everything together. She had been kitted out with a diving bell and mobile saturation system that had been craned on board in a series of containers. It wasn't the full system he would have liked, as would be present on a true dive support vessel, but it would have to do for what they had in mind.

The main bell was attached to the A-frame at the rear of the ship. This would winch the bell in and out of the water and swing it over to connect to the top of the recompression chamber that had been secured to the deck in a precise position to mate with the bell. If the weather deteriorated, they couldn't have the two being pulled apart and breaking the seal, which could kill anyone inside. It was in the chamber the divers would live between dives, at the same pressure as the depths they would be diving to, which at this point was unknown. It would also allow them to travel up and down to the seabed without any decompression issues, as they would spend the whole time with their body tissues saturated with the gases they would absorb at the full pressure of the depths they were diving to, hence the name 'saturation diving.' After completing the job, they'd stay in the chamber until their bodies had been safely decompressed.

At this point they still had to determine a final depth for the plane wreckage, but Richards had managed to narrow the search area down based on the information Carlita had given him, as well as taking into account the wind, water currents and other atmospheric conditions that records showed for around the time of the crash. They would still have to do an extensive underwater search, but Richards was fairly confident that when they eventually found her she'd be above a thousand feet and maybe as shallow as five hundred. He could but hope—the shallower they were the safer and easier things would be, but any diving at that depth was fraught with danger, particularly given the hastily rigged system they had on board. McCready, though, had been adamant this was the only way to go given the timeframe.

Richards walked out onto the flying bridge to join McCready, who was looking out over the water ahead. There were few waves and the weather was hot. Everyone was in shorts and it was a welcome change from Scotland.

"How are you feeling?" asked Richards. "You haven't been to these depths for over a year."

McCready looked up.

"I'll be fine. Like riding a horse."

"Yeah, a horse that can kill you at the first wrong step."

"I'll be okay," he said, smiling.

Richards watched him closely. He could tell he was tense, though whether this was at the prospect of diving to the depths they were likely to encounter or the situation with Carlita, he couldn't tell.

"You sure you want to do this, John? We've no idea what's down there." He paused. "Is she really worth it?"

McCready looked at Richards. His expression became more set.

"You know I have to, Craig. She came to me for help. How can I not do this?"

"I'm just worried you're getting in over your head, and I don't mean with the diving."

McCready paused and looked back out over the water.

"I'm alright. I can't see there being a problem."

"I hope not. As I've said before, Clare's the best thing that ever happened to you. And don't you bloody well forget it!"

McCready glanced up. "Don't worry. I know what I'm doing."

Richards looked at him dubiously but said nothing. They both stared out over the water.

A minute later Carlita joined them.

"Hi, guys, all going well?"

Richards smiled at her, glanced at McCready, and then left to go and check on their progress.

"Did I say something wrong?" she said, looking upset at Richards' departure.

"No," said McCready. "He's just overly protective sometimes."

Carlita looked slightly confused but then moved so she was close to McCready at the rail. She closed her eyes and let the sun warm her face. She then stared out over the water.

A couple of dolphins leaped through the surface close to the bow. She squealed with delight.

"There! Look there. Dolphins!"

McCready saw them. They watched the animals cavort and play in the bow wave for several minutes before zipping off at a sharp angle and away to other distractions.

"John," said Carlita, "do you think we will find the plane?"

"We've got a pretty good chance, so long as the information you had is correct. Craig has narrowed it down to a manageable area. It'll take some work to find it, but once we do it'll depend on the depth and its condition as to whether we can bring anything up."

"You have to, John. You have to bring it up. We can't let anyone else get hold of this. The consequences are unimaginable."

He looked at her.

"So what do you think it is?"

"I don't know. All I know is that from what we found at

the facility many thousands could die—if not right away, then over time, if whatever it is, is used."

He looked at her and smiled.

"Hey, I won't let that happen, okay. You were right to come to me. I won't let you down."

She looked up at him. He could almost see tears in her eyes.

Ten minutes later Richards poked his head out of the bridge door.

"Chopper's inbound. Five minutes."

McCready made his way back onto the bridge and up to the helipad at the front where he would shortly be meeting his dive partner, Mac Logan.

Sure enough, a few minutes later he could hear the distinctive far-off WHOMP WHOMP of helicopter rotors. He watched as the machine drew closer. The speck grew larger and larger, and then suddenly it was upon them. The 'Huey' circled around, allowing the pilot time to judge the best approach given the position of the ship and the wind direction. After a circuit, he flew in over the bridge and slowly set down on the moving ship. There was no time to slow the rotors. A few seconds later McCready saw a tall man with a thick scruffy beard jump from the back, dragging a large kitbag behind him. He waved to the pilot, who acknowledged and then pulled back on the controls, heaving the helicopter up into the air and banking steeply away for the return journey back to shore.

Once the downwash had subsided, McCready walked forward to greet Logan, a big smile on his face.

"Hi, John, great to see you," said Logan. He dropped the bag and bear-hugged McCready, almost winding him in the process.

"Great to see you too, Mac. How was the flight?"

"Flights! Took four, including the chopper, to get me out of darkest Mexico."

"Sorry about that. Hope we didn't call at the wrong time."

"Nah, it's alright. We'd explored about five miles of caves no one had ever been into. Truth be told, they were at a bit of a dead end, so the call came at a good time."

"Come on in. Craig's worked miracles to pull this all together. I'm sure he's dying to see you."

"That old bastard!" said Logan with a grin. "Always biting off more than he can chew. And I hear there's a lady on board. The reason we're here?"

"That's right," said McCready.

And with that, McCready took Logan inside and showed him to his cabin.

An hour later Logan had settled in and met everyone else.

But it was then time to go to work.

Richards had devised a three-stage operation.

The first was to locate the wreck.

This would be done with autonomous underwater vehicles, or AUVs.

The second was a reconnoiter of the wreck to determine its condition and the best way to get inside to retrieve the object they were after. This would involve a tethered remotely operated vehicle, or ROV, which could survey the wreck at close quarters with cameras, and possibly even go inside if the condition of the plane allowed. From this they would hopefully be able to get an idea of where the object was—it's size, weight, etc., and what equipment would be needed to recover it.

At this point they didn't have a clue what they were dealing with.

If all that went to plan, the third stage was to use lifting bags, which would be filled with gas pumped from cylinders around the bell. These would be controlled up to a shallow depth. From there, a cable from the onboard crane would be attached in mid-water to haul the object up and onto the deck of *Ocean Challenger*.

What happened then would be determined by what they found. Right now, they had no idea whether it contained any hazardous or explosive material.

One concession Richards had obtained from McCready was that if the object was a danger to the ship and crew in any shape or form, there were two options. The first was to throw it back in the water, however much concern that might bring—at the end of the day the safety of the ship was paramount. The second was to contact Martin Steel and let him handle things from there. This might leave McCready with a problem between himself and Carlita, but again, there could be far greater factors at play than her brother's safety, and they had to do what was right once they understood what they were dealing with.

So it was into this three-stage operation that work started straight after lunch on the first day.

Stage one began with the lowering of two twenty-foot torpedo-like AUVs into the water. They were controlled from a large metal shipping container on the rear deck and were equipped with sensors that could map an area completely autonomously at a speed of up to ten knots.

Richards had managed to narrow the search area down to around two thousand square miles. It would still take a while to cover all of this, but assuming the target's location was within the area, there was always the probability they wouldn't need to search it all to find the wreck. It would be incredibly unlucky if that were the case.

The two machines were lowered into the water one at a time. As they touched the surface, the controller in the container checked the preprogrammed flight plans for each. Once he was happy all was well and the systems were working, he let them off the leash to go do their thing.

The AUVs had forward-facing wide-angle cameras that would show anything underwater within a fifty-foot distance depending on visibility. Other than that, the range was limited by the lights they carried.

But their main capability was that they could survey the seabed from a height of three hundred feet, completely autonomously and work 24/7.

The sonar images were relayed in real time up to the monitors on the ship and showed in high detail an image of any objects the AUVs flew over on the seabed. If there was something of interest, manual control could be enabled and the pilot could investigate the target. If it turned out to be nothing, a flick of a switch put them back on autopilot and they continued the search from where they had left off. If all went to plan, they should have covered the search area within a few days.

Richards watched as the two sleek machines set off into the depths to do their master's bidding. He then walked over to the container that housed the control center. It was also from here that the ROV would be operated when they found the wreck and needed to inspect it more closely.

There was one technician at the controls. He was an experienced pilot Richards had worked with over the years at Ocean Oil.

"Hi, Harry, all looking okay?"

Harry Bishop looked up from the screen.

"All good so far. I won't turn the cameras and lights on unless we find something, to conserve battery life, but you can see the sonar track on the screen here." He indicated a flat line on the display in front of him. There were two lines across two screens, one for each AUV. We won't see anything until they come within range of the bottom. Current depth below the ship is eight hundred feet, so should be in the next couple of minutes."

Richards watched the screen. Sure enough, a couple of minutes later the flat lines on the display suddenly grew more of a profile as the AUVs leveled out three hundred feet above the seabed and started scanning the bottom for any anomalies.

Initially there was just flat terrain, but then gradually bumps and slopes became apparent. After a couple of minutes there appeared to be some old junk that had found its way to the bottom. There was what looked like a couple of barrels and steel girders from somewhere. These passed by and then the ground returned to bland, uninteresting topography.

Richards watched for a few more minutes and then walked back outside. Even with an air-conditioning unit in the corner the container was stifling hot. He let his face cool down in the breeze that had started to pick up and savored the fresh air.

Underwater searches were often slow and boring. It usually took many weeks to find wrecks where an approximate location was known. But technology was advancing all the time and Richards was pretty sure that if the wreck was in the area he'd designated, they would locate it before too long. It could be, though, they wouldn't find anything. After all, they were only going on some vague information Carlita had come across.

The plane might not even be there.

Chapter Twenty

As it was, it took until the following morning for everything to change.

Richards, McCready and Carlita were in the mess hall having breakfast when one of the deck hands ran in.

They looked up.

"You'd better come quick. I think they've found something!"

They made their way out to the container on the rear deck. The doors were wide open and a breeze was blowing through, making it more bearable inside.

As they entered, Bishop glanced up. He looked tired. The result of a long night and far too much caffeine.

Behind him, one of the screens showed a continuous readout of the sonar scan moving over the seabed, while the other showed a static display. On it was the image of a large aircraft lying on the seabed. It was incredibly detailed—not like a photograph, but like a black-and-white 3D model of what an aircraft would look like. They could even see cracks and damage to the wings that had been caused by the crash. Around the edges of the image were a number of smaller objects that were part of the debris field of items that had detached themselves from the plane when it had fallen into the depths.

"Take a look at this," said Bishop, indicating a screen above the main displays. They crowded closer. It showed a view of the wreck from the video camera in the nose of the AUV. Bishop rubbed his eyes and sat up straighter in his chair. He grabbed hold of a joystick on the desk in front of him.

"We definitely have an aircraft; the only question is—is it yours?" He glanced at Carlita. "Can you tell me, are there any markings or anything specific we should be looking for?"

Carlita leaned in. "Not really. I don't even know what kind of plane we're looking for. But maybe if there's something out of the ordinary it would be a giveaway, but there's nothing definite. I'm sorry."

Bishop took a deep breath.

"Okay, here goes."

He nudged the joystick forward and the image started to move. At the bottom of the screen was a series of numbers and figures. They indicated the position of the AUV and the direction it was facing. They also showed the depth—currently seven hundred and twenty feet with the AUV being about thirty feet off the bottom. Deep, but not as bad as it could have been—assuming this was the right plane of course.

They watched the screen, mesmerized by the images displayed in front of their eyes. While the AUV could provide perfectly good pictures, it wasn't that maneuverable, so for now it would effectively be just a flyby of the wreck.

If they wanted a detailed, close-quarters inspection they'd have to launch the ROV.

The AUV moved over the fuselage of the plane. They could see it was large and relatively intact. There was no growth of algae or other marine life on its surface, suggesting it hadn't been down there for long.

They could see windows along the side, which gave McCready pause.

"I really hope that isn't filled with people."

Everyone glanced at him.

McCready looked at Carlita. "And you've no idea where it came from? Who owned it?"

"No," she said.

"Okay, I'll take her round for another pass, then we need a decision, folks," said Bishop.

They watched as the AUV circled the plane again, but there was no new information to be gleaned from the images. When he'd completed the circuit, Bishop let go of the joystick and leaned back in his seat.

"Okay, what do you want to do?" He glanced between Richards and McCready.

Richards was watching the now static image of the plane on the screen.

"The odds of there being more than one aircraft, in this condition, in this area, are too much to contemplate. This has to be it. Are we agreed?"

McCready nodded. They glanced at Carlita.

"Sure," she said. She seemed glad to have been included in the decision.

"Right, Harry, you can recall the AUVs. I'll get the captain to head over to the location. When they're back on board and we're on-site we'll send the ROV down to take a closer look and maybe see if we can get inside."

"On it," said Bishop returning to the screen.

Richards and McCready walked outside. Carlita followed them.

"This has to be it," said McCready.

"Looks that way," said Richards. "We'll confirm before I put you and Mac in the water. We don't want you going down there only to find you're on the wrong flight."

"That would be nice," said McCready.

"Where is he by the way?"

"I thought I'd let him lie in. Sleep off the jet lag."

"Okay, good idea. He's going to need all the rest he can get if this is the target… Right, I'll go see the captain, and then we'll meet back here when we're on-site to get the ROV in the water."

But before Richards could leave there was the sound of an aircraft in the sky. They looked up to see where it was coming from. It didn't sound like a high-altitude airliner, more like a fast, low-flying jet. A second later they saw a speck approaching from the east. It was low down and coming fast. A few seconds later it shot past, barely a hundred feet above them. The noise was deafening. They watched as it swept up vertically into the sky and then proceeded to fly in a tight circle around the ship at a height of a couple of thousand feet. It had swept-back wings, a high canopy and twin tail fins. Richards watched it for a few seconds.

"Looks like a Sukhoi Su-35—a Russian jet."

He ran back into the container and grabbed a pair of binoculars. He looked up and focused the image.

"It's not Russian. It's Chinese. Red star with a yellow border on the wings. What the hell is that doing here?" He continued to stare at the plane. "Also, there's something strange under its belly."

"Weapon of some sort?" asked McCready.

"No, I don't think so," said Richards. "It's too long for a missile or torpedo, and too narrow for an auxiliary fuel tank."

"Maybe a surveillance pod—cameras, sensors, that sort of thing," said McCready.

"Yeah, could be. That would make sense," said Richards, dropping the glasses around his neck.

They watched as the plane continued in a constant bank around the ship. A minute later it leveled off and headed back east, the twin afterburners lighting up as it sped away.

Richards and McCready shared a look.

"You don't think it could have anything to do with what we're looking for?" asked McCready.

"I'm starting to get a bad feeling about this," said Richards. They both looked at Carlita, who had also been watching the plane.

"Guys, I don't know any more than I've told you. I wish I did."

Richards shook his head. His expression was grim, but he noticed Carlita was looking scared. She really didn't know.

"Okay, we'd better get this done. I have a feeling we'll need to be out of here sooner rather than later."

And with that he headed off to ask the captain to steam at full speed to the position of the wreck.

While the attention on the ship moved to the next stage of the operation, all thought of the Chinese jet was forgotten.

But if anyone had looked, as the jet sped away, they would have seen the long, strange pod Richards had seen beneath the fuselage detach and drop into the water.

Once below the surface, the casing split in two, allowing something to emerge from inside. After a few seconds it headed into the depths.

Two hours later, *Ocean Challenger* was in position over the wreck, her dynamic positioning system engaged. This would allow them to remain on station directly over the plane. It used a series of thrusters in the hull, controlled by a computer with data from a network of satellites, similar to a navigation system in a car. If the ship drifted off position by even the smallest amount, the computers would detect the movement and power up the relevant thruster to bring her back on station—all automatically. Once the system was engaged there was no danger of losing the wreck site. They had noted the GPS position just in case, but hopefully that wouldn't be one of the problems they would no doubt encounter moving forward.

Richards watched as McCready helped the deck crew swing the sophisticated ROV over the side and into the water. The thick umbilical that provided power and video, and acted as a tether, unspooled from a giant drum on the rear deck.

The AUVs had been hauled back on board and were now sitting peacefully in their cradles, their task complete for now.

The ROV was highly capable. It was something Ocean Tech had been developing as Ocean Oil when they were involved in the North Sea oil industry, before the name change. ROVs formed the backbone of much of the work on the rigs and there was a time when it was thought they would completely replace divers, along with the costly operations required to support them. But regardless of how sophisticated they'd become, divers would always be needed in the final analysis, as with current technology the machines were still not dexterous enough and unable to make on-the-spot decisions, even though their every move was monitored by a controller on the surface.

They watched as the $200,000 machine sank below the waves and headed for the seabed seven hundred and fifty feet below.

Once it had gone, McCready and Richards walked back into the confines of the container and watched as Bishop maneuvered her down to the wreck.

As the power supply came through the umbilical there was no danger of running the battery down, so the lights were on all the way to the bottom. It might seem boring to look at a screen of water passing by, but the water wasn't empty. The lights attracted marine life as she headed deeper.

There were millions of zooplankton, the tiny animals that made up the bulk of biomass in the oceans, and without which there would be no food chain of life in the seas—but then there were the larger animals. A strange octopus swam by, and then an eel glided past. Before they reached the bottom, even a shark had swum into view, but when Bishop had tested the pan and tilt of one of the remote cameras, it had shot off into the darkness, frightened by the sudden movement.

As well as the cameras, the ROV had an array of equipment that enabled it to interact with its surroundings. At the front were two manipulator arms with mechanical claws on the end. These could hold something with an iron grip, or be delicate enough to pick up a marine creature and place it in a specimen jar unharmed. For this particular operation the ROV was equipped with a cutting tool that could slice through sheet metal like a knife through butter and would make light work of the aluminum fuselage of the aircraft. There was also a series of proximity sensors that could relay the position of the machine and provide a warning if it was getting too close to an obstruction that might ensnare it. The last thing they needed was to have to dive to free it from entanglement with a trawl net that had been abandoned on the wreck, or a twisted piece of metal that could trap the umbilical.

Half an hour later the down-facing sensor started beeping, indicating they were approaching the seabed. Everyone drew closer to the monitor.

At first, all they could see was sand, and then, as the ROV touched down, a cloud of sediment sent up by the thrusters covered the cameras. Bishop moved the machine forward to take it out of the cloud, but they still couldn't see the wreck. He checked the readout on the screen. It gave him the direction he needed to head in. He twisted one of the two joysticks and the image changed on screen. The ROV moved forward and over about thirty feet of seabed. Then, suddenly, out of the darkness, the lights reflected off something white. It was the starboard wing coming slowly into view. It was massive, extending off into the black beyond.

As the ROV rose up over the wing, the lights illuminated its surface, the white paint making it glow as though it had a power source all of its own. The visibility was good—about sixty feet, with little plankton or particulate matter to bounce the light back into the camera lens.

They watched as Bishop headed toward the fuselage. The one thing that struck them was just how intact it was. There were a number of cracks in the wing, but other than that, from what they could see, the pilots had done an amazing job of putting her down. Only time would tell if they'd managed to escape in time.

Bishop steadied the joystick in his right hand and leaned back in the seat.

"Okay, where would you like to start?"

Richards moved forward to take a closer look at the image. The wreck stretched off either side of the screen.

"If we think there's something strange, and it's not a passenger plane, but carrying cargo, then the whole interior could just be open space. Let's check out the cockpit, see if the pilots are still there, and then head back to look through the windows, see what we can see inside."

"Roger that," said Bishop.

They watched as the ROV lifted up off the wing and headed toward the nose. An eel swam through the shot, slithering away into the darkness.

When they reached the cockpit, Bishop pulled in close and moved the lights so their beams were unobstructed. He then pushed the camera forward on an extendable arm so it could see inside.

When the image became clear, Carlita let out a cry, throwing a hand to her mouth. The body of one of the pilots was strapped in his seat, while the other floated in the cramped confines behind. They clearly hadn't managed to get out. Even the door was closed. Maybe something had jammed it shut. Carlita gasped again as the light fully illuminated one of the faces, revealing a half-eaten cheek and no nose. A crab scuttled over the eye sockets and disappeared inside the skull. Nature was already setting about recycling the organic material.

They all took a breath.

Bishop backed the ROV away from the grizzly scene and moved further along the fuselage. He was close to the side so the lights and cameras could look in through the windows. At first there just appeared to be a void beyond. There were no seats and mercifully no passengers. But as they moved further aft, something appeared in the middle, secured to the floor. When they reached halfway, they could clearly make out some sort of object. It was around thirty feet in length, stood six feet high with an equal width. Bishop stopped the ROV with a clear view of the interior framed by a window.

"Is that what you're after?"

He glanced back at the three people watching over his shoulder.

McCready and Richards let Carlita closer so she could see. The object was some sort of cradle. It was made up of steel bars that enclosed what looked like a long, fat cylinder with curved ends.

Carlita's face looked blank.

"I've no idea, but it's the only thing there, so I guess it must be."

Richards looked at McCready and shrugged. "Looks like that's it then." He leaned closer, appraising the cradle more carefully. "She's big. Going to need a fair amount of buoyancy to bring that up."

"But doable," said McCready, glancing at Richards.

"Oh, everything's doable, John. It's just at what risk?" He took another look. "There's no way we can get in from any hatches, and with the size, we'll have to cut through and bring it out over the wing. At least that'll make a good platform to attach the bags. It should then be a straight lift to the surface where a couple of guys in a Zodiac can drag it over to the ship and winch it on board... Sound good?"

"Works for me," said McCready.

Carlita just looked at them, but there seemed to be a

sense of relief on her face. They'd found the plane and it was likely they were going to be able to retrieve the object that could do so much harm.

Richards turned to Bishop.

"Okay, Harry, if you cut a rectangle half the length of the object over the wing area, John and Mac should be able to ease her out with a bit of grunt. You okay with that?"

"Sure thing, boss. I'll shout if I need anything."

Bishop pulled the ROV back over the wing and parked it so it was looking at the fuselage.

As McCready and the others left the container, Bishop stood and crossed over to a kettle to refill his mug. He stretched his tired body, and after walking around for a couple of minutes, he returned to his seat and prepared for the task ahead.

What he'd missed, though, was a shadow fall across the body of the plane. A shadow that was no eel or shark.

This was way bigger.

Chapter Twenty-One

Harry Bishop made himself comfortable in his seat and took a firm grip of the controls. He yawned and then settled back to concentrate on the job at hand.

He pulled back on the right-hand joystick and moved the ROV forward to find a starting place for the cut into the fuselage. The equipment used liquid oxygen burning at 10,000°F, which would scythe straight through the metal on the side of the plane.

He piloted the small machine over to a point around ten feet to the left of the center position of the cradle inside and then brought up the controls that operated the cutter. A flick of a couple of switches and a turn of a third joystick and he saw a brilliantly bright flame leap from the end of the rod in the right-hand manipulator claw. He moved it forward so it was in contact with the metal and started the long task of cutting a twenty foot by ten foot hole in the side.

An hour later he'd cut through the top, the bottom and the left-hand side. He set about the last section on the right.

There was plenty of gas left and the flame ripped through the fuselage as though it was barely there.

He made the final movement that completed the rectangle and then withdrew to check the cut was complete all the way around. He then moved in close to the middle of the section and reached out with the mechanical claw to grab hold at the top. Once the grip was secure, he reversed the ROV slowly. With a whine of metal on metal, the large section of fuselage fell away as though in slow motion, landing on the top of the starboard wing.

He was about to move forward to check out the interior of the plane when the image from the camera jerked to the left.

What the hell is that?

A moment later it moved again, only this time it was more violent, as though the ROV had been pushed through the water by something.

And then the screen went blank.

He stared at it in disbelief. He tried rebooting the system, checking the telemetry—but nothing. He moved the controls, but there was no indication he was having any effect on the vehicle. It looked like it wasn't just the video feed that was out—the ROV was dead in the water.

He'd had system failures before, but not as suddenly as this. There was usually some sort of warning that indicated one was imminent. This time, the only clue was the sudden movement before contact was lost. It had to be some sort of marine creature—maybe a shark—possibly an eel, but the movement seemed too dramatic for an eel. As it was their only ROV, there was no option other than to pull it up and see what the damage was.

He spoke into a mike to instruct the deck crew to get to work.

An hour later, Bishop, Richards and McCready watched as the final length of umbilical was hauled in. Although the panel had been cut in the side of the wreck allowing them access, it was always good to have another pair of eyes down there when the divers were in the water, so if they could repair the ROV, that's what they'd do.

They watched as the umbilical was hauled over the side of the ship. But as they reached the point where the machine would break the surface, they stared in shock and disbelief.

There was nothing there.

McCready and Richards exchanged glances as one of the crew reached out with a grapple pole and pulled the end of the umbilical over to examine it more closely.

When it was lying on the deck, a tingle of fear crept up McCready's spine. No sea creature had done this. The cables had been cut cleanly through. Whatever was responsible was man-made, and right now, it was seven hundred and fifty feet directly beneath them.

Richards chased after McCready as he strode toward the recompression chamber, fully kitted in a thick drysuit with collar seal at the neck to clamp to a commercial dive helmet.

"John, wait up!" said Richards.

McCready stopped and turned, determination and focus in his eyes.

"Look," continued Richards, "you can't do this. We've no idea what the hell we're dealing with. Clearly someone else knows about the wreck and wants what's inside. It could be the other company Carlita is going on about, or it could be the owners of whatever is down there. Either way, it's too dangerous. And what's Mac got to say for himself?"

At that moment Logan walked past, fully kitted like McCready.

"Not a problem, Craig. If John's going, I'm going." He carried on walking to the chamber, where he proceeded to climb in.

Richards threw his hands in the air.

"Has everyone gone mad?"

McCready turned to him. "Look, Craig, we need to check this out. If it turns out to be dodgy, we'll make a judgment call down there and, if necessary, back off. You know me, never one to take a risk," he said with a grin. Richards looked as though he was about to throttle him.

"You're the exact opposite of that! Jesus! Doesn't anyone have any common sense around here?"

Carlita had been watching the exchange. She stepped forward.

"John, maybe you should reconsider." She looked up at him. He could see the worry on her face.

He took a deep breath and looked at her closely. She was clearly conflicted. On the one hand this was why he'd flown halfway round the world—for her—to find and retrieve what she'd said was so dangerous, but on the other, he knew how she felt about him—clearly, she was torn between the two. But when he thought about it, he didn't have a choice. It wasn't up to her anymore. If the device, whatever it was, was as dangerous as she said, many lives could be at stake. He had a duty to stop that from happening. He looked at her and smiled.

"I'll be fine. Really," he said, as he crossed over to the hatch at the end of the chamber.

She rushed forward and hugged him.

"Be careful."

When she pulled back he could see there were tears in her eyes.

"Always am. I'm only going for a quick swim. You know I've always loved the water." He looked at her seriously. "This was what you wanted. We're here because of you, remember?"

"I know," she said. "Maybe I was wrong. Maybe I shouldn't have contacted you. It's dangerous, John. I don't know what I'd do if anything happened to you, and it would all be my fault." She looked up at him, her eyes pleading.

"Well, we'd better make sure nothing does then." He smiled. "I'll be back in no time."

He kissed her on the forehead and then climbed into the chamber. Before he disappeared, he nodded at Richards. Richards nodded back and then pulled the round metal door to with a clang. It was the last fresh air they would breathe until the job was done and they'd fully decompressed, which could be several days away.

McCready held the door closed until the pressure inside increased enough to seal it shut. He then made his way into the main part of the chamber.

Half an hour later the pressure had been increased to that of the seven-hundred-and-fifty-foot depth they'd be diving to, and they'd transferred into the bell that was attached on top. With an okay from McCready over the comms, the bell was winched up and over the side of the ship and into the clear blue water. Within seconds it was heading for the bottom.

Carlita watched briefly, but then turned to look out to sea, seemingly hardly able to watch as the bell disappeared below the waves.

Inside the small round space it was tense. McCready and Logan carefully prepared for the dive ahead. It was deep, but well within the range both of them had dived to before, though for McCready it had been well over a year. In fact, the poignancy of the moment was not lost on him. The last time he'd descended in a bell like this, his brother had been with him. It was a dive from which Sean would not return alive. He was adamant nothing like that would happen this time.

Neither of them spoke as the light from the portholes slowly dimmed and they headed ever deeper into the darkness and a rendezvous with whatever awaited them below.

The equipment was complex and state of the art. Even though the operation had been put together last minute, Richards had managed to combine the infrastructure of the boat with the latest in deep-dive technology to keep Logan and McCready as safe as possible.

Their main gas supply came from on board *Ocean Challenger*. It consisted of a mix of helium and oxygen. This would eliminate the possibility of nitrogen narcosis, or drunkenness of the deep, which occurred when breathing air that contained nitrogen deeper than a hundred to a hundred and fifty feet. Beyond this, the mind was pretty much lost to the condition. As well as being unable to work, it meant you would likely pass out and die. A side effect of breathing helium, though, was that it distorted the voice. This was due to the gas being a different density to air, one which the vocal cords had not been designed for, so you got the high-pitched squeaky voice people had at parties when breathing from balloons filled with helium. To counter this, sophisticated computer descramblers were used to process the conversations and convert them into intelligible speech. This meant the divers could talk to each other and dive control on the surface without any problem.

If things went wrong and there was an interruption to the gas supply from the ship, each of them wore bailout rebreathers, again using a mix of helium and oxygen. These were controlled by wrist-mounted computers, which provided the perfect mix of gas to ensure a minimum of decompression if they had to ascend without the bell for any reason. However, if this situation arose, it could still leave them with severe decompression issues depending on the duration of the dive, even with the high-tech algorithms controlling the gas mix. In this scenario they would have to transfer straight into the chamber to be recompressed from there.

All this was going through their minds, not as issues to worry about, but as a checklist to make sure they responded automatically to any eventually, should it occur.

McCready had just finished strapping on his rebreather when the speaker in the bell crackled to life.

"Okay, guys, you're approaching the bottom," said Richards. They felt a slowing of their downward movement. "Everything looks good from up here. Give us a 'go-no-go' when you're ready."

McCready grabbed the mike.

"Roger that. Will do."

He turned to Logan.

"All ready?"

"All ready. Let's do this."

They helped each other on with their helmets, carried out a final equipment check, and then McCready grabbed the mike again.

"Okay, Craig. Leaving the bell now."

"Roger that. Stay safe," came the reply.

Chapter Twenty-Two

McCready dropped down through the round hatch in the bottom of the bell and stood on top of the starboard wing of the aircraft. They had landed exactly where the skipper of *Ocean Challenger* had said they would. He was earning his keep. As both of them were diving, there would be no bell man, so they had each paid out a length of umbilical that would allow them to move as far from the bell as was needed for what they had to achieve.

It felt good to be back in the water. The depths had never bothered McCready. Once you were beyond a certain point it made no difference to him. As it was, it was pitch-black where they were, and if it wasn't for the large rig on the top of the bell that flooded the plane with light, they could have been at any depth.

McCready watched as Logan eased himself down onto the wing. When they were both happy, they crossed over to the rolled-up lift bags on the outside of the bell and detached them from their straps. They pulled them onto the wing and laid them out ready to attach to the cradle once they'd extracted it from inside the plane. McCready then moved back to the bell to grab the high-pressure hose that would allow him to fill the bags using compressed air from the cylinders attached to the bell.

Once everything was ready, McCready looked around.

Everything was quiet. There was no sign of whatever had damaged the ROV.

As they started to move toward the hole in the side of the fuselage, they could see the crippled machine lying on its side at the trailing edge of the wing. They moved slowly over to it. As they were staying in close proximity to the bell on a flat surface, they had no fins. This, though, meant their movement was slow-motion walking, so it took a while to reach the ROV. When they did, it was clear no animal had been anywhere near it.

"You seeing this?" said McCready, as he looked at the damage on the top.

Wherever he looked, the camera and light mounted on his helmet would send images back up to the control room on board the ship.

"Roger that," said Richards over the comms. "Keep an eye out, John. There's something down there, and it ain't friendly."

"Roger that," said McCready.

He indicated for Logan to follow him over to the fuselage. When they reached the large hole that had been cut in the side, they could see the cradle strapped to the floor. It appeared to be completely intact. They could also now see that the sides were made up of a series of metal bars, beyond which was a long, cylindrical object that ran the full length, width and height of the cradle. As they moved closer, a number of symbols stood out on the side. A couple were in Chinese, which didn't bode well, but then McCready saw one that made his blood run cold.

"Look at that, Mac. That's a radiation symbol. What the hell is this thing?"

Logan moved closer and saw what McCready was indicating.

"Jesus!"

McCready was now all focus. Carlita had not been kidding when she'd said it could do some damage. Whatever happened, there was no way they could leave this down here to fall into the wrong hands.

McCready aimed the camera at the symbols.

"You getting this, Craig? We have to get it up."

"Copy that, John. Be careful. Whatever was down there earlier could still be around… and now we know this is serious."

"Move over to the far end," said McCready to Logan. "Let's see if we can move it."

Logan made his way slowly to the end of the cradle deep inside the plane. They undid the straps that held it to the floor, and then, on McCready's mark, tried to lift it. To his surprise it moved. It was heavy, but that might have been due to the cradle rather than the object inside. McCready couldn't be sure, but he had a feeling what they were looking at was some sort of AUV, like those they'd used to scan for the location of the wreck, only this one was far larger and, by all accounts, with an entirely different purpose. If that was the case, it would be neutrally buoyant in the water and therefore weigh nothing down there. It also meant they were dealing with a highly sophisticated machine with a radiation symbol on the side, and whichever way you cut it, that wasn't good.

They strained to lift the cradle, and they were able to

raise it enough to shuffle slowly out through the side of the plane.

They were just clear of the fuselage when everything went to hell in a handcart.

Logan was still inside. McCready was out on the wing. The cradle was between them when there was a high-pitched whine from behind McCready.

He spun.

Something was coming at him out of the darkness. Two lights suddenly flicked on, blinding him. And then he was hit in the side. He fell over. He could vaguely make out some sort of shape above him. It looked like a snake.

When he struggled to his feet he could see it was no snake.

He stared incredulously at the serpent-like machine. It was about twenty feet long and a foot and a half wide. It was made up of numerous segments with thrusters at various points along the side, but what made McCready pause was its movement—it slithered through the water like a snake or eel, while its nose looked left and right, just like an animal.

He hit it hard from underneath.

Immediately, the 'head' whipped round to stare at him —there was no other word for it.

It moved closer.

As it did, while the head continued to stare via a bank of cameras and lights, the other end bent round toward him. McCready could see a claw-like device protruding from the rear. Clearly, whoever was controlling it was watching them—but where was it being controlled from? McCready didn't have time to think about any of that as the claw advanced, opening the large pincer and coming straight for him.

"John, look out," yelled Logan.

But it was already there.

McCready managed to move to the side but the pincer struck him hard on the head. He collapsed onto the wing, dazed for a moment. When he hauled himself to his feet he could see the machine moving inside the plane, heading for Logan.

Logan dropped his end of the cradle and stood his ground. As the machine bore down on him, he shouted at McCready.

"Get the lift bags attached and get the cradle out of here! I'll try and hold this thing off until you're clear."

McCready didn't even reply.

He moved as fast as he could to the first lift bag. He grabbed the straps and looped them through one end of the metal frame of the cradle. He then grabbed the high-pressure hose and injected air into the bag, forcing it to take shape and rise up in the water until it was straining at the leash. He could now pull the whole thing further out onto the wing and clear of the fuselage.

He then repeated the action with the second bag.

The cradle was now sitting there primed, ready to shoot to the surface when he injected more air into the bags. When he did, the ascent would accelerate as the bags expanded when they rose higher due to the reduction in water pressure. Excess gas would escape from underneath, preventing them from exploding, but it would be a wild ride to the surface.

He was about to put the final blast of air into the bag to start the lift when he heard a scream over the comms. He looked up. He could see lights jerking around inside the plane.

He had to help Logan.

He left the cradle and moved as fast as he could over to the fuselage. He pulled himself inside. When he saw what was happening his mouth almost fell open.

The ROV had split in two. One section, consisting of two segments, was hovering a few feet away, almost as though it was conducting the operation through the cameras at the front. The claw on the second section was holding onto the side of the hole in the fuselage, just like a hand would. But what was more terrifying was that the other end of the second section contained a spinning saw, which was advancing on Logan, who was pinned in the corner. As it closed in on him, he put out his hands to hold it off. He struggled fiercely, but it was too powerful. There was nothing he could do. McCready watched in fear as the machine brought the saw closer and closer. He could see it heading for Logan's umbilical.

"Noooo!" shouted McCready.

He pulled himself down the collection of hoses until he reached the ROV. He grabbed hold of anything he could. He tried to pull wires out of connectors—anything to draw its attention away from Logan. He noticed the second section of the ROV turn to look in his direction.

"Come on. This way!" he yelled at it.

But while the cameras continued to watch him, both machines stayed where they were.

McCready moved round the side. The saw was close to cutting through Logan's umbilical. He tried to grab it, to pull it away, but it was hydraulically operated and he had little chance. He could only watch in horror as the spinning blade cut through the pipes as though they were spaghetti. As they split, gas erupted into the confined space.

"Switch to your rebreather, Mac. Now!"

He could see Logan reaching up to his helmet to

operate the valve that would switch his gas supply over to the bailout. It would barely give him enough time to decompress but they had to get him breathing quickly or that wouldn't be a problem they would have to deal with.

But then he had it.

McCready could see Logan's look of relief through the faceplate.

But the operator of the ROV could also see it. Before McCready even had a chance to react, the saw changed direction. All McCready could do was watch in horror as it moved in on Logan's helmet—and didn't stop.

The saw pushed through the helmet straight into his face.

McCready could barely move. He watched as his friend's body spasmed and convulsed and then fell to the bottom of the plane, a thick red trail flowing from the helmet's faceplate.

But he had to snap out of it.

With Logan gone, the machine would turn its attention to him.

He headed as fast as he could back to the entrance.

He had to get the cradle up and out of there.

He crossed over to one end and injected air into the bag. It expanded slowly and started to lift off the wing. He was halfway to the other bag when he felt his foot grabbed in a vice-like grip. He turned to see the claw of the ROV holding him fast. The machine was still split in two. The second section watched from around ten feet away.

But what was more alarming was the spinning saw. The machine had moved round and the saw was heading straight for his head.

He had the high-pressure hose in his hand. He brought it forward, aiming at the camera section of the ROV. When he turned it on, high-pressure air shot into the front of the machine. He held it there. If nothing else, the chaos of bubbles would obscure the operator's view and might give him a few seconds.

Clearly something had happened, as the grip on his foot lessened a fraction. It was all he needed to pull himself free. He kicked at the ROV, trying to disable it. He then grabbed hold of the cradle and pulled himself over to the second lift bag.

But the ROV had other ideas.

Before McCready had time to reach the second bag, he saw the longer section heading for the bell.

He now had a choice to make.

Stop it attacking the bell and his way out of there, or inflate the second bag and send up the cradle. If he waited too long, neither would be an option.

"Bollocks!" he said to no one, and went for the second bag.

He'd almost reached it when he heard a mass of bubbles explode from the top of the bell. He looked over. The bell was falling onto the wing of the plane, all connection to the umbilical severed. The collection of pipes thrashed around, spewing gas out into the water. It also meant all comms and video were gone—they were blind on the ship above.

A second later he found it difficult to breathe. He immediately switched to his bailout. Once it was working, he discarded the now redundant umbilical by detaching it from his helmet. He then headed back to the lift bag. The high-pressure hose would still work as it was fed from cylinders on the bell, and that line hadn't been cut. He reached the bag and injected air into it. He then watched as it rose up in the water, starting its long journey to the surface that would only accelerate as it rose higher. He stayed with it as it started to ascend.

The operator of the ROV must have also seen this. The machine turned in its own space and sped over to attack the lift bags. If it succeeded, everything had been in vain.

McCready stood on top of the cradle as it headed up. He still had the high-pressure hose in his hand but that would soon be coming to the end of its length from the bell as the bags rose ever higher.

The ROV headed for the nearest bag, its lights the only illumination now the bell's power supply was gone.

McCready moved to intercept.

As the machine started to cut the straps to the lift bag, McCready kicked it viciously in the side. It whirled round and came straight for him. At the same time the camera section also advanced. He now had two machines to deal with.

He looked over the side of the cradle. They were about thirty feet above the wing and coming to the end of the length of the high-pressure hose. He had one chance and one chance only. If he screwed this up he was dead and the machine had won.

The ROV approached, its body winding through the water, the deadly saw out in front. There almost seemed to be a swagger about it, as though it could smell victory. But as it reached him, McCready ducked. The underside cruised inches above his head. He waited until it was almost past and then grabbed the claw at the rear. He took the high-pressure hose and wrapped it round the base of the claw so it was securely attached. The ROV was now effectively tethered to the bell, which acted like a massive anchor. He then moved round to the front and found the hydraulic lines that fed the mechanical control system. He pulled a knife from a thigh pocket on his drysuit and cut them in quick succession. Immediately, all power and strength went from the saw—it was impotent.

The camera section of the ROV looked like it had gone berserk. It moved quickly from the rear of the tethered section and then back to the front. It advanced at McCready and moved round him, circling him. McCready couldn't see any weapon on this section, but he was still wary of it.

Finally, it rushed at him, seemingly out of frustration. He fended it off, but when it came round for a second attack, he took his knife and hit the camera on the front as hard as he could. He could see the glass covering the lens crack. He grabbed one of the small thrusters on the side and hit the glass again and again. Harder and harder. The crack enlarged, growing bigger with every strike—and then it splintered. The pressurized housing of the machine couldn't take any more impacts. With a violent explosion of bubbles, the integrity of the seal was broken.

It imploded.

A second later it was full of water and the electronics shorted out.

Now, motionless in the water, it drifted slowly down to the seabed. It would provide no food or sustenance for the creatures of the deep but McCready was just glad it was dead.

For the first time on the dive he relaxed a fraction.

But he still wasn't safe.

He now had a major decision to make.

There was no way he could fix the bell—that was gone. But if he stayed on the cradle as it rose to the surface he'd come up so fast he'd be crippled by the bends before he even reached it. His only chance was to try and ascend on his own using the gas in the rebreather, and hope the computer managed to control it enough so he'd still be able to decompress safely in the chamber when he got there.

He was loath to jump off the elevator on which he was currently standing, but to carry on would mean almost certain death. It was rising just too fast.

He shut his eyes and stepped off.

He hung motionless in the water as the cradle disappeared above him. He only hoped they were ready to retrieve it topside when it got there. He'd seen a lift of a heavy object before which had gone out of control. When the bag had reached the surface, it had shot so far out of the water the underside had been exposed to the air—all the gas had spilled out, deflating the bag and causing the object to plummet back into the depths. They couldn't afford to let that happen here.

Below him, he could hear the distant whine of the electric thrusters of the larger section of the ROV as it desperately tried to free itself from its plight, but McCready knew how to tie knots.

It wasn't going anywhere.

As he started the long, slow ascent to the surface, the light from the ROV slowly faded until it was gone. His only friend now was the dull glow from the computer screen on his wrist. The small package of electronics was all that was keeping him alive.

As he rose, one thought filled his mind—he was leaving Logan dead on the bottom and there was nothing he could do about it. The image of his death was seared on his mind forever. Someone, somewhere, was going to pay for this. It was no longer about helping out a friend from the past.

Now it was personal.

Chapter Twenty-Three

On the deck of *Ocean Challenger* all they could do was watch as events unfolded hundreds of feet below. They were powerless to help. They knew things were bad, and that Logan had been killed. They had seen the images from McCready's camera. Carlita had cried out in shock as they had watched Logan die. She'd had to go outside to get some air, away from the confines of the container. But she'd come back shortly after—McCready was still down there.

They'd watched until the cameras had been taken out when the cables had been cut. After that there had been a few seconds of stunned silence.

Richards had been the first to react.

"Okay, we have to be positive. John will have managed to release the lift bags and they'll be on their way up. So, we need to get ready for their arrival. It's unlikely he'll come up with them. He knows it would be suicide. We need someone looking out for when he surfaces. When he does he'll have to go straight into the chamber. Carlita, can you keep watch?"

She nodded, but Richards could see she was shaken and frightened. She hurried out of the container. Richards looked around at the remaining members of the crew.

"Right, get two Zodiacs in the water ready to grab this thing when it arrives. It'll probably be going like the clappers, so stay back until you see it surface, but then go in fast. We can't afford for it to drop back down… Okay, get to it!"

The crew ran off to launch the boats and prepare for what would happen next.

When they'd gone, Richards took a deep breath. Bishop looked over from the control panel. He looked crushed. They had both known Logan well.

A short while later there was a shout from one of the crew in the inflatables. He pointed at the water between them and the ship. Richards and Carlita looked down into the depths. Sure enough, they could see something rising up toward them. It was surrounded by a cauldron of bubbles as the air vented from the lift bags.

And then it was upon them.

The two bags were the first to burst through the surface, their bright yellow color contrasting vividly with the blue of the water. And then the cradle surged up through the surface.

Before it had even fully emerged the two Zodiacs raced forward. Crewmen in each reached out to grab the straps before the bags could deflate. They managed one, but the second fell over on its side, air exploding out in a massive rush. The bottom of the cradle dropped away. Shouts went up as everything was now hanging on the single strap at the other end. The driver of the Zodiac leapt to help his crewmate secure the cradle. They hauled what they could of the bag into the boat. Once it was tied on, they slowly made their way back until they were beneath the A-frame at the rear of *Ocean Challenger*. Once there, a diver jumped into the water with a line to tie onto the other end of the cradle.

Within five minutes they had it secure. With an okay from Richards, the operator swung the A-frame up and over, bringing the cradle, and the sad-looking lift bags draped over it, out and onto the deck. Once it was on board everyone crowded round. All, that was, except Carlita. She continued to stare out over the water, watching for McCready.

Richards started to walk around the large, long object that now sat on the deck dripping water. When he was halfway, he stopped, crouched down and peered closely at what was held within. He could see the symbols McCready had mentioned. They were indeed Chinese, but what was universal was the black and yellow symbol for radiation. Whatever the hell this thing was, it was dangerous and it totally changed the game. As had already been demonstrated, serious people seriously wanted it back.

He told the crew to cover it with a tarpaulin so it couldn't be seen from the air. He then had a decision to make. He had to tell someone. And that someone had to be Martin Steel, though he didn't want to make the call until McCready was up.

But that was the next question. What happened if he didn't make it up?

He crossed over to Carlita at the side of the ship. He could see the hurt and pain in her face. She looked up as he approached.

"Is it bad?" she asked.

"Yeah, it's very bad. Whatever that thing is, it's radioactive. There's no detection equipment on board, so I've no idea if it's a danger to us, but if someone gets their hands on it and uses it, you were right, a lot of people are going to die."

She continued to stare at the water.

"I wish I'd never got John involved."

Richards could see the genuine sadness.

"He's tougher than you think," he said with a reassuring smile. McCready was tough, but he wasn't indestructible. Who knew what had happened down there after he'd sent the cradle heading for the surface?

"Also," continued Richards, "now we know some of what we're dealing with, John would have come anyway, with or without you. That's just who he is."

She smiled at this, and then looked back at the water.

"How long should it take him to come up?"

"Well, given he only has his rebreather, and assuming it's functioning okay, he should be here within a couple of hours, but he'll be in the chamber far longer. Which reminds me, I have to go make sure it's ready. Just keep an eye out, okay?"

Richards left and walked over to the chamber. They had enough gas and equipment to recompress and treat McCready. The only problem was, what shape he would be in, when—no, IF—he made it back to the surface.

McCready had managed to settle into a slow but steady rhythm. As soon as he'd left the wing of the plane on the cradle, the gas in his drysuit had started to expand—just like the lift bags—so getting up was not a problem. He didn't even need to expend much energy. All he had to do was vent off the excess gas every now and then from a valve on his shoulder to ensure he didn't ascend too fast.

He was currently within the profile the computer had set him to reach the surface safely, so long as he stopped at the intervals indicated. The only problem was, it was telling him he had four hours to go, but he only had a gas duration of two hours—the sums didn't add up.

He had carried on, though, and had been doing fine, right up to the point one of the alarms had started beeping. It was just after he'd begun to discern a brightening in the water above. It was faint, but if the depth readout was not enough to reassure him he was rising, the lightening of the water was a welcome sight.

The alarm was not.

He looked at the figures and the message that was now flashing on the screen.

Shit!

It indicated that the oxygen levels were dropping fast. There must be a leak of some sort. In a heliox rebreather, the helium provided the diluent that made up the inert gas the body did nothing with during respiration—the important bit was the oxygen. Only about a fifth of the oxygen breathed was used by the body with each breath—the remaining four-fifths was recycled to be breathed again—hence the name *rebreather*, unlike with a scuba cylinder where all the exhaled gas was lost to the water with each breath.

Now, with the leak, the oxygen would be gone before he could make it safely to the surface. With no comms to ask for more gas to be sent down, he was left with only one option—ascend before time and take his chances in the chamber. That was one thing he wasn't looking forward to. Apart from the fact the outcome was unknown, he'd recently spent far too long in a chamber in San Diego, and the thought of going back into one was not appealing.

But there was no other choice.

He checked the computer again. He was at three hundred feet. He'd continue to rise relatively slowly, trying to stay within safe limits for as long as possible. And then, when he only had a few minutes gas supply left, he would ascend from whatever depth he was at, at the time.

That depth turned out to be just shy of two hundred feet.

The oxygen was now showing zero and the screen was doing its best impression of a video game, flashing all sorts of warnings. There were also multiple alarms going off. He clicked the right-hand control button to silence them. He didn't need a headache as well as whatever else greeted him when he reached the surface.

And that was the next problem. In the few hours he'd been ascending he could have drifted miles from the ship. He hadn't noticed any current when he'd been on the bottom, but he'd been weighted down and was within the area of the wreck for most of the time. Now he was in open water he wouldn't notice any current as he'd be drifting with it, so would effectively be staying still in relation to the water. It could be running at twenty knots and he'd never know.

A minute later and he took his final breath. The rebreather froze, refusing to give him any more gas as the mixture would be too dangerous to breathe without any oxygen.

It was now or never.

As he looked up, it was definitely brighter. He couldn't make out the surface, but that was where he was heading, and fast.

He refrained from venting the gas from the suit for a while, to increase the expansion and therefore the buoyancy and subsequent speed of ascent. He also leaned his head back and slowly breathed out, trying to match the exhalation of gas from his lungs with the expansion as he rose.

It was getting brighter and brighter. He started to feel light-headed. He let out more gas. He could see the surface coming up faster now. It was almost like ground rush when parachuting at low altitude.

He was at what he deemed to be a depth of sixty feet when he blacked out.

The light that had seemed so welcoming now faded down a seemingly endless tunnel. He tried to fight it but couldn't. The last thing he remembered was how happy he was that he had seen Carlita again, and what the possibility of life together might have been like.

But then he had to correct himself.

The last thing that flashed through his mind was of the small velvet box he'd left in his sock drawer at Clare's house in Los Angeles, and that he'd never be able to give her the contents.

And then everything went black.

Carlita had been sitting at the side of the ship for several hours. No one had been able to persuade her to leave, or that it was maybe too long now and there was no hope. She refused to move. Richards had brought her some food and a cup of coffee and sat with her for a while, but had left when it was clear she would rather be on her own.

Now, as the light was fading, she continued to stare out across the water. If something had happened to John she would never forgive herself. She was about to finally concede there was no hope—he wasn't coming back—when she saw a glint of light way out on the calm surface. If the sun had been higher and the sea glistening with light, she wouldn't have seen it, but now, with dusk approaching, the glint shone out like a beacon. It was about a quarter of a mile away to the stern of the ship.

She looked more closely and then ran over to the container where Richards was looking through some of the video footage from McCready's camera.

"Craig! Come quick. I think I see something!"

Richards grabbed a pair of binoculars and followed Carlita back to the side of the ship. He looked where she was pointing and put the glasses to his eyes. At first, he couldn't see anything. It was getting darker, and anything in the water would blend in with the color of the surface, but whatever it was must have moved slightly as he saw a reflection off something. It was only for a moment, but he knew, without a shadow of doubt, it was coming off the faceplate of McCready's helmet.

He didn't wait for anyone else. Most of the crew were inside eating.

"Come with me!" he said to Carlita.

She ran with him down to one of the Zodiacs moored at the rear. Richards jumped in, started the engine, and as Carlita untied the mooring line he knocked the Zodiac into gear. A second later they were speeding over the smooth surface to where they had seen the glint in the water.

As they approached, they could see it was a body lying face up.

It was McCready.

Richards ran in at speed and then slowed at the last second, flicking her briefly into reverse, and then neutral. He reached down and grabbed the rebreather on McCready's back. It would be too heavy to drag into the boat. He made sure the computer was still securely fastened to his wrist. The information within it was vital to determine any treatment for him in the chamber. Next, he released the helmet and pulled it off. He then undid the rebreather and let it fall into the depths. With Carlita's help they hauled his inert body into the boat. Before he was even on board, Richards checked for a pulse.

He was alive.

But there was no time to lose.

Richards slewed the Zodiac round and headed back to *Ocean Challenger*.

When they arrived, the crew were waiting. They'd heard the activity and come out to see what was going on.

Eager hands reached down to carry McCready up onto the deck. Without even removing his suit, he was carried into the chamber airlock. A dive medic climbed in with him and the door was sealed. Richards was an experienced chamber operator and could carry out any protocols required, but there needed to be a skilled medic inside in case of complications and if any drugs needed to be administered.

It was all over within minutes.

Once the airlock had been pressurized to that of the chamber, the medic had hauled McCready through and onto a bunk. He quickly placed an oxygen mask on his face and plumbed in a drip. Only then could they take a moment—but they couldn't relax. They had no idea if there had been any bubble damage within his tissues.

Only time would tell.

Over the next half hour Richards worked out a treatment protocol with the medic and then the long wait started. It looked like he would need to be in the chamber for at least the next ten hours. He would be monitored at all times—and then, what would happen would happen.

Richards instructed the skipper to head for shore as fast as he could. While they could carry out basic treatment in the chamber and stabilize McCready, if he needed surgery of any kind, or things deteriorated, they needed to be at a shore-based facility where they could cope with more serious issues.

By the time there was some calm on board, and the ship was underway, it was dark outside.

Richards walked out onto the deck and leaned against the rail at the stern beneath the A-frame. He stared down at the black water passing beneath the ship and felt the wind on his face from the movement across the sea. There was nothing more he could do. He turned round and saw the large cradle sitting on the deck and realized their problems were only just beginning. It was clearly Chinese, and with the jet that had flown over earlier, and the ROV on the seabed that had killed Logan, he knew trouble was coming.

He glanced over the deck to the main superstructure. Most of the crew were inside, either eating or catching up on some much-needed sleep. He noticed someone on a companionway on the deck above. Their outline was lit up with the glow of a cellphone. He smiled. They were back in range of a signal now, and someone was no doubt calling home to their family.

He looked back out over the water, his thoughts returning to Logan and the fact they would never be able to recover his body. He knew McCready would want payback for this. He just hoped he would be able to restrain him long enough until he had recovered.

Ten minutes later he walked over to the side of the chamber and looked in at his old friend. They had been through a lot together—you could rightly argue too much—but McCready was someone who never gave up. He was someone who would always do the right thing, whatever the cost, which along with being one of his greatest strengths, was one of his greatest weaknesses, at least for those around who loved and cared about him—but that was just the way he was. This was no more true than when he noticed Carlita staring in through one of the other ports of the chamber. He could see she had tears in her eyes. It must be so much worse for her.

Chapter Twenty-Four

It was nine and a half hours later when McCready emerged from the chamber into the sunshine of another day. Richards was there to greet him. Carlita was just behind.

"Do you always have to nearly die?" said Richards.

"No," said McCready, wearily. "But it seems Mac did." There was an emotionally charged moment where Richards nodded solemnly. They looked at each other for a second and then he indicated Carlita behind him. "She didn't leave the side of the ship all the time you were down. She was the one who spotted you on the surface." His expression showed he was starting to see how much she cared for McCready and could understand his feelings for her.

Richards drew back and let Carlita step forward. Her eyes were moist and she looked up at McCready with relief and hope.

"John," was all she could manage before throwing herself in his arms and hugging him tightly. He hugged her back. They clung to each other for a minute before he eased her away.

"I thought I'd lost you," she said with a sniffle.

"You won't get rid of me that easily."

He was about to say more when Richards beckoned him over.

"We have to make a decision about this." He pointed at the cradle.

McCready glanced up, gave Carlita another hug, and then walked over to the large cradle that was lying on the deck.

"You have to call him," said Richards.

McCready looked at the long torpedo-like object behind the bars. He nodded slowly.

"Yes, I know. I'll do it now."

Carlita had overheard the conversation.

"John, what are you going to do?" She clearly looked nervous.

McCready stopped and smiled at her.

"I have to call the man I told you about. I know what you said about your brother, but this is bigger than that. I have to tell him. We'll deal with anything else if it happens, and I promise, I'll do everything I can to keep him safe."

Carlita looked up at him, but her expression had hardened.

McCready watched her curiously, but he knew how much she loved her brother. He smiled again and then walked over to the control room in the container to grab his phone.

He came back out and took a series of photos of the cradle and the object within. He focused on the symbols, both the Chinese and the radioactive ones. He then took a deep breath and dialed.

It was answered on the fifth ring.

"Martin Steel."

"I have a little problem," said McCready.

There was a slight pause.

"Nice to hear from you, John. Where are you? Connection sounds distant, shall we say."

"I'll tell you in a minute, but there's something I need to confess first."

"I'm listening…" But the tone had changed.

"Carlita did give me some information that I've acted on. I was going to call you but she was convinced that if more people knew it would put her brother in danger. I thought I could keep it contained until I knew what was going on. At the end of the day it might all have been nothing."

"Go on. I assume, therefore, it isn't nothing… By the way, what are you doing in the Bay of Bengal?"

Now it was McCready's turn to pause.

"How the hell do you know that?"

"It's what we do, John. How many times do I have to tell you?" McCready could hear a sigh at the end of the phone. "It's called 'Find my Friends.'"

"But I didn't enable that."

"Yeah, I know. We did."

McCready had to smile.

"She told me the information she'd found in Africa related to the company trying to acquire something—she didn't know what—that was potentially dangerous. She contacted me because it was in a crashed plane that was too deep for the company to salvage, so she wanted me to get it before they did."

"Okay, so I guess you're going to tell me you found whatever it is and it's not good."

"Yeah, you could say that. In fact, that's probably the understatement of the year."

There was silence for a moment.

"So what did you find?" asked Steel.

"I'm sending you some pictures. Hang on."

McCready tapped his phone and listened as the whoosh of the files being sent came over the speaker. He put it back to his ear.

"Should be coming through."

There was a pause at the other end.

"Okay, coming in now," said Steel.

"From what I can see, it looks like some sort of AUV," said McCready, "but the worrying thing is the radiation symbol on the side. There are some close-ups at the end. Once I saw that, I realized you needed to know."

He waited while Steel checked the pictures. He then heard an outrush of breath over the phone.

"Anyone else know you have this?"

"Possibly. We had a flyby by a Chinese jet a while ago and when we were diving on the wreck we were attacked by an ROV with Chinese writing on the side. The machine is dead in the water, along with a good friend of mine."

"Okay, this is serious, John. Really serious. What you have is a Chinese nuclear AUV. A bit like the Russian Kanyon/Poseidon nuclear-powered version, only this one is more compact and with greater firepower."

"So what you're saying is that this thing is a nuclear weapon?"

"That's exactly what I'm saying."

"Jesus!"

"Yeah, right."

"The Chinese are going to want it back."

"Yeah, right."

"So, what do we do?"

"Well, you got yourself into this mess. I'd love to just say *get yourself out of it*, but I think, even for you, that might not be possible."

"Can't we just let the Chinese take it? It is theirs, after all, and it would keep it out of the hands of the company in Africa that wants to use it."

He could almost hear the gears working in Steel's brain over the phone.

"That would be one way to go," he said slowly, "but it would be rather useful to bring it back to take a closer look at."

"Oh great," said McCready. "I really don't want to get tied up in your games again. People died last time. And someone's already died this time."

"Look, John, you may not have a choice. If the Chinese come for it, you won't be able to stop them. I'm assuming you're not armed."

"Not exactly. There're a couple of Very pistols on board and I think the captain has a rifle somewhere, but that's it."

"Like I said, you're not armed." He paused. "What are you doing now?"

"We're heading for Chennai. Should be there sometime tomorrow."

There was a pause.

"Okay, I'm coming out. I'll be in touch nearer the time, but head for port as fast as you can. Keep an eye out and report anything out of the ordinary. When you get close to land, stay a mile offshore. I'll talk you in when I get there. Okay?"

"Yeah, okay."

"And John, do exactly as I say. This is serious!"

And with that Steel hung up.

McCready set the phone down and walked out onto the open deck. He told Richards and Carlita what Steel had said. They were shocked at the thought of a nuclear weapon being on board and slowly backed away from it, as though that would make a difference.

As it was, they were steaming for port. All they could do now was keep an eye out for over-inquisitive activity from any ships or planes. Richards went to tell the captain. Carlita walked up close to McCready. He looked at her.

"I had to tell him."

Her expression was still hard, but it had softened a little. She nodded and put an arm around him, holding him close.

"I know, John. I just hope it doesn't get out."

They both stood and looked out over the water. It was still calm, but a breeze had sprung up. The forecast was for increasing winds, which would make the water choppy, maybe even stormy. It looked like there were rough waters ahead—on all fronts.

Chapter Twenty-Five

Nyah's week had been relatively quiet, with a break in excursions out onto the ice due to the weather that had finally closed in.

She'd been catching up on paperwork and filling out reports on the progress of her research. Much of this involved analyzing computer data collected automatically from the sensors they had been installing across the region. Not the most exciting way to pass the time, and the work probably wouldn't show any dramatic results for many months, if not years, but it was all part of the job and key in determining long-term trends that, in turn, could predict the health of the planet moving forward.

The storm had meant no one was supposed to be out on the ice, and those who had been caught short were holed up in tents and vehicles wherever they'd been when the weather had hit. Everyone had been accounted for, though. It was just one of the hazards of having your office in an extreme environment.

She was looking forward to today. They would finally be

able to go back outside. The trip was further into the interior to fix some more sensors, and she was just glad to be getting out into the fresh air again.

She made her way to the gear store, which was the last module at the end of the base. It was where all the scientific equipment was kept and serviced by the technicians.

She was just checking over the allotted kit and associated equipment when she heard a faint beeping coming from one of the shelves at the back of the room.

She crossed over and looked for the source. It was coming from the second shelf up from the bottom. It was where they kept the Geiger counters that were used to check for any background radiation that might be emitted from ancient rocks or other items found out on the ice, including meteorites and the like. Any readings could reveal a whole history of an object, be it from this planet, or indeed, any other.

She scrunched down and looked along the shelf. Sure enough, the sound was coming from one of the units at the back. Normally they were turned off before being put back in the storeroom, or else put to one side for charging. She reached in and grabbed it. When she pulled it out she could see the soft glow from the display on the front. The ID number on the side indicated it was the one they'd packed, but never used, on their last trip—the one when they'd landed in the middle of nowhere at the location where the black helicopter had been.

She looked closely at the screen. It showed all recent readings that had registered. On the last trip they'd never needed it, so it had remained in the equipment crate, unused. But somehow it must have been turned on, as the log showed the readings were from the date of that trip. She looked closely at them. After double-checking, she sat down on the floor in stunned amazement.

As she looked at the display she could see that around the time they'd set down on the ice, the readings had gone off the chart. They had remained there until the time corresponded with when they'd left the area.

She picked up the device and headed back to the main section of the base. She had to tell someone about this.

She found Murphy in the canteen eating breakfast. He was stuffing a piece of fried bread with bacon, egg and tomato on top into his mouth as she walked over. He looked up as she reached him. He swallowed the mouthful, took a swig of coffee and grinned at her.

"Hey, Nyah, fancy some gourmet cuisine before we head off into the unknown?"

"Urgh, no thanks. I have standards," she said with a smile.

But then her expression turned serious. She set the Geiger counter down on the table. Murphy looked at it suspiciously.

"What have I done now?"

"Nothing. But I found this in the equipment store. It had been left on. No idea how that happened, but it's the one we took on the last trip."

He picked it up and looked at it. When he saw the screen was displaying information, he took a closer look. As he did, he frowned.

"This can't be right. There was nothing anywhere we went that should have had any background radiation, let alone reading off the scale."

"I know… except…"

He looked up. "Except?"

"Except when we stopped on the ice where that helicopter had been. We knew something had been disturbed there. That's where the readings are from."

Murphy looked at it closely, checking through the figures.

"This is not good. We have to go back, check it out."

"We're going close by today. I'll see if I can get Matt to take a detour."

"Oh, and what will that cost you?" said Murphy with a grin. "Two hours in the hot tub together!"

She thumped him.

"Come on, quit stuffing yourself with that crap. We don't want you having a heart attack out on the ice!"

Murphy rammed the final piece of fried bread into his mouth, swilled it down with yet more coffee and then followed Nyah out to prepare the equipment for the trip.

Half an hour later they were airborne. Bowman had at first grumbled at having to deviate from the planned route. It meant refiling the flight plan, but a few fluttered eyelashes from Nyah and the predicted outcome had been achieved. Nyah knew Murphy would never let her live it down, but hey ho.

They flew directly inland from the coast before turning in along the mountain range that would take them to the location they had stopped at before.

As they got closer, Nyah looked at the surrounding area —the ice, the mountains, the landscape, but she couldn't see anything out of the ordinary. At one point she thought she saw a flash of light off something halfway up one of the rock faces about a mile from where they were headed, but she soon forgot about it. It was probably a piece of ice catching the sun.

They circled the location in a wide arc, in case they could see anything from the air. When they were directly over the site, it seemed there might be something below the ice, but it was difficult to tell.

Bowman brought the helicopter in for a smooth landing fifty feet from the point of interest. Once the rotors had stopped turning and the whirlwind of snow had calmed, Nyah and Murphy jumped down carrying the Geiger counter. They walked over to where the GPS told them the location was. Much of the disturbed snow they had seen before was gone following the recent storm. It would have been blown away anyway, but there was a new layer a couple of feet deep. When they were at the exact spot, Murphy pulled out the wand from the Geiger counter and turned it on. He held it close to the ground. Immediately there was a rapid clicking. The readings shot off the scale. He glanced at Nyah, who looked concerned.

"There shouldn't be anything like this out here. We're miles from anywhere," she said.

"I know," replied Murphy. He stood up and looked around. "Okay, let's do some digging."

They walked over to the chopper and pulled out a couple of small foldable shovels from the rear. They walked back to the spot and Murphy started to dig in the newly fallen snow.

As he did, Nyah heard a soft PHUT sound from behind. She turned round but couldn't see anything. She went over to join Murphy digging in the snow. She shoveled away a portion and then heard the PHUT sound again. She also saw a piece of ice three feet away flick up into the air. It seemed strange but she carried on digging. Suddenly she struck something hard. She glanced at Murphy.

"Found something."

He looked up and walked over. At the bottom of the shallow hole was something dark buried in the ice. It looked to be about five feet in diameter and was circular in shape.

He brought his shovel down into the snow. As he did, there was an almighty CLANG and the shovel shattered into pieces.

They stood there staring at it. A moment later there was a CLANG from the helicopter. Bowman leaned out of the cockpit door. He was screaming for them to get back in. The rotors were already beginning to turn.

They ran back to the chopper and leapt inside. When they had their comms units on, they could hear Bowman shouting at them.

"Someone's shooting at us!"

Nyah and Murphy stared at each other in horror.

As they lifted off the snow and banked away, a massive SMACK reverberated through the airframe as something hit the metal side just below the engine.

Nyah and Murphy leaned back in their seats, fear written across their faces. But then Nyah sat up and groaned—they'd left the Geiger counter on the ice, along with all the evidence. But right now, that was not foremost on her mind. She'd come to Antarctica to conduct science, not get shot at. She took a deep breath and tried to steady her rapidly beating heart.

Halfway up the cliff face, there was a whirr of an electric motor as the small waterproof camera tracked to follow the departing helicopter. To one side, on a tripod on a ledge, sat a remotely controlled Accuracy International sniper rifle with a suppressor attached to the barrel. A small wisp of smoke drifted up into the freezing air, the gun's work done for now.

The whole episode had been streamed from the camera to a location thousands of miles away, and at that precise moment, someone was thinking what to do. The outcome of those thoughts would determine what happened next.

Bowman slewed the helicopter round to land back at Halley an hour later.

After they'd lifted off from the ice he'd flown a zigzag pattern to throw off the shooter. They were a long way from any firing position he could see, and a rifle shot over that distance would be heavily affected by the wind. The sniper would either have to be incredibly skilled or incredibly lucky to hit them again. Even so, he had felt a few beads of sweat run down his neck.

As soon as he was sure they were out of range he'd radioed the incident back to base. He'd been met with incredulity by the duty controller but told to report to the base commander on their return—immediately on their return.

Nyah, Murphy and Bowman walked into the base commander's office twenty minutes after they landed. They told him the story and then watched as he looked between them one at a time.

Jerry Patcher was a veteran of Antarctic expeditions. He was in his mid-fifties, had short dark hair and a hardy face that had seen many extremes of nature over the years on many continents. He was someone who didn't flap easily under pressure and was a respected leader in times of crisis.

He'd been down to Antarctica on ten tours and nothing ever phased him. But this was different—people were being shot at. Wind rain, snow, ice, plummeting temperatures, he could handle—outward aggression designed to kill, he could not. At least, it was something he wouldn't stand for. However, he had a role to play there, and that was scientific research, and as much as he might have liked to head out and confront whatever this was, they had no weapons, and he hadn't a clue what he was dealing with.

After he had looked the three of them over and determined they weren't high on anything and had not been drinking, he leaned back in his chair.

"Okay, we've actually had more sightings of these black helicopters across the continent." He picked up a sheet of paper. "In fact, there have been six so far. Some could be the same machine, but others were so far apart on similar dates, they were definitely different aircraft. If what you say is true, and I'm not doubting you, just being cautious, there seems to be something going on down here that is against every treaty and international agreement ever written. I would immediately lay blame on the Russians, but we have a pretty good relationship with them. I'm sure I'd be aware if they were up to something. That, of course, leaves the Chinese—the current villain of choice. They've always been pretty secretive as to their activities, and I'm sure they're up to more than they admit, but these actions seem pretty extreme, even for them." He paused. "So, you didn't manage to see where the shots came from, or what was buried in the ice?"

As project leader, Nyah replied. "No, sir. We hit something hard with the shovels and then all hell broke loose. I'd actually heard something just before but didn't think anything of it. It must have been bullets hitting close by."

"And you didn't hear the shots?"

"No," continued Nyah. I guess they were using a silencer. The air was clear and quiet. We'd have heard a shot from miles away. Also, whoever it was must have been a heck of a way away as there was open ground to the mountain range of close to a mile."

Patcher studied them again.

"Which means whoever was firing knew what they were doing." He thought for a moment. "Okay, I don't want you to tell anyone about this…"

"But sir…" spluttered Murphy.

Patcher shot him a look. "We don't want a panic on our hands. I'll put the word out that people should report and steer clear of the black helicopters if they see them. Other than that, all excursions on the ice will be more tightly controlled. And leave anything you find alone until we know what we're dealing with. Oh, and always carry a Geiger counter with you. We don't know if there are any more of these sites out there."

"Yes, sir," said Nyah. "What will you do about it?"

Patcher thought for a few seconds.

"There's nothing I can do from here. We're not equipped to handle something like this. I'll have to pass it up the tree to London. Maybe they'll have someone who can deal with it."

Nyah nodded.

"Okay, that's all," said Patcher.

Nyah, Murphy and Bowman filed out. When they were outside the room they all looked at each other. Murphy was the first to speak.

"What the fuck is going on down here?"

Chapter Twenty-Six

McCready stood on the bridge of *Ocean Challenger* and looked out over the waves, which were increasing in height by the minute. He sipped a mug of coffee, and considering what he'd been through, he didn't feel as bad as he thought he would. The physical side was as well as could be expected, but the emotional side was trying to deal with the loss of Logan—something he would never forget, and, if he ever found out who was responsible, would never forgive.

He was still thinking about the past few days, and what the next step should be, when the captain called him over. McCready walked over to the radar plot, which the captain was looking at intently.

"You expecting company?"

McCready looked at the display. He could see their position in the center of the screen. There were a couple of other targets that represented nearby ships, but the captain pointed to a fast-moving dot that was approaching from the west. McCready checked the scale of the screen—a hundred miles across, which meant the target, whatever it was, was about thirty miles away, but if it was heading their way, it wouldn't take long to reach them. And it wasn't a ship. It was airborne. He glanced at the captain.

"No, we're meeting my guy at the port. But I'll check, just in case."

McCready pulled out his phone and dialed. After a few rings, Martin Steel answered.

"You here yet?" asked McCready.

"No, we're still in the air. Landing in the next hour or so. Why?"

"We're about fifty miles out from Chennai, and we've got a target approaching on radar. Could be innocent, but just wanted to check it wasn't you."

"Be careful, John. It's not us."

"Okay, thanks. I'll be in touch if we have a problem." He clicked off the phone and turned to the captain, his expression hard.

"Nothing to do with me."

The captain nodded. He walked over to the rear of the bridge and undid a combination lock on a tall locker. He pulled out an AK-47 rifle. It looked old and McCready was doubtful whether it would even fire, but he guessed it was better than nothing.

"You need to go tell the others. We have to be ready, just in case," said the captain.

McCready nodded. He made his way out of the bridge and down the steps to the rear deck.

He gathered Richards, Carlita and the crew together.

"Okay guys, we have a target approaching by air from the west. No idea what it is, but it'll be here shortly. It may be nothing, and the cradle is covered, so they may just overfly us. But we need to be prepared."

Richards headed for the control container to look for

anything he could use as a weapon. McCready turned to Carlita.

"I want you to stay inside and don't come out whatever happens, okay?"

"But I want to help," she said fiercely.

"I know. But if they're armed it could get ugly. Please, for me... just stay inside."

He looked at her seriously. Eventually she relented.

"Okay, but if I see you in trouble..."

McCready smiled.

"Okay, if I'm in trouble you can take them all on and throw them off the ship... alright? Seriously, stay inside!"

She nodded slowly.

McCready returned to the bridge to keep an eye on the target's progress. He could just be being paranoid. It was probably nothing and would pass them by. But something told him that wasn't going to happen.

It was a fear that was confirmed twenty minutes later when he watched the approaching blip turn into the sound of an aircraft outside. He ran out onto the flying bridge and looked to the west.

As he watched, he saw a small shape in the sky grow larger. A minute later there was the roar of rotors and a large black heavy-lift helicopter swept overhead. He watched it bank round. Two men were leaning out of a door on one side. They were dressed in black combat gear. One of them had binoculars and was carefully surveying the ship.

"Get ready!" said McCready to the captain before heading down to the rear deck.

When he got there Richards and the others were watching the circling helicopter.

"This doesn't look good," said Richards.

"No, it doesn't. We have to stop them. If this thing gets into the wrong hands…"

"But what if they're Chinese? They only want back what's theirs."

"Yeah, but that doesn't look like a Chinese chopper to me."

They exchanged glances.

There wasn't enough room for the helicopter to land. If it had attempted to the rotors would have hit the A-frame. Also, the large cradle filled most of the rear deck. But this didn't seem to deter them. The massive machine came in to hover directly above, fifty feet up. The pilot kept it expertly aligned with the forward motion of the ship.

Four men, all in black, threw ropes out of the side doors. Before anyone had time to react, they'd abseiled down onto the deck. They wore body armor. Kevlar helmets covered their heads, while balaclavas and assault goggles covered their faces. There was no way to determine their nationality.

The crew took up defensive positions.

Three of the men pulled the tarpaulin off the cradle.

The remaining one, presumably the leader, stepped forward. He was the only one holding a weapon, though the others had sidearms. He pointed the gun at McCready, who had moved closer to confront them.

"We're going to take this." The man indicated the cradle. "Don't try to stop us!"

McCready moved forward.

"We can't let you do that. We salvaged it from the seabed in international waters, and under international law we claim ownership."

The man raised the weapon from his side.

"You don't want to do that," he said.

At that moment a shot rang out. It had come from the flying bridge. McCready looked up and saw the captain brandishing the AK-47. The bullet hit the deck inches from the boot of the leader. He didn't flinch, merely looked up at the bridge. A second later, though, he raised his gun to his shoulder. He fired, hitting the captain in the arm, who cried out, dropping the weapon. He leaned against the side of the bridge, moaning in pain.

"You bastard!" said McCready.

"He'll be fine," said the man with the gun. Now, no more stupidity, please. We have no intention of hurting anyone, unless we have to."

He glanced up at the helicopter and spoke something into a throat mike McCready couldn't hear. McCready then watched as a lift cable was lowered. When it reached the deck, the men ran to grab the attachment and secure it to the cradle.

The man had turned his back on McCready for a moment. In that instant McCready ran forward and made a grab for his weapon. The man was off guard and stumbled backward, but he didn't lose his footing. Instead, he turned in a flash, knocking McCready to the ground. He grabbed his gun back and aimed down at him.

"I wouldn't do that if I was you," said Richards.

He was brandishing one of the Very pistols in his hand. While it wasn't exactly accurate, it could be dangerous at close quarters. It fired an explosive flare with the force to shoot several hundred feet up into the air.

The man glanced at him, and while no one could see his face, his body language took on that of an exasperated father, whose children wouldn't behave.

Another quick action and the pistol was shot from

Richards' hands. He just stood there—what else could he do?

"I'm getting tired of this," said the man. He then took his weapon and was about to smash the butt into McCready's head when Carlita ran out from a door in the main superstructure.

"Stop! Don't hurt him!"

She ran to McCready, flinging a protective arm around him. McCready looked at her, furious she'd not stayed inside, but overwhelmed that she would do this to try to protect him when the odds were clearly impossible.

The man with the weapon stared at her and shook his head. He then turned to his men and gave a winding-up signal with his hand. The engine noise increased above. The helicopter rose to pull the lift cable taut. A few seconds later and the cradle was a foot off the ground. The other three men jumped onto it. The man with the weapon turned to McCready.

"In case you get any foolish ideas about shooting at the helicopter with any other weapons you may have on board, I'm taking an insurance policy."

He grabbed Carlita and dragged her over to the cradle.

"Noooo!" shouted McCready. He jumped up and ran toward them.

The man lifted the weapon, aiming at McCready, but Carlita forced it down.

As McCready ran, the cradle lifted higher off the deck.

By the time he reached it, it was too high to do anything. He stared up at Carlita. Her terrified gaze was fixed on him.

"It'll be alright," said McCready. "I'll find you."

But all he could do was watch the cradle with the nuclear weapon inside, and Carlita's face wracked with fear, disappear up into the air, with no way of knowing where they were going or who had taken them.

Chapter Twenty-Seven

McCready and Richards watched the helicopter until it was a small dot in the distance.

"So, who the hell were they?" said McCready. "They weren't Chinese, that's for sure."

"I guess they must be the people who took Carlita back in Algeria. The company she talked about."

"Tranter Chemicals. At least that's what Steel told me."

"So what are you going to say to him?" said Richards.

"The truth. What else can I say?"

"He's gonna be pissed."

"Yeah," said McCready wearily, "I suppose he will be."

Before calling Steel, McCready climbed up to the bridge to watch the track of the helicopter on the radar. Over the course of an hour, it headed first west and then south. It then suddenly disappeared off the screen. But it was still in the middle of the sea over water.

"What happened?" McCready asked the captain, who had also been watching. He was in some pain after being shot and had a tight bandage around the wound on his arm.

"No idea. She could be flying low enough to evade radar, but she's still some way from shore. Could have landed on another ship, I guess."

McCready glanced at him. He took a final look at the screen and then made his way down to the container on the rear deck and grabbed his phone. This was one call he wasn't looking forward to making.

It rang three times before being answered.

"John, everything okay?"

"Er, no, not exactly."

Two hours later, *Ocean Challenger* pulled into the docks at Chennai. As the large ship was nudged up against the side by a couple of tugs, mooring ropes were thrown to the stevedores on shore. They caught them deftly and ran to secure the vessel.

As McCready stared down, he could see Martin Steel standing on the dockside. Behind him were two men who looked like they'd come from the same regiment Steel had commanded years previously. Behind them was a black Range Rover.

As suspected, the call had not gone well. When Steel had heard the weapon had gone, and most probably not taken by the Chinese, he had at first gone quiet, presumably thinking of a suitable response, but when he'd spoken he had been calm, measured and entirely in control. He'd said he'd meet McCready at the docks as soon as they could get there to go through a full debrief. He had then hung up, saying nothing more. McCready secretly thought Steel would, on one level, be enjoying it. While the situation was serious, he seemed to live for moments like this, when he had to react at a heightened level to resolve a problem or situation where failure could have catastrophic consequences.

As he looked down now at him, he was the definition of cool calm. He wore tan chinos, an open short-sleeved white shirt and a pair of Ray-Bans fit for an American aviator. He looked like a man without a care in the world, but when McCready looked more closely, his stance was strong, determined and primed, like a racehorse waiting to be let out of the gate. He just needed McCready to tell him everything he knew and effectively fire the starting gun.

McCready walked down the gangplank onto the dock carrying his belongings in a small bag. He was followed by Richards. It was a hot day and swirls of dust on the dockside were set off by the strong wind. The sounds of the bustling city beyond the docks filled the air.

They walked over to Steel. When they reached him he looked at them with a questioning expression and then shook their hands. He threw a glance at the ship and then turned to McCready.

"Okay, I need to know everything you know."

They told him over the following hour.

When they'd finished, Steel looked between them.

"I'm sorry about your friend." He paused. "Okay, we have a number of options. I would agree it probably wasn't the Chinese who took the weapon. They would have been more ruthless…"

"More ruthless?" blurted out Richards.

"Yeah, they could have shot you all. It appears from what you say they went to great lengths not to kill anyone. That's the one bit that puzzles me. Given they may well be planning something horrific with the device, why risk leaving you alive? It doesn't add up."

"Okay, I know there are bigger things at play here, but

they also have Carlita," said McCready. "So we're back to square one."

Steel looked at him, and as he did, his expression softened a little.

"You said they took her so you wouldn't fire at the helicopter, yes?"

"Yes," said McCready.

"Okay, so at the risk of being somewhat blunt, that's probably all they wanted her for. When they had her before, they were going to kill her when they found out what she knew. Now they have the weapon, other than to ensure their safety when leaving the ship, why would they need her alive?"

The realization suddenly dawned on McCready. He looked down at the table.

"They wouldn't."

"I'm sorry, John," said Steel, "she's probably already dead."

McCready stared at him hard and then stood and walked away. Steel watched him go.

"He'll be okay," said Richards, "but I wouldn't try and stop him being part of what happens next."

Steel looked at Richards evenly.

"What happens next is out of his hands. I can't have civilians—even John—getting involved. With the weapon out in the wild and the potential consequences it could create, this is now on the international stage. Way above his pay grade. We can't have a repeat of what happened in the Pacific, where he went off all half-cocked jeopardizing a long-planned operation."

Richards could see from his expression that Steel was serious.

"I'll talk to him," said Richards.

"You do that," said Steel. "Oh, and tell him I want my helicopter back."

After the men had left *Ocean Challenger* with the weapon and Carlita, they had flown due west before turning south. An hour later they had rendezvoused with a large cargo ship. As the ship steamed into the wind, the pilot brought the chopper into a hover directly above one of the open holds in the middle. The weapon was then lowered inside. It was released from the lift cable and secured away from prying eyes.

Once this was done, the helicopter descended gently onto the deck and cut the engine. When the rotors had come to a stop and the wheels had been secured and the blades swept back in line, Carlita had been led into the main superstructure of the ship.

Next, a large camouflage tarpaulin, designed to look like a stack of containers, was stretched over the helicopter. From the air, nothing could be seen.

Within the hour the ship was sailing serenely on its way as though nothing had happened—as though it didn't have a weapon of mass destruction in its hold.

Chapter Twenty-Eight

The wind swirled around the high Alps sending flurries of snow off the steep slopes. It howled as it rushed along cliff faces and through narrow canyons, but in the warm, enclosed confines of his home, Victor Solano lay back in his bed and stared at the ceiling.

He knew he had only a few months left to live, but he'd had a magnificent life. And he was about to end it with his most masterful act—one the world would never forget. And one that would hopefully save the world. There would be hard times to go through before that happened, but nothing done right was ever easy.

But what made him smile was that the most important thing in his life was back in his possession. The one thing that could make him pause. He eased himself up onto one elbow and looked at her sleeping form lying next to him. She was everything he had ever dreamed of in a woman. Strong, decisive, determined, beautiful—but also, as he had found—compliant. It had been like breaking a thoroughbred racehorse, and it had been a challenge. But he loved challenges, and this one had been his greatest success. Once he had found her weakness, the rest had followed from there.

Yes, Carlita Fuentes was beautiful.

She was spectacular.

And she was his.

He watched her naked form as she slept. The smooth soft skin. The rolling curves of a firm, lean body that was toned to perfection. He could see the bruising she still had on her face. It was unfortunate she'd had to endure that, but she'd accepted his conviction that it was necessary for the deception to have worked. It was she who had told him about McCready, and that he would be a way for them to retrieve the weapon after the plane had come down earlier than planned. He had, at first, not been convinced, but gradually he'd realized it was the only way to achieve their aims in the given time. It had been her original idea but she had gone along with all his suggestions, like a puppy lapping up the love she desired and he always gave her. He knew exactly how far to go before he reined her back in with the ultimate threat—one he had only ever used once. The fact that he had, meant she had never wavered again. And even throughout this latest endeavor he was never worried, despite what she'd told him about her original feelings for McCready.

But she was back now and the weapon was with his men. Soon the world would have a demonstration of what was to come. Hopefully the final act would not be required, but he didn't hold out much hope: human beings were human beings—largely stupid, selfish and self-important, particularly their leaders, which was why preparations continued.

The body next to him stirred. He looked down into the

beautiful brown eyes as they flickered open. For the briefest of moments they showed confusion, even a hint of disappointment, but the change to a cat-like smile and a look of love was so instant, so seamless, Solano nearly missed it. It was enough to make him pause, though.

He moved on top of her and they locked lips in a sumptuous, erotic embrace.

"You did so well, my darling. You were magnificent. Everything is nearly ready."

He felt her move beneath him. He knew exactly how to give her pleasure and he could tell she was craving it. She drew him to her and they kissed deeply again.

An hour later Solano walked from the bedroom into the adjacent large walk-in shower. He was breathing heavily and his body was covered in sweat. He turned on the jets. They assaulted him from all sides with forceful sprays of water. He let them massage his spent body. As he soaped himself down, he smiled.

Carlita lay on her back on the bed, her soft tanned skin glistening from their exertions. She breathed in deeply to steady her racing heart. She loved Solano in a way it would be difficult for most to understand. He was like a drug. She couldn't get enough. She couldn't survive without him. She lay back and thought of how her tumultuous life had led her to this point.

She knew exactly when her life had changed and set her on the path she had pursued—it was when an eighteen-year-old man from Scotland, whom she had given her heart to forever, had left her and never contacted her again, as though she had never existed.

Carlita had cried for days. She had thought the gift of the poncho she had put in his backpack would have meant something, but clearly it hadn't. Her family had tried to console her—even her brother had appeared sad and tried to comfort her, but nothing had done any good. She had always seen the best in people, that people always had a good side to them, and when it came to love she had always had a fairytale image in her mind—that two people would find each other and be together forever. But that was not the real world. In the real world there was hurt and pain, and she vowed there and then never to let anyone else in again —ever.

What had changed that was when a tall, dark, mysterious stranger had come into her life. He had helped her brother when no one else would. She had always been protective of her brother, which was why she had been so taken with McCready—he had been there, selflessly trying to protect him with no concern for his own safety. So when someone else came along, she knew he must be a 'good' man. On the surface he was hard and sophisticated, and treated her like a queen, but as she got to know him, she found he had a darker side, one that meant he would ruthlessly pursue what he wanted without rules, without inhibition, and without a thought for the consequences. And when she realized he was pursuing her, those darker aspects to his character excited her, making her want to be with him. He was only the second person she had ever slept with, and once she had, she'd never looked at another man. He had been so experienced, so tender and loving, but then in an instant he could be violent and harsh. In fact, she didn't realize it, but the further he pushed in a certain direction, the further she allowed her limits to go, until, when she was so far in, there was no turning back in what she would let him do—and she loved it. When he went away, she yearned for his return. She would do anything for him, though she sometimes wondered if maybe it was the price she had to pay to keep her brother safe, and that she had just convinced herself she was happy.

She wanted for nothing and had a life many would dream of—but deep down, all the acts she had committed were being stored away in a hidden ball of pressure that would one day surface. If it ever did, she didn't know how she would react, but for now it was under control.

One thing that had reminded her of that pressure was when she'd walked into the living room at McCready's house and seen the poncho on the wall. She had, for a moment, been unable to speak. It had reawakened a time where everything, life and all its facets, was innocent and beautiful. She hadn't been prepared for it and it had shaken her to the core. She couldn't understand why it was there, but as on so many occasions, she had compartmentalized what she was experiencing and seeing, and locked it away as an anomaly—one that might be revisited at another time.

She also realized she had a job to do—something for Solano, her beloved Victor—and she couldn't fail. She knew, ultimately, she was tied inextricably to him in pleasure and pain. She could see no way out, and so she never looked for one, but the poncho on the wall had ripped a deep hole in the fabric of her being—something she didn't understand and maybe never would.

She looked up as a distant, growing howl in the background indicated the storm outside was getting worse. She climbed out of bed and pulled a black satin robe around her. She walked over to the window and stared out over the valley. The storm was raging. The wind echoed through the mountains. Moments later, large raindrops pelted the thick triple-glazed glass. She stared at it, inches from its awesome power and strength. It felt amazing to be so close to, and yet so detached from, the entity outside.

A noise behind her made her turn. Solano walked naked from the shower. When he saw her he crossed over and embraced her. She reached up hungrily for his lips. When they broke apart she turned back to look over the valley.

"I hear the doctor visited recently," she said.

"Yes, it was routine. He gave me some more pills."

"Are things getting worse?" At this she turned to face him, worry etched in her eyes.

"Maybe a little, but no more than we expected."

She looked up at him. The sadness was evident.

"I am so sorry, Victor."

He smiled down at her and wrapped his arms around her.

"I have you, don't I? What else do I need?"

She smiled a contented smile and luxuriated in his embrace.

It was 'kind' Victor who was with her now.

Chapter Twenty-Nine

When the cargo ship had sailed out to a point due south of the Indian peninsula, it had stopped at a predetermined position based on longitude and latitude.

The helicopter had long since gone, taking Carlita back to the mainland, and so the main deck was clear, save for the weapon sitting in its cradle, which had been raised from the hold. The camouflage tarpaulin had been completely removed, making the AUV visible from the air, but it wouldn't be staying there for long and the chances of being overflown this far out to sea were virtually zero, even if someone had been looking for them, which was highly unlikely.

The first out onto the deck was Juliano Mendes. He was followed by a nervous-looking Chinese gentleman wearing a gray jumpsuit and large octagonal glasses. He was slightly balding and kept glancing around as if someone was about to call out his name and he would be found out.

In fact, his name was Doctor Joseph Chang, a former

employee of the People's Republic of China's nuclear weapons program, and he was only there because his family had lived in Hong Kong and been persecuted for the privilege. He'd been given a way out for them all to be together, and he had taken it—but it had come at a price.

That price had been the information of where and when the weapon was being transported, as well as the technology to command and control it. What he had to do now, to complete his side of the bargain, was to program the final target into the computer and hand over control to the people he was working for. This was something he was very happy to do, as his family was now living it up in a sumptuous villa in the South of France—one he soon hoped to join them in. He was particularly looking forward to swimming in the thirty-foot infinity pool and watching the sunset with a glass of Chablis from the hot tub that looked out over the Bay of Antibes.

He approached the weapon he had helped develop. It was one of the most powerful underwater devices in existence. Taking its initial design from the Russian Kanyon nuclear AUV, it could travel the world for years at a time, completely autonomously, and then, when instructed, be capable of delivering a nuclear warhead to a target in any ocean, or along any coastline, anywhere on the planet, without detection. It was the perfect first-strike weapon. Chang didn't know who he was ultimately working for and didn't really care. Nothing could have been worse than the regime he had left and their growing need to exercise power and threats over their neighbors, and ultimately the rest of the world. But when Mendes handed him the target to be entered into the navigation system, he looked at it twice and glanced up at the South American with a quizzical expression. But Mendes remained impassive and just looked at him. Chang shrugged and started to get to work.

He took out a small laptop and plugged it into a port on the side of the AUV. He entered a code into the laptop and wrote in specific commands. He then instructed the machine to only comply with commands using a certain protocol. This would mean it couldn't be hijacked even by its original masters. The whole process took twenty-five minutes. When he'd finished, he pulled out the lead, sealed up the small hatch and turned to Mendes.

"It's done. Your boss will now have complete control as discussed. Should you wish to abort or change the target coordinates, it can be done by the software he has been sent." He bowed slightly at the end of his short speech.

Mendes looked over the lethal machine that sat there so patiently waiting to be set loose to do its deadly bidding. He turned to Chang.

"Thank you, doctor. Your help is greatly appreciated. You may not realize it now, but your assistance is going to help change the world, and for the better." Chang looked at him dubiously, and then watched as Mendes pulled a satellite phone from his waistband. He dialed a number and waited for the connection.

"It's ready," he said when the call was answered. "Yes, you have full control. We're about to launch. It will be free in around ten minutes." He listened for a moment. "Thank you, sir. I'll be back as soon as I can." He hung up the phone and turned to the deckhands who were waiting for his order.

"Okay, put it in the water."

The men quickly set to work. The top of the cradle was removed, revealing the weapon fully for the first time. Large slings were hooked underneath and attached to a crane that was at one side of the deck. The AUV was then carefully raised into the air and swung out over the water. Two of the crew held on to guide ropes to stabilize any violent swinging motion. Once it was steady it was lowered into the water.

A couple of minutes later it had been detached from the crane.

Chang opened his laptop again. At a signal from Mendes, he pressed a sequence of buttons on the keyboard that would activate the AUV. A moment later the vehicle started to hum, the motor systems firing up remotely. After a final check that was confirmed on Chang's laptop, the propeller engaged at the rear and the AUV headed off into the sea. A second later it dived below the surface.

It would never be seen again.

But its dangerous payload would soon be on display for the whole world as it headed for its final destination.

The curved string of islands that made up the Florida Keys.

Several thousand miles away, Solano sat in his office. In front of him was a bank of displays that showed information and video feeds from his interests around the world. Some of these included stock prices and updates on businesses. Others showed upcoming conference calls and security cameras. But the screen dead center was currently showing an image from a camera in the nose of the AUV.

He watched the water slip by in front of his eyes. It grew darker and darker as the machine dived into the depths.

He felt hands on his shoulders and then arms around his neck. He smiled and glanced up at Carlita as she stared with passion at the video from the AUV.

"It's begun," said Solano. "We're going to change the world."

Carlita leaned down to kiss him on the neck. She squeezed him tight and then watched the screen before the light became too low and darkness enveloped the image.

The world had no idea what was coming.

Chapter Thirty

It was dark when McCready and Richards finally arrived back at Aberdeen a day and a half after leaving the dockside at Chennai. Rather than drive all the way across Scotland to his home on the west coast, McCready went to stay with Richards at his house just outside the small village of Drumoak, ten miles to the south-west of the city. The large granite building was situated in five acres of land at the side of the River Dee and had impressive views over grass and trees to the river below.

When they walked in through the large oak door, it was dark and cold—somewhat similar to the feelings of the two men, and maybe more so for McCready. They had both lost a friend in Logan, and for McCready, he had the added anguish of Carlita being taken from him again. His emotions were mixed—sorrow and sadness for Logan, and anger and vengeance for what he had let happen to Carlita. He couldn't think what must be going through her mind—if she was even still alive.

Once they'd dropped their bags in the hallway, Richards went straight for the drinks cabinet at the far end of the spacious lounge. He pulled out a bottle of whiskey and grabbed a couple of glasses and poured two shots. They then both sat down in the deep leather sofas either side of the stone fireplace and savored the spirit as it slipped down their throats, going a small way to ease their pain and distress.

McCready barely even glanced at the myriad of diving mementos Richards had displayed around the room. There were muskets from wrecks dived in Cornwall. An old Siebe Gorman standard dress dive helmet sat in a corner, the brass and copper gleaming in the light. There were even two cannonballs on the hearth that had come from a centuries-old wreck off the west coast of Scotland.

All this he knew was there and normally he might have indulged himself, but for now they were exhausted from the trip, both physically and emotionally. Not only had Logan died and Carlita been taken, they had also failed to stop the weapon from falling into the hands of the very people the whole exercise had been designed to avoid.

It was not their finest hour.

McCready took another swig from the glass, leaned back and closed his eyes. It was a low point for both of them, but somehow they had to go on. They had to work out a way to put things right. There was nothing they could do about Logan, except maybe ensure whoever had been responsible paid for their actions, though, as it looked like it was the Chinese, there was little chance of that happening.

But then there was Carlita.

How could he have let her be taken?

He tried to think if there was anything else he could

have done—but there was nothing. The men had guns and they'd been prepared to use them. Any resistance, and he, or she, could have been killed, which would have achieved nothing. At least now he could regroup and he could plan. He could react and he could face them, whoever they were, on his terms. That was the one thing that kept him going. So long as there was the chance she was still alive, there was the hope he could rescue her. That, at least, gave him solace.

He turned to glance over at Richards.

His old friend was as tired as he was.

He looked back at him warily.

"No, no. I know that look. Whatever it is can wait till the morning when you've had time to rest and think about whatever it is you were going to say, which would, no doubt, be completely inappropriate given feelings are running high and we're both knackered—okay?"

McCready was about to say something but relented. Craig was right. The morning would bring a new day with new hopes and a new perspective—and a clearer mind.

He'd leave it till then to plan the next move.

The next day dawned bright and sunny and raised the mood slightly. They were both more rested when they awoke just after nine, the jet lag contributing to their tardiness. After lengthy showers to wash away the cobwebs, and a full cooked breakfast, they were ready for whatever lay ahead.

They arrived at Ocean Tech at half past ten to find the place a hive of activity. They had recently received a number of orders for the Skyline system from scientific expeditions operating in remote areas, and they were also working on a series of contracts for the military.

Richards led McCready up to the conference room. As they passed through the design studio, the head technician, Graham Evans, pulled Richards aside to show him some design specs for one of the projects.

McCready wandered into the conference room and made a couple of coffees. Despite the rest, caffeine certainly wouldn't do any harm, and they would need to be sharp to work out what to do next.

A couple of minutes later Richards walked in. He sat down, took a sip, and then eased back in his chair and looked at McCready.

"Okay, we need to talk about this," he said seriously.

"How could it have gone so wrong?" said McCready.

"We didn't know what we were getting into. The question is, how did the guys who stole the weapon"—McCready glanced at him—"and took Carlita, know we were there? It doesn't make any sense."

"Yeah, but don't forget where the information came from. Carlita stole it from them, so they could have found out who we were and been monitoring us, waiting for us to bring it up, and then move in."

Richards was quiet for a while.

"Okay, so what do you want to do?"

"We have to try and find out who these people are—then we can get a handle on what we're up against. Are they just some small, well-funded operation? Or are they a large conglomerate? The company in Africa looked like it was pretty big—Tranter Chemicals."

"But I thought you said Steel looked into them?"

"He did, but he also had concerns over the reliability of the information. There were some 'anomalies,' as he put it, and he didn't mention anything about them being involved with something that would use a weapon like this."

"Maybe the name is just a cover for who's really behind it—using the company as a front for other activities?"

"Possible. But what could be the endgame? From what Steel said, that weapon is pretty formidable. You don't just go setting one of those things off. There would be repercussions at an international level. You'd never get away with it."

"Unless it's a bluff. The authorities know the weapon's capability and so would likely give in to any demands that were made—they couldn't risk it being used."

McCready nodded, but he was suddenly distracted by something—something he remembered.

"Hang on a minute. There may be something from when I was in Monaco."

He jumped up and walked out of the room. Richards took another sip of coffee.

A minute later McCready came back in. He was carrying the binoculars he'd borrowed from Steel—though he couldn't imagine when he'd be giving them back—a bit like the Chinook, if he thought about it.

He put them down on the table and ran a cable into a laptop that was connected to the projector. A couple of minutes later and a menu showing the video files recorded by the binoculars was displayed on the screen.

"What are you after?" asked Richards.

"Anything out of the ordinary. Anything that could point somewhere to focus our search."

"You didn't see anything when you were on board?"

McCready glanced at him.

"Not really. I was kind of busy trying to find Carlita and avoid the crew. It was just another boat."

Richards raised his eyebrows. "Yeah, just another multi-million-dollar mega yacht. Seen one you've seen 'em all."

It broke the mood and McCready grinned.

"Okay, wiseguy, let's see what we can find."

He flicked on the playback and the footage played on the wall.

As he watched the images, McCready relived what it had been like at the time—what he had felt and what he had been thinking. Most of it concerned what he'd been trying to do to get Carlita out and how he had thought he would feel when he saw her again, but in the back of his mind, the subconscious side, he had been storing away the images he was seeing.

They watched the fast boat head out, away from shore, and approach the *Freedom Seas*. But then something happened that he'd noticed before but paid little attention to—the helicopter took off and headed over the bay toward Monaco. He freeze-framed the aircraft in mid-air. He then leaned in to take a closer look. It was an Airbus AS365 painted black with a silver underside. It could well be a charter machine, but McCready had a sense that whoever was flying out from the yacht was connected to what was going on and most likely in a position to use the helicopter as their private transport.

He moved the image forward, frame by frame, to see if there were any identifying figures or numbers on the fuselage. And then, just before it disappeared out of frame right, he saw it—at the back, next to the closed-in tail rotor. It was the aircraft registration number, or tail number, all aircraft had to carry. He couldn't make out all the letters and numbers, but he had half of them, and along with the make and model he felt sure they could track down the owner.

It took the best part of an hour, but after numerous calls

and being stonewalled a couple of times, McCready came up with an owner—Euro Action, a company that was involved with the green revolution. Further digging revealed the executive director of the company was one Victor Solano.

When they had all the information on the table, McCready thought for a moment and then looked at Richards.

"That's who we have to go for."

"Who?"

"This Solano guy. He's the head of the company. We go to him. He may not even be aware of what's going on in the company itself."

Richards looked at him with a comical expression.

"You do know who this guy is?"

"No, should I?"

"Er, yeah, he's one of the richest men in the world, if not the richest."

McCready hesitated, floored for a moment.

"Okay, so it's highly unlikely he's involved with any of this then. But if we bring it to his attention he'll probably want to investigate. He wouldn't want his name associated with this sort of thing. In fact," said McCready, warming to the idea, "it would be perfect. He could use his resources to help find Carlita and get the weapon back."

Richards gave him an incredulous look.

"So, you're just going to walk up to this guy, who will have so many barriers to reaching him, and tell him someone in one of his companies has kidnapped an ex-girlfriend and stolen a nuclear weapon?"

"Yeah, what's wrong with that?"

Richards shook his head.

"Even for you, John, that's a bit off the grid."

"Got a better idea?"

And that stopped Richards.

He didn't.

McCready moved over to the laptop and did a Google search on Solano.

As he read about him, he had to admit he was impressed. He'd achieved so much in his life. He also appeared to be passionate about the environment and saving the planet. But it was when he came across a recent video on YouTube about a speech he'd given at Basel that he became really interested. He watched it through once and then put it up on the screen for Richards. At the end, they both stared at each other. Richards was the first to speak.

"This threat he makes against governments. You think it could have anything to do with the weapon?"

"But how? He seems to be serious about saving the planet. How could letting off a nuclear bomb have anything to do with that? They're polar opposites. It must be something else. But Mr. Solano is beginning to interest me. Like I said, we need to talk to him."

"Shouldn't you call Steel first? He might know a way to contact him... have back-channel access. He might even have some thoughts on any connection."

McCready thought about it for a minute.

"No, if he even listens, which he probably won't, he'd just tell me what he said to you in India—stay out of it, like in the Pacific. And even if he did take me seriously, what's going to be his priority, the weapon... or Carlita?"

"And when you have a rational brain cell functioning in your head, you can obviously see why," said Richards, raising an eyebrow.

McCready glanced at him. "I can't think like that right

now. I can't afford to go there. Also, he might want his helicopter back, and that would be a shame."

Richards suddenly remembered. "Ah, yeah, right. He did actually mention something about that."

It was now McCready's turn to raise an eyebrow, but with a *told you so* expression.

Chapter Thirty-One

Victor Solano watched the plot of the AUV on the large map displayed on the screen in his office. It had crossed the Atlantic and was around fifty miles from the east coast of the continental United States. At the side of the screen was a readout of depth and speed.

Solano had done all the calculations, along with Mendes, who had triple checked everything. They'd worked out a position twenty miles from the coast and a depth of three hundred feet as the optimum location for what Solano wanted to achieve. The AUV would be on station within the hour. It was time to make the call.

While contacting the United Nations would be the politically correct way to go, Solano was under no illusion at the speed, or lack thereof, with which the organization worked. He had therefore decided to call another number—the president of the United States.

When the phone rang at the White House switchboard, it was put through with little fuss. Solano was known in these quarters. The president had even played golf with him on a number of occasions—though the outcome was a closely guarded secret.

In the Oval Office, President Galt Stevens was having a relaxing day. There were no major crises to deal with around the world, other than the usual fire-fighting that had to be done on a daily basis, and he was still recovering from his ordeal in California where he had been held hostage for several harrowing days. He had also been hard at work trying to repair relations with Russia after the death of their president on American soil. Something that had been impossible to avoid. He finally thought he might be getting through to Kostas Slavov, who had taken over from President Petrovich. He had respected the former president, despite butting heads on numerous occasions, and in the most dramatic way possible toward the end of their incarceration. The newcomer was an altogether different animal, but the world had to go on, and he was sure some form of working relationship would develop in time when everything had calmed down.

He answered the call with a hearty, "Hello, Victor, what can I do for you?"

"Galt, thank you for taking my call," said Solano, making the opening words conciliatory in preparation for what was to come.

"Of course. Any time for you. Maybe one day you will even win at golf!"

Solano let it go. He then turned serious.

"Galt, you need to listen to me very carefully. You need to evacuate the Florida Keys from the tip of Key West all the way to the mainland at Homestead. And you need to do this immediately."

Stevens froze on the phone. He knew Solano. He knew he could joke around over games of golf and football scores, but he had never known him make light of serious matters. He chose his words carefully.

"Victor, what are you saying to me? Why would I need to do this?"

There was a pause on the line.

"The speeches I have made recently, both in Basel and at the United Nations. These were not for effect. They were not some sort of stunt. They are real and they should have been taken seriously. And as you know, I am a man of my word."

Stevens remained quiet.

"So, what is going to happen is that in eight hours' time a tsunami is going to hit the Florida Keys. It will raise the water level to a height of around fifty feet. The wave will be powerful enough to sweep across the islands. It will wipe out all habitation and structures, and I am afraid…" he paused here, "…many lives will be lost. The sooner the evacuations start, the more people you will save."

Stevens was speechless.

"But why? And how is it possible?"

"The 'how' is not important. The 'why' will become obvious. To save the world, Galt… To save the world."

Solano hung up.

Stevens replaced the receiver slowly in the cradle. He leaned back in his chair, thinking. Victor Solano didn't bluff. This, Stevens knew to be true. A moment later he realized he had a crisis on his hands no president in history had ever had to deal with.

And he had eight hours to save as many people as he could.

The action happened as fast as was humanly possible, but it was never going to be a complete success. The National Guard was mobilized in the south of Florida and all residents, tourists, and anyone else who could be found, were asked to leave the area. To some degree they were told the truth—a new early warning system had predicted a massive earthquake some twenty miles off the Keys that would create a tsunami that would cover the islands. This was a threat people could understand. They had all seen videos of what had happened in Japan back in 2011, where a massive wave had swept all before it, leaving a trail of devastation and killing over twenty thousand people. A tsunami was not something that could be avoided or beaten. When people heard a hurricane was coming they often thought they could batten down the hatches and tough it out—you couldn't do that with a wall of water.

The mass exodus was carried out in as orderly a manner as possible, but as always in these situations, there was a certain amount of panic. This had resulted in the highways in the south of Florida being clogged solid for hours. The navy had brought an aircraft carrier into the area that had been conducting exercises off Miami to airlift people onto the decks. But even that had to leave within a certain timeframe or risk being capsized by the massive wave that was due to strike at 3pm local time.

In the end, they did the best they could, but it was never going to be enough.

From his cliff-face home in the heart of Europe Solano watched the evacuation on numerous news channels across the screens in his office. He knew people were going to die and he knew he would be responsible, but he had to make a point. Millions more would die if he did nothing. Something had to be done that would make the world sit up and take notice before he had to go that one final step from which there would be no turning back.

He had wrestled with the dilemma over many months while he had planned his actions.

What gave him the right to decide over life and death?

He had resolved the issue relatively quickly.

What gave a president, or the leader of any country for that matter, the right to send his or her people to war, where thousands, tens, maybe hundreds of thousands could die?—no one, other than the electorate of arbitrarily created countries giving a certain individual the right. The way Solano saw it, humanity was at war with climate change, and the resultant destruction of the human race itself, along with millions of animals that lived on the planet—that's what gave him the right. The fact was, his ultimate goal was to protect life—the classic case of the lives of the many outweighing the lives of the few. He could live with that. And he would have to—but not for very long.

He checked the position of the AUV. It had maneuvered to a depth of three hundred feet and was sitting at the predetermined position twenty miles off the Keys.

Solano typed into the keyboard. The message was sent through the internet to an island he owned near Mauritius, five hundred and sixty miles off the east coast of Madagascar. From there it was fed into an underwater acoustic system transmitting on a secure frequency that could be picked up by the AUV.

When the signal arrived at the AUV, the internal technology took over. Circuits were joined, and within five seconds the sequence of events that would detonate a nuclear weapon off the Florida coast was put in motion, and nothing could stop it.

The bomb was designed to create as much force as possible, coupled with minimizing fallout and radiation. Taking into account the depth of water, it was unlikely much radiation would spill above the surface and create any long-term damage. What Solano needed was the force of the explosion to disturb the water column on a massive scale.

The position had also been chosen with regard to the depth of water.

When the blast came, part of it was directed down, hitting the seabed, destroying anything in its way but redirecting the force upward. This, coupled with the main blast, pushed the water up, creating a rolling wave that radiated out in all directions. It rose up to a height of thirty feet, obliterating all in its path.

The first to go was a trawler that had been pulling in its nets at the end of a week's fishing trip. Next, two dive boats taking sports divers to the wreck of the US Coast Guard cutter *Duane* were tossed aside like toys. Unlucky in its angle to the onrushing wave, a cargo ship that had been heading for the Bahamas was capsized and sank within minutes.

But then, as the wave hit the shallows of the Keys, the reduction in depth compressed the water, causing it to rise even higher. It topped out at sixty feet, thundering in over the islands, sweeping all before it.

When the surge was finally gone nothing was left standing.

The water slowly started to subside, but it left behind a desert of destruction.

In the final tally, it turned out that two hundred and fifty people had lost their lives. Hundreds of homes and businesses had been destroyed. Thousands were now displaced and homeless.

It was a microcosm of what was to come if the world didn't change.

As Solano watched the footage from the armada of news helicopters now circling the region, he took no pleasure in what he saw. Nothing from now on in his life would be pleasurable. All he could do was wait and see the reaction to what he had done, and to see if anyone would now take him seriously or just write him off as a delusional crackpot. Only then would he decide whether he had to go the final mile.

He also realized he would now be a wanted man. The world would be after him. They would know what he had done and they would not understand. He had to make preparations to leave and leave soon.

When the phone rang he knew who the caller would be. However much he'd rather not take it, he had to, it was the least he could do. It was the last chance for the world.

He lifted the receiver and spoke carefully.

"Hello, Mr. President."

The voice at the other end was incredulous and shaken to the core.

"Victor, what have you done?"

"What was necessary to get the world's attention. And if you want to avoid what comes next, the world needs to listen."

"So what comes next, Victor? What could possibly be worse than this?"

"It seems you have little imagination, Galt. Be under no illusion, this is a drop in the ocean compared to what is coming, and it's coming regardless of what I do. The only difference will be the timeframe."

"They'll come for you, Victor. They will all be coming for you."

"Then you'd better hold them off, because if they do, there is no going back. If they come, there can be no negotiation, no agreement. There is still time to create a way forward. But you have to listen to what I have said—what the scientists around the world are saying. The world is going to change whether you like it or not. The only question is how fast it changes, and that depends on what you do next. My deadline is one week. I expect to hear from you on behalf of the other world leaders by then."

And with that he hung up on the president of the United States.

He had no idea how he would react, but he knew that while Stevens was a tough president who didn't suffer fools gladly, he was also not impulsive. He had been given a demonstration of what Solano could do, and more importantly, what he was prepared to do—and while Stevens had no idea of what was to come, he did feel he would take his threats seriously and keep the dogs at bay for now.

Still, it was time to start what he knew would probably be his final journey, whatever happened in the next few days.

Chapter Thirty-Two

Now that McCready had a task to get his teeth into, all thoughts of doom and gloom were blown away. He was never happier than when having a problem to solve, and it really didn't matter how big the problem was or how insurmountable the odds were of achieving it—often, the harder the task the more he relished it.

He would now focus solely on Victor Solano.

For some reason he was convinced Solano held the key to finding Carlita, and if that meant he had to physically get to him, however difficult that might be, then so be it.

He was currently poring over a computer screen in the conference room at Ocean Tech, reading everything he could about him. And while there was much about his life and achievements, what really interested McCready was the fact he was largely a recluse, only coming out in public for announcements to do with his businesses or on special occasions for his birth country of Brazil, or to assist friends in their endeavors. The rest of the time he seemed to be holed up in what appeared to be an amazing residence halfway up a mountain in Switzerland. To McCready that was ideal. He would be confined to one place—easily located—and, by all accounts, without an easy exit should he decide he didn't want McCready's company.

He clicked a link in the Safari browser and up came a *Vanity Fair* article on Solano's home. They had tried to do one of those exposés on celebrity homes but had never been able to get Solano to agree, so they had done the next best thing—find architects and others to speculate about the house in the cliff face and what might be behind the striking glass frontage that could be seen from afar.

By all accounts there had been some wild ideas as to the internal layout and structure, but it was clear from the well-known names and faces credited in the article that some serious thought had been put into it, and it wasn't just some cheap made-up piece without considered opinion to back it up.

Among the things of which there was no argument was the location and how you accessed it.

He clicked on a link and an illustration popped up. It was bit like the ones for ski resorts where you had a plan layout of the mountains in 3D showing all the cable cars, chairlifts, ski runs, etc. In this case, it showed the transport systems to get someone from planet Earth up to Solano's hideaway. And it was truly impressive.

There were two options.

The first was to fly by helicopter to the Mayor Observatory at the top of the adjoining Alp. Named after the Swiss astronomer Michel Mayor, it provided world-class facilities for studying the heavens. The public were allowed to look around and were encouraged to take full advantage of the visitor center, restaurant and gift shop while they were up there, as well as the incredible views of course.

The second was to take a cable car from the village in the valley below up to the observatory.

Once you arrived at the top, whether by helicopter or cable car, from there on, it was private territory to get to Solano's home.

A small pod transit system led from the public area down into the mountain. It consisted of three capsules, or pods, which were connected together, one behind the other, on a linked chassis. Each was able to rotate, so as the steepness of the track increased, so the pods would turn to keep the occupants horizontal—and they needed to be. After fifty feet of tunnel, when leaving the top station, the track then traveled two hundred feet horizontally in a tunnel along the mountain ridge. For this section the tunnel side was transparent, allowing occupants to look out at the amazing view. The track then started to descend at an angle of forty-five degrees, before turning completely vertical and heading straight down into the rock, like an elevator, all the way to Solano's home, eight hundred feet below.

McCready had to give him credit. It was impressive—and so was the price tag, no doubt. How the other half lived. He knew an Arab prince who wasn't shy of spending a buck or two, but this was on a whole other level.

As the transit system was the only way to access the residence, people had speculated how Solano would get out if there was a fire or the system failed in some way. Numerous suggestions had come up, but the one that seemed to have the most traction was that he had a locker full of parachutes to enable him to jump if things got too bad. To be honest, it wasn't such a crazy idea. Solano was known to indulge in adventure sports, including scuba diving and BASE jumping, which was where you jumped off a fixed structure rather than out of an aircraft, so McCready could easily see how he might have that as a contingency. People did it from high-rises in New York, so he was told—this would be the perfect place.

Next, he turned to see what he could find on the interior of the home—but here things became a little vague. It was fairly clear there were at least two levels, as there was glass frontage in the rock face. The lower level had the large circular balcony in the middle, but above, there was a level that had small, regular oval-shaped windows running the full length of the floor below. However, beyond that, there were no pictures or diagrams of the interior. Still, that wasn't the main problem—the main problem would be getting in, with or without the owner's consent, McCready didn't mind which. The former would obviously be easier, but as he'd always told himself—he wouldn't do it if it was easy—so plan for 'not easy' and see what happens.

He was thinking about his options when Richards hurried into the room and flicked on the TV that was suspended near the ceiling in the corner. Immediately, a newscaster appeared on screen. Behind her was an aerial view of flooded land and destroyed buildings.

"This just happened in Florida. Complete devastation of the Keys and surrounding area," said Richards.

McCready watched the TV closely. He could hardly believe what he was seeing.

"So what was it? A tsunami from an earthquake or something?"

"That's the official line," said Richards. "But you know the media. Wild conspiracy theories are flying around that our new friend Solano could be involved."

At this, McCready turned to look at Richards.

"What do you mean?"

Richards took a deep breath. "Well, you know those

videos we saw, where he was making threats if something wasn't done about climate change?"

McCready nodded.

"There you go."

McCready looked incredulous. "Hang on a minute. They're saying Solano caused this? But how could he…?" McCready trailed off, as in his mind he was already answering the question. "Unless he used an extremely powerful bomb of some kind."

Both men looked at each other seriously.

The game had now completely and utterly changed.

"Jesus!" said McCready.

"Yeah, right," said Richards.

McCready was thinking fast. "Okay, so he has to get the weapon to carry out this action. He somehow manages, through his resources and contacts, to force the plane down—but it comes down in the wrong place. He doesn't have the equipment or people who can dive to those depths, so he's stuck. When Carlita broke into one of his companies she came across the plan to steal the AUV, not knowing what it was, nor what it was for. I'm not surprised Solano wanted to stop her from telling anyone. It could have ruined everything."

"Yeah," said Richards, "but then we just end up doing his dirty work for him." He paused before continuing a little softer and reiterating what Steel had said on the dock in India. "But when he had the weapon, what would he need Carlita for?"

McCready glanced up sharply. But he knew he was right. She was almost certainly dead, and while he would never give up hope—he never did—things had changed from a rescue mission to a payback mission. If it was the last thing McCready ever did, the richest man in the world was going to wish he'd never been born.

The gears were turning over now.

"Well, if those rumors are true, and they seem pretty credible, knowing what we know, there are going to be a lot of people after him, which means…" said McCready.

"…you need to back down and let them do their thing," said Richards.

McCready looked at him incredulously.

"No, the opposite. We have to do something now. If Carlita *is* still alive, every minute means one less minute for that to be so."

Richards shook his head.

"We've been here before. There's going to be so much attention on him, you'll never get close."

"I didn't seem to have a problem in Los Angeles."

Richards hesitated for a second.

"You can't just fly straight into a mountain, John!"

"I know, but we have a helicopter and we have a pilot and we have options."

Richard sighed. He wasn't in the mood for a fight but sometimes he was pushed to the limit.

"That's not your helicopter, and as I've mentioned before, he wants it back. And don't you go dragging my niece into any more of your harebrained schemes."

"She seemed to quite enjoy the last one."

"Yeah, well that side of the family always was a few cans short of a six-pack."

Martin Steel eased back in his chair in his office at 10 Downing Street. He stretched and yawned. It had been a long few days.

After he'd returned from India there had been many things on his mind. The location of his helicopter, though, had not been one of them. He knew where it was and he didn't need it right now. Also, it had a tracker on board, and when he'd last checked, it was still parked up at Ocean Tech in Aberdeen, so he could relax.

What his main concern had been, was that there was a nuclear weapon loose in the world. In fact, he had to worry about nine of them, as eight Russian nuclear devices had also gone missing a couple of months previously, but the trail had gone cold on those. But for someone like Steel, the trail on these sorts of things never went cold.

What had now made matters more interesting was the fact he'd been told by his counterpart in the US about the real cause of the flooding in Florida—one down eight to go. However, while that weapon no longer posed a problem, looking to the future, it was what Solano did next that worried him. He had made other threats, and those were to the whole world, not just the US, and that did concern him.

In fact, he had been so busy he'd merely brushed aside —to be dealt with later—a note about some scientists being shot at in Antarctica.

That was at the bottom of the world—far away from everything.

It was the least of his worries.

Chapter Thirty-Three

The Security Council at the United Nations had met many times over the years in controversial and difficult circumstances, but none of them had ever been in a situation such as this.

The fifteen members, made up of five permanent and ten non-permanent, were sat around the horseshoe-like table. There wasn't a smile to be seen anywhere. First, there had been the condolences to the Americans for the losses in Florida, then there had been outrage that such an action could have been perpetrated by one man.

There had been confusion as to what he was trying to achieve, and what was to come next. The tapes of the two speeches he had given, TED and at the UN, were replayed. The grievances were well known—indeed they were well publicized, and had been for many years by scientists both credible and incredible. But it always came down to the inevitable—the actions that were required to resolve the climate change issues were just too unpalatable for the leaders of developed nations to take. There was no way any of the leaders, however much they might agree or sympathize with the arguments, would be prepared to commit political suicide by advocating the draconian measures required—it was never going to happen.

As speaker after speaker made this clear, through different interpretations and with different excuses, a gradual dawning descended on the group of men and women. And that was that the human race was sleepwalking into a calamity it knew existed. It knew it was possible to fix it. But that it would never be fixed—could never be fixed—because of the way the world worked. They realized they had failed their fellow man.

And there was no way out of it.

Once this truth was accepted, the question was, what to do next?

The conclusion they came to was that Solano had to be stopped. He had warned them of worse to come. But what could he mean? It was felt they had to proceed cautiously. They had, after all, seen what he was prepared to do, and since none of them had any idea what he was planning next, they could not risk something being unleashed without warning. The final decision was that President Stevens should be a go-between with Solano, and that he should try to see if he could talk some sense into him. But even as they said this, it was clear none of them had the convictions of their statements.

It was a hopeless situation.

And so they packed their bags and returned to their countries with their heads in the sand and no resolution to the crisis in sight.

What that meant was that when Solano learned of the outcome, there would be only one way to go—and the world wasn't going to like it.

Chapter Thirty-Four

In Antarctica the black helicopters had been busy.

Over the previous two months they had been preparing for a mission that would change the world. Their crews were made up of mercenaries who knew not to ask questions. All the kit had been provided for them, from the aircraft to the weapons systems they installed at eight locations across Antarctica. They had merely been given the coordinates of where to bury the large cylindrical drums. They had a depth and a precise location, but beyond that they had no idea of the contents or the purpose. All they knew was that they were heavy and, despite their weight, they were delicate. They assumed it was some form of highly secret military sensing equipment. This deduction was made on the basis they also had to set up monitoring posts within a one-mile radius of the sites of the buried drums. At these locations would be a camera linked to a satellite network and a high-precision remotely controlled sniper rifle with suppressor. The distance was important as the rifle was only accurate within the one-mile range, and that was dependent on the wind.

The mercenaries went about their task clinically and professionally. All the drums had now been installed, along with their guardian angels. Their final act was to turn on the equipment. Once this had been done, they had left the scene and returned to their base—a ship several miles offshore in the Weddell Sea. There they awaited further instructions, which would come if there was any interference to the drums that couldn't be taken care of by the remote weapons. They were quite happy with that. They were being paid handsomely for their work, even if that meant sitting with their feet up on a ship, playing video games and watching movies. It could take as long as it took as far as they were concerned.

In his office, Solano checked the array of monitors that displayed the incoming feeds from the cameras across Antarctica. Many of them were currently obscured by bad weather, but that also meant there would be no helicopters in the air that could cause him problems.

Many of the locations had been specifically chosen for their proximity to the thickest regions of ice across the continent, and most were far away from areas of research by the scientists. But just in case, there were sensors that indicated activity within a mile radius of the sites, and so far, just the one had been triggered. He would have to monitor that carefully. It was the most important one. It was the relay station that triggered all the others when he sent the signal.

He was still musing whether to give a warning to those working down there. It was the right thing to do, and he wanted to do the right thing, but at the same time he didn't want anything to jeopardize the plan. Still, there was time yet. The world had no idea what he was proposing to do and he would keep it that way—it was too finely balanced to risk any interference at this stage. There was one chance for humanity and this was it.

He was still pondering the issue when his Apple Watch alerted him to the arrival of the transit pods at the small station in the heart of the mountain. He clicked a button and watched the train pull into the station on a display on the desk. The pods stopped automatically at the end of the line and Juliano Mendes climbed out. A minute later Solano heard the inner door of the airlock on the upper level open and Mendes walked into the atrium.

Solano made his way out of his office and over to greet him. He smiled.

"All good?"

"Yes, sir. Everything went like clockwork."

"Okay, we need to clear up here. Make sure all systems access and protocols are transferred to the island. We won't be coming back."

"Yes, sir."

Solano made his way down to the lower level while Mendes headed to the office to make the final preparations to leave. As he did, he saw Carlita emerge from one of the rooms. When they saw each other, they stopped and stared for a moment. Mendes glared at her before heading away. Carlita watched him, a distressed look on her face. She then walked downstairs to join Solano at the front, looking out over the valley below.

"Are you ready?" he asked.

"Yes, I am. It's what we planned for. What we dreamed about. It's finally coming true."

Solano looked at her. He knew this was what she wanted, but he detected a slight uneasiness in her voice. He put it down to the enormity of what they were about to do.

"I shall miss this place," she said. "I feel safe here, like we're on top of the world. No one can touch us."

He put his arm around her and held her close.

"You will have other places. Other homes. You will want for nothing."

Carlita looked out over the valley. "Maybe, but it will be without you," she said, looking up sadly into his eyes. "And they will come after me."

At this, Solano looked at her fondly. "Maybe, but you have Juliano, and you will have all my money. You'll be fine."

She glanced at him for a moment. "I wish you wouldn't call him that."

"It's his name now. Always remember that." He paused. "I have things to do. Make sure you are packed, ready to go. Leave nothing behind that you ever wish to see again."

And with that he walked off, leaving Carlita with her head full of conflicting thoughts.

Chapter Thirty-Five

"Wow, it's so beautiful!" said Charlie as she sat at the controls of the Chinook that was still *on loan*.

They were flying up a wide valley in Switzerland, the massive snow-covered peaks towering high above them. From the co-pilot's seat McCready watched the stunning scenery sweep by on either side. While he loved Scotland and the wildness of the country, it couldn't compare to the pure spectacle and postcard beauty of Switzerland. Everything here was more epic, as though designed for a movie as opposed to TV.

"It certainly is," said McCready.

The last few days had been frantic, trying to pull a plan together as quickly as possible. McCready had convinced Richards and Porter to come along and Charlie had leapt at the chance for more crazy flying, which usually seemed to be involved when McCready was around.

He had to somehow get to see Solano. He knew, given the current climate, that was highly unlikely. It had also crossed his mind that with all the resources at Solano's disposal he might somehow have come across McCready as part of the team that had raised the AUV. He therefore couldn't give him any notice of his presence or what he was trying to do.

After careful consideration of all the information, it looked like they had two options.

Option A involved getting into one of the transit pods that linked Solano's home with the cable car station at the top of the mountain and arrive as any normal guest would. The problem with that was that he would no doubt have to go through layers of security, all covered by cameras, which would probably be monitored from the residence. They'd see him coming a mile away.

Option B—the more daring one—was to abseil down from the Chinook onto the curved steel top of the residence that stuck out ten feet from the cliff face. He would then be able to drop down onto the balcony and hope he could enter through the glass frontage. Porter had given him some small shaped charges that would do the job and not cause too much damage—Porter had been rather disappointed at this particular restriction—and hopefully not injure anyone. A slight problem with Option B was that due to the angle of the rock above the residence, the helicopter would have to be at least five hundred feet above it in order to be able to get the rotors close enough for McCready to abseil down. That was a hell of a drop and any number of things could go wrong.

He was still considering the options when Craig stuck his head into the cockpit.

"Got a minute?"

McCready left the cockpit and walked back into the small office-like area between the cockpit and the cargo bay that was, in fact, the place where he'd had his first encounter with Martin Steel. They sat down. It was quieter in there, the soundproofing having been improved to make it less like standing in a factory.

"So, what do you want to do?" said Richards.

"I think I have to try the easier route first."

"Okay, but there's a good chance you'll be stopped, maybe even detained."

"True," said McCready, "but I might at least get to speak to him, or someone in the residence. I can be pretty persuasive when I want to be."

Richards raised his eyebrows as though to say, *oh really?*

"Fair enough… Okay, we'll drop you off at the private airstrip just down from the village. It was where we were going to park up anyway while you're up there. They think we're a scientific team doing research in the area, and we're not far away if you need anything. You got the comms set?"

McCready nodded. He leaned down and reached into a backpack on the floor and pulled out the comms unit he'd had in Monaco. It fitted into his ear and there was a throat mike that attached around his neck he could press to speak. He tucked it under his black turtleneck sweater. Next, he checked the shaped charges Porter had given him. They were pretty easy to use. They had the option of magnetic or sticky-tape attachment, and a timer that could be set for up to a minute. Although they were powerful, they would not be dangerous unless you were extremely close. All the energy was expended in one direction. They'd be enough to blow through the toughest glass windows, however many layers of glazing they had, and the residence in the cliff was at least triple. They could also, at a pinch, blow through steel and concrete, but it would depend on the thickness. Porter had refused to give any guarantees—glass was what had been requested and glass was what he got. It wasn't like they came with a year's warranty or anything, but McCready was pretty sure they would get through most things he was likely to come up against.

"Okay, I'd better go tell Charlie," said McCready.

He climbed back into the cockpit and informed Charlie they were good to go once they reached the airfield they could see coming into view further up the valley.

Ten minutes later, after Charlie had cleared the landing with the small air traffic control building, she swept the large machine round in a wide arc and landed at one end of the short runway. She then taxied past a hanger that had its doors wide open. A sleek Learjet was parked inside. Once she was clear of the building, she crossed over to an area of tarmac out of the way and killed the engines.

When the rotors had come to a stop, McCready thanked Charlie and Richards, and told Porter he'd take good care of his equipment—that was, unless he had to use it, in which case he hoped it would be blown to smithereens. He pulled on his Berghaus climbing jacket and a baseball cap to keep out the bright sun, and then climbed down from the side door onto the tarmac.

He looked back at Richards.

"Just be ready to pick me up at the helipad if I run into trouble."

"Don't worry. Give us the word and we'll come to the rescue."

"Thanks. Let's hope it doesn't come to that."

"Yeah, there's a first for everything," said Richards with a grin. "Go on, get outta here!"

McCready gave a final wave, hoisted the backpack onto his shoulders and headed off on the half-mile walk to the village and the cable car station. The air was fresh and it felt good in his lungs, but he barely noticed it as his mind was focused on the task ahead.

When he reached the village, he found it was busy. Being the start point for the trip up the mountain, there were many tourists waiting in line to take the cable car. McCready joined the queue and watched the excitement of families, particularly the kids, many of whom would no doubt be having their first ride.

When it came to McCready's turn, he optimistically bought a return ticket and then filed through with all the others into the next car. Once inside, they were given a quick briefing as to what they could see on the way up, and then the car rolled out of the station and started the long climb to the top of the Alp.

McCready had always liked cable cars. He had a head for heights, so seeing the massive drops that were often below the flimsy glass and metal boxes had never worried him. Any tension this time was centered around what he would do when he got to the top—if it would work, and if it did, what he would discover. Would Carlita be alive? And if she wasn't, what would he do to the man whom he held responsible? The thoughts caused him to zone out the hubbub around him as the kids raced from side to side to get the best view.

McCready became more focused after they'd crossed the lake and cleared the second pylon on top of the low Alp. They were now moving up toward the main cliff face and he could get a proper look at the sheer rock and Solano's home embedded halfway up.

Not many of the others in the car were aware of the structure. Some had read the guide books that mentioned it, but most were oblivious. McCready took a particular interest. If Option A didn't work, he might find himself abseiling down from above. It would be risky. Whenever helicopters hovered close to a rock face they could be subject to updrafts and downdrafts, which could spin them into the wall, giving those inside—or anyone dangling from a five-hundred-foot rope, for that matter—no chance. His expression hardened as he looked at the sheer scale of the mountain.

He hoped Option A would work.

As they climbed higher he took a pair of binoculars from his pack and focused on Solano's home. He could see the wide balcony along the front with the extra area extending out in the center. There were lights on throughout, but the privacy glass restricted his vision, and although he thought he caught a glimpse of someone moving around inside, he couldn't be sure.

As he swept the glasses over the structure, he could see a large flat metal area on the rock at the left-hand end. It was about fifteen-foot square. He couldn't think what it could be, unless it was where some of the machinery was housed that kept the residence functioning.

A few minutes later and they were approaching the cliff face. As he turned his gaze upward, he could see the top station coming into view. He hadn't even noticed the other car descending on the parallel cables, he'd been so absorbed with Solano's lair.

His attention was suddenly drawn to the small pod transit system that linked the cable car station to Solano's residence. He could see the series of pods emerge from the rock and make their way along the track to the station just down from the ridge of the mountain. They were enclosed behind what looked like a glass wall to protect them from the weather. He reached for the binoculars again. There were three distinct pods. The rear two were empty, but there was someone in the first one. It was a man dressed in a smart business suit carrying a slim briefcase. He couldn't make out his features—he was too far away. A moment later the pods disappeared from view into the rock. He placed the binoculars back in his pack and prepared for their arrival.

The cable car pulled smoothly into the upper station and came to a stop with a gentle sigh. A moment later the doors automatically swung open and the gaggle of excited tourists rushed out to sample the thrills that awaited them. McCready waited until everyone had gone and then made his way into the main entrance lobby.

He wandered over to a map that showed a plan layout of the top of the Alp and all there was to see and explore on your visit. It showed the ridge line of the mountain, and at the highest point, the observatory. Between the two was the helipad. The map also highlighted the visitor center and the things you could discover there—from the conditions of the environment in the region, to the advantages of the location for the observatory, and why it was the perfect place from which to study the stars. Much of this had to do with the fact that at this altitude the air was clean and pure with little pollution—toxic and light—to obscure the heavens. He wished he had more time. It would have been interesting to look around.

He turned from the map and glanced around the lobby.

One exit led out to the walkway to the observatory, but another led down a short corridor to a door at the end. There was a decorative red rope slung between two gold-colored bollards blocking off the route. A sign to one side stated the area was private in five different languages. He thought it must be the way to the transit system. He noticed a camera above the entrance to the corridor and pulled the peak of his baseball cap further down, shielding his face.

He was about to turn away to go outside when the door at the end of the passage opened and the man with the briefcase he'd seen in the pod walked toward him. He seemed to be preoccupied, and as he walked past, McCready got a good look at his face. There was something about him that made McCready stop dead. It wasn't a face he recognized, but for some reason he had a strong feeling he'd seen him somewhere before. But where? He definitely didn't recognize the face, but there was something about the eyes and the way he moved. McCready followed him through the concourse. But rather than head for the cable car, he instead walked out onto the walkway that led up to the observatory.

McCready hung back, watching him. Halfway to the observatory the man turned to his left and climbed a small set of metal steps onto the helipad. McCready could see a black and silver Airbus AS365 helicopter on the pad, its rotors spinning. As McCready looked closer and read off the tail number, his heart started beating faster. It was the same one he'd seen in Monaco.

The man walked confidently up to the rear door and climbed in. A couple of seconds later the helicopter lifted off and swept round over the walkway. As McCready glanced up, he noticed the man looking down. When the man saw him, McCready thought he detected a look of shock, but the chopper was moving fast. It swept away over the mountain and was gone.

McCready stood there, still not able to place him. He gave it a minute but nothing came to him. He then looked around. The walkway was built on a rigid metal frame secured to the rock. It had a glass floor through which you could see the precipitous drop below.

McCready crossed over to the sturdy handrail at the side and looked down into the valley. He could see the cables for the cable car stretching away over the lower Alp and then on to the village way beyond. He pulled out the binoculars and focused on the airfield to the south of the village. He could see the Chinook. It looked as though his friends were lying on the grass near the helicopter enjoying the sunshine. He clicked the throat mike.

"Hi, Craig, I'm at the top. Going to check out Option A. Will be in touch when I've made a decision."

Through the binoculars he could see one of the small figures pick something up off the grass and bring it up to his head. He heard a crackle in his ear.

"Roger that, John. Be careful. Stay in touch," said Richards over the radio.

McCready turned from the view and walked back inside the lobby to work out what to do next.

As the Airbus AS365 flew away, Juliano Mendes sat in the back with his briefcase on the seat beside him. They were dramatic and traumatic times they were living through. His task now was to travel to Solano's private island for the final phase of the operation. He was glad to be going to the island. He loved it there. But the trip would be tinged with sadness because of the finality of it all. Also, he was concerned for Solano—his condition was worsening. He knew he didn't have long. And he was also still mad at Carlita. When he had been told about the plan to acquire the weapon when things had gone wrong, he'd been against it from the start. Not that it wouldn't work. In fact, given the factors involved, he was pretty sure it would work—and that was the problem. He had big personal issues with it, and he was furious Carlita had not understood. It had driven a wedge between them and that was something he'd never wanted to happen. And what had suddenly made matters worse was that when the helicopter had swept across the mountain top before heading down into the valley, he thought he'd recognized someone looking up at him.

It was impossible. It couldn't be.

But he was sure it was.

He pulled his cellphone out of his pocket. He knew that with one call he could cause the man on the walkway to have a very bad day. He thought about it for a moment, but he knew he had already decided.

He put the phone slowly away.

What would be would be.

Chapter Thirty-Six

It was clear to McCready there was no way he could bluff his way onto the transit pods. There was too much scrutiny with the camera and the security guard, whom he had seen when the door at the far end of the short corridor had opened. He still didn't want to go with Option B, but there might be another way.

When he'd been looking through the binoculars from the cable car he'd seen the pods make their way close to the ridge at the top of the mountain, enclosed behind a transparent wall of some kind. If he could climb round there, there might be a hatch or a way of getting onto the track and picking up the pods as they passed.

With the plan formulating in his mind, he looked around for the best place to make his way along the ridge without being seen.

Most of the group he had come up with had long since left to head to the attractions further up the mountain. He crossed over to the far side of the area outside the lobby that looked down the other side of the mountain. Over here there was little activity. He was at the edge of the platform where the viewing point joined the outside of the lobby building. The rock beyond the guardrail was not quite as steep as the vertiginous drop on the other side. McCready checked no one was looking and then quickly climbed over. He was now on the outside of the glass barrier and still holding on to the railing. There was about ten feet to go before he would be completely obscured from view. He shimmied along the side keeping his head down.

He made it to the rock with no one raising the alarm.

Once beyond the rail there was a flatter area he could safely stand on, but with a massive drop to the right. He walked across this and found himself at the far side of the cable car station. He could look along the top of the mountain ridge, which extended for about a mile. On both sides was a near vertical drop, but around fifty feet further on, he could see where the transit pod track emerged from the rock into the section with the transparent side. This was around two hundred feet in length. Beyond this, the pods disappeared into the rock again to drop down to Solano's home eight hundred feet below.

McCready sat down and unslung his backpack. He rummaged through and pulled out a climbing harness and rope, a number of pitons, a hammer and a string of karabiners that he slung around his neck. He climbed into the harness and secured it tightly. He then made sure all the pockets in his backpack and jacket were zipped up and then stepped forward to the edge of the ridge.

He had climbed a lot in Scotland in the Cairngorms and was used to cliff faces and the equipment needed to keep you safe. But this was at a whole different height and on a whole other scale. Still, a drop was a drop. Thirty feet could kill you—so several thousand would make little difference—when you're dead, you're dead.

Before he stepped off onto the face, he clicked the comms unit around his neck.

"Craig, you there?"

"All here," came the crackly reply several seconds later.

"Okay, I'm going for a mix of Option A and B. There's too much security inside so I'm going to make my way along the ridge to the transit track and see if I can get in through the glass side."

"Okay, but be careful, that's a hell of a drop up there."

"You'd noticed? Talk later."

He clicked off the comms, then took a deep breath and stepped out onto the rock face.

At first, the going was easy. There were numerous cracks and ledges to hold onto and he was able to maintain the golden rule of climbing, of always having three points of contact.

But about twenty feet along, the rock became smoother. He pulled the hammer from the harness around his waist and banged in a piton. He then clipped a rope, attached through a figure of eight knot to a karabiner, to the piton. This would give him a safety line in case he fell. Now, feeling more secure, he started to inch along the rock, the rope paying out through a descender attached to the harness around his waist.

He made it all the way across the smooth section. There was a moment when he lost his footing with his right foot but he didn't fall. When he was at the other end he sighed with relief and started to move more freely. Not far ahead he could see the section of track enclosed by the transparent side.

When he reached it he took a breather.

He looked around.

The view was spectacular. He was close to the ridge line and could see down the drops on both sides. As he looked out over the mountain range to the north, it was almost obscured by gathering clouds. They weren't that close, but they did seem to be heading this way and were thick and muddy-looking. He was sure there would be snow before the day was out.

He turned his attention back to the job at hand.

He looked down at the section of track behind the glass side. There didn't appear to be a hatch or any kind of access point. He was going to have to do it the hard way.

He banged another piton into the rock and clipped the rope through a karabiner. He then abseiled backward down to the glass and locked off the rope with the descender.

As he looked along the two hundred feet of exposed section, he could still see no hatch or anything that looked like a means of entry.

That left him with no other choice.

He leaned back in the harness and reached round to pull his backpack to the front so he could remove the small pouch containing the shaped charges. He unzipped it. There were four in all. Porter had said he wasn't exactly raiding the Kremlin or anything, so he couldn't think he'd need more than that. At the end of the day, all he needed them for was to get into the residence. If he managed that, he could always get out the same way he had come in.

As the glass wasn't magnetic, McCready peeled away the sticky-backed tape Porter had said could stick to anything—think gaffer tape on steroids. He'd said not to touch the surface when he peeled off the backing, else he'd need surgery to remove it, and until that happened he'd be wandering around with a bomb stuck to his hand or wherever.

McCready carefully removed the backing and placed the charge about two feet down from the top of the glass side. He then repeated the action with the second charge about five feet further along. That should give him enough room to get through. It also left him with two more charges for whatever else he might encounter.

He set the timers at twenty seconds and pulled himself up out of the blast area.

Knowing Porter, he thought there was every chance of being blown off the rock face even if he'd been a hundred yards away, but true to his word, when they ignited, there was a small, sharp crack and that was it. McCready felt nothing from his protective position. When he lowered himself back down there were two perfect large holes in the glass that met in the middle. All he had to do was bash though the area between them with his climbing boot, knocking the damaged section into the space below. He now had an area six feet long by three deep that he could easily fit through. He pushed the backpack through first and then dropped down onto the track.

He'd barely had to time to pick up his pack and catch his breath when he realized he'd made a big mistake. He heard a noise from the cable car station end of the tunnel.

There was a train coming.

Victor Solano looked out over the valley from the wide expanse of glass at the front of his home. He would be sad to leave the place—after all, it had been his sanctuary for many years, a place away from the world yet totally connected to it by the view he was now experiencing.

But then he turned back. There was something he had to do for one last time.

It was something he knew he would miss, and there was a pang of regret as he realized it was the last time he would ever do it.

He walked along Main Street, heading for the room at the end. He reached it and placed his palm on the reader. The large door slid open revealing the Aston Martin beyond. He walked in, pulled open the door and sat in the driver's seat. The smell of the leather was still strong. He glanced around the interior of the car and recalled all the memories it brought back to him, both of the films and the time he had spent sitting in her. He flipped up the center console that hid the controls for the 'optional extras.' Even though he'd had them all fitted for real—just because he could—he would have liked to have tried them out one day, but to do that would have meant revealing to the world that the car was in his possession, and that was something he could never do.

When he left the residence, the place would be destroyed, along with the car. He wanted no trace of his life and its secrets. When he had done what he had to do, all his life and possessions would be crawled over for years to come, and he wanted as little left as possible.

McCready stared up the dark tunnel that led to the cable car. The noise was getting louder and there was nowhere to go. The tunnel was a snug fit for the pods, so whatever was approaching, there would be no way he could move to one side. He hoped it wouldn't be traveling fast. If it was, he was going to be squashed like a bug on a windshield.

He waited for the inevitable.

The noise grew louder.

It was an electric humming, along with the rattle of wheels on a track. He stared into the tunnel.

And then it was upon him.

It wasn't moving fast but it also wasn't going to stop. He ran along the track toward the tunnel at the other end. He knew beyond that was the vertical drop down to the residence below. He looked for something he could hold onto. The end of the pod had a wide, curved window flush with the metal side—nothing there.

He ran further.

He was now entering the tunnel. It was dark and he was wary of the upcoming drop. He undid a karabiner from his climbing sling and attached a small piece of rope to it. In the center, at the top of the pod, he could see a metal attachment point—somewhere a crane could be secured to allow the pod to be lifted off the tracks.

At the last second, as the pod was about to hit him, he leapt up and grabbed hold of the rim at the top. There were only a few inches clearance between his fingers and the roof sweeping past just above. He clung on with one hand and reached up with the other to clip the karabiner to the eyelet in the middle. He then secured the other end to his climbing harness and leaned back, placing his feet on the bottom of the pod. He was now in a classic abseil position and would be going nowhere. He glanced inside. It was empty. Presumably the occupants down in the residence had called it back for some reason.

A second later the pod swept into the tunnel. As it did so, headlights flicked on automatically. McCready glanced round to see where he was going. Ten feet in front of him the floor disappeared. A moment later and the string of pods moved slowly over the edge to descend vertically down the tunnel like an elevator. As they did, he swung out below, hanging vertically over the hundreds of feet of void.

He found the descent was fairly leisurely, but once he reached the bottom he presumed the track would level out and he would have time to unhook himself and jump onto any platform at the end.

He found out five minutes later.

As the pod leveled off, he could return to his upright position with his feet braced against the glass. He tried to twist to see where he was going. There were lights further down the tunnel. A moment later they swept into a small platform. The end was coming up fast. It looked like there would be little room between the pod and the rock wall. McCready gripped the rim at the top and quickly undid the karabiner. He just managed it, jumping to his right and landing on the platform as the pod came to a halt, inches from the wall.

He unslung his backpack and pulled off the climbing gear. He stuffed it inside the pack and then looked around.

He was standing on a small stretch of platform the length of the three pods. Ahead of him was a glass door that led through what looked like some kind of airlock, which would presumably keep the interior protected from the harsh temperatures outside. As there was no one there to confront him, he assumed he had not been discovered.

He crossed over to the door, but there was no handle or button. There didn't seem to be any way to open it. He should have thought of this. For security reasons the occupants would want to know of anyone who was visiting them and have control over whether they gained entry or not. He looked around. There was nothing he could use to try and lever his way inside. He would have to use the charges, but he had to be careful—there were only two left.

Before he went any further he clicked the comms unit around his neck. He wanted to update Craig on what he was doing and to be ready to come and get him in case anything went wrong.

"Craig, are you there?"

Static.

"Craig, do you copy?"

But there was nothing.

He was too far into the rock for the signal to get out. He took a deep breath and reached into his backpack. He pulled out the two remaining charges. As it was an airlock, he would need both of them—one for each door.

He figured the best place was probably the middle of the glass and stuck the first charge there. He retreated further down the platform and waited for the blast. It was a bit louder than before in the confines of the station, but it cracked the glass and blew out the central section. He climbed through and then repeated the action with the second door. At least he knew he could get out if things went wrong, but he would still have to get up the vertical shaft somehow.

Solano was enjoying the pleasures of the Aston when he thought he heard a distant CRACK. He paused, listening, and then returned his attention to the car. He pushed the gearstick through its motion, shuffling it through the gears —it was still perfectly fluid after all these years. A moment later and he heard a second sharp CRACK, only this one was louder. There was also a sudden beeping from his watch. He glanced at it and frowned. There was an alert indicating a breach in the airlock at the pod station.

He quickly climbed out of the car and walked up the

stairs to his office. Once at the console, he flicked through the series of cameras until he came to the one showing the platform and the airlock.

He stared in fascination as he saw the figure of a man smash through the inside door and walk cautiously through into the corridor that led to the main part of the residence. As he progressed, he was caught on a different camera and Solano got a good look at his face.

He sat there, stunned and intrigued. He was looking at John McCready. He leaned back and watched his progress. He then flicked a switch on the panel on the desk in front of him and watched the monitor as a large metal sheet shot down from the roof above the outer airlock door, sealing off the exit. He saw McCready spin round and look at it for a moment.

Solano then stood up and reached into a drawer below the desk. He pulled out a Glock 38 and stuck it into the waistband behind his back.

This was going to be interesting.

Chapter Thirty-Seven

Martin Steel walked up to the oak-paneled door, knocked once, pushed the door open, and walked into the Prime Minister's office. It wasn't large but it was tastefully decorated. The walls were a pale cream color and there were paintings from English artists over the years strategically positioned for maximum impact.

Dominic Carter looked up as Steel entered. Since Carter had been elected Prime Minister he had achieved much. High among his list of accomplishments had been a complete revamp of the UK's security, which he had largely handed over to Steel with a carte blanche remit to do what had to be done to achieve the objectives and keep the nation safe. This Steel had excelled at, and while there had been some touch and go moments, it had all been for the good of the country.

"How are the Americans reacting to what happened in Florida?" asked Steel.

Carter pushed himself back into his plush leather chair and sighed. He looked weary. There were a lot of world leaders who were having to face up to the problems that had been presented to them over the previous few days.

"They're mad as hell, as you can imagine," said Carter. "It seems this Solano fellow is on some sort of crusade to save the world, and while, when you listen to his speeches, he has a point, there's no way countries can U-turn their policies to resolve things as he would like. Somehow he has to be stopped from whatever he's planning." He paused. "Are you hearing anything?"

"Not specifically, but there is chatter coming from a number of sources, which on its own wouldn't amount to much, but in the context of recent events could be connected. I have some people to reach out to. It may give us an edge."

"The Americans?"

"No, I want to keep this in house at the moment in case I'm wrong, but I have a feeling we'll have to move fast if I confirm what I'm thinking."

Carter nodded. "Okay, Martin, do what you do best," he said grimly. "This is one we can't afford to get wrong."

"Will do," said Steel.

He walked back out of the room, up a level, and into his own office. While much of his work was done shuffling between the various security agencies, he was based at Downing Street. It gave him access to the PM at all hours and was the perfect place to be, given his role within the government.

Once back in his office he turned to his computer. He pulled up a number of files and incoming intel reports he'd received over the previous few days. He resized and spread out the various windows so he could see them all at the same time.

Included in the information was the intelligence he'd

received regarding the missing nuclear devices lost from Russia a number of months previously. It showed a cover-up in the Kremlin that had tried to hide the loss from the world. Even the Americans didn't know. It was only through Steel's pipeline into the heart of Russia's security networks that he had even come across it at all. It appeared the devices had been en route by rail to somewhere in Ukraine when the train had been hijacked.

Also on the screen were the reports coming out of Antarctica.

While he normally wouldn't spend much time on scientists and their problems at the far end of the Earth, something in the most recent report had made him take an interest. Following the initial account of shots being fired at one of the teams in the field, there were now reports of suspicious helicopters operating in the region. What was even more worrying was that, at the location where one of them had been seen, high levels of radiation had been detected. It was the same location where the shots had been fired.

Steel was pondering the implications of this when he noticed a small window in the corner of the screen with an ALERT message blinking away. He looked at it more closely, frowned and then clicked on it. A new window opened up. It showed a map of Europe and a small blinking red dot in the middle. It was the transponder on his Chinook helicopter. He frowned again and zoomed in on the map. The scale altered until it showed the dot at a small airfield in the Swiss Alps. Steel thought for a moment—the place rang a bell—and then typed into a secure search engine. A moment later a file opened showing a picture of Victor Solano and associated details and information. It also showed the location of his home. Steel clicked a series of keys. A new flashing dot appeared on the original map. It was about a mile distant from the first one.

"Oh shit, John! What the hell are you doing?"

Chapter Thirty-Eight

McCready stared at the large metal barrier that had sealed off the airlock. He realized now that his presence was known. He also realized there was no way out—he'd used the last of the charges.

He turned from the exit that was no more and headed cautiously down the corridor. It wasn't very long. He soon came to a door at the end. It had a frosted glass panel in the middle. He pushed it slowly open and walked through into another world.

He found he was in a large, low-ceilinged atrium. As he walked forward he could see he was on a wide balcony. It encircled the whole level and extended out to what looked like windows at the far end—the cliff face. The floor was covered in thick pile carpet and the walls were a soft pastel shade. It gave a serene and calming tone to the place. Also, where there had been the gentle hum of generators in the transit area, now there was complete silence save for the sound of classical music wafting up from below.

McCready hadn't known what to expect, but this was amazing.

He walked forward to the edge of the balcony. Across at the far side, a man emerged from a room. He looked straight at McCready. He appeared to be appraising him, as if deciding what kind of threat he posed. He then started to walk around the balcony toward him. As he did, McCready could clearly see it was Solano. He had that air of confidence all rich people had. He also looked like a man with nothing to lose.

He stared straight at McCready.

"Mr. McCready, I presume," he said. His words were not said in anger, or indeed with any hint of hostility, yet he must surely have been surprised to see McCready there. "I see you didn't call ahead, or"—he nodded toward the transit station—"ring the bell."

"Ah, sorry about that," said McCready, still working out how to play this. "I've come here looking for something, or, should I say, someone."

Solano nodded. "I see, and what makes you think this *someone* is here?"

"I have no idea if she is, but I think given recent events in Florida, and the potential cause of those events, it would be logical to assume you were responsible for taking the weapon from us. A woman called Carlita was also taken. Do you know where she is?"

Solano looked at him with a steely gaze. "What concern is that of yours?"

"Is she still alive?" asked McCready, barely able to conceal his growing anger.

At this, Solano looked slightly bemused and then smiled.

"Come with me. Let me show you something."

"Not until you tell me if she's alive."

McCready stood there poised for action. He could feel the blood rushing to his face. He wasn't sure how long he could restrain himself.

Solano gazed at him for a second. He then walked casually over to a wide staircase that led to the lower level and proceeded to walk down it. When he reached the bottom and McCready still hadn't moved, Solano gave him an impatient look.

"Do you want to find out or not?"

McCready walked slowly after him, glancing at the rooms as he passed. One seemed to be like some sort of control room with panels and screens on the walls and desks in front of them.

When he reached the lower level he followed Solano toward the glass at the front. Solano stopped when he reached the windows and turned to McCready. He put his wrist to his mouth and spoke into his watch.

"Where are you? There's someone here to see you."

McCready watched with puzzlement. They both waited. A few seconds later he heard someone approaching from behind.

He turned and his jaw literally fell open.

When he saw Carlita, she was dressed in a casual set of slacks and a peach-colored top. Her hair was damp from a shower and glistened in the light. She was very much alive and very much safe. When she saw him she also stopped dead. Her expression then hardened and she shot a gaze at Solano, who was standing beyond McCready.

"What is he doing here?" she said.

McCready stared at her, shock written across his face. He felt a knot of realization starting to grow in the pit of his stomach.

"Are you okay?" was all he could manage.

Carlita had regained her composure, and when she spoke, it was a with a tone that carried total disdain.

"Of course I am okay, John. Why wouldn't I be?"

"What the hell is going on?" He looked from Carlita to Solano.

"Why don't you explain it to him," said Solano. "I have work to do before we leave for the island." And with that he headed for the stairs that led to the upper level.

McCready turned to stare at her. He was sure she was acting under duress for some reason but couldn't work out why. He moved quickly over to her.

She backed off.

He stopped.

"What's going on?" he repeated. And there was now a worry in his voice as though the reality of the situation was starting to hit him, but he wasn't prepared to accept it.

Carlita continued to look at him with an expression that tore him apart inside.

"Are you really that stupid, John? We needed you. You had the skills to get the AUV from the wreck. That's what all this was about."

McCready was trying to think fast.

"But what about on the yacht in Monaco? They were hitting you. They cut you. They drugged you."

"Yes," she said, defiantly. "We had to make it convincing, so you would help me. So you would want to do everything you could to look after me after what I'd been through. And you did. You came through perfectly. But you would never have really been harmed. Even the guns had blanks in them."

McCready was absorbing this.

"What about Porter, the guy who was with me—what were you going to do with him?"

She hesitated for a moment.

"He wasn't needed, let's just leave it at that."

McCready stared at her. He couldn't believe it. If he'd had a seat to fall into, he would gladly have done so. The facts were coming too fast. How could he have been so gullible?

"And Tranter Chemicals—all that was a sham?"

"Oh no. Tranter Chemicals is real. We *were* targeting them as an environmental group, but they had nothing to do with everything else. The local police were bought off to hand me over to the *Freedom Seas* crew, and from then on it was all Victor's plan. He has a very nice yacht, don't you think?"

But McCready couldn't reply.

Carlita looked at him with pity.

"What, you think I actually cared for you after what you did to me?"

McCready was now even more confused.

"Did to you? What did I do to you?"

She looked at him with utter contempt.

"I loved you. You were my whole world, my whole life, and you left me. I would have done anything for you, gone anywhere with you, but you never even wrote. I wrote every week for a year. You never replied—not once." She said this now with bitterness in her voice.

McCready found a deep wave of nausea breaking over him.

"But I did," he said, almost in a whisper. "I wrote every week for… for months." He was trying to think fast. "I never received your letters." And finally he had it. He looked her straight in the eyes and he could almost see her waver.

They were now close.

"Your father. It must have been your father. He wanted me to leave because he thought I would take you away from him, so out of respect I left, but I never received your letters. He must have stopped yours from being sent somehow and prevented mine from getting to you."

They stared at each other for several moments. He thought he was getting through to her. The tears were forming in his eyes. He thought he could see her hesitate, but then she seemed to recover, and she was back to the hard, harsh person he didn't recognize.

"Whatever. It was a long time ago. Everything is different now. Victor found me. He took me in. He loved me. He has given me everything."

McCready was finally beginning to absorb what had happened. He looked up at her, any fight drained out of him.

"In fact, think how lucky you are, John," she continued. "What you have done is going to help change the world. After all, that's what we always talked about, wasn't it?"

He looked at her.

He was completely broken.

"So what are you going to do?" said McCready, stumbling for words. "How are you going to do this? Many people have dreams—making them a reality is something else entirely."

At this, she smiled and her eyes shone. "Not when you are with someone like Victor. What happened in Florida was just a taste of what is to come."

"But how can you say that? People were killed…"

"Millions will die if we don't do this!" she yelled at him. "There are plans for the Antarctic. It's nothing that won't happen anyway, we're just speeding things up a little."

"That's enough!" shouted someone from the balcony.

McCready looked up to see Solano staring down. A moment later he had made his way downstairs. When he reached them he glanced from one to the other.

"I think Mr. McCready has heard enough." He looked at Carlita and his tone was harsh. "Go and get your things. We're leaving now. Everything has come a little too close to home."

McCready noted a flick of fear cross Carlita's face, but then it was gone. She hurried away. Solano turned to McCready.

"It's a shame you won't be able to see what transpires, but you're too much of a liability to leave running around. As you know, the way you came in is now closed off, and there is only one other way out of the residence, which I am afraid you will also not be able to take.

"As I know the authorities will no doubt be here shortly, I cannot afford for any of what I have to fall into their hands. It would be too inconvenient. So, what is going to happen is, when Carlita and I have left, the residence will be destroyed. You won't have long, but rather than wasting time trying to escape, why not put on some music and enjoy the view. Everyone should enjoy their last few minutes on Earth, don't you think, Mr. McCready?"

He smiled, but there was no humor in it.

From behind, Carlita rejoined them. She carried a lightweight bag and was wearing a thick sports jacket and thermal leggings. They both stood there and stared at McCready for a moment.

Nothing was said.

Solano then turned and walked down the long glass frontage to a door in the wall at the end.

Before she followed, Carlita looked at McCready. He could sense something in her eyes that didn't match the way she had behaved earlier. Maybe the minutes she'd just had away from him had given her time to get over the shock. Maybe realizing he had written to her all those years ago and had never received her letters was having some effect. But whatever she was thinking, it wasn't enough to save him now.

She reached up and gave him a kiss on the cheek.

"I have to go. I'm sorry things had to work out this way, John. Truly sorry."

She was about to turn when he tried one last thing.

"So why did you contact me?"

"What?"

"If you thought I thought so little of you, why would I help you?"

She hesitated.

Again McCready could see the conflict within her. It was as though two sides were fighting for supremacy. But then she seemed to reach an equilibrium. After a final stare she turned and walked to join Solano at the end of the room.

When she reached him, he lifted a cellphone and dialed.

"Wait for us, we'll be there sooner than expected," he said into the handset.

He ended the call and looked back at McCready. He had a rueful expression on his face. He then turned and typed something into a panel at the side of the door. A second later the lights dimmed. A computerized voice echoed over the hi-fi speakers.

"Self-destruct has been activated. You have ten minutes to leave the building. Self-destruct has been activated. You have ten minutes to leave the building."

"You know, Mr. McCready," said Solano, "Carlita has told me a lot about you. I read what you did in Los Angeles.

In another time I think we could have been friends. This is nothing personal, but I cannot let anything stop what has to happen." He paused. "We won't be meeting again. I think, somehow, despite everything I have heard about you, even you can't fly."

He placed his palm on a reader. Immediately the door at the end of the room slid to one side. At the same time McCready saw a sheet of metal on the rock face side of the new room open upward—it must have been the large panel he'd seen when coming up in the cable car.

Wind blew into the newly opened space.

McCready could see a small capsule-like object beyond, suspended from a sharply angled metal gantry above. Solano walked through and opened a door to the capsule. He beckoned Carlita through. McCready watched as she took one last look back.

Their eyes met.

He couldn't be sure, but despite everything she'd said, he thought he could detect a flash of regret. It had been the same when he'd told her about the letters—as though she was realizing she'd made a terrible mistake. But then she turned and climbed into the capsule. McCready could see two seats, one behind the other. Carlita climbed into the rear and Solano quickly joined her. He then flicked a switch on a control panel. The door slid closed. McCready saw the gantry extend thirty feet out over the void. He realized what was going to happen.

There was a pause of about half a minute, and then, without warning, the capsule slid down the gantry and out into thin air.

It dropped like a stone.

Five seconds later a large parachute billowed from the top and the plunge into the abyss was halted.

But McCready didn't have time to watch.

He raced back to the center and the way out to the balcony. He was right by the window—the comms should work. He pressed the throat mike.

"Craig, do you copy? Do you copy?"

After an agonizing few seconds there was a crackle, and then the reassuring voice of Richards came on the line.

"John, what's happening? You okay?"

"No! I need immediate evac from the residence. I managed to get in, but things are bad. The place is set to blow and I have to get out of here. The only way is if I can get onto the balcony and you pick me up from there. But it needs to be now!"

There wasn't even a second's pause.

"Okay," said Richards. "We're on our way. Be there quick as we can." And he clicked off.

McCready had to now see if he could stop the countdown and find out what Solano's plan was.

He sprinted to the keypad where Solano had initiated the self-destruct. But there was no clue how to deactivate it.

He couldn't waste time.

He had to find out the endgame.

He ran back into the main part of the residence. He was about to head up the stairs to the control room he'd seen earlier, when he spotted a well-lit room at the back.

He walked toward it.

When he reached the entrance, he stopped dead. He stared at the Aston Martin, hardly able to believe what he was looking at. Something told him it was the real thing. Solano wasn't the sort of guy to have a replica. It took all his willpower to tear himself away and concentrate on the task at hand.

He ran up the stairs to the control room. He had to try

and find out what Solano was going to do, and if he couldn't, at least where he was going. He had mentioned an island, but what island—and where?

And then he hesitated.

He realized he was more concerned about stopping Solano than what happened to Carlita.

Where she was concerned, he was beyond caring.

She was dead to him.

What she'd done had changed everything—changed him.

He thought a part of him would never be the same again.

And he didn't like it.

Chapter Thirty-Nine

When Richards received the call from McCready, he could hear the tension in his voice and realized the seriousness of the situation. But he also heard something else. It was a neutral, almost vacant tone he'd never heard before. It didn't sound like his friend, and it concerned him. But there wasn't time to worry about that now.

He turned to Charlie, who was lying on the grass next to him.

"Okay, we've got to move. John's in trouble."

Immediately Charlie jumped up, and, along with Porter, they ran into the Chinook.

Charlie ignored the pre-flight checks and went straight to the engine start-up. A couple of minutes later the rotors were spinning at full speed and the chopper lifted off with a roar of power. As they cleared the airfield Richards noticed the Learjet had been pulled out onto the tarmac and was preparing to leave.

He looked up at the mountain and wondered what the

hell had gone on up there. McCready had never mentioned Carlita and that had to be bad.

McCready ran into the control room. He looked around desperately, trying to get a sense of the place. All the computer screens were still on. Solano clearly didn't expect McCready to get out of there alive.

"Self-destruct has been activated. You have five minutes to leave the building," said the computerized voice.

"Shit!"

He clicked on a file on the center screen, but all that happened was a small window opened saying to enter biometric ID. He glanced at the keyboard and saw a fingerprint sensor. There was no way he could get into this.

Alongside the computer was a pile of folders. He grabbed them and flicked through them.

In one was a map of Florida with a marker on it. For a moment he thought it might be where Solano had gone, but then other papers were related to the weapon they'd brought up from the wreck of the plane. The marker was the detonation location. He grabbed them anyway and stuffed them into a plastic zip folder he found on the desk.

The next file had another map with a number of markers on it and a series of figures next to them. Could be where Solano had gone. It went into the folder.

He was looking for anything that might be of interest, when he heard the roar of helicopter rotors from below. He checked his watch—three minutes.

He ran back downstairs and raced to the windows at the front.

It was going to be tight.

As he reached the glass he could see the Chinook, its

nose right outside the balcony, but it was way off the edge—too far.

He ran to the door that led out to the balcony and pressed the DOOR OPEN button.

But nothing happened.

He felt a rise of panic. He clicked the comms mike.

"The door won't open."

Richards' calm voice came over the comms.

"John, we can't get close enough. The rotors will hit the rock. Is there any other way out?"

McCready paced around, trying to think. He could see Richards and Charlie in the cockpit only fifty feet away. He held up a hand, as though for them to wait.

He ran to the end where the wind howled around the escape capsule bay. He walked into it and checked the walls and floor in case there were any parachutes. There weren't. He'd been right about the escape route—he just hadn't figured on the capsule.

"Self-destruct has been activated. You have one minute to leave the building."

He ran back into the main room and then stopped dead. He had an idea. But he almost dismissed it as soon as he'd thought of it—it could never work. But there was no other option. He smiled to himself. *If you're gonna go out, it may as well be in style!*

He ran back into the main part of the residence, clicking the comms as he went.

"Craig, I haven't time to explain. Turn the chopper round. Hold station as close to the center of the balcony as you can… And open the loading ramp."

"Open the loading ramp?" came the confused reply.

"Yeah, and stand back."

McCready was still at speed. He ran into the space

where the Aston Martin was sitting pristine in the middle of the spotlessly white room.

He pulled open the driver's door and climbed inside, throwing the plastic folder onto the passenger seat. He almost wanted to savor the moment, but there was no time. He turned the key. The throaty roar echoed around the chamber. He flicked up the central console and looked at the switches for the optional extras. He shook his head. There was no time to play.

And then he wondered something.

But he didn't have time to think about it.

Above him there was a massive explosion. It was followed by several others. Ahead, he could see the upper level of the residence start to collapse.

He pulled the door shut, pushed down on the clutch, rammed it into gear and floored the accelerator.

The DB5 leaped forward as though unleashed from its cage after so long. He fishtailed out into Main Street and sped down past the various rooms on either side. He marveled at the surreal nature of what he was doing as he flashed past the gym and spa on his left—the pool on his right.

But now he had to concentrate.

Ahead was the exit to the balcony through the wide double glass doors. Beyond, he could see the Chinook maneuvering into position. The rear was coming into view but it was a hell of a lot further out than he'd hoped. It looked to be about thirty feet, and it was also too high. The loading ramp was coming down slowly—painfully slowly.

It may not be enough.

But he was approaching the glass doors at fifty miles per hour. He glanced down at the controls in the center console.

What the hell!

He flicked the switch for the machine guns that were located in the indicator lights. Immediately there was a roar as they opened fire, smashing the glass to smithereens.

"Jesus Christ, they work!"

He could hardly believe it.

But then something in the rear-view mirror caught his eye—a fireball racing toward him. He put his foot to the floor and wanted to close his eyes, but he daren't. The car shot through what was left of the doors. Another blast of the guns took out the balcony surround.

And then the Aston flew off the end of the balcony and out over the thousand-foot drop.

Ahead he could see the beckoning safety of the cargo bay of the Chinook that was finally in position.

Time seemed to stand still.

He could see the open mouths of Richards and Porter as they stared in shock at the car flying toward them, and then flinging themselves against the sides of the helicopter.

The Aston crashed down into the cargo bay.

McCready jammed his foot on the brakes, but they were old and clearly hadn't been used in years. They barely stopped his onward charge.

Great, the machine guns work but the brakes don't!

He yanked the handbrake for all it was worth. It made a slight difference but he still slammed into the end of the hold with a mighty CRUNCH. The lack of air bags and seatbelt meant there was nothing to stop him smashing his head into the windscreen.

Through a daze he could see Richards and Porter coming to help.

But they weren't out of danger yet.

The fireball exploded out into the valley, engulfing the Chinook. A piece of a metal girder flew out with the force of the explosion, smashing into the rotors. There was the terrible sound of screaming metal from the engines.

The helicopter lurched forward.

It started to go out of control and it was headed in only one direction.

Down.

Chapter Forty

Inside the escape pod, everything was calm. Both passengers were securely fastened in their seats with five-point rally harnesses. The main chute had deployed as planned and a computer-controlled guidance system had taken over to fly them in to land at the airfield in the valley.

As they glided down toward the field, Solano noticed a Chinook lift off and head for the mountain. He watched it closely. But he didn't worry. Even if it was in any way connected to McCready, there was no way they could help him now. They were too late.

A minute later the capsule drifted down for a smooth landing on the grass in the field at the end of the runway. After the capsule had come to a halt Solano glanced back at Carlita. He was so proud of her. He had watched her with McCready, and while he had noticed a slight waver when he had told her about the letters, she had remained strong. She had remained loyal. And he could look forward to their final weeks together as he saw through his pledge to the world.

A few seconds later Mendes came running up to the capsule. He eased open the door and looked inside.

"Are you okay, sir?" He nodded at Carlita.

"Yes, thank you, Juliano. Is the plane ready?"

"Yes, sir. Anytime you like."

"Right now would seem like a good idea."

Mendes helped Solano and Carlita out of the capsule.

They headed over to the jet that was waiting at the end of the runway. There was no worry about a take-off delay. Solano owned the airfield—anyone else would have to wait.

Ten minutes later the Learjet sped down the tarmac and up into the clear Swiss air.

Solano didn't even look back at the home he'd lived in for more than ten years—he would never be returning.

He reached over and kissed Carlita on the cheek. Then gripped her hand. She turned to smile at him, but then, as she looked out of the small oval window to her side, her expression was one of faraway confusion and regret.

The Chinook was falling, and falling fast.

In the cockpit, Charlie was in the fight of her life to save the stricken aircraft and everyone on board. Helicopters were difficult to fly at the best of times, but with one of the twin rotors damaged and providing little lift, it was like driving a truck on ice with no steering.

She slowly managed to control the spin the giant machine had entered. But there was nowhere to land. She scanned ahead, but there was several thousand feet of air before the valley floor below. The low Alp was too far away —they'd miss it by a mile.

And then she saw something.

There was no way.

But she didn't have a choice.

She gripped the controls harder and set her mind on what she had to do.

In the cargo bay Porter had helped McCready out of the car. He was still dazed from the crash, but he was alive, which was something not entirely expected.

Porter looked at him and then the car, and then back at McCready.

"Don't tell me, it's McCready, John McCready!"

McCready was about to give a wiseass reply when they were hurled forward against the bulkhead as the helicopter started to drop. Porter and Richards clung on for dear life. McCready managed to stagger into the cockpit.

When he got there, Charlie's face was a mask of concentration as she tried to control the plunging machine.

Ahead, McCready could see the deep valley and the cables for the cable car strung across it. He couldn't believe what he thought she was trying to do, but he knew now was not the time to ask questions.

Charlie wrestled the controls. And while she had managed to stabilize the fall, the Chinook was rocking from side to side. The cables were a hundred feet below. It was a couple of thousand feet to the pylon on top of the low Alp.

They were coming up fast.

At the last second she stalled the helicopter, bringing the nose up so the wheels at the rear would hook around the first cable—like a slow-motion landing on an aircraft carrier.

There was a tug back in the forward motion. It looked like the wheels had caught securely. She then dropped the nose gently, but it was still a fifteen-ton aircraft straddling two cables, and there was no telling if they could support the full weight for very long. She kept the rotors spinning to try to provide as much lift as possible.

She turned to McCready.

"Get the others ready. I'm going to try and slide down to the pylon. The door should be opposite it. Hopefully you'll be able to just step out when we get there."

McCready stared at her. He'd always thought he thought outside the box, but this was an entirely different box.

"What are you waiting for?" said Charlie. "Last time, you crossed over from a crashing C-130 on a refueling hose. This is child's play!" She grinned, but McCready could hear the strain in her voice.

He gave her a smile and a nod and then headed back to the cargo bay.

When he told the others what was going on, they just stood there, incredulous. McCready was the first to move. He crossed over to the door and pulled it open. The wind swept into the hold. As he looked out, he could see they were moving down the cables, but there was very little control. There would be moments of acceleration and then a sharp braking that jerked them to a halt—and then more sliding.

They could see the pylon. It was now about three hundred feet away.

"I'll go and get Charlie," said Porter.

"No," said McCready. "Let her concentrate. She'll be here as soon as she can."

They watched in fear as the helicopter continued its unstable ride down the cables.

And then they were there.

They came to a crashing halt at the top of the pylon.

The screaming rotors added to the sense of drama and urgency. McCready helped Richards out onto the pylon first. His clothes were whipped and slammed in the downwash. Porter wanted to go for Charlie, but McCready insisted he get out. A second later, Charlie ran in from the cockpit.

Moments later there was a grinding, wrenching sound from the cables. They were starting to give way—stretching, causing the Chinook to tip alarmingly. McCready fell back into the cargo bay. Charlie helped him up. They climbed up to the door that was now above them. Porter reached over and grabbed her hand, pulling her up onto the pylon.

The Chinook slipped some more. The nose dropped sharply. Eager hands reached for McCready, when he remembered something.

"Shit! The folder!"

He let go of Richards, who was waiting to haul him onto the pylon.

The cables groaned. They were coming apart.

McCready slid down to the Aston. He pulled open the passenger door and grabbed the folder he had taken from Solano's office. He managed to pull himself up what was now an almost vertical slope to the door above. He grabbed the side of the door and reached up for Richards' hand. It was inches away, but suddenly it was as though his friend was pulling his hand back.

What the hell is he doing?

But Richards wasn't pulling his hand back.

With a final ear-piercing groan, followed by an almighty crack, one of the cables gave way. The whole nose of the Chinook tipped down. The rotors smashed against the side of the pylon, disintegrating in a demented spinning death.

The helicopter was now hanging from the rear wheels

looped over the second cable. But this was too much for the undercarriage. With another crack, both of the wheels broke off, sending the helicopter plummeting into the valley below with McCready still inside.

Chapter Forty-One

All McCready could do was hang on for dear life. He was pinned against the bulkhead leading to the cockpit. As he looked up he could see the sky and the side of the cliff face flying past through the open rear of the Chinook.

It seemed like he'd been dropping forever but then there was a massive crash as the helicopter hit a steep snow slope in a rock gulley. What was left of the rotors were smashed off with a grinding, wrenching scream. Snow and ice flashed past the tail ramp at the rear, but the helicopter was still upright, albeit almost vertically.

From what McCready could remember, the slope leveled off to some degree, before ending in a rock wall that dropped a thousand feet straight down to the lake in the valley below.

He didn't have much time.

He managed to stand and make his way into the cockpit. The view ahead was terrifying. The slope did level off but not by much. They were on an unstoppable headlong charge over the edge if he couldn't do something about it.

He looked at the controls. But there was no point. The rotors were gone. The wheels were gone, and the underside was acting like the ultimate toboggan.

He had to get out.

He pulled himself back into the hold and looked out the back. If he tried to jump he'd almost certainly be killed.

And then his gaze fell on the Aston.

It was the only option.

He jumped into the driver's seat and started the engine. It took several agonizing attempts but then it fired. He heard that glorious growl once more. He rammed it into reverse and looked out the back.

"Here goes nothing!"

He released the clutch and the car shot backward. Within seconds he was in bright sunlight as the DB5 flew out of the rear of the doomed helicopter and onto the snow.

But his problems were far from over. He was still sliding down the slope out of control. The only difference was he was now in a car and not a helicopter.

The slope was at more than forty-five degrees, and the car was heading after the Chinook—fast.

He spun the wheel from side to side trying to slalom to slow down like a skier, but it didn't work. In frustration he turned the wheel all the way and yanked on the handbrake to try to skid to a stop. And it might have worked, but for a rock hidden beneath the snow.

It smashed into the side, throwing the car into roll. It spun, over and over, tossing McCready around as though he was in a washing machine.

Finally it righted itself.

But it hadn't stopped sliding.

Ahead, he could see the drop at the edge of the thousand-foot cliff approaching fast. If he needed any more proof, the Chinook suddenly disappeared over the edge.

He had to get out.

He grabbed the door handle and pushed.

Nothing happened.

He tried again, but the mechanism must have been damaged in the roll. He climbed into the passenger seat and tried the other door—but it was the same.

Shit!

He was trapped.

He looked ahead. The drop was rapidly approaching. He realized this was it.

This was how he was going to die.

He was almost resigned to his fate when for some reason the film the car had featured in popped into his head.

And he almost laughed out loud.

"I hope you had *all* the extras fitted, Victor!"

And without hesitation, as the DB5 flew out over the edge, he flipped up the top of the gear lever and pressed the little red button.

Immediately there was the sound of small charges blowing the roof panel above him. There was then a loud roar as the rockets in the ejector seat below him fired. He only just managed to grab the folder as he was shot upward.

The seat flew in a high arc behind the car. He traveled about fifty feet into the air, but because of the angle of the slope, he only had about ten feet to fall before landing on a cushion of snow.

He watched as, way below, the Aston crashed down in the center of the lake with a massive splash, the sound barely carrying up the mountain.

McCready lay back, hardly able to believe he was alive. The cold seeped through his jacket, but he didn't care. He spread his arms and legs, making the shape of an angel in the snow, and he laughed. He then took in a series of deep breaths of mountain air.

When he had calmed down, he lifted his left hand. It was still gripping the folder. There was work to do—but for now, McCready enjoyed the best feeling in the world.

Being alive.

The only question was how was a St. Bernard with the brandy going to find him up there?

He was still pondering the question, when he looked up and smiled.

It had started to snow.

Chapter Forty-Two

The following day McCready sat opposite Martin Steel in his office at 10 Downing Street.

He ached all over. He'd suffered severe bruising to his left side and a slight compression of the neck as he'd ejected out of the car, and was still feeling slightly shell-shocked from the experience.

After gathering together in the small village, the four friends had made their way back to the UK. Porter, Charlie and Richards had returned to Scotland, while McCready had arranged to meet Steel and finally tell him everything that had gone on.

McCready looked grim as he stared across the desk at Steel. Since recovering from surviving the previous day he'd slumped into a subdued state of mind following what had happened.

Steel looked through the documents McCready had retrieved from Solano's office and then glanced up at him, a curious expression on his face.

"And you won't tell me what happened with the girl?"

McCready was stony-faced.

"You don't need to know, other than things were not as they seemed, okay?"

Steel gave him a final look and then turned back to the file. Before he continued, he passed a sheet of A4 over to McCready.

"Here, this is for you."

McCready picked it up, glanced at it, and frowned. He looked at Steel with raised eyebrows.

"Really? You're serious?"

He dropped the invoice for 'One Chinook helicopter' back onto the desk.

"It was all I could do to stop the Americans from adding a Blackhawk, but then I did remind them you'd saved their ass, to put it mildly." And then he added, "It's not like you can't afford it."

McCready glanced at the file Steel had just been reading.

"How about that for payment?"

Steel looked at him. A wry smile spread across his face.

"We'll see."

McCready smiled, but then the tone turned serious.

"So, what do you think?"

McCready had had a chance to look through the papers more closely, and he'd seen that the map with the markers on was of Antarctica, and the numbers written on it were coordinates, but beyond that he had no idea whether it was important.

"I'm not sure. We've no idea what the markers represent. Antarctica is a massive continent, and there's no clue as to the significance of the positions. I'll pass it over to some of the intel guys, see if there's anything they can match it up to. We've had some concerning messages coming out from down there, so this could be of interest. The important thing now is where Solano has gone. Whatever he's been planning in this grand gesture of his is for real. You don't go through what he's just shown the world and then call their bluff."

"No? What if that's exactly what he wants you to think?"

Steel thought on that for a moment. "I don't think so. Having listened to his talks and videos, what he says makes perfect sense from one standpoint. And he's right—the problems will never be solved, again, for the reasons he gives. Governments just aren't prepared to do what's necessary to stop what's coming."

"So you agree with him?"

"I'm not saying that. He's looking at it from a higher perspective—the richest man in the world perspective, where anything is possible if you throw enough money at it. Back down in the real world things don't work like that."

"So there's nothing the world can do?"

"Yeah, there's plenty, but it won't."

"So mankind just walks off the proverbial cliff?"

"Pretty much."

The words hung in the air.

McCready eased himself into a more comfortable position in his chair and groaned as he did so.

"You okay?" asked Steel.

"I'll live."

"Look, John, I can maybe guess what happened with the girl up there, and thank you for bringing the information to me. We'll see what we can do from here. Go home, have some rest. Lick your wounds and live to fight another day." He paused. "Anyway, I thought there was someone over in California." He raised his eyebrows.

"Is there anything you don't know?"

The question wasn't meant to be serious, but Steel thought about it for a second before answering.

"No, I don't think so."

McCready smiled again.

"One final thing. Do you have any idea where Solano has gone? We have to find him."

McCready shook his head slowly.

"The only thing he said was that they were going to an island—which doesn't exactly narrow it down."

Steel was thoughtful.

"Okay, we'll take it from here. Go home. Relax. Your part's over."

McCready stood slowly and stretched. He reached out to shake Steel's hand.

"Oh, before you go, give me the invoice," said Steel.

McCready glanced at him and then handed him the invoice for the Chinook. Steel took it and tore it into pieces.

"Needed a new paint job anyway!"

McCready grinned and they shook hands.

As he left, he thought it would be sometime before the two of them saw each other again.

When McCready walked into his home it was going dark. The house was uninviting and the depression he had been feeling only deepened.

He crossed over to a cupboard below the stairs and flicked on the heating. He left the lights off and walked through to the oak bar by the moonlight that was flitting in through the windows. He poured himself a brandy and made his way to the lower level of the living room and stared out over the bay. He was about to sit down on the sofa, exhausted, when his eyes fell on the poncho on the wall. He stared at it for several seconds. He then put the brandy down on the glass table and walked over to the wall.

There had been three objects hanging there. One, a pair of gold-plated pistols Prince Khalid Yassin of Saudi Arabia had given him. They had hung on the wall for many years as a reminder of the reprobate Yassin had been in McCready's eyes, and also to remind him of the true value of things as mere objects. But when Yassin had proven to be the best of friends, McCready had seen the gift in a new light, and after having them valued, he had now secured them in a vault at a bank in Oban.

The second object was a spear he'd been given by a Masai tribal chief for saving his daughter when he had been working in Kenya many years previously. The third item had been the poncho Carlita had given him.

As he stared at it, his face hardened. How could he have been so stupid—so taken in? The anger would come, but for now it was just shame, disappointment and a deep hurt inside. He had never felt so used, so betrayed, in his entire life.

Without another thought, he walked up to the wall and pulled the poncho from it. He then made his way out of the house and down to the large double garage at the back with the garden beyond.

He opened the roller door, found a small incinerator and a box of matches. He also grabbed a can of petrol. He carried them down to the garden, careful to avoid the small grave of the otter pup he had buried there the year before.

He set up the incinerator, bundled the poncho up and placed it in the wire frame. He then splashed some petrol on it from the can.

He stepped back for a few moments, and then, without

any emotion, struck a match and tossed it onto the pile of material. Within seconds the petrol ignited. It burned with a fierce intensity—reflecting the same fierce intensity of feelings McCready had had for Carlita.

He watched the flames as they flickered in the night, the embers flaking off and spiraling up into the black sky above, like parts of his soul, forever gone—forever lost.

Never to be whole again.

Chapter Forty-Three

Martin Steel sat in one of the twenty padded chairs around the conference table in Cabinet Office Briefing Room A, or COBRA for short. The room was fairly small, which enhanced the tension that was felt by the four people who were at the table. They were joined by two others on a wall-sized video screen at the far end.

The room was used in times of crisis, usually in respect of the United Kingdom, but this time it was a crisis facing the world, and one that was about as serious as it could get.

Sitting next to Steel was Dominic Carter. Also present was Dr. Sarah Marks, the UK's leading climate change scientist. She was a tall brunette in her mid-forties and just the kind of person you needed in moments like this—intelligent, quick-thinking, and what Steel liked most about her, she didn't suffer fools gladly or stand for any bullshit. The final person at the table was Professor Helmut Bressler, one of Germany's leading meteorologists. He was someone Marks had recommended attend, given the analysis she had come up with in the short space of time she'd had to study the information Steel had given her. This, in turn, was a summary of what McCready had given him, combined with the reports coming out of the Antarctic—something Steel was more and more beginning to think were linked.

Joining them on the video wall was Jerry Patcher, base commander at Halley, and Major Frank Carswell, a nuclear weapons expert.

It looked like they had all had very little sleep.

The mood around the table was somber.

"Okay everyone," started the Prime Minister, "you know why you're here. The world is facing a growing crisis that we don't yet fully understand. There are meetings like this going on in countries across the globe. I hope today you will be able to shed some light on what we might face." He looked over at Marks. "Doctor Marks, if you would like to begin."

"Thank you, Prime Minister."

Marks looked around the faces, both in the room and on the wall.

"I'm afraid what we've come up with is a terrifying prospect. As you know, Victor Solano has made a number of unprecedented threats. His justification for these is to make countries come together to work toward a solution for climate change." She paused. "And in a way, if what I think he is intending to do is correct, he may well achieve his goals. But we can't take that chance, because if he doesn't, millions are going to die."

There was complete silence in the room.

She shuffled the papers in front of her and clicked a key on her laptop. It was connected to a screen that all could see. A map of Antarctica appeared.

"This, as I'm sure you're aware, is a map of Antarctica. The continent holds around seventy percent of the world's fresh water tied up in snow and ice. The predictions are not new. If the ice disappears through global warming, the water the ice is made up of will result in a massive rise in sea level. We've been warning about this for years."

She advanced the slide on the presentation. The map of Antarctica was replaced by one of the world.

"This is the world as we know it today."

Everyone could see the familiar outline of countries. She clicked another key. Immediately the blue of the ocean started to encroach on the land masses, changing the shape of many of the countries until some were completely unrecognizable. The Florida Keys were gone. Much of coastal Asia was gone. After a minute the simulation stopped. All stared at the screen in shock. They had heard the predictions and some may have seen similar graphics before, but now it all seemed very real.

"Not only will the land be underwater, but coastal habitation will disappear. Currently, forty percent of the world's population live within sixty miles of the coast. Much of this will be gone. Ports will have to shut down. National security will be put at risk. Many nuclear power stations are situated on the coast—they will be gone. And not only that, people will have to move. The exodus will make a chapter in the Bible look like a day out for a small village. Put another way, the world will have changed forever. Society will break down. Borders of countries will be irrelevant. In short, the human race will cease to function as a coherent, stable whole, if indeed it ever did."

All eyes were glued to the screen.

"But all this is known. This is coming whether we like it or not. The new issue, that Solano has stated on a number of occasions, is that he is going to play with the timeline. What you have just seen on the screen will take place over many years—not that many, but certainly ten to fifty at least, maybe more. What we think Solano is going to do is compress that into one to five years."

There was an intake of breath around the table.

On the screen Patcher looked out with incredulity on his face. "But how can he do this? It's impossible!"

"Well actually, Mr. Patcher," said Marks, "no, it's not."

She again had their complete attention.

The map of Antarctica appeared back on the screen.

"If we go back to the snow and ice and look at it in conjunction with some information acquired by Mr. Steel, we have this." She clicked a key and eight red markers appeared on the map—three in the west and five over to the east. "These markers are thought to be locations of interest to Victor Solano. There have been reports of unregistered helicopter flights in the regions associated with these locations provided by Mr. Patcher. There has also been a report by a team of scientists that at one of the sites they found something buried in the ice, and it was giving off an extreme amount of radiation."

"What was it?" asked Carswell.

"I'll let Mr. Steel take it from here."

Steel leaned forward. He looked up at the screen and then around at everyone in the room.

"Several months ago, eight nuclear weapons were stolen from a Russian train operating in Ukraine. It never made the news. The Russians wanted to keep it quiet for obvious reasons. The weapons disappeared off the face of the Earth, and to our knowledge, which is pretty good, the Russians never managed to recover them. I believe these nuclear weapons are now located at the red markers you see on the screen."

There was another collective intake of breath.

"That's why you're here, Frank," said Steel glancing at the screen. The army major nodded seriously.

"But what would that achieve?" This from Patcher.

Steel continued. "These weapons are hydrogen bombs. Each one has an explosive equivalent of ten million tons of TNT. Put into perspective, the bomb dropped on Hiroshima was equivalent to fifteen thousand tons of TNT." There wasn't a sound in the room. "If they were detonated, they would produce blast waves that would travel many miles in all directions. But more importantly they would massively raise the temperature within that radius and beyond."

He paused, and as he looked around, he could see they were starting to put two and two together, and they weren't looking happy about it.

Steel indicated for Marks to continue.

"If that happened," she said, "the combined blasts would raise the temperature over a significant proportion of the continent for a period of time. Compressing years of global warming into a few minutes. And he's been clever with the placement of the weapons, if indeed that's what they are. There are five over to the east, where the ice is at its thickest—up to 16,000 feet, and three in the west, which could be designed to trigger the destabilization of the glaciers that run into the Amundsen Sea—principally the Thwaites and Pine Island glaciers. If these are caused to break off, move faster into the sea, or are vaporized, they alone could contribute to over three meters of sea level rise."

She let that hang there.

"I think you can all realize the implication of this. The water that wasn't vaporized in the initial blasts would be melted and run off into the sea. Then there are the physical effects. The initial shock and following ground tremors could cause ice shelves to become unstable—break off, also contributing to sea level rise."

She paused. All the faces were masked in shock.

"Don't get me wrong. He's not going to blow up a continent. Even if he carries out his plan, Antarctica will still be there, along with much of its snow and ice, but the effect of the combined blasts *will* raise sea levels worldwide and in a very short period of time."

"But surely the ice that's vaporized will just be gone," said the Prime Minister.

"You might think so," said Marks, "but it's not as simple as that. Helmut, perhaps you could explain."

Bressler moved forward in his chair.

"Of course. When the ice is vaporized, it isn't destroyed as such. It condenses as droplets in the atmosphere and then falls later as rain, and while much of this might fall on the land, this would then enter the river systems and make its way down to the seas and oceans, contributing to the rise in sea level. I'm afraid there's no getting away from it, any ice that's 'destroyed' will still eventually add to sea level rise."

"Thank you, Helmut," said Marks.

She looked around at the shocked faces.

"So, he wasn't lying. And he's not bluffing. And it looks like he will do this unless he can be stopped." A curious smile crossed her lips.

She looked up.

"In fact, you know, it's quite brilliant. He is going to do exactly what he threatened to do, and it could work."

"Yeah, in a Thanos sort of way," said Steel under his breath.

"But it would only work," said Marks, "if everyone came together to solve the subsequent rise in sea level."

"Yes," said the Prime Minister, "if everyone came together."

"We can but hope," said Marks.

"I'm afraid I don't survive on hope," said Steel pointedly. He paused before continuing. "So, as you can see, we have a massive problem on our hands." He looked at the screens. "Frank, you know the weapons we're dealing with here. I'll talk to you privately later, but I need you to draw up a simple protocol to disarm them. We may have to get unqualified people in the field to carry this out. Mr. Patcher, I'll be in touch with you as well re the next step, so please stand by for now and I'll call you shortly." Patcher nodded on the screen, but he was clearly looking numb. "Okay, if anyone has anything to add, please say it now." He looked around at the faces, but they were all so shocked no one had anything to say. "Right, that will be all. If you think of anything else, you know where I am."

The meeting was concluded. The screens went blank. Marks and Bressler packed up their things, and, after a "thank you" from Carter for coming, left the room. When they'd gone, Carter poured two cups of coffee from the heated jug on the table and pushed one over to Steel.

"Okay, Martin, what's the plan?"

Steel looked at his old friend.

"The way I see it, we have to do two things. We have to work on the assumption Solano is going to do what he says he will do. If there really are nuclear weapons at those sites, he's clearly prepared to use them. We've seen that in Florida. To have gone this far means he'll carry out the threat. Coupled with that, the admission that he's dying of cancer means he's nothing to lose if he's found and caught. So, the first thing is to evacuate the teams out of Antarctica. It's something they do every winter anyway, so the systems and procedures are in place to do that quickly. We also need Major Carswell to talk to the men and women down there and see if there is a way they can try and locate and disarm the bombs. They would probably be suicide missions, but we have to try everything, and people down there are, by their very nature, up for a challenge. Also, being one of the guys or girls who tried to save the world wouldn't look too bad on your resumé, even if it was posthumously."

Carter was making notes.

"Okay," he said, "and the other thing?"

"We have to find Solano. See if we can stop him before he detonates the bombs. We've no idea of his timeline or even where the hell he is, so that's a long shot, but we have to try everything."

"So, no one knows where he is?"

"On an island somewhere. At least that's what John McCready says."

At this, Carter raised an eyebrow.

"Doesn't exactly help much, does it?"

McCready stared out over the bay in western Scotland from the raised deck at the back of his house. The weather was turning and the wind was starting to whip up the waves and roll the water in further up the beach. He liked it like this. It reflected the mood he was currently in.

He had slept fitfully, the events of the previous weeks filling his thoughts. But the one thing he couldn't shake was how he had been used. The morning had brought a new perspective, but as his gaze fell on the incinerator in the garden, the ashes of the poncho were still there. It had left a large gap on the wall and a large hole in his life. The wall could be fixed—there was now just the spear, which he would have to move to the center, and that would be for another day—but his life, that was a whole different matter.

There was nothing more he could do to help Steel with Solano. He had to try and focus on what was important now. And to be more accurate—*who* was important now. And that was a question with an easy answer.

When he thought of Clare he thought of the entire opposite of what Carlita now meant to him. Clare was the embodiment of what he had thought Carlita might have been in his life—but she was gone, a memory, albeit a painful one, that would fade with time but was still raw. What he needed was time with the here and now.

Time with Clare.

And without further thought he knew he had to speak to her.

He walked back inside and grabbed the phone. He checked the time and dialed. It would be the middle of the night in Los Angeles, but he needed to talk to her. It rang six times and was answered.

"Hello," said a clearly sleepy Clare.

"Hi," he said.

There was a pause and then a more awake Clare answered.

"John, how are you? Where are you?"

He paused, just glad to hear her voice.

"You got a minute?"

He felt she was waking by the moment, her voice sounding happier and more eager.

"Of course. I've missed you so much."

McCready paused. He felt a lump in his throat. It was just what he needed.

And so over the next half hour he told her everything. About the drama on the wreck. The death of Logan. That

Carlita had been taken and he'd gone to try and find her. And then of the ultimate betrayal and how he had felt so used. He skipped over some of the details of the escape from the mountain in Switzerland, but he could hear, as the story unfolded, that she was living every minute of what he was telling her. When he finished he was sure he could hear a sob at the end of the line. There was silence for a moment.

"John, I'm so sorry. I can't believe she did that to you." But McCready could also hear relief in her voice. "When are you coming home? When can I look after you?" He could now hear the joy in her words.

"Soon. Really soon," he said. In fact, he wished he could jump on a plane right there and then, but there were some things he had to sort out first, and one of them had to do with the small velvet box at the back of his sock drawer in LA.

It was time.

He was about to say something when he heard the PING of an incoming text on his phone. He pulled it away from his ear for a second to see what it was. The message was short and it was cryptic. He suddenly stood very still. Then put the phone back to his ear.

"I have to go, something's come up. I love you. I'll call you soon. I promise."

McCready slowly lowered the phone and looked at the message carefully and deliberately so he didn't miss any of its meaning. He then walked into the living room and sat down and read it again.

It looked like he wouldn't be heading to Los Angeles anytime soon.

Chapter Forty-Four

Victor Solano looked out of the oval window of the Learjet at the turquoise water rushing below the port wing.

The flight to a small island off the north coast of Mauritius had taken eleven hours, and although he had slept, he knew the next couple of days would be the most important of his life.

He felt the light bump as the wheels touched the ground and then the roar of the reverse thrust as the pilot slowed the aircraft to prevent it disappearing into the water of the lagoon at the end of the short dirt strip runway.

The hideaway had been built five years previously and Solano had an arrangement with the president of Mauritius that the identity of its owner should remain confidential. This had benefited the Mauritius government because of the funding of numerous projects about which the president was extremely happy. The country had received new buildings and infrastructure and in return Solano received the ultimate in privacy and discretion. Other than his home in the Alps, it was the one place he could go to get away from the rest of the world. The difference here was that no one knew he was here, and right now that was of paramount importance.

The jet taxied round from the end of the dirt strip and pulled to a halt at a small hut halfway down the runway. An open-top jeep was waiting to pick them up.

The steward lowered the steps at the front of the plane and Solano, Carlita and Mendes walked down into the hot sunshine. It was like a new world after Europe and the tension they had experienced there. Carlita leaned her head back and let the rays wash over her face before putting on a pair of stylish sunglasses to protect against them.

When they were all aboard, the jeep set off.

The island was a mile long by half a mile wide. It was surrounded on all sides by a fringing reef that shielded it from the fiercest of storms that could blow in off the Indian Ocean.

They drove along a narrow track through vegetation on both sides, before coming to a wall of palm trees with a small gap through the middle. Among the trees was a security building and a few small villas where the staff lived.

And then they emerged out onto the shoreline.

A covered parking area was right in front of them. Beyond that, a walkway extended into the lagoon. At the end of it was Solano's home, though it was unlike any home most people lived in.

It floated on the water and was shaped like a large curved Y. It was three hundred feet from front to back and four hundred feet at its widest. It was built in such a way that the whole structure could be towed to a new location should the need arise.

You entered from the walkway into an enclosed, air-conditioned atrium. This led to the rest of the building through wide open-plan spaces that spread out on either side to make up the Y shape.

Its surface was wooden planking like the deck of a boat. On this was built a comprehensive array of rooms, layered back over three levels. There were even areas of grass with small palm trees around the edges to provide an eco feel to the structure. At the tip of one end of the Y was a helipad.

On the first level, on the seaward side, a large oval infinity pool looked out over the lagoon and the reef beyond. On the uppermost level was a covered space where you could relax on sofas with deep cushions, as well as, at one end, an open-air dining area for meals with a view. To one side, a tall mast carried an array of communications aerials, satellite dishes and radar equipment.

One of the staff was waiting to greet them at the end of the walkway. They said their hellos and then walked into the amazing home. Their luggage followed not far behind.

Mendes immediately headed off to make sure everything was in order and the provisions were well stocked. It was an almost unnecessary act as the staff were efficient, discreet and loyal.

Solano was keen to unwind after the trip, but he had to check on any progress from the world leaders and the status of the operation in the Antarctic. Time was running out and there were decisions to be made if he didn't receive the response he was looking for.

He made his way down a set of wide stairs to a lower level where he had an office not dissimilar from the one in Switzerland. From here he could monitor and control his empire. Basically, all the systems and information was duplicated from his home in the Alps.

He walked over to the computer and switched it on. He accessed the server that handled the secure communications and then logged in. There was a short message from President Stevens. It basically said to hang tight. There were developments, and he should hold back from whatever he was threatening to do. Solano shook his head. He knew they were playing for time. And while he would give them a certain amount of it, he had a deadline from which he was not going to be persuaded to go beyond. At the end of the day, the issues were so profound he could not see how a few short hours, even a day or two, would make a difference. The problems had been staring at them for years, and at some point someone had to say enough was enough.

He fired up the screens around the room and checked the camera feeds that were coming in from the Antarctic. Everything appeared normal. When he was sure everything was in order, ready for the final stage, he felt he could start to relax. He would talk to Stevens later. Right now he needed a drink.

He walked back up onto the main level and over to a cooler in the kitchen. He pulled out a beer and popped the top. He took a sip and enjoyed the flavor. He then made his way up to his bedroom on the second level. The suite stretched over an entire floor of the complex. It had an unrestricted view over the lagoon. As he walked in, Carlita had already changed into a svelte black bikini that showed off her body to perfection. She walked into his arms.

"We're on the final leg, my love. I am so happy," said Solano. She reached up to kiss him on the lips. They held each other for a full minute.

"I have something to do and then I'll join you," he said.

Carlita made her way out onto the wide balcony that encircled the suite. There was a small pool at one end, with a view as equally impressive as the larger one on the main deck.

She slipped into the cool water, feeling it caress her skin. She dipped below the surface, pushed off and allowed her body to float the full length of the pool. Once at the other end she stood up and leaned her elbows over the side. She looked out over the beautiful reef that surrounded the island just inches below the surface. On the shore she could see some birds ducking and diving through the air, their cries drifting on the wind.

She took a deep breath and thought about the momentous events that were unfolding around her, and those that had happened in the last forty-eight hours.

And she was thinking of John McCready.

And what he had said to her in Switzerland.

She wanted to dismiss it—to assume he was lying, but why would he? He'd always seemed so honest. So real. Everything she had ever known he had done had been to help others—her brother twenty-five years ago, and then, when she had called him out of the blue to help her with a dangerous mission that was nothing to do with him, he had come for her, no questions asked. She just couldn't equate that with a man who would have used her and ignored her all those years ago. What if he had written to her, and her father had stopped her getting the letters? What if her father had taken those she had sent to John? She didn't know how to process it. It had all happened so long ago. It was as though she'd been living in another world, which, in effect, she had. A life with Victor Solano was not reality as most people experienced it. It was a life of privilege and wanting for nothing. She had allowed herself to be drawn into this hypnotic man's grasp and found it impossible to escape. Even during his darker moments she had stayed.

She loved him, of that she was sure, but she was equally sure his hold over her was not healthy. And if she was prepared to face up and question that, what about this whole endeavor? Should she question that too?

On one level, she knew what he was doing was for the right reasons, but did he have the right to inflict what was coming on the world? It was a question she couldn't answer and one she had to wrestle with—or should she just accept what he said? She knew deep down he loved her. The lengths he'd been prepared to go to to keep her demonstrated that.

But had those lengths meant the opposite?

How could he truly love her and treat her the way he sometimes did—as a possession, not a partner?

There were so many questions.

But in that moment she had a flash of realization.

There was no way in a million years McCready would ever have treated her like that—no way.

Maybe she had the answer she'd been looking for.

Her thoughts were interrupted as Solano placed a margarita down on the poolside next to her. He then jumped in the water and swept her up in his arms. He kissed her. She embraced him back, but maybe not with quite the same conviction as before.

"Are you alright?" asked Solano.

She turned to him, a smile on her face.

"Of course, why wouldn't I be? It's just all a lot to take in."

He watched her, his expression one of slight concern.

"I don't know. You were quiet on the flight. In fact, since Switzerland. You're sure seeing him again has nothing to do with it?"

She turned to him sharply—too sharply.

"No, of course not. It's just everything we're doing." She paused. "Are you sure we're doing the right thing, Victor?" She looked him straight in the eyes.

The look of concern on Solano's face only grew.

"I have never been more sure of anything in my life. It's what we've worked so long for."

She turned to stare out over the water.

"I know. I'm sure you're right."

Solano watched her. The concern had not gone away, but along with it there was a certain sadness in his eyes.

Chapter Forty-Five

McCready sat in his office on the first floor of his home. It was situated at the rear and had a wide panoramic view over the bay. The weather was still deteriorating and he could see the clouds scurrying across the sea, growing blacker by the minute. A light drizzle had started and he knew from experience heavy rain would follow. While he would normally welcome such weather, right now he had more important things on his mind.

In front of him was an open laptop. He had come up to the office to work out what to do next.

He was still reeling from the text he had received on his phone. It had been short. It had been cryptic, and it had left him with more questions than answers.

He picked up the phone again and read through it.

It simply said:

> TO REPAY A DEBT.
> MAYBE YOU CAN STOP IT ALL

It was followed by a series of numbers, which, by how many there were and their grouping, were clearly longitude and latitude coordinates.

A seagull squawked outside, distracting him for a moment.

He turned back to the message and opened Google Earth. He watched as the globe spun up on the screen, centering itself on the UK. When it was stable, he entered the coordinates in the search bar and clicked RETURN.

He then waited as the globe moved round and enlarged until the small red marker appeared at a location.

It was positioned on an island off the northern coast of Mauritius. At the scale, it was too small to see clearly. McCready drew two fingers down on the trackpad to zoom in.

As the island grew larger, he could see it in more detail. Overall, it was pretty unremarkable, except for one thing.

It was about a mile long by half a mile wide and much of it was covered with vegetation. There was what looked like a small dirt strip diagonally across one end. It was maybe large enough to land an aircraft—its straightness certainly suggested that was its purpose. There were no roads, though a meandering track led from the dirt strip and disappeared into the vegetation. There were also no large groups of buildings, though he thought he could see what looked like some houses where the trees were thinner on the ground.

However, what was interesting and drew the attention was a large structure built out into the lagoon on the western side of the island. McCready had no idea what it was. From above it looked like the profile of a champagne glass built over the water.

He zoomed in further.

He could see the structure more clearly now, and he let out a breath. It was spectacular. It was like looking down on a superyacht, yet one that had been created with none of the restrictions of the design of a boat. There were a series of decks with pools, dining and lounging areas—even green areas with palm trees. On the top was what looked like a seating area, and to one side, a mast-like structure with radar and communications equipment, but why that would be needed McCready wasn't sure.

He stared at it for several minutes taking in the design and layout.

He then leaned back and reread the message.

And as he looked at the image on the screen showing the structure in the lagoon, three things started to come together: the word DEBT, an island, and the image of an amazing home the equal of the residence in Switzerland.

McCready was in no doubt whatsoever that he was looking at Victor Solano's current location.

But that left a number of questions.

Who had sent the message and what the hell did he do now?

The first was puzzling. The only person he could think of was Carlita, but they had parted so badly, and she had been so cold to him, that he couldn't see that she would have had a change of heart in such a short period of time. Also, as far as she was concerned, he was supposed to be dead, so what made her think he would ever read the message? Also, the fact the message suggested there was a way to stop what Solano was planning to do seemed to go against everything she had told him, which had been her whole life for many years—it was puzzling.

So, could it be a trap of some kind?

Maybe there had been reports on the news about the

incident in Switzerland and his name had come up as being alive. If so, maybe he was being lured there for some reason—but that also made no sense. He could just tell people where Solano was and that would cause all sorts of problems for him. No, this was something else, but he couldn't put his finger on what it was.

For some reason, he believed the message was genuine—everything fitted. He was sure Solano was on that island. So that left the other question, what did he do now?

He looked out over the sea and pondered this for some time.

Eventually, it boiled down to two things.

Should he even bother to do anything? It wasn't his problem, after all. He'd originally become involved because of Carlita, and even if she had sent the message, he had no feelings for her anymore, so what would be the point? But then he thought of the implications of doing nothing. What if Solano carried out his threat, and it did indeed change the world—but for the worse? What if he had been able to do something and hadn't acted? How could he live with himself? So, if he was going to try and do something, that begged the next question, did he tell Martin Steel?

It was entirely possible the whole thing was a hoax—how, he wasn't sure, but would Steel even believe him? He was concerned with the bigger picture, trying to deal with the situation on a global scale—but people would still need to know where Solano was, to be able to try and stop him.

After some more thought, which included contemplating the weather that was progressively closing in, he came to a decision. He would go to Mauritius and see if Solano was really there. If he was, then he would contact Steel. If he wasn't, he'd have a week in the sun and a complete change of scenery. He could maybe even fly Clare out and they could have a much-needed break together.

With the last part of his thoughts seeming more attractive by the minute, he picked up the phone and dialed. It was answered on the fifth ring.

"Hi, John, how's it going?"

"Hi, Craig, we need to have another chat."

Chapter Forty-Six

"Okay, settle down!" shouted Jerry Patcher over the babble of conversation in the canteen at the Halley VI Research Station.

He looked around at the assembled group that had come together in the largest internal area at the complex. What he had to say was for the whole base to hear. It would have far-reaching consequences and mean the upheaval of numerous projects, not to mention the possible death of a number of their complement.

There were fifty people in all. Nyah and Murphy were seated about halfway back. Nyah spotted Bowman entering with a couple of the other pilots and beckoned him over. Murphy groaned and shuffled up to give him space on the already crowded bench seat.

When the last of them had arrived, Patcher turned to everyone, his expression serious.

"Okay, now we're all here"—People threw jeers at the stragglers who had just come in—"I have some news of extreme importance."

At this, everyone quietened down. Patcher was a great base commander and he joked around along with the best of them, but to survive in an environment such as this you had to know when frivolity was allowed and when concentration was necessary.

He had their complete attention.

"There's no easy way to say this, so I am going to be direct and I am going to give you the facts with no sugar-coating. At the end you will have many questions, but there won't be time for that. We need to act on what I am going to say and we need to act now."

He glanced around. All eyes were on him.

"I have just come off a conference call with the British Prime Minister; the UK's national security adviser; Doctor Sarah Marks, whom some of you may know; and Professor Helmut Bressler. There was also an army major present. The reason for this will become apparent shortly." He paused. "You may have seen in the news recently a catastrophe that occurred in Florida." There was muttering in the group. "The explanation given was that the tsunami that killed two hundred and fifty people and flattened the region was caused by an earthquake off the east coast of the Keys." He paused. "That is not what happened."

If he hadn't had their attention before, he did now.

"It was actually caused by a stolen Chinese nuclear AUV that was detonated off the coast deliberately."

There was an intake of breath from all present. Some of the mutterings of earlier now turned into outraged expletives.

"It was carried out as a message from the world's richest man, Victor Solano. The message was something we, and many scientists, have been shouting from the rooftops for many years—that climate change is coming. It's coming fast, and if the world doesn't come together to combat it, many of our coastal cities will end up like Florida—and that will just be the beginning."

The muttering stopped. Many of those present were sympathetic to the cause. The message he was sending was a hundred percent correct.

Patcher continued. "Unfortunately, it doesn't end with Florida. In case the message wasn't enough, which I am led to believe it was not, the main threat he has made is to accelerate climate change from the decades it may realistically take… into a few years."

At this, the gasps were back and everyone started talking at once.

"But how can he?" shouted one of the scientists.

"That's impossible!" shouted another.

Patcher let them have their moment then raised his hand. Gradually they calmed down.

"Unfortunately, it is possible, and I'm about to show you how he intends to do it."

The attention was back.

Patcher flicked on a video projector and stood to the side of the screen behind him. The familiar map of the continent appeared on the wall.

"As you may have heard, there has been some unexplained activity by a number of helicopters in the region. They're black and have been sighted by some of the teams working in the field. It was unclear what the helicopters and their crews were doing—until now."

He clicked the mouse and eight red markers appeared across the white backdrop.

"These are eight locations we believe the occupants of the helicopters have visited and worked at. It appears they have been burying equipment at these sites. For those of you working in this field, you might recognize that five of the locations are centered around the areas of the greatest thickness of ice.

"What has been buried at the sites are Russian nuclear weapons."

He paused, but no one said anything—they were too shocked to respond.

"This is not a joke," continued Patcher. "It's real... Solano's plan is to detonate the weapons if he doesn't receive some sort of cast-iron guarantee from world leaders about cooperating and moving forward to change the way the world and society works. And we all know that will never happen. When the weapons detonate they will vaporize huge areas of snow and ice, and much of what doesn't go up instantly will melt from the subsequent rise in temperature. This will ultimately raise the sea level significantly within the space of a year, with the aim of forcing governments to work together to solve the problem."

There was complete silence.

"We have to assume he will carry out this threat. So, with that in mind, the whole continent is being evacuated of all personnel. It's not like you haven't done it before for the winter season. But this time we're taking *everyone*."

He let this sink in. There was some talk, but most were so numb they sat there staring around, not sure they'd really heard what they'd been told.

Patcher raised his hand again for quiet.

"There is one caveat to that last statement." They fixed their eyes on him again. "Eight teams need to stay behind. This is being coordinated and selected from bases across the territory. Not all bases will be involved, but we have been selected to provide one of them. No one will be forced to participate but we need to send one team."

"What will they do?" asked Murphy. There was a mumbling as others also wanted the answer.

Patcher looked around the group and then took a deep breath.

"They will have to go out to the sites and attempt to disarm the nuclear weapons."

At this there was stunned silence—and then murmurings.

"We're not qualified for that," shouted someone.

Patcher again raised his hand.

"I know, which is why no one will be forced to do this, but they can't get enough specialists down here in the timeframe. With more bad weather coming in, we'll only just be able to get everyone out, and that will be cutting it fine.

"Whoever decides to go will receive step-by-step guidance from Frank Carswell, the major I mentioned earlier. The weapons are thought to be a group that was stolen from a train in Ukraine several months ago. Their type is known and therefore a fairly accurate protocol for their disarmament is known. Major Carswell will talk you through it via a video link in real time. He'll be able to see your actions and stop anything he considers to be dangerous. But people, you must understand one thing—these are unprecedented times and I will not lie to you. Whoever does this… may not return."

He let them talk for a few seconds, then raised his hand again.

"Okay, I know you have questions, but time is of the essence. Go away, think about what I've said, but not for long. I need anyone who is prepared to take on this task to be at my office in half an hour. Everyone else, you need to plan to leave as soon as possible. Pack the basics and report to the transport center when you're ready. Flights out will be arranged on a first come first served basis. It will be fraught. There'll be a lot of waiting around, but we all need to work together to get this done." He looked around at them all again.

"Right, that's it. Good luck!"

When he left the room there was immediate uproar. Some left straight away to go and pack, clearly wanting to be the first out of there. Others stayed to talk. The main topic of conversation was who would be crazy enough to volunteer for a suicide mission. But as the conversations continued, it became clear the type of person who would work at the bottom of the world was also the type of person who was up for activities with a certain element of risk.

So it was that half an hour later there were six people standing outside Jerry Patcher's office.

And one of them was Dr. Nyah Hawthorn.

Chapter Forty-Seven

As the helicopter rotors spun up to speed, Nyah glanced across at Murphy in the back. There were no jokes, no jibes toward Bowman in the front. All of them knew what they were heading into.

Nyah had been standing in line outside Patcher's office for ten minutes, while others had been interviewed inside, when Bowman had walked past. Initially he'd done a double-take when he'd seen her. She had then spent the next five minutes trying to explain why she was there and that she felt compelled to try and help—whatever the cost. He had looked at her with a new respect, and then, to her great surprise, had said that if she was going, he would go. This had completely blindsided her. Although they had a friendly banter and she fancied him like hell, she thought it was all just boys having fun from his side. To hear him say he would come with her into the unknown made her smile, but also feel warm inside.

Shortly after, Murphy had wandered past on his way to pack his things ready to leave. When he saw Bowman and

Nyah, he too stopped. He looked between the two of them and then pushed into the line next to Nyah.

"Oh no, I see what's going on here. You two numpties just want some time on your own. Well I can't be having that now, can I? Don't know what you might get up to. I'm coming too."

Bowman had glared at him, but Nyah had again been amazed by his words. Now they had three.

The chopper lifted up into the air. The wind was increasing and the weather slowly deteriorating, but the circumstances were so dire, so unprecedented, that all convention, all regulations were out of the window. At the end of the day, they only had to get to the bomb. It was highly unlikely they would ever be coming back.

As they climbed higher, Nyah looked down at the camp below. There was a hive of activity as the scientists and crew worked to ready the base for shutdown and evacuation. A C-130 transport had already arrived. There was a string of small vehicles loading her up. This would be going on across the continent. And seven other teams, just like her merry band of three, would be heading out to the bomb locations as she sat there.

In the end, the choice of who would go had come down to her and two others. The thing that had swung Patcher's decision was Nyah's conviction, and that it had been her crew who had first drawn attention to the black helicopters and been shot at, so it seemed only fair that had she wanted to go, she would have been given first refusal.

As she sat in the aircraft now, heading out over the snow and ice, she wasn't so sure she should have been so enthusiastic.

On the one hand she knew she was doing the right thing —someone shouldn't be allowed to detonate a series of nuclear bombs on the planet's last untouched environment. Not only would it destroy much of its surface, but it would leave radiation that would make it uninhabitable, even for research scientists, for years, maybe decades to come. But on the other hand, Nyah was conflicted. What if Solano was right? She knew from years of working in the field and listening to climate specialists that the world was on a path that would cause it to implode climatically, and that, as things stood, nothing was going to stop that. There were things that could be done but weren't being done. Maybe Solano's way was the only way to make people focus—because they had to act now and not tomorrow.

She wrestled with the thoughts as the helicopter sped on.

An hour later they approached the site. The weather was worsening. Low cloud reduced visibility and increasingly strong winds swept in. They were about half a mile out when Bowman's voice came over the comms.

"We need to check out the position of that gun. I'm not prepared to land at the bomb site unless we've removed the threat. It would be too dangerous."

"Good idea," said Nyah.

"Did you get a fix on it last time?" asked Bowman.

"Not precisely, but from where we were, and the side of the chopper that was hit, I'd say it was the mountains on the right."

Bowman glanced to the right. He slewed the helicopter round to track over toward the range. They were close to the cloud ceiling. The mountains stretched for several miles and were covered in snow and ice. Bare rock showed in gullies and the steeper sections.

He flew in at a close angle, trying to make it difficult for any shooter to track him. The helicopter was about a quarter of a mile to the south of the bomb position and close to the rock when there was a PING off the bodywork. Bowman immediately flew in a zigzag pattern, trying to make further shots more difficult. Murphy and Nyah peered out of the side window, trying to see anything on the rock face. They were almost directly opposite the bomb site when there was a large SMACK on the windshield. At the same time Murphy shouted.

"There, over on the small ledge!"

"You see it?" said Nyah.

"Yeah, there was a muzzle flash."

"Matt. Matt, you see that?" asked Nyah.

But there was no reply over the headset. Nyah leaned forward and looked at Bowman. He was gritting his teeth.

He'd been shot.

The helicopter was now veering down at a steep angle, heading for the rock and snow on the side of the mountain. A second later and another bullet slammed into the bodywork above them. There was a loud bang and the helicopter started to spin violently.

The engine was hit.

Nyah screamed in the back. She clung to her seat. Murphy stared over, fear written across his face. He was clearly terrified. All they could do was hang on and wait for the inevitable.

Bowman was fighting the controls, but there was little he could do—the rotors had been damaged. He could direct their course but had no control over power or altitude. They were going down. It was just a matter of where. He was trying to get them out of the line of sight of the gun. He slewed round to the right. Ahead was a snow slope that extended down to a steep drop-off below. The gun position was some way to their left. It was unlikely anybody shooting would be able to angle to where they were going to crash.

A second later they found out.

The helicopter hit the slope hard, head on. The skids buckled with the impact. Nyah and Murphy were thrown violently into the bulkhead between them and the cockpit, smashing their heads, dazing them.

But in front, things were far worse.

As the nose hit the rock, it crumpled the front of the helicopter. The instrument console was pushed violently into Bowman's legs, breaking both of them. He cried out in pain before his head smashed into the side door, knocking him unconscious.

The chopper slid down the slope, coming to a stop as the buckled skids caught round a protruding rock. It stopped them from falling further down and over the edge, but the machine would never fly again.

They were going nowhere.

In the back Nyah groaned. Her head hurt. She glanced at Murphy. He was checking himself over. She then glanced forward.

"Matt?"

No reply.

"Matt? Are you okay?"

Still no reply.

She eased herself up. As she did, pain rushed through her head. She tried to peer round the front seat to check if Matt was okay, but she couldn't see. She opened the side door and looked out. Their position was not good. The slope dropped steeply away to the valley below, and as she looked along the side of the mountain, the clouds were now even lower, starting to swirl around them.

And it had started to snow.

She climbed out onto the slope, holding onto the seatbelt to stop herself from falling. She inched round to the front and opened the cockpit door.

And gasped.

Bowman was lying slumped over to one side, unconscious. But what was worse was that the instrument console was embedded in his legs, crushing them. There was no way they would be able to get him out, and even if they could, there was no way he was going to be able to walk. In fact, if he survived, he might never walk again.

Nyah climbed back into the rear. She looked at Murphy. "You okay?" she asked.

He groaned, rubbing his head.

"Feel like I've been on an all-night bender."

"Matt's in a really bad way. His legs are crushed."

Murphy looked at her, shock on his face.

"Shit!"

It took them half an hour to work out what to do, but in that time they came to one inescapable conclusion—whichever way you looked at it, they were screwed.

Bowman had come round but had been in so much pain they'd had to inject him with morphine from the medipack. A radio call to Halley confirmed there could be no rescue as all the aircraft were dealing with the evacuation and the weather was closing in. No helicopter would be able to reach them.

They were on their own.

They now had a decision to make. Either stay and try and look after Bowman, or press on and go for the bomb.

It was an impossible decision, but if you were able to take emotion out of the equation, it was simple.

There was no choice.

But for Nyah it was not so simple.

She couldn't take the emotion out of the situation. She had been heartened when Matt had agreed to come with her, and she knew it was not for the 'good of the mission'—it was for her.

Murphy had finally convinced her they had to go. He couldn't do it on his own. It was a two-person job, and to put it bluntly, it didn't look as though Bowman was going to make it.

Their next problem was they couldn't go down to the valley floor, several hundred feet below, until they'd disabled the gun. They knew it was further along the range from where they were, but they were unarmed and no match for whoever might be there.

They grabbed what weapons they could—hammers, ice axes, the flare gun from the chopper, as well as packing all the gear they'd need at the bomb site. This resulted in two one-hundred-pound packs, but there was no other choice.

It was then time to go.

After a final conversation with Bowman, they left him wrapped in all the spare thermal clothing they could find and with food and drink he could reach in the cockpit. He had been aware of what they had to do, and understood, but the look on his face when they'd left had been something Nyah would never forget.

As they headed off, the wind was increasing and the snow thickening.

The side of the mountain was steep but manageable. They had both completed numerous mountaineering and survival training courses, so for the moment things weren't too bad.

They found the gun position twenty minutes later. They had been approaching cautiously along the slope, not wanting to give prior notice of their presence to anyone who might be there. In the end they needn't have worried. When they found it, they glanced at each other in surprise. The position was completely unmanned. They could see the rifle on the motorized tripod with the sophisticated sights on top. To one side was a camera that also looked like it was controlled remotely.

Once they had ascertained it was no threat, Murphy pulled all the wires from the control system and wrenched the gun from the tripod. He threw it to one side and buried it in the snow. Nyah did the same with the camera.

They were now safe from the gun, but they shouldn't get ahead of themselves—there was still a nuclear weapon to disarm. Put in that context, their achievement didn't seem quite so amazing.

After a brief stop to decide their next move, they pulled their jackets tighter around them, roped themselves together, and started the tricky job of descending to the ice below and then heading out to the bomb.

The call came through to Solano after dinner on the first night on the island. It was preceded by a beeping and a light flashing on the main control desk in his office.

Solano crossed over to it and clicked on the video call. Immediately the face of the lead mercenary appeared on the display. Solano could see the movement behind him and the motion of the ship.

"I have a report, sir," said the face on the screen.

"Go ahead," said Solano.

"It would appear the packages have been discovered. Teams have been sent out to investigate."

"Are you able to stop them?"

"Negative. There's a storm moving across the continent. We're confined to the ship. That will mean some of them will probably not reach the locations, but we have had activity at Site A."

"Go on."

"No one is there yet, but we had to fire on a helicopter that had come to investigate. We hit the chopper and it went down. I'm not sure of the damage as it was out of camera range, but a while after it disappeared, the rifle and camera were put out of action. We're blind at that location."

Solano thought for a moment.

"Okay. Let me know any further developments."

"Yes, sir." The man's image vanished from the screen.

Solano pressed some keys on the keyboard. The computer display showed images from the camera positions at the bomb sites. As the mercenary had said, the image at Site A was blank.

He eased back in his chair. All was not yet lost, but Site A was important. It was the hub that triggered the other bombs once he'd sent the signal. He thought about it for a minute. He would have to pressure Stevens and move up the deadline.

Chapter Forty-Eight

It was a twelve-hour flight to Mauritius from London's Gatwick Airport and it gave McCready and Richards time to go over everything they had discussed during the previous two days.

After he had told Craig about the cryptic message, which had been met with a certain amount of incredulity, McCready had managed to convince his friend to go with him. There would be no massive operation with high-tech equipment this time—just a comms set to stay in touch. It would also be just the two of them. They would hire a local boat and some dive gear and McCready would try to find out if Solano was on the island. If he was, he could then decide what to do—whether to try and stop him alone or call in Steel and the cavalry. It would all depend on how much time there was. Richards had already made up his mind on this, but things often changed on the ground, so they would see how it went.

McCready glanced up as the stewardess of the BA flight walked along the aisle making sure everyone had their seatbelts fastened for landing. When she had moved on, he looked out of the window as they approached the island in the middle of the Indian Ocean.

He had never been to Mauritius before, but he had heard of the welcoming locals and laid-back atmosphere. He was half hoping Solano wasn't there so he could ask Clare to come and join him, but they were a way off that just yet.

The wheels touched the sun-drenched tarmac with a squeal, and shortly after, the plane taxied to the side of the large, modern-looking terminal. After the usual wait to disembark, McCready and Richards walked down the steps and over to the Arrivals hall.

Once they were through customs and had retrieved their bags, they hailed a cab at the front of the airport and set off for the forty-five-mile drive to the LUX Grand Gaube Resort at the northern end of the island where they had rented a villa for a week.

Mauritius was located around twelve hundred miles off the south-east coast of Africa. It was forty miles long and thirty miles wide, and was surrounded by one of the largest coral reefs in the world. It had been formed by long-dormant volcanoes that made up a string of mountain ranges that were heavily forested.

The drive was enjoyable and gave them time to relax after the flight, taking them across the center of the island before heading up to the northernmost point.

The cab pulled up at the front of the resort an hour and a half later. After the usual check-in requirements, McCready and Richards were escorted through the beautifully laid out grounds to their villa, which was situated, at their request, away from the main activities and facilities of the resort.

Once they'd unpacked, changed into something more appropriate for the tropics, and washed away the fatigue of the flight with a cool shower, they grabbed a couple of beers from the minibar and sat down in wicker chairs at a glass table on the veranda at the front of the villa. The calm waters of the Indian Ocean were a stone's throw away and the sounds of holidaymakers enjoying the idyllic location drifted on the breeze. It was going to be hard to concentrate on the job at hand, but they had to.

McCready laid out a chart on the table. It showed the whole island, as well as a number of smaller ones to the north, including where the coordinates had led them.

There were two ways forward they had considered.

When they'd been checking out resorts, they'd found that Grand Gaube had a helipad and could arrange sightseeing flights of the area. It would be the perfect chance to recce Solano's potential property before working out the best approach. If they were lucky they might even get a glimpse of Solano himself, which would seal the deal—and they could end things there. If not, then the resort ran dive trips to the local wrecks and reefs. They could use that as an excuse to get close to the island, most likely at night, and then investigate further.

With that agreed, Richards walked over to the phone and booked a helicopter flight for two that afternoon.

When it turned up at the helipad, the helicopter was a Bell Jet Ranger, the workhorse of the skies for many a destination. It was everyone's classic image of a small helicopter. They had seen service the world over, but this one looked as though it was fairly battered and bruised from a lifetime flying tourists around the islands.

Their pilot's name was Cody. He was an American in his sixties with a balding head and bronzed skin from years out in the open. He had been a US Navy pilot and was seeing out his years "bumming around in the sun" as he put it.

They all seemed to be on the same wavelength and it was clear Cody was up for anything they wanted to do. Somehow McCready felt the guy was more than a little bored with delicate tourists who got airsick at the slightest maneuver other than flying dead straight, dead level. McCready told him they were doing a recce for dive sites so wanted to look at some of the offshore islands that would be less explored.

They took off with McCready up front and Richards in the back. Both were equipped with high-powered binoculars and McCready had those Steel had lent him in Monaco so he could record anything they saw for analysis later.

The flight was slightly calmer than the last time they'd been in a helicopter.

McCready always marveled at the way the machines could lift off from a standing start and maneuver on a dime —even fly backward.

They swept out over the water.

Below, they could see paddleboarders and swimmers enjoying the shallow waters of the reef. As they crossed over some light surf breaking over the coral, the water turned deep blue as it dropped away into the depths.

Ahead of them was open ocean. The wind had picked up and was blowing white caps off the tops of the waves. In the distance they could see the island of Gunner's Quoin. It was a small volcanic cone sticking out of the water. Beyond that to the north-east was Flat Island and Round Island. McCready didn't want to be too obvious, so he let Cody fly them on a circular route around Gunner's Quoin, but then, when they moved on, heading for Flat Island, McCready pointed to an island more to the north-west, several miles out.

"How about there? Can we take a look at that one?"

Cody glanced at the chart and shook his head.

"Ain't nothing to see out there. Also, it's a restricted area. Something to do with the government. Why don't we take a look over at Flat Island? Some good dive sites there from what I've heard."

"We'd really like to go the other way," said McCready, with a slight raise of the eyebrows.

"More than my license is worth," replied Cody. "All the pilots have been told to stay away."

This was making McCready even more sure he was on to something.

"Couple of hundred bucks make it worth it?" asked McCready, bringing out two hundred-dollar bills.

Cody glanced at the money, then McCready.

"I guess I could say the navigation was off a bit, but we can't get too close. No flyovers or anything like that. Okay?"

"Sounds great," said McCready.

A few minutes later McCready could see the small island rising out of the water. It could equally have been called Flat Island. There was no raised elevation at all. As they approached, Cody said he would fly past as though en route to somewhere else.

As they came closer, McCready could see the features he'd seen on the computer. The fringing reef, the small dirt airstrip, and the lagoon with the large structure stretching out from one end. He trained the binoculars onto the building. The glasses brought it into sharp relief. He pressed record and scanned the facility from the edge of the reef to the foliage and undergrowth on the land. By the time he'd finished he had a pretty good idea of what was there. As the chopper turned to head back, he pointed the binoculars at one of the upper decks. He could see a woman swimming in an infinity pool. A man came out to talk to her. It wasn't Solano, but his gait reminded him of the man he'd seen at the cable car station at the top of the mountain in Switzerland.

He was also sure the woman in the pool was Carlita.

He was silent for a minute, but then turned and nodded to Richards. He nodded back.

"Okay, Cody, my man, take us home," said McCready.

When they were back at the villa, McCready plugged the microSD card from the binoculars into his MacBook Pro. A few seconds later the video was playing back in iMovie on the screen.

They watched as the island came into view.

The layout was fairly simple. There was nothing really there except the structure in the water and a few houses in the trees onshore, which McCready assumed would be staff quarters. He had thought there would be a fair amount of security, but there didn't seem to be anything obvious. But, then, as he looked more closely, he could see a number of posts around the periphery of the buildings, and there was the tall mast in the middle—all good mounting points for cameras, so it was likely everything was monitored through video surveillance. He was also betting there were at least a few armed guards on standby in case of problems. In normal times Solano would probably feel well protected by the location, but these were not normal times. He was sure the cameras would be monitored 24/7. If anyone approached on the surface, or over land, they'd be seen coming a mile away, even at night. Any cameras would, no doubt, have night-vision capability.

That left only one realistic way to approach—from underwater.

Once that had been agreed, Richards went off to secure a boat. When he left, McCready checked back through the footage. He had to memorize every inch of the place to be able to try and gain entry later that night.

As he watched the final few minutes of video, he was drawn to the woman in the pool. She swam with easy, powerful strokes that propelled her smoothly through the water. He was in no doubt he was looking at Carlita. He wondered why she had sent the message, and he wondered how he would react if he got to see her again after everything she'd done. And although there had been no sign of Solano, McCready was sure he was there.

He had to be.

Two hours later they were ready to go. The hotel had been only too happy to rent them a fast boat. It was a RIB with twin hundred and fifty horsepower engines. They loaded two spare fuel cans, as while they weren't going that far, you never knew when they might come in handy.

McCready had been down to the dive school and rented a full set of kit. The only thing he'd brought with him was his Suunto dive computer, which doubled as a watch. And while he wouldn't be going that deep, if he had to act fast with developing circumstances, he would rather have a computer keeping an eye on his decompression status than trying to work it out for himself. He had also hired a diver propulsion vehicle, or DPV, to allow him to travel a distance underwater without expending any energy, along with a compass to determine direction.

As well as the dive gear, they took a couple of powerful waterproof torches and the comms kit McCready had used in Monaco. It would comfortably work over the range from the main island all the way out to Solano's island if necessary. They also took some coffee in a thermos and a couple of sandwiches. They had no idea how long they'd be out there for.

Once they had everything on board, McCready cast off the line and Richards took them sedately out of the small harbor. They had informed the dive center they were going out to Gunner's Quoin for some night diving and would probably be back in the early hours. They'd been told "no problem"—just to sign in when they got back so anyone coming in first thing would know they were safe.

Once clear of the small harbor, Richards pushed the throttles forward and they headed out into the night.

Chapter Forty-Nine

It had taken only thirty minutes to get to the island. The water had been calm and the RIB had powered over the surface at over forty knots.

As they approached, Richards slowed to reduce their profile and the size of the wake. It would be a dead give-away in the calm conditions. McCready's biggest concern was how close they could get without the risk of being seen. He didn't know the range the night-vision cameras would have. The other thing was the radar he'd seen on the top of the mast. He was sure it wasn't there just for show. They would have to act as though the boat was just passing by, heading somewhere else, and not interested in the island. McCready could then drop into the water and make for shore. The comms would work even if Richards and the RIB were a mile or two away.

As Richards kept the boat heading forward, he angled in slightly to the island to give McCready the shortest distance to travel.

McCready pulled on the shorty wetsuit and weight belt.

Next, he checked the buoyancy compensator and regulator on the dive cylinder and ensured all was well. He lifted them onto his back and then strapped on his fins and mask and did a comms check. Once he was happy everything was working, he checked his dive computer was set and active. It should automatically turn itself on when he hit the water and submerged but he never liked to leave things to chance.

Richards slowed the boat to a crawl and knocked it into neutral. There was nothing more to be said between them. They both knew what had to be done and the potential stakes. McCready merely nodded to his old friend and rolled over the side.

Once he was in the water Richards passed him the DPV. He then eased her back into gear and headed slowly away from the island. He would go out about half a mile and wait.

In the water, McCready did a final check to make sure all the straps were tight. He then took a compass bearing on the entrance to the lagoon and attached it to the small bar on the top of the DPV. It would give him an easy position from which to monitor their course as he traveled to the island.

He took a final glance at the departing RIB and then submerged.

The water was cool, and it felt good to be back beneath the surface. Also, with the basic equipment he was wearing, he felt free and unrestrained, unlike the cumbersome bulky commercial gear he had worn when diving on the wreck of the aircraft.

He descended to a depth of twenty feet, checked the compass, and then secured a short strap from the DPV to a karabiner on his BC. This would allow the strain of the pull of the machine to be taken around his waist rather than through his arms.

He then pulled the trigger. Immediately the small electric motor started up with a whine, and the propeller at the back shot him forward. It would take a while to reach the island, so he settled in for the ride.

It was peaceful and calm in the water. He had no lights other than a pencil torch that lit up the compass. It gave him time to think of what might come when he reached shore, where things could end up being far from peaceful if anything went wrong.

Half an hour later he detected a brightening in the water. There had been some moonlight that had penetrated the surface, so things hadn't been completely dark, but now, ahead, he could start to see a slight glow from a more horizontal angle. He must be getting close to the structure in the lagoon.

He stopped the DPV and hung there for a moment, unmoving. Silent.

He then carefully rose up until he could just see above the surface. Several hundred feet ahead of him was the front of the structure. From this angle it looked massive.

McCready scanned for any guards. If they were there, they certainly weren't showing themselves, but there would be the ever-watchful cameras.

He corrected the compass bearing and dropped back below the surface. As he wasn't using a rebreather, his bubbles would give him away if anyone was watching, so he moved as fast as he could to get himself under the shelter of the main structure.

The visibility in the lagoon was not great. The area was

full of silty water that had run off the island. With nowhere to go except out of the entrance when there were currents to clear it out, the upper end of the lagoon remained clogged with murky water.

After about five minutes he could see things getting darker. He must be directly beneath the structure.

He could relax.

He finned over until he reached a solid wall made of metal. He slowly followed it all the way to the surface. As he broke through, he found himself in what looked like a large open space. There was about ten feet between the water and the bottom of the structure.

He glanced around. He could see something in the center that looked like a wide shaft disappearing into the water below. He risked turning on his torch. On the surface was a pontoon with a selection of watercraft moored to it that was accessed by a door in the shaft. Among the high-powered boats McCready spotted a Seabreacher, which he had spent what could best be described as 'an interesting time' in when he had been in Palau earlier in the year.

He glanced underwater and swung the torch around. There was some sort of large shape further down, but the visibility was so poor he couldn't tell what it was. A reflection of light from the torch suggested something that could have been glass. Maybe there was an underwater observation room of some kind.

But there was no time to investigate. He pressed the transmit button on the comms unit around his neck.

"Craig, you there?" he said quietly.

There was a moment's silence and then a reply.

"Still here. Where are you?"

"I'm under the structure. There seems to be some sort of garage for boats, but no one's around. I'm going to try and get up onto the main deck area. If things go wrong and you get a rapid beeping it means I've been discovered and you'll have to get yourself out of there."

"Okay, we'll see about that," said Richards.

"I mean it, Craig. Don't try to come and get me. There's no point us both being caught. Get a message to Martin Steel. Let him handle it from there."

"Be careful," said Richards.

"Always," replied McCready.

He then swam further along the side of the structure until he reached the end.

As he peered around the high wall, he could see what looked like a swim platform on the outside about thirty feet away. He finned carefully over to it. When he looked down he could see the sand of the lagoon twenty feet below. He dropped the DPV and then pulled his BC and cylinder from his back. He dropped them down as well. At least he had a reference point if he needed to find them quickly later. Once he was sure he was going to climb out, he sent his fins and mask after them.

He slowly climbed up onto the platform.

There was a set of wide steps that led to the deck above. He made his way up cautiously, trying to stay in the shadows. On the deck was a pool at the end closest to the water. There were rooms and some steps to the upper decks to his right. He ran across to the nearest wall. It was late. No one was around, but what he failed to notice was a camera high on the mast in the middle turn and follow his every move.

He walked cautiously along the wall and peered round the corner at the end. He found himself in a wide atrium with glass-sided walls. At the far end was what looked like a central hub of some sort, surrounded by a large open-plan interior. There were chairs and some low tables. It was dark inside.

He walked into the atrium and made it halfway across when the area was flooded with light.

McCready froze.

There was nowhere to hide.

When he realized that, he relaxed. He heard footsteps behind him and turned to see a security guard—they did have them after all. He was dressed in a one-piece black jumpsuit. But what was more concerning was the weapon in his hand that was pointed directly at McCready.

A moment later he heard someone else approaching. He turned to see Solano walk into the atrium. He wore a gray toweling robe and was barefoot. He had clearly been asleep and was bleary-eyed. When he saw McCready, he stopped dead. A slightly perplexed expression crossed his face.

"You seem to be a somewhat resourceful man, Mr. McCready. I can see why Carlita suggested we use you."

At this, McCready's expression hardened. He was still wearing the wetsuit, and the comms unit was in clear view around his neck.

"So, who else knows you're here?"

"It's just me," said McCready. "My boat's moored over by the reef. I swam in from there."

Solano didn't look as though he believed him.

"Somehow I doubt that. But as you're here, let me extend my hospitality."

"You're too kind. At least I doubt you'll be destroying this place anytime soon."

Solano smiled. "You would be right. I would love to know how you made it out in Switzerland, but I'm tired and tomorrow will be a busy day, so that will have to wait. André here"—he indicated the guard—"will put you somewhere safe. Please don't try and do anything stupid. You really have nowhere to go, and I have no intention of harming you."

"You sure about that?"

Solano pondered this for a moment.

"Yes, for now."

He was about to leave when he noticed the comms unit around McCready's neck. He crossed over and reached for it. But before he could grab it, McCready undid it for him. As he passed it over he repeatedly hit the transmit button. He managed five presses before Solano took it from him.

"So, who have you been in contact with?"

"No one."

Solano sighed. He then turned to André. "Take him away. Make sure he's comfortable, but secure."

"Yes, sir," said André.

"Sleep well Mr. McCready." You won't have much else to do anytime soon."

Solano violently twisted the comms unit, snapping it in two. He then turned and walked from the atrium.

McCready glanced at André.

"Come along, we don't want any trouble."

McCready half raised his hands to indicate he was going to play nice. André then led him into the main part of the building.

The inside was beautifully equipped. It looked like the interior of a superyacht, only without the restrictions of space. He was directed to an elevator at the center of the hub he had seen earlier.

They walked into the car when the doors opened. Once inside it was cramped, but André knew what he was doing. He kept a safe distance from McCready to be able to keep the gun trained on him. After a gentle woosh, the car came to a stop. The indicator said they were two levels down. The doors slid open.

McCready was ushered out into a brushed steel walled corridor. It led away in both directions. Along the sides were regularly spaced doors. They looked like cabins or storage rooms. It was most likely the staff/maintenance area. After they'd walked about thirty feet André opened a door on the left and indicated for McCready to go inside. Once he had, André shut the door firmly and McCready heard the secure, unarguable click of a lock being turned.

The room was small but comfortable. It was a cross between a cabin and a cell. There was a bed and an area with a small desk and chair. To his immediate left was a door that led to a toilet, basin and shower. There was a TV on the wall opposite the bed, but no window. Up in one of the corners, close to the ceiling, was what McCready was sure was a camera. He had the sense he was in the middle of the structure, rather than at the side. But one thing he was sure about—he wouldn't be able to escape from there anytime soon.

He pulled off the wetsuit and walked into the shower. After he'd soaped himself down and washed away the salt, he found a comfortable robe in a small wardrobe and wrapped it round himself. He then lay down on the bed. As Solano had said, there wasn't much else to do.

As he looked at the ceiling, two things ran through his mind.

First, he was pretty sure somewhere above him Carlita was sleeping, oblivious to his presence; and second, he hoped to hell Craig had got his message when he'd repeatedly pressed the TRANSMIT button on the comms unit, and that he would, right now, be heading back to the main island to get help, rather than attempting some harebrained rescue attempt—that was his forte, and he couldn't have anyone stealing his thunder.

Richards had indeed got the message. He'd been watching a pod of dolphins playing in the moonlight, not a hundred feet away, when the comms unit had beeped five times in rapid succession. His first response was to groan. If he'd really thought about it, he knew this was going to happen, but he had hoped, for once, that McCready would be able to pull something off without it going pear-shaped and escalating to a whole different level. And while the message indicated trouble—that was it. No detail. No idea what had gone wrong. Had he just been caught and was being held? Was he injured? Was he now dead? All required a different response with a different urgency.

Richards sat there for a moment trying to work out what to do. The options had been going through his mind since McCready had left. He knew what he wanted to do, but he also had to consider the bigger picture. If McCready was in trouble, it likely meant Solano was on the island, and if that was the case, there was far more at stake than McCready's life.

He took a deep breath and picked up the satellite phone.

John, why the hell can't it ever be easy for once?

He dialed a number and waited for it to be answered.

"Yeah, hi, I need to speak to Martin Steel. Tell him John McCready has a problem."

Chapter Fifty

When Nyah and Murphy made it to the bottom of the mountain they were numb from not only the worsening weather that was causing the temperature to drop by the minute, but also the thought of Bowman sitting trapped in pain in the helicopter. But there had been nothing more they could do. It was hitting Nyah harder, and it was only now that Murphy could see how much she really cared for the pilot.

"He'll be fine," he said, more out of reassurance than anything based in fact.

Nyah looked at him skeptically.

"You know that's not true. He was in a bad way when we left him. There's only so much morphine, and the temperature's dropping. With the chopper's engine out there's no heater." She took a deep breath. "You know he's not going to make it."

Murphy looked at her.

"You can't think like that. We both have to focus on the

bomb. The sooner we can disarm it, the sooner we can get back to Matt. Okay?"

She nodded, but it was no reassurance.

They took a final look up the mountain. They could just see the tail of the crashed helicopter sticking out over the ledge. They hoisted their packs onto their backs and headed out over the ice.

Although the weather was closing in and visibility was down to less than a quarter of a mile, with snow coming down harder all the time, the GPS unit Murphy carried could pinpoint a location with military precision. He had no doubt it would put them right on the spot they had visited before—the time when they hadn't known they were dealing with a nuclear weapon.

The going was not too bad to begin with, but as the wind picked up, blowing straight across the ice, by the time they were a mile out, it was getting tough. The snow had brought the visibility down to less than fifty yards. Once they were the correct distance from the mountains, it took a further twenty minutes of walking and checking the GPS until they found the spot. Nyah held out a Geiger counter to make sure. Within a couple of minutes the readings were off the scale.

They were there.

Now came the difficult part.

They hadn't been sure how long they would need, so they'd come prepared. They had access to all the equipment they could possibly have wanted from Halley, as no other teams would be out on the ice due to the evacuation.

The first thing they had to do was to erect a shelter. This would give them protection from the elements, as well as somewhere to cook and sleep, if necessary.

It took an hour to complete, but once done, they were

sure they would be able to survive whatever the weather could throw at them.

They then had to clear a work area around the bomb itself.

They dug a ten-foot hole, fifteen feet wide. This exposed the drum the bomb was contained in and gave them unrestricted movement around it.

Next, they had to set up communications.

Although, back at Halley, they had gone through the procedure with Major Carswell over a secure video call, he had not been a hundred percent sure what the eventual protocol would be. He knew the workings of these kinds of weapons, but they were always being adapted and updated, and there could also be booby traps and unfamiliar components he would have to observe on the fly to give instructions and procedures to adopt. To do this, it would require a reliable video link so he could talk them through it, step by step, in real time, while observing what they did.

While Nyah arranged the equipment inside the shelter, Murphy set to establishing a comms link back to Halley fifty miles away. It consisted of a compact satellite dish on a ten-foot pole. This would be connected to a video-conferencing laptop in a hardened waterproof case.

It took him half an hour to set up the dish. It had to be secured against the winds that were increasing by the minute and were whipping at the shelter and anything else not tied down.

Inside, Nyah set up the cameras. One was positioned so it could look straight down into the drum. A second was fixed to the side to give a wide view. There was also a thin SnakeCam they could use to move in close if there was anything of particular interest or concern. It consisted of a tiny lens on the end of a long flexible fiber optic cable that could be maneuvered into small gaps between the bomb components—a bit like special forces and police units used to spy on rooms with people under surveillance.

Once the cameras were ready, Nyah fixed a series of lights to illuminate the nooks and crannies of the bomb workings so nothing would be missed. She was sure this was going to be a terrifying experience, but as in all things, preparation was half the battle. They didn't even want to look at the bomb until they knew they had protection from the elements and reliable comms in place.

After two hours they were exhausted, but there was no time to rest.

Before they did anything, Nyah grabbed the walkie-talkie and contacted Bowman. He didn't sound good. His voice was becoming weaker all the time, but it only spurred her on to get the job done as soon as possible so they could return to help him.

She glanced up at Murphy.

"Okay, ready?"

He nodded and switched on the video link.

There was a connecting sound out of the speaker and then the comforting image of Jerry Patcher came on the screen.

"Hello, Nyah, I heard about Bowman. I'm sorry. Once you have this under control we'll do everything we can to try and get help to you, but let's concentrate on this first, okay?"

"Yes, sir. Thank you, sir."

Then Patcher's face turned even more solemn, if that were possible. "It also seems only three other teams have managed to reach their devices—the Scandinavians, the French and the Japanese. The others have been unable to make it through the storm. The weather is deteriorating and worse is heading your way, so the sooner we can get this done the better."

"I'm with you there, sir," said Nyah. "Okay, what do we need to do?"

On the screen Patcher looked like he was adjusting something to one side.

"The next image you'll see will be Major Carswell. He'll talk you through the procedure. Good luck."

The screen flickered for a moment and then the image of Carswell appeared—all the way from London. He peered out, glancing left and right slightly. He could clearly see Nyah and Murphy to either side of the screen. He looked calm and collected, which went a little way to reassuring them.

"Okay," he said. "Let's get this show on the road."

Chapter Fifty-One

Solano rose early, and despite the interruption to his sleep caused by the arrival of McCready, he was feeling fresh and awake. The deadline for the response from the world community was the following day, so everything hinged on them finding a way to work together. But given the news that action was underway to try and disarm the bombs, he thought he might have to bring everything forward. Also, McCready's presence concerned him. It meant that others might not be far behind. He would have to put the final phase of the plan into operation.

He had enjoyed a light breakfast by the infinity pool on the deck outside his bedroom with Carlita, and was now in the control room assessing the situation. He checked his watch. It was time to contact the president.

While he waited to be put through, he thought about how he felt.

Others might have thought Solano would be highly stressed with everything that was on his shoulders. In fact, he actually found he was as calm as he had ever been in his life. His plan was hours away from coming to fruition. He knew he only had months to live. There was nothing to be stressed about.

"Hello, Victor," said the weary voice of Galt Stevens.

"Mr. President," said Solano. "What progress is there?"

The president paused before taking a deep breath. "I am afraid very little, but we are still waiting to hear back from the Security Council with a final answer. It could be a day or so. I know what your plan is, Victor. You cannot do this. It's madness."

"No, Galt, I am afraid it's the sanest thing I have ever done. In the future, generations will come to see that. It's a shame it has had to come to this, but things cannot carry on as they are. The deadline is final."

"Time, Victor, we just need more time."

"I'm afraid that will not be possible. I am aware of certain actions to disarm the bombs. You will not succeed. You would be better served by getting everyone out of the region if you want to preserve life."

Stevens paused again.

"Victor, I will be back in touch when I have a final answer. In the meantime, please do not do anything foolish."

The line went dead.

Solano thought about the president's words. He knew the man was stalling to allow time for the bombs to be neutralized, but equally, Solano knew that would never happen. He lifted a small rectangular box off the desk. It was plugged into the panel in front of him, which in turn was connected to the communications equipment on the roof. On the front was a screen that had a display like a digital clock. Currently it was blank. But all he had to do was turn the device on, enter a code, and press a red button on the front, and a signal would be sent via satellite to the control equipment at Site A. Once the computer at the site had verified the code, it would initiate a countdown of its own and transmit activation codes to all the other bombs in Antarctica. A minute later his work would be complete.

He turned the small box over in his hand. So much power in such a small space—the world was full of anomalies.

He heard a noise behind him and swiveled in his chair to see Mendes walk into the room.

"Morning, Juliano."

"Morning, sir. Did you hear something last night? I thought I heard people moving around and some voices."

Solano looked up at him. "Yes, we had an intruder. He's down in the lower level." Solano flicked a switch on the desk. One of the security cameras on a display showed an image of McCready in the cabin. He was lying on the bed watching TV.

Mendes moved in closer. When he saw who it was he breathed in sharply. Solano looked at him curiously.

"You, okay?"

"Sure," said Mendes, "I'm just surprised anyone would be out here."

"Yes, it is a bit of an issue. I'm going to keep him down there until everything is over. I can't afford any screwups at this stage. After tomorrow it won't matter."

"Yes, sir."

"Oh, and don't tell Carlita about this, okay?"

Solano looked at him pointedly.

"Of course, sir," said Mendes.

Solano then turned to other matters.

"Now, is everything ready? We are likely to be leaving soon."

"Yes, sir, all systems are prepared and provisions are loaded to last several weeks. We just need about half an hour's notice."

"Good," said Solano. "It looks like this is the last day, Juliano. We've finally made it."

"Yes, sir. I hope it will not come to that though. You know my thoughts on this matter."

Solano eased back in his chair and looked at Mendes.

"I know, but you're wrong. You'll see."

The two men stared at each other for a moment.

"I'll go and check with security on the island," said Mendes, "make sure we don't have any other uninvited guests."

When Mendes left the control room he walked a safe distance and then leaned against a wall, breathing hard. When he'd seen McCready in the cabin he'd had a surge of hope. What came next, though, would be far from easy.

He walked quickly through the complex to the elevator. As he approached the doors, he saw a security guard also heading for the elevator. He spoke briefly to him, telling him it was thought there was some issue on the other side of the island and that he should take two men and go and investigate. The guard headed off obediently.

Mendes then entered the elevator and descended two levels. Once he exited the car, the only sound he could hear was the distant electrical hum of machinery that kept the complex functioning.

He moved quickly down the corridor to the cabin where McCready was being held. He took a deep breath, unlocked the door, and pushed it open.

He walked in. There was noise coming from the small

bathroom. A moment later the toilet flushed and McCready walked out into the room. When he saw Mendes, he stopped. The two men stood there staring at each other.

McCready took in the features and the frame. It took him a few moments, but then he recognized him as the man from the cable car station. The one who'd left in the helicopter. Now he was up close, he was sure he had never met him before, but there was something familiar he couldn't put his finger on. It was the eyes. There was something about his eyes.

"Mr. McCready," said the man. "My name is Juliano Mendes. I am the personal assistant and adviser to Victor Solano." He held out his hand. McCready took it. The grip was firm. He remained silent.

"Firstly," continued Mendes, "I am sorry you have been confined like this. I have only just heard of your presence. This may sound strange, but I am going to let you out."

McCready looked at him curiously.

"Now why would you do that? Did Solano instruct you to?"

Mendes glanced around, and also up into the corner of the room, as though he suspected they were being watched.

"No, and we may not have much time, but you need to stop what he is doing. He's going to go through with his threat if nothing is done, and judging from the way the world is reacting, that's not going to happen."

McCready looked at him closely again. The thought was still there.

"Have we met before? There's something really familiar about you."

Mendes paused for a second and then looked straight at McCready.

"No, you have never met Juliano Mendes before."

McCready thought it was a strange way to phrase it, but he couldn't worry about that now. It appeared there was a way out and he wasn't going to miss the opportunity.

"Okay," he said, "let's go."

Mendes turned and McCready followed him out of the room. As they left, the small camera in the corner moved to follow their movement.

The elevator rose smoothly up through the levels until they reached the main deck. The doors opened to each side. Waiting for them was Victor Solano and an armed guard.

Mendes looked shocked. He walked out slowly.

"Juliano," said Solano, "what are you doing?"

Mendes hesitated. "I was taking Mr. McCready for some exercise. He has been cooped up in the room for hours."

Solano gazed at him with sadness.

"Juliano, after all I have done for you. Now? Now you do this?"

Mendes didn't know what to say. He just stood there looking at his feet. McCready was about to say something when Carlita walked down some steps and headed toward them. When she saw McCready, she let out a cry and flung a hand to her mouth. She glanced rapidly between McCready, Solano and Mendes.

"John!" she said. "You're alive. What are you doing here?"

"Becoming a nuisance," said Solano. The earlier friendliness had gone. He must have realized his problems were growing, and from within—from those he trusted. He was starting to lose the easy-going demeanor.

"I think Mr. McCready has outlived his usefulness." He turned to the guard. "André, take him away and dispose of him. I no longer have time for distractions like this."

André nodded and moved toward McCready.

"No!" cried out Carlita.

Solano looked at her.

"Enough of this! Take him away."

But Carlita ran in front of McCready. André stopped and glanced at Solano, not sure what to do.

Solano sighed. He looked at Carlita with a piercing glare and gritted his teeth.

"No, Victor, you cannot kill him. I will not allow it. I will make sure he's no trouble. I promise."

Solano weighed up the options. It looked like he was torn. Eventually, he sighed with frustration.

"Carlita, if he does anything to disrupt the plans, I will hold you personally responsible, and you know what that will mean." He glanced pointedly at Mendes. Carlita grew quieter. She nodded gravely at him. With a tired shake of his head he turned to Mendes.

"Come with me, Juliano. We have things to discuss."

Solano then gave a slight gesture to André, who stood down. Mendes followed Solano over to the control room.

Carlita turned to stare at McCready, but his expression was hard.

"I hope you don't expect any thanks."

She looked at him, and he could see there was conflict in her eyes.

"John, you should not have come here."

He looked at her with confusion.

"So, you didn't send the message?"

She looked back at him, equally confused.

"What message?"

Chapter Fifty-Two

Nyah and Murphy stared down at the top of the large round drum they had excavated from the ice. It still lay in its position five feet below the surface, but they had an area around it in which they could work. The shelter overhead was holding, even though it was being thrashed by the gales that were increasing by the minute. When Murphy had looked earlier, snow had been piling up around the side that he would need to check didn't get too deep. The temperature had also dropped considerably, but at least inside they were warmed by a small gas stove they'd brought with them. There was also plenty of illumination from the bank of battery-operated lights, so they could concentrate on the task ahead.

Nyah had checked the position of the cameras, and the laptop had been set up at the side of the drum on a small ice ledge so they could both see what Carswell was instructing them to do.

Nyah glanced at Murphy. She took a deep breath and

turned to Carswell, who was looking out of the screen at them.

"Right, Major, where do we start?"

Carswell smiled. "I think given what we're about to go through, you can call me Frank."

Nyah smiled back. "Thanks, Frank. Probably a good idea."

Carswell then turned serious.

"Okay, if you follow my lead, step by step, you should be fine. Don't forget, the words 'nuclear weapon' sound really scary, and on one level they should, but it's not like in the movies, one slip and the whole thing goes off. This is more about making it inoperable so no one can remotely detonate it or start some form of countdown, okay?"

"Sure, if you say so." The realization of what they were about to do was starting to sink in.

"Right, the first thing is to remove the top of the drum. This is just a container and not an integral part of the weapon. Once you have the top off, I should be able to get a better idea of what we're dealing with."

Murphy jumped down into the area surrounding the drum and helped Nyah remove the top. There were three clamps around the circumference. They weren't locked. It was just a matter of unclipping them. Once they were undone they lifted the lid off and placed it up on the ice. They could now see what was inside.

"Okay, stay back so I can take a look," said Carswell.

They moved to one side. On the screen they could see Carswell concentrating on what he saw.

As they peered in, all they could see was a jumble of components and wires and a central metal cylinder. It meant absolutely nothing to them—but that was why

Carswell was there. They watched him concentrating on the screen. After a couple of minutes he looked up and scowled.

"Right," he said, "most of what I can see seems pretty standard, but there are a couple of oddities."

Nyah and Murphy exchanged glances.

"Okay," continued Carswell, "if you see this box here…" On the screen they could see him using an electronic pointer to indicate a small box on the side of the drum away from the main components. "Not sure what that is. It's not consistent with the rest of the device. We'll leave it for now, but we may have to come back to it later. Also, there's a connecting cable lower down that's at odds with what should be there, but don't worry, this was to be expected. We'll just have to take it nice and slow and be prepared to backtrack when necessary."

"But, like you said," said Nyah, "it can't just go off?"

Carswell took a worryingly long time to answer. "Well, hopefully not."

Nyah swallowed and glanced at Murphy. The Irishman's wit seemed to have abandoned him.

"Okay," said Carswell. "Let's make a start."

And so they followed his instructions.

The first task was to unscrew a large metal threaded top to the cylinder within the drum. It took up most of the space. Wires led into it from boxes at the side. When they had it unscrewed, they carefully removed the top and peered in. There wasn't a lot to see—just what seemed to be a white Styrofoam substance that the wires from outside the cylinder disappeared into.

"Okay," said Carswell. "Let me explain how this works in simple terms. Embedded in the Styrofoam are two objects, neither of which you can see at this point. At the bottom will be a fusion bomb. This is made up of a cylinder filled with lithium deuteride powder, which is essentially the fuel. In the middle of this is a plutonium rod. This is very hard to set off. In fact, it won't do anything unless the object embedded in the Styrofoam above it is set off."

"What's that, a firecracker?" said Murphy with a nervous grin.

"No," said Carswell, looking deadly serious. "It's an atomic bomb of the kind dropped on Nagasaki."

Both of them gulped. The grin vanished.

Carswell continued. "The atomic, or fission, bomb at the top is itself set off by a surrounding chemical bomb that has to detonate in an exactly symmetrical action all around it at the same time. So, our aim today is to stop the chemical bomb from going off. No chemical bomb—no fission bomb. No fission bomb—no fusion bomb. No big bang. Okay?"

There was silence for a moment. Then Murphy cleared his throat.

"Yeah, I think we got that."

They followed more of Carswell's instructions, which concentrated on clearing away a number of components so they could disconnect the power source that would activate the initial chemical bomb. There were times when he hesitated before telling them to cut a wire or remove something, but as they worked through the task they became more confident. They seemed to be making progress. After twenty minutes there were a number of items out of the drum and sitting on the ice. Nyah was waiting for the next instruction when there was a *Hmmm* from Carswell.

"What is it, Frank?"

"Never seen one of those before."

He was looking at a circular metal box that was wedged between the main cylinder and a control panel of some sort.

It had just been revealed by the last component they'd removed.

"Right, we need to hang on a minute before we go any further."

Nyah relaxed. She hadn't realized how stressed she'd become. When every move you made could be your last, you had to give it your total concentration, and despite Carswell assuring her nothing was suddenly going to go off, you never knew. She looked back at the screen after taking a swig of coffee from a thermos.

As well as talking to them, Carswell was also giving instructions to the Scandinavian, French and Japanese teams who had made it to their bombs at around the same time. None of the others had managed to get through the weather. On the screen, Nyah could see Carswell looking urgently at a feed that must have been coming through from one of the other sites. She saw his expression turn to one of fear and then she heard what he was saying.

"No, Sven, do not remove that component!"

Nyah couldn't hear the other end of the conversation, but Carswell's expression was becoming more agitated by the moment.

"I don't care that you want to get this done," continued Carswell. "It's a delicate process. We can't rush anything. If you... Oh no!" Nyah saw Carswell slump back in his chair, shock and pain covering his face. She didn't want to interrupt, but eventually she had to.

"Frank, what is it?"

Carswell turned slowly to look at her.

"I was wrong."

"What do you mean, you were wrong?"

"It went off."

"What went off?" said Nyah, the pitch in her voice

rising. She was sure she knew, but she wanted him to tell her she was wrong.

"The bomb. The Swedish team proceeded when I told them to stop. They were convinced they had to move fast in case it was activated. As they were removing a component, they inadvertently connected a circuit that triggered the bomb… They're gone."

Nyah moved back in shock, unable to speak. The Swedish team were operating on the other side of the continent, so there would be no effect where Nyah and Murphy were, but it meant a nuclear explosion in Antarctica and all that entailed. She looked at Murphy, who was equally shocked. She turned back to the screen.

"But you said it couldn't do that."

"I know."

Nyah took a couple of deep breaths.

"Okay, what do we do now?"

Carswell returned his attention to their screen.

"Proceed *very* carefully." He paused. "Maybe we should take a break. I know I could do with one."

"Sure, said Nyah. "We could do with one here as well."

"Right, say fifteen minutes."

The screen went blank.

Nyah turned to Murphy. She was shaking.

"I can't believe it, Josh. It blew up."

"I know. We need to stay cool." She raised her eyebrows, looking around at the ice.

"Yeah, like that's going to be a stretch!"

They both smiled. It cut through the tension.

"I'd better check on Matt. See how he's doing," said Nyah.

She moved around the small space and grabbed the

walkie-talkie from her pack on the side. She lifted it and pressed the TRANSMIT button.

"Hey, Matt, you there, over?"

There was silence for a moment.

"Nyah, is that you?" His voice was weak and she could hear the pain and stress.

"Sure is. How you doing?"

"Not great. I've used the last of the morphine and it's starting to hurt like hell."

"Just hang in there. We'll be done in no time…" She gave a hopeless shrug to Murphy, but she had to give Matt something to cling on to.

"Okay, the sooner the better," said Bowman. "How's it going down there? You not cut any wrong wires yet?"

"It's a slow process, but it's all going great."

"Okay, please be quick. I'm not sure how long I'm going to last." His voice was growing fainter by the minute. A tear crept into her eye.

"Stay strong, Matt. We'll be there before you know it." There was no reply. She clicked off the walkie-talkie and turned to Murphy.

"He's not good. I don't know how long he's got."

"He's tough. He'll be fine," said Murphy.

But Nyah could hear the hollow despair in his words.

Chapter Fifty-Three

Craig Richards watched the large gray Royal Navy Merlin helicopter come in to land on the helipad at the side of the beach at the Grand Gaube resort.

He stood back, shielding his eyes from the sand and dust kicked up by the rotors. A moment later he saw Martin Steel, along with another stockily built man who was dragging a large, wheeled metal case, climb down and head toward him, ducking beneath the spinning blades above.

When Steel reached him, they shook hands.

"Hello, Craig, thanks for the call. This is Duffy Jenkins," said Steel.

Jenkins stepped forward. Richards shook his hand as well.

Jenkins was a former sergeant major in the SAS, the regiment Steel had commanded for a number of years before taking over as Dominic Carter's national security adviser. In his new role, Steel had requested Jenkins join him as his assistant cum driver cum bodyguard—something he was perfectly suited to, given he'd already saved Steel's life when they'd been on operations in Afghanistan in previous years. And Jenkins had been more than happy to oblige his former commanding officer.

"Can we base ourselves in your room for now?" asked Steel.

Richards nodded and led them through the grounds to the villa.

While Jenkins proceeded to unpack the large case he'd been pulling and set up the equipment, Steel and Richards sat down at the dining table in the open-plan living area.

"Okay," said Steel, "we've got to move fast if Solano is on the island. To bring you up to speed, the documents John found in Switzerland laid out a plan to detonate eight nukes in Antarctica. This would melt a significant amount of ice and result in meters of sea level rise over the coming months. We have to stop him."

"Jesus!" said Richards. "I never knew it was that bad."

"Yeah, well it is."

"So how long do you think we have?"

"The US president is due to speak to Solano shortly. The deadline is soon. The president is going to try and stall him, as there's no way world leaders are going to agree to his demands—that's just not going to happen. So, right now, people are working in Antarctica to try to defuse the bombs. If they can do that, it won't matter what Solano does. But if he has time to transmit a signal, it'll set off a countdown on the bombs, which will ultimately decimate the planet. One of them has already gone off, and some of the teams can't reach theirs because of bad weather, so it's imperative we get to Solano to stop him. Sooner or later he's going to realize what's going on, and then who knows what he might do. He could send the signal anyway, even before the deadline."

Richards was trying to absorb all this but it was so crazy he could hardly believe it.

"Ready, sir," said Jenkins from across the room.

Steel looked up and walked over. He beckoned Richards to follow him.

When Richards reached the equipment he could see a widescreen monitor sitting upright in a protective case. Below the monitor was a keyboard, along with other controls. A thick cable led from the back of the case out onto the veranda where Jenkins had set up a portable satellite dish.

Steel typed into the keyboard. An image of the world appeared in the center of the screen. A couple more clicks and the words ACQUIRING SATELLITES appeared. After about thirty seconds, SATELLITES ACQUIRED appeared. A window then opened in the center with a cursor in it.

Steel typed into it.

Richards could see it was the set of coordinates McCready had been sent in the message he'd received.

Immediately, the image of the Earth rotated and started to zoom in—a bit like Google Earth, but when it eventually homed in on the island, it was clear this was no Google Earth. The final image steadied out at around a thousand feet, but even at that height, everything was crystal clear. The resolution was phenomenal.

"Okay," said Steel, "what can you tell me about security?"

Richards looked at the image.

"From what we could tell from the chopper, there didn't appear to be that much. As you can see"—he pointed as he continued talking—"there are a few buildings under the trees, so I guess they could have a security team there. But it looked like most of it was by remote cameras on the main structure."

Steel looked closely at the screen. "That thing is interesting. Some high-tech comms gear on there, radar. Is it floating?"

"John said it was, and there was a hollow area underneath where they kept a number of boats."

Steel again examined the image closely. He then zoomed in further and looked around in detail. Jenkins had also joined them to watch. Finally, he zoomed back out so they could see the whole island.

"Okay, with the radar, if anyone's watching, they'll see us coming at a distance, so they might try and escape. They've got to be pretty edgy, particularly this close to the deadline. The boats John mentioned shouldn't be a problem for the chopper if they go that route. And while there is a helipad, there aren't any helicopters. The only other way off is by the jet on the runway. We need to disable it so it can't take off."

Jenkins nodded. "No problem, sir. I can knock it out with some C4."

Steel nodded.

"So, how many more of you are there?" asked Richards.

Steel and Jenkins exchanged glances.

"Just us three," said Steel. "At such short notice, and not being sure how reliable the intel was, I had to make a quick decision. Duffy here fancied a couple of days in the sun, and I needed to get back in the saddle so to speak." He turned to Jenkins. "Let's get ready. Wheels up in half an hour." He then turned to Richards. "You okay to come along, Craig?"

Richards just stared at him and gulped.

"Wouldn't miss it for the world."

Half an hour later Richards ran up to the Merlin, which had its rotors turning. Steel and Jenkins were already aboard. Jenkins helped pull him inside. A couple of seconds later it lifted off into the air.

Steel and Jenkins were dressed in black one-piece combat clothing. Each wore a harness secured over their clothes, and spare ammunition bulged from pockets on the webbing. Both also had large, evil-looking knives sheathed on their thighs and a handgun holstered on their hips. Beside them, on the bench seat, each had a Heckler & Koch submachine gun.

Jenkins was going through a backpack that Richards could see held small explosives charges and other military equipment. They all wore comms units around their necks.

Steel checked an iPad-sized display that showed a real-time satellite feed of the island. It looked as before. Nothing new. He clicked the TALK button on his throat mike to speak to the pilot.

"Okay, Shane, soon as we can we need to drop down low and approach from the south. The trees on the island will shield us from their radar. Come in to land in front of the jet on the runway. Duffy can take it out and then we don't need to worry about them leaving that way."

"Sure thing, boss," said Shane over the comms.

Steel glanced at Duffy, who nodded at him. He then

nodded at Richards, who looked at him nervously but nodded back—he was as ready as he was ever going to be.

"Okay, let's do this," said Steel, as the helicopter swooped down low to skim mere feet above the water, heading north.

Chapter Fifty-Four

Solano checked the screens in the control room. He watched the cameras from around the large floating structure and checked the radar display that showed if anyone was approaching the island. He had been sure McCready had not been alone and had to prepare for whatever might happen. This was the one reason he had left Switzerland. While he was secure at that location, he was trapped if anyone tried any form of assault on the residence—here, however, he was on an island, and while on one level it might also appear as though he was trapped, he knew otherwise.

He turned to Mendes, who was standing to one side.

"Make sure all is ready. We're going to have to leave at short notice. And Juliano, I want no more talk of what happened earlier. We move on and we forget."

"Yes, sir," said Mendes as he turned to leave to carry out Solano's request.

When he'd gone, Solano checked his watch. There were

only hours left before the deadline. He knew there was activity in the Antarctic and he knew one of the bombs had gone off. He could not allow anyone to interfere with the others. But he was a man of principle. He had given the world leaders until the deadline to agree to his demands and he would give them that time.

McCready sat on a chair overlooking the pool on the main deck area. Carlita sat opposite him. He had explained to her about the message. At first she'd been confused, but then a certain understanding came over her. He'd asked her what it was, but she had refused to be drawn. He now watched her, not sure where he stood.

As he stared at her face he could still see some of the girl he had known back in Peru; maybe some of her compassion and dreams were still there.

"You know what Victor is doing is crazy," he said. She turned to him, hostility on her face. "Look, he might have the best intentions, but no one can know what the consequences will be if he carries out his threat. He's just one man. He doesn't have the right to inflict this on the world—and he's not going to be around to see the result." He said the last words more harshly than he'd meant. She looked at him sharply.

"You don't know anything about him. What he's achieved in his life. He has always wanted to do good in the world. But the world does not want to do good for itself. It takes someone with his vision, his determination, his courage, to do something like this. There is no one else. There is no other hope."

"You really believe that?"

She looked away from him. When she turned back, he could see her eyes were teary.

"Yes… yes I do."

McCready was silent for a moment.

"What did he do to you, Carlita?"

She looked at him.

"What do you mean?"

"This isn't the person I knew. The one so full of life. So kind. So caring. So wanting to change the world, but in a positive way. Now you seem so tense, as though there's a scared, lost little girl beneath all the bravado. It's like he has complete control over you."

For a moment hesitation covered her face, as though she'd been found out, but then the composure was back.

"You know nothing of my life. What has happened."

"I know, but there's always time to understand, to accept the truth… to change."

She looked at him but didn't reply.

Mendes walked into the control room. Solano turned to him.

"Everything is ready. You just need to say the word."

"Good," said Solano. He was about to continue when a handset on the desk rang. He glanced at it and then picked it up. It could be the president. Instead, it was the calm voice of his security controller in one of the buildings on shore.

"Sir, there's something you need to see."

"Yes?"

"Check the satellite view, range ten miles," said the controller.

Solano turned to the screen in front of him. He selected the satellite view of the island with a ten-mile radius.

"Okay. What am I looking at?"

"South-east of the island. Coming fast. We have a helicopter inbound."

Solano looked closely at the screen. He then adjusted the controls and zoomed in. He could see the dark gray top-down outline of a fast-moving helicopter skimming over the surface of the water.

"Thank you. We're leaving now. Make sure preparations are ready on the island. Delay them as long as you can. But minimum casualties."

"Yes, sir," replied the controller.

Solano turned to Mendes.

"We have to leave now. Get Carlita."

Mendes hurried off while Solano walked out of the control room and made his way up a level to the central hub. On the way, he collected André, who was carrying a weapon.

When they arrived, they found McCready and Carlita waiting with Mendes.

"We have to go now," said Solano to Carlita.

"What's the hurry? Have you spoken with the president?"

"Not yet, but something's come up that means we have to leave, and I mean now!" He glanced at McCready, then turned to André. "Keep him under guard. I don't want him talking to anyone."

"Yes, sir," said André. He walked toward McCready, his weapon raised.

McCready looked confused. "So, who am I supposed to talk to? There's no one else here."

"Goodbye, Mr. McCready. I trust this will be for the last time."

Solano crossed over to the elevator with Carlita and Mendes in tow.

McCready watched as they waited for the doors to open and then stepped inside. As the doors closed he could see Carlita staring at him. He wondered if he'd ever see her again.

As the elevator disappeared, André nudged him with the gun and pointed in the direction of a room to one side. But before they reached, it McCready heard the roar of a helicopter in the distance. Suddenly everything made sense. Someone was coming and Solano had to leave.

But where the hell was he going?

The elevator descended.

It went down to the level where McCready had been detained and then carried on further, stopping two levels below.

When the doors opened, Solano stepped out first. They were in a small circular room about fifteen feet in diameter. It had a hard-wearing floor covering but little else. At one end was a door. Solano walked up to it and pressed a button on a control panel. It slid smoothly to one side with an electric hum. They all walked through. Once on the other side, Solano pressed another button and the door closed.

They were in what looked like the interior of a superyacht. The floor was covered in plush carpet and the walls and ceiling were a light pastel shade. The lighting was unobtrusive, but there was the constant background hum of a generator somewhere deep within the space.

As Solano strode forward it became clear this was no yacht.

The width was limited to twenty feet, and as they passed through various sections there were no dividing doors. There were also no wide panoramic windows. Instead, a series of oval windows, three feet in diameter, looked out underwater. There was little to see through the glass as they were beneath the large structure and it was dark, but dim light spilled in from the surface some way above.

They were in a submarine.

Mendes followed Solano to the control room. They passed through a lockout area, where an airlock led beneath the sub to allow divers to explore the reefs and environment below the surface. Scuba gear hung on racks on the walls.

They walked on until they reached the control room. It was fitted out with the latest high-tech equipment to provide full automation and ease of use by a minimal crew, which in this instance would be Solano, Mendes and Carlita.

"Take her out to a distance of a mile and a depth of a hundred feet," said Solano. "Close to the drop-off, in case we need to dive deep."

"Yes, sir," said Mendes.

Solano carried on further forward while Mendes set about taking the sub to sea. Carlita followed Solano.

They stopped and sat down in deep leather seats in a luxurious area that had larger windows, though the view beyond was still of dark water.

"So this is it?" said Carlita.

Solano looked at her and smiled a weary smile. "Yes, this is what it has all been leading to. In forty minutes I will talk to the president and see if they have met the demands. I am sure they won't have, so there will only be one thing left to do—send the signal. It will start a half-hour countdown. Then it will be over."

Carlita looked at him, her face showing the enormity of the situation.

In the background they heard the engines start up. The whole structure began to vibrate slightly. Shortly after, they felt the slow movement as the submarine left the dock heading for the open water beyond the lagoon.

Chapter Fifty-Five

The helicopter flew low and fast on a direct line for the island. Steel was sure they wouldn't have been seen on any radar, and on that point he was correct—they hadn't been seen on the radar screen in the security control room on the island. There was no way he could have known, though, that Solano had access to the latest military-grade satellite technology, and that they'd been spotted as soon as they'd left the shoreline of Mauritius.

It was tense in the back.

They were readying themselves for action. Steel knew that as well as the element of surprise, speed was essential. They had to disable the jet on the runway and then approach the structure on the water as fast as possible. He didn't want to give anyone time to escape by boat, even if they could catch up to them pretty quickly in the helicopter. It was far simpler to confront Solano on land—in his home.

"Thirty seconds," said the pilot from the front.

Steel and Jenkins checked their gear. Jenkins had his

backpack already in place and his weapon at his side. Steel grabbed his Heckler & Koch and was ready to go.

Richards clung on as the helicopter swept up over the palm trees at the end of the island and swung in to land in front of the Learjet on the runway. Before the wheels had even touched down, Steel and Jenkins were out of the door.

Jenkins ran straight for the Lear while Steel checked the perimeter and scanned for any hostiles. Richards carefully climbed out of the helicopter and stayed close by it, which Steel had told him to do until he was given the all clear.

When Jenkins reached the jet, he slid underneath and pulled two charges from his backpack. He pushed them into the nose wheel and main landing gear, and then ran back over to the chopper. He checked everyone was clear and pressed a small red button on a black box he held in his right hand. Immediately there were two large BANGS as the undercarriage was blown out from the jet. It collapsed onto the ground with a THUD. It was going nowhere.

Steel then led them toward the trees at the side of the runway, which from the satellite showed a track leading to the main structure in the lagoon.

They ran through the palms and made their way along the edge of the tree line toward the walkway.

As they approached, still under the cover of the trees, they saw two armed men standing at the entrance. There were some buildings to the left. Steel indicated for Richards to stay with him and for Jenkins to go round and check the buildings.

Steel and Richards walked forward, keeping low. A few minutes later Steel received a coded beep in his earpiece. He signaled for Richards to follow him and do as he did. He couldn't afford to be delayed any longer than necessary—they had to get to Solano before he realized they were there. Worst-case scenario, if Solano felt trapped, he might blow the bombs and not wait for the deadline.

Steel stood up and walked casually toward the men at the head of the walkway. Richards followed him. As they approached, the men pointed their guns and told them to stop. Steel let his weapon fall to his side on its shoulder strap. He put his hands out to show he was no danger and continued to walk forward. When they reached the walkway both of the guards blocked their progress. One who appeared to be the leader spoke first.

"You're trespassing. This is private property."

Steel smiled at him. "We just want to talk to Victor Solano, that's all. We don't want any trouble."

The man stared at him with a humorless expression. "Do you have an appointment?"

"Not exactly," said Steel.

As he spoke, he maneuvered round so the men would be between him and the trees behind. Richards followed his lead. It all seemed extremely casual and took about ten seconds.

"Do you think there's any chance we might see him? It's really important," said Steel.

This time the man smiled.

"Not a chance."

A second later there was a sharp wolf-whistle from behind the men.

They spun round to see Jenkins with his gun aimed squarely at them. One of them attempted to fire, but he'd barely got a round off that went wide before Jenkins had shot him in the arm forcing him to drop the gun.

"Now, now," said Jenkins, "that's no way to treat guests."

In the same moment, Steel had raised his Heckler &

Koch and pointed it at the second man—the one who'd been doing the talking.

"Now, if you'll just lower your weapon, we can sort out an appointment. Okay?"

It seemed as if it wasn't okay, as the man tried to aim the gun. Steel smacked him in the head with the butt of the Heckler & Koch. He fell to the floor, out cold.

"No trouble?" Steel asked Jenkins.

"No, sir. There's a control center back there. They're all sleeping like babies now. But they must have seen us coming. They've got real-time sat coverage of the whole area."

"Yeah, well I guess he can afford it. Okay, come on, let's go talk to Solano."

The three of them ran down the walkway to the floating structure. When they reached it, Richards stayed at the entrance in case anyone tried to leave, while Steel and Jenkins spread out to search for Solano.

Steel made his way cautiously through the complex. He was impressed. He had been in many exclusive properties around the world in his official capacity, but this one took the ticket.

He had moved through to a large hub-like area when he heard whistling coming the other way. He peered round a corner. A guard was walking toward him. He had his hands in his pockets and his weapon slung behind him. Steel stepped out and leveled his gun. The man was so surprised he didn't know what to do—but the whistling stopped.

"Who are you?" he asked.

"Don't worry, I'm not going to hurt you. I do need to know a couple of things, though. First, is there a guy called John McCready here, and second, where is Victor Solano?"

The man hesitated.

"I don't know anyone called McCready. Someone came

aboard last night and has been detained. It could be him. And Solano has gone."

"Gone, Gone where?"

The man shrugged. "Gone."

"Okay, take me to McCready."

For a moment the man looked as though he was thinking about resisting, but Steel raised his gun higher and the guard realized it would be pointless. He turned and headed down the corridor. He came to a door, unlocked it, and then pulled it open. Steel indicated for him to walk in first. As he did, Steel saw someone stand up from lying on the bed.

"Hi, John, quit lying around, we've things to do."

McCready just stared at him, and when he'd got over the shock, he grinned.

"What the hell are you doing out of the office?"

"Yeah, well, thought I'd do some real work for a change. Come on."

McCready didn't need any further bidding and walked out of the room. The guard was about to follow when Steel shook his head.

"Oh no you don't."

He closed the door, locking him in.

"Craig is here," said Steel, "but the guard said Solano had gone… any idea where?"

McCready followed Steel back through complex.

"Last I saw, he was heading down to a lower level, though why, I've no idea. There are some boats down there, so he could have left that way."

"We didn't see any leave, and I have someone in a chopper at the airstrip monitoring the island by satellite. He's said no one's left."

"That's odd," said McCready, "unless…"

"What?"

"Follow me."

As they moved, Steel spoke into his comms unit.

By the time they were back in the main hub Jenkins and Richards had joined them. After Jenkins had been introduced to McCready and McCready had given Richards a welcoming hug, he turned to the elevator.

"Down here."

They crammed into the small space.

McCready pressed the button for the lowest level. It took them past where he'd been confined overnight and then stopped at the bottom. When the door opened they found themselves in a small fifteen-foot diameter room. At one end was a door with a control panel next to it. McCready walked over to it and looked out through a window in the door. All he saw was water. He turned to Steel.

"Thought so. They're in a sub."

Steel looked around the group.

"Shit! We have to move! Okay, everyone, back to the chopper."

Chapter Fifty-Six

Mendes brought the submarine to a stop a mile to the north-west of the island. The depth reading was a hundred feet as Solano had requested. While he enjoyed piloting the vessel, it could work completely autonomously in so much as you could designate a depth and location and it would navigate there all by itself.

He informed Solano of their arrival and then they both walked back to the control room. Carlita followed. They all knew what this meant.

The time had come.

Solano sat down at the main panel and took a moment. He looked up at Mendes.

"Okay, release the buoy."

Mendes clicked a switch on the communications panel. A light changed from red to a flashing amber.

On the top of the hull a small hatch opened and a satellite transceiver spooled out from the sub attached by a cable. Once the buoy was on the surface and had connected to the satellites, Solano would be able to communicate with anyone anywhere in the world.

While the system was priming itself and locking on, it gave Solano time for quiet contemplation. This was it. There would be no going back from what was going to happen in the next few minutes.

Eventually the comms system was ready. The amber flashing light on the panel changed to a steady green.

Solano glanced at Mendes and Carlita, and then dialed a number on a keypad on the desk in front of him. He clicked it onto speakerphone.

It rang four times before being answered.

"Hello, Galt," said Solano. "We come to the moment of truth, you and I."

They could hear Stevens sigh over the speaker. He sounded weary.

"Victor, we are not there yet. You have to give us more time. We have agreement from a number of countries, but for this to work as you need it to, we need more time."

But Solano couldn't give him any.

"I am sorry, Galt, the deadline has been reached. There is no more time."

"Then I am sorry too, my friend. It looks like this is the end."

"You still don't get it." Solano sighed. "This is the beginning."

He clicked off the call and glanced at Carlita and Mendes, a grim look on his face. He shook his head slowly.

"Now is the time."

The chopper lifted off from the dirt strip with Steel, Jenkins, Richards and McCready on board. Steel had given instructions to the pilot that they were looking for a submarine—no idea what size—but that it must have left within the last half hour. It couldn't have gone far, but then subs could operate in three dimensions, so even if they knew which direction it had gone, it was unlikely they would find it unless it was shallow, and given the sub didn't want to be found, that was even more unlikely.

"As I understand it," said Steel, "the deadline for President Stevens to have some sort of coalition together is coming up shortly. Presumably they need to communicate to do that. If they do, either the sub will have to surface, or if they have a comms buoy, they could extend it and remain submerged. If there's no sign of the sub, that will be our best bet—look out for the buoy. It's likely to be dark in color and about the size of a small navigation buoy, so it's needle in a haystack time."

They moved over to the square windows in the side of the helicopter, while McCready made his way to the cockpit to have a clearer view.

They found it twenty-five minutes later. While the sea was relatively calm, there was a slight chop, making the search more difficult. There had been a false alarm when Jenkins had seen something, but on closer inspection it was a discarded fishing net attached to a number of floatation buoys. What had been distressing was that they could see a large turtle trapped in the nets, and despite the desire of all on board to go and help, they had more pressing matters.

In the end, Richards found it. He'd noticed something creating a disturbance in the regular outline of the chop. When they had circled round and hovered in low at about thirty feet, it was clear it was man-made and was attached to something below. They could see the thick black cable heading down into the depths. Steel was pretty sure he could see a large shape further down, but with the spray kicked up by the rotors he couldn't be sure.

"Okay, I have to go down there," said McCready, when it had been agreed they had found the buoy.

"What can you do?" asked Steel. "Can you get inside?"

"Maybe. I'm not sure. It'll depend on what type of sub it is. Knowing Solano, he'll have the best. It won't be some off-the-shelf military or tourist sub. It'll be a bespoke model with all the bells and whistles, which means all the toys, fitted out for diving and exploration. It won't be too highly depth rated, but for divers to enter and exit it would need to have a simple airlock system, which can be operated from inside and outside in case of emergencies. If I can find it and open it, I can get inside."

"Okay," said Steel, "I'll leave that to you, John. Now, while you don't have any military training, you have far more dive experience than Duffy and me, so okay, so long as you're sure."

"Piece of cake," said McCready.

"Right, there's kit in the lockers at the back. Let me know if there's anything else you need."

"Thanks."

McCready headed for the lockers. Richards followed him.

"You okay doing this?" asked Richards.

"Don't really have a choice, do I? These guys may well be ex special forces, but that was a while back, and they'd be unlikely to cope with anything unexpected in the water."

He looked through the lockers and pulled out a wetsuit, weight belt, mask and fins and then a small pony cylinder that would be lightweight. He attached a regulator and slung it onto his back. He checked all was working, and then walked over to the side door of the chopper.

Steel watched him. As they looked out, Steel had some last-minute instructions.

"Okay, John, the easy way would be to just cut the comms buoy, but Solano could still surface and set things off from there, so, if you can, you have to disable any form of transmission system that can arm the bomb. I've no idea what it will look like or how you do it. Remember, millions of lives are potentially at stake, so the life of one man is expendable, okay?"

McCready looked at him, his expression hard.

And then Steel added, "Or one woman, if it comes to it."

"I'll do what I can," said McCready.

The chopper dropped down and hovered twenty feet above the buoy. McCready gave a last look at Steel and Richards and then jumped into the water.

He hit smoothly and swam quickly for the buoy. He wanted to make sure he grabbed the cable linking the buoy to the sub before any current could sweep him away. This would either come from the sub itself, if it was moving through the water, or from a sea current doing its thing. Given a diver could only comfortably swim against about one knot, any water movement could ruin his day. As it was, the sub was stationary but there was water movement. He had to swim hard to reach the buoy before being dragged away. On one level he was glad he'd brought the small pony cylinder as there was less drag through the water, but by its very nature it held less air, so it wouldn't last long.

He let his legs stream out in the flow on the surface for a couple of minutes and removed his mouthpiece to get his breath back and save the precious air in the cylinder. When he was happy, he threw a wave up at the chopper, kicked his fins in the air, and submerged, heading down.

The cable was thick and easy to hold on to. Once he had started to descend, the visibility was good. He could make out the large shape of the sub below. It wasn't anything like a military-sized vessel, but it looked impressive nonetheless.

He pulled himself down until he was about thirty feet above the hull. He needed to get a sense of the layout and try and work out the best way to get aboard.

The first thing was that it was big, well over two hundred feet long. From what he could see there were large viewing ports toward the front on either side. Just forward of the midpoint was a small conning tower with windows in it. To the rear of this must be where the elevator station back at the island had docked onto the sub. If there was going to be a way in through a lockout hatch it would be underneath.

The current was still strong. He held on with a firm grip as he pulled himself down until he was standing on the top of the hull. The exertion had caused his breathing rate to increase. He checked the air supply on the cylinder gauge. Not good. It was down to a quarter of a cylinder. He still wore his wrist-mounted watch/dive computer so he wasn't concerned about decompression. When he entered the sub he'd be entering a one atmosphere environment, similar to the surface, but he wouldn't have been in the water that long—still, he couldn't hang around.

He pulled himself along the side and then under the white-painted hull. As he glanced below he could see they were some way off the bottom but also close to a drop-off that disappeared into the depths. The underside of the sub was smooth and clean, except for a large hatch just aft of the center of the vessel. He had nothing to grip onto here, and as the current was still flowing, he had to fin hard. He was almost at the hatch when he sucked for air and nothing happened. He had no time to check the gauge. Instead, he threw off the useless cylinder to make him more streamlined. He then finned as hard as he could to the hatch while holding his breath.

When he reached it, there was a handle to grab onto. The center of the hatch was transparent. He could see through both airlock doors to the interior above. There was a control panel at the side. It took him precious seconds to work out he had to press and hold a button and turn a recessed handle before it would open.

There were more agonizing seconds when nothing happened. Then the red lights at the side of the panel flicked to green and the hatch automatically swung down.

McCready scrambled inside, but the water had to be evacuated before he could breathe. He looked desperately round for the controls. He found a HATCH CLOSE button and rammed it hard. The outer hatch swung to, and an automatic evacuation of the water took place. As the level dropped he pulled off his mask and gasped for air. Once the water had gone, he leaned against the side and sat there getting his breath back for a few moments.

When he had calmed down, he removed his fins and pressed the DOOR OPEN button for the inner hatch. When the lock had disengaged, he pushed the door up and climbed into the interior of the sub.

The space he was in had dive equipment on the walls. A door led out from each end.

He closed the hatch and checked which way to go. To his right was heading toward the stern where the engines and maintenance rooms would be.

He headed forward.

As he walked through the vessel, he stared around in

awe. It was unlike any sub he'd ever been on. He could have been walking through a luxurious superyacht. In fact, it reminded him of the *Freedom Seas*, but given Solano owned both vessels, it wasn't surprising they had similar styles.

He noticed he left damp footprints on the carpet. He smiled.

He'd gone about fifty feet when he heard voices. He slowed and crept forward. He was in a corridor that seemed to lead to a control room of some sort, maybe from where the sub was driven. He inched up to the entrance of the room and risked a quick look. He could see Solano, Mendes and Carlita at a panel on the far side.

Solano was speaking.

"I am sorry, Galt, the deadline has been reached. There is no more time."

"Then I am sorry too, my friend. It looks like this is the end," replied a voice through a speaker. McCready thought he recognized the voice of the president of the United States. He should know, after all.

"You still don't get it." Solano sighed. "This is the beginning."

Solano clicked off the call and leaned back in his chair. He glanced up at Carlita and Mendes, a grim look on his face. He shook his head slowly.

"Now is the time."

Chapter Fifty-Seven

Solano picked up the small control box and plugged it into a connector on the panel in front of him. The top of the box had a hinged transparent screen which he lifted up. Beneath it was a small display and a keypad. He pressed a button on the side. A start-up process was displayed on the screen. When it was ready there was a simple command—ENTER CODE.

Solano looked at it for a few seconds. He was about to lift his finger to type in the code when Mendes stepped forward.

"You're really going to do this?"

Solano paused and then swiveled in his chair to stare intently at Mendes. Carlita watched from the side.

From his position behind a bulkhead, McCready could sense a sudden rise in tension in the room. It looked like the box Solano held would transmit the code to start the countdown to detonate the bombs. Somehow, he had to stop that from happening. He'd been ready to run forward, but this new development was interesting. He'd wait a little longer and see what happened.

"Juliano," said Solano, "this is what I have planned. You know this."

"But I never thought you would actually go through with it," said Mendes.

Solano looked at him with sadness, and not a little frustration. Carlita also wore a look of concern.

"It is happening, Juliano. Now, do not displease me. You owe me your life, remember?"

At this, Mendes hesitated.

From where McCready was hiding, it looked like Mendes was saying a quick prayer. And before he realized what was happening Mendes had leapt for the control box.

But Solano had expected it. In a movement that was impressive for a man of his age, Solano jumped up and pushed Mendes aside, knocking him to the floor. In the same instant he pulled a gun from his waistband and aimed at him.

McCready could see the fear on Carlita's face. She put a restraining hand on Solano's arm, but he ignored her, brushing it off.

Mendes struggled to his feet and again advanced on Solano.

Solano kept the gun steady, his finger tightening on the trigger.

"No, Victor!" cried Carlita, throwing herself between them.

The sound of the gunshot was amplified in the confined space, echoing off the walls.

Carlita's movement was enough to put off Solano's aim, but the bullet still hit Mendes in the chest, before embedding itself in the control panel behind.

As Mendes went down, sparks and a loud bang came from the panel.

Then, as McCready watched, he heard a name he had not heard for twenty-five years.

"Fernando!" shouted Carlita.

She ran to shield him from Solano.

McCready stood there, rooted to the spot. Mendes was her brother. He knew there had been something familiar about him. But he had to act now. Solano was aiming the gun at Carlita, who was completely shielding her brother—protecting him to the end.

Solano grabbed her and flung her aside. McCready could see an uncompromising determination in his eyes. Carlita hit the side of the control desk, smashing her head. She cried out. In the same instant McCready ran into the room and charged at Solano.

Before Solano had time to react, he hit him in the chest, hurling him back and onto the floor. When he was down, McCready kicked the gun from his hand and slugged him in the face. He went out cold. McCready then moved to Carlita. She was lying on the floor in a daze. He brushed her hair away from her face. She looked up at him and her eyes went wide.

"John?" was all she could manage.

Once he was sure she was okay, he crossed over to Fernando. He was groaning on the floor, a wide pool of blood flowing onto the pale carpet, staining it red. McCready supported his head and looked down at him.

"Fernando," he said, kindness and caring in his eyes. "I never knew it was you."

Fernando smiled weakly. "I am sorry, John. I wanted to tell you, but I didn't want to put you in danger. He helped me years ago. He gave me a new life, but I never thought he would do this." He paused, growing weaker all the time. "I always remembered you. For the help you gave me and for caring for Carlita. I knew you would want to help—that's why I sent the message. That is why I chose Juliano Mendes —J. M."

McCready just stared at him, stunned—not knowing what to say.

Carlita came over. She held her brother's hand. The tears were flowing freely from her. McCready backed away to allow her this time. It didn't look as though there was long. It would be the one time she had not been able to protect him.

Carlita held Fernando as he became weaker. She whispered words in his ear that McCready couldn't hear. He watched her as she rocked him, like she must have done when he was a baby, but eventually Fernando stopped moving.

Stopped breathing.

McCready gave her a minute and then gently put his hand on her shoulder. She turned to him, her face a mask of desolation. He pulled her to him and she clung on hard, all the bravado of before gone. She was a broken, frail human being who had lost everything.

McCready was so wrapped up in the moment he had failed to see Solano slowly getting himself to his feet. He had no gun, but when McCready noticed he was moving, he watched as he stumbled across to the control panel. It was only when McCready saw him pick up the small box that he realized what he was going to do. He unwrapped himself from Carlita and tried to run at Solano. But it appeared as though everything was happening in slow motion. He had only made it halfway across the room when he heard a computerized voice.

CODE ACCEPTED
ACTIVATION HAS NOW COMMENCED

McCready grabbed for the box, but when he had it he could see the same message on the small screen. He turned to Solano. The man had a thin, resigned smile on his lips. He wasn't gloating. He wasn't triumphant. It was merely satisfaction at the culmination of his life's achievements, and that even now he hadn't failed. He slumped down into a chair and stared around the room, his eyes finally coming to rest on McCready.

"You can't stop it now," he said, "the world's fate is in its hands."

McCready stared at him evenly.

"You had no right."

Solano looked off into the distance for a moment and then back at McCready.

"Something had to be done. There was no other way."

"But you're gambling with the lives of millions."

Solano smiled ruefully.

"Life is one big gamble Mr. McCready. It's just how you play the game."

McCready was thinking of a response when he heard a wail from Carlita. He turned to again see her holding Fernando's body in her arms. He was about to move to her side when there was a bang and more sparks from the panel where the bullet had hit. A warning light started flashing and an alarm sounded.

He rushed to the panel.

AUTONOMOUS CONTROL DISENGAGED
ALL SYSTEMS OFFLINE

The lights flickered and he felt a sudden lurch in the sub's attitude. A second later the hull tilted down at the nose. He felt them moving deeper. He was about to try to regain some form of control when there was a gunshot from behind.

He whirled round, his heart in his mouth at what he might see.

Carlita was standing over Solano's body, the gun in her hand. Her face was expressionless. The tears had stopped, but their tracks streaked her cheeks. She just stood there, staring at him. McCready crossed over and slowly took the gun. He then pulled her away and looked at her. It was as though she was in a trance.

He shook her.

"Hey!"

Nothing.

"Hey! We have to move. The sub's sinking. We have to get out of here."

He shook her again, and this time there was a response. It was slow but she seemed to be understanding what he was saying.

"Come on, you have to help me."

And now he felt she was back. She glanced briefly at the body of Solano on the floor and then she looked at her brother, and he saw her face harden.

And then she was all focus.

"What do we have to do?"

At that moment the sub hit the seabed with a massive crash. They heard a loud BANG and then the sound of rushing water.

Chapter Fifty-Eight

Above the shelter they'd erected over the site to keep out the weather, the weather was fighting back.

Nyah and Murphy could hear the gale tugging at the fabric. The pitons Murphy had fixed into the ice were being tested to the limit.

A minute later one of them broke free.

The canvas whipped around like a crazed banshee, sending snow scurrying inside and sucking out the warmth. Murphy jumped up. He zipped his jacket tight and pulled on his gloves. He then climbed out into the screaming gale. Nyah watched him go.

This was all they needed.

The screen in front of her came to life again with the face of Major Carswell.

"Okay, Nyah, are you good to continue?"

"Yes, thanks. Let's get this over with."

"Right, now take a look at the wires next to the cylinder."

Nyah shone the light down into the drum and looked closer.

Outside, it was all Murphy could do to stand up. He struggled to find the loose corner of the canvas. It was nighttime and pitch-black. He found it and grabbed the unsecured end, bringing it under control. He knelt down, forcing it to the ground, then pulled a piton hammer from his belt and started to knock in a new one. He added a second to make sure and then leaned back to check it was secure. He was just standing up to go and check on the rest of the pitons when there was a loud CRACK from the darkness ahead of him. A second later, the satellite dish hurtled toward him out of the storm. He didn't even have time to fling his arms up to protect himself when the small curved dish hit him in the head.

He slumped to the ground, unconscious.

In the pit below, Nyah thought she heard a THUMP from outside, but she couldn't be sure because of the noise of the gale. At the same time, the video feed on the screen went blank. She stared at it in shock, and then glanced above her.

"Murphy! You okay?" she shouted.

Nothing.

"Murphy!"

She was about to go outside to check on him when there was a whirring sound from the bomb. She turned to look at it in fear. The noise was coming from deep within its workings, but a small red light on the steel box at the side of the drum had also come on—the one Carswell had told her not to worry about. But now Nyah was worried, and she definitely didn't like the sound the bomb was making.

She didn't know what to do.

The video link was dead. Whatever she did to try to regain the connection failed—it was gone. She also didn't know what had happened to Murphy—and the bomb was whirring—talk about information overload.

She decided the bomb was the most pressing.

She looked closely at the small box. It was sealed, but on the top were four Phillips screw heads—one in each corner. She grabbed a screwdriver and quickly undid the screws, careful to collect them and put them safely to one side. She then took a deep breath and lifted the top off the box.

Inside she saw something that made her gasp and her heart beat faster.

There was a countdown timer displaying minutes and seconds. It currently showed twenty-five minutes, ten seconds. The numbers were decreasing. Also, below the timer was a series of red lights—eight of them. As she watched, they started blinking, and then, one by one, they turned green—all except one. She thought for a moment. Eight lights—eight bombs. And she realized this must be the master control system for the other bombs. The reason one of the lights wasn't green was because it had exploded—it wasn't there anymore.

She looked around for anything else: a switch to turn it off—*that would have been nice*.

Anything.

Clearly the box was designed to trigger the bomb when the countdown reached zero, so in other words the bomb would not go off if the countdown stopped. Just speculating, it might also not go off if the timer was disconnected from the bomb. While she'd seen enough movies to realize there was always a conundrum as to which wire to cut to disarm a bomb, there had so far been no booby traps that Carswell had seen that would have set the bomb off. Her only hope was that this had been constructed in a similar fashion and that if she managed to disconnect the timer, the bomb would not explode.

It was her only hope.

She peered into the drum to see how the box was connected to the explosives. It was tight, but as she looked underneath she could see two wires strapped to the side, leading from the box down into the components below.

She smiled wryly—they were red and blue.

Okay, she wasn't worried about color. Her only chance was to break the circuit—either wire would do.

She checked the timer—twenty-two minutes, fifteen seconds. She had some time to think. Twenty-two minutes, fifteen seconds of what could be the rest of her life.

But first she had to see if she could find Murphy—to check she wasn't doing anything stupid. It was a big decision.

The wind was still tearing at the shelter. She climbed out of the pit and pulled on her jacket. She then put on her gloves and unzipped the entrance. Immediately snow blew inside and the wind tugged aggressively at the canvas. She poked her head out. They must have been in the heart of the storm. Snow flew past horizontally. She tried to shout for Murphy, but it was no good. He'd never have heard her. There was little hope. If she went out there and searched for him she could get lost in the darkness. She turned round and zipped the front back up.

She sat down on the floor and leaned against one of the poles that supported the roof. There wasn't even the chance of getting any help for Murphy, whatever had happened to him.

Her mind drifted back over her life. What she had achieved. What her dreams had been. And as she did, she found herself starting to cry. Everyone had dreams. Everyone thought they would have an amazing life—but it rarely turned out that way. She thought back to why she had gone to the Antarctic in the first place and realized that while she loved science and all it could teach her, it had been an excuse—she had been running away… away from the world, all points north. There had been nothing for her there.

She crossed over to the drum and glanced at the timer.

Eight minutes.

She thought of Matt and the fact that for the first time in a long time she had dared to dream she could maybe be with someone, and that they might have had a future together, but that had all gone. He had to be dead.

And then she came to a realization.

They had been told what the bombs were designed to do. To change the world—and in a flash she realized that was what she wanted too—it was one of the reasons she'd come down here in the first place, to do the research to prove to the world how serious the issues of climate change were.

Now she wouldn't have to—they would see for themselves.

And in that moment, she knew what she had to do.

She relaxed on the floor, a calm and serene composure coming over her.

She leaned back and closed her eyes.

She no longer wondered what would happen if she cut the wires.

She no longer wanted to cut the wires.
She wanted the bombs to go off.

Chapter Fifty-Nine

The sub was filling fast. McCready crossed to the panel and checked the depth gauge—a hundred and seventy-five feet. Outside it was almost black.

He looked around and then turned to Carlita.

"Can you dive?"

She shook her head. He could see that the look of trauma from losing her brother and shooting Solano was now changing to a look of fear as she realized the situation they were in.

He had seen the dive gear when he had come on board, and he would have easily been able to make it to the surface, but with Carlita it would be a different matter. If it was the absolute only option he would take it. He was sure he could get her to the surface okay, but they were lying on the seabed and the lockout hatch was on the bottom. The only way would be through the upper hatch, which would mean flooding the sub before leaving, and it would not be a pleasant experience. It was the final option.

He looked around the control room for anything that might give him an edge.

"What else do you have on board? Anything that might help?"

She thought about it.

"I don't know. There are some watercraft—Jet Skis, a small boat you can access from a compartment when on the surface. There's also an ROV on a cable that can inspect the seabed. That's about it."

"Show me."

She led him through the sub. The water level was rising. It was sloshing around their ankles everywhere they went now.

They eventually came to a compartment just past the lockout hatch through which he'd entered. As they passed the hatch, he noticed the inner door was sticking upright. He hadn't left it like that. The impact with the seabed must have knocked it open.

In the ceiling, through a transparent hatch, was a small ROV. It wasn't as sophisticated as the one they'd used on the wreck of the plane, but it had a camera and lights, and, most importantly, a small manipulator arm at the front. He checked out the control desk at the side. There were two joysticks and a screen to view what the camera saw.

A plan was coming to him.

"Okay, great. Come with me."

He led her back to the main control room.

"Do you know how to unspool the comms buoy they put out?"

She looked around the controls.

"I think so."

She eventually found it.

"Here."

McCready looked it over and then operated the switch that allowed the winch to pay out more cable. He needed the buoy on the surface.

After a couple of minutes there was a BEEP that indicated it was there.

Next, he looked around for the radio controls. He found them and retuned to Channel 16—the international distress channel.

He picked up the mike and spoke into it. When he received a reply from the pilot of the Merlin, he asked to talk to Steel.

"John, what's happened? We watched you for a while, but then the buoy disappeared."

"Long story. Solano is dead but he managed to transmit the code to Antarctica. I would assume the bombs are going to detonate. The sub is filling with water and we're dead on the bottom. There's dive gear on board, but I can't get Carlita up that way except as a last resort. Do you have lift capability on the chopper?"

"Yeah, we have cables and a winch. What do you want to lift?"

"A submarine."

"What?"

"There's an ROV on board. If you can get a cable down to us, I should be able to attach it to the sub. You can then pull us up to the surface and we can get out. The sub is getting heavier by the minute with the leak, but you should be able to hold us long enough to escape."

There was silence for a moment then Steel was all business.

"Okay, we'll see what we can do."

"Thanks," said McCready.

He glanced at Carlita and then they headed back to the ROV controls.

When he reached them he fired up the small machine. He checked over the launch protocols and opened the outer hatch. He then piloted the ROV out into the water. He watched the screen from the onboard camera. It was dark outside but the high-powered lights soon lit up the hull of the sub. Once he was in position he set the machine down on the hull and let go of the joysticks.

He then crossed into the adjacent area and over to the dive gear. He assembled two aqualungs and grabbed some masks and fins, before giving Carlita a need-to-know crash course in scuba diving—just in case.

He then returned to the controls.

There was nothing on the camera. He thought it best to move up to the top of the conning tower, which was pretty central, and scan the water for the cable, assuming they could get it down to him.

He didn't have long to wait.

Five minutes later he saw it.

The cable was swinging in the water. There was a large hook on the end with a failsafe that would keep it attached to anything it was secured to.

McCready maneuvered the ROV to grab the hook. He then searched around for something to attach it to on the sub. The easiest was the railing around the top of the conning tower where people could stand when the sub was on the surface. It wasn't the strongest attachment point, but there would be no real weight put on it as they weren't actually going to lift the sub out of the water, just get it up to the surface to give them time to get out. There would be no time to take the bodies of Fernando and Solano off with them, but they could be recovered another day.

A few minutes later McCready had attached the cable. He ran back to the control room and told Steel they could start to lift. They needed to keep it slow and steady, otherwise the drag of the water might break off the attachment point.

He then returned to the lockout room and helped Carlita put on the aqualung. He had no idea what was going to happen next. They made their way to the hatch. As they prepared to leave, they could hear the metal of the hull groan as the helicopter started the lift. It was slow but there was definite movement.

Inside, the water was still rising. It was now up to their knees. He hoped it wouldn't increase too much as the strain might become too great.

They sat there for what seemed like an eternity. Carlita looked nervous. They didn't speak but McCready gave her a reassuring smile every now and then. They could see it getting lighter through the transparent door of the lockout hatch.

There was another groan from the structure.

He pulled on his aqualung in case they had to make a fast exit. The groaning increased. Then there was a sudden jerk and the sub started sinking.

The cable had broken.

"Oh shit! We have to move, now!" he yelled.

Carlita hadn't even had time to put on her fins. She managed to pull her mask over her face and put the mouthpiece in her mouth when McCready grabbed her and pushed her into the hatch, which was already full of water.

The sub was starting to roll over.

He pulled the door closed—but it wouldn't stay shut. When he let go of the handle it sprang back up. He yanked it shut again.

"Hold this closed," he shouted through his mouthpiece.

She gripped the handle nervously as McCready moved down to the lower door. Then he pressed the control that would open the outer door.

Nothing happened.

He pressed it again, but all he got was a loud BUZZ and a red light flashed.

A message appeared on the panel at the side.

HATCH CANNOT BE OPENED UNTIL INNER DOOR IS SECURE

He looked back at Carlita.

"Pull it to. Hold it tight."

She pulled down as hard as she could.

He tried the button again, but with the same result.

She shrugged. It was all she could do.

All the time the sub was sinking.

Carlita looked down at McCready. Even though she was scared to death, her mind was still sharp. And suddenly everything became clear.

She knew what she had to do.

She quickly pushed the inner door up and climbed back into the sub.

McCready looked at her questioningly. But when he saw what she was going to do, he shook his head violently and moved up toward her.

But she was now in the room above.

She pushed down on the door, sealing McCready inside. She then turned the locking handle to secure it shut and crossed to the controls on the wall. She pushed the OPEN

OUTER DOOR button. As she looked through the glass, she saw the door open behind McCready.

McCready turned and looked up at her. He banged on the glass.

"No, Carlita! We'll find another way."

She could see the anguish in his eyes. And in that moment, all the feelings she'd had for him came racing back. How she wished life had turned out differently.

She knew, now, what she had done to him, that all the years with Solano had been a lie. She had lost everything: her brother; the man she had thought she had loved for all those years; and the only man she had ever truly loved— McCready.

She had nothing to live for.

She put her hand to the glass. McCready did the same from his side.

Their eyes locked.

And in that moment they lived a lifetime together. Everything that might have been flashed between them.

She could see the pain in his eyes, and she knew he had forgiven her.

McCready continued to stare at Carlita through the glass. There was nothing he could do. Without her keeping the door locked from above, the outer door could not have been opened, and to open the inner door now would have resulted in an explosion of water into the sub that would have killed her.

He checked his dive computer. They were at a hundred and fifty feet and getting deeper by the second. If he didn't go now, it would be too late.

He took a last, agonizing look, and he could feel his eyes

welling up. He could faintly hear her voice through the glass as the tears flowed down her face.

"I'm so sorry, my John. I am so sorry."

He touched the glass one last time, staring deeply into her eyes.

"I'll come back for you. I'll get you out."

But he had to go.

He turned and pulled himself through the outer hatch.

As he pushed away from the hull, he looked back. The sub was now almost vertical and descending fast. He watched as it hit the seabed close to the drop-off, but rather than fall flat onto the bottom, it started to slide, and then McCready watched in horror as it plunged over the edge into the abyss.

"Nooooooo!" he screamed in despair.

While Carlita had made questionable decisions in her life, she had been set on a path that had been out of her control—but no one deserved this. He could barely imagine the terror she must be feeling as the sub sank further. Eventually it would reach its crush depth and then it would all be over.

There was no hope.

When his breathing had calmed, he realized *he* was not out of danger. He checked the depth and remaining air supply and looked up to the world above—one that, for him, would never be the same again.

He slowly ascended to the surface.

Five minutes later he burst through into a maelstrom. The water around him was whipped into a frenzy by the downwash from the helicopter fifty feet above.

As McCready looked up, he could see Richards leaning out of the door, scanning the water. He saw him point and look back inside. A moment later Steel joined him. The chopper descended lower. A rescue harness followed.

When it reached him, he let it touch the water to earth any electrostatic charge generated by the helicopter before grabbing it. He then scooped it under his arms and gave a whirling signal with his finger for them to lift. A second later he felt himself swept out of the water and rising up toward the waiting aircraft above.

Strong arms pulled him inside.

When he was free of the harness he threw off the aqualung and slumped to the floor. He leaned back against the side, exhausted. Richards bent down to check he was okay.

He looked up at him with pain etched across his face.

Not only were Carlita and Fernando dead.

The signal had been sent.

The bombs were primed.

Chapter Sixty

Nyah had almost lulled herself to sleep. After she had made the decision to let it happen, her mind had drifted. She wondered what it would be like when the explosion came. What happened in the afterlife? Was it like the stories—your life flashes before you and you see all your loved ones there waiting for you, or was it just a blank emptiness forever, and the whole of your life was for nothing and meaningless?

She was just thinking how terrible that would be when she thought she heard a noise. She was so zoned out she almost missed it. But no, there was something there.

A faint crackle.

Slowly she came to focus. But she couldn't hear anything.

But then it came again.

It was definitely a crackle of some sort, and in with the distortion she thought she could hear a voice.

Suddenly her eyes flicked open. She jumped up as fast as her state would allow and hurried over to the walkie-talkie. As she reached it, it came again.

It was Matt.

She had convinced herself he was dead. He hadn't responded to any of the calls she'd tried to make earlier, and with the onset of night and the ever-increasing gale, the temperature at the helicopter must have plummeted. Couple that with his injuries, and she'd tried to put it in a place in her mind she couldn't access. But now he was there speaking on the walkie-talkie, or was it just her mind playing tricks? Was she hallucinating?

But it came again.

"Nyah, do you read, over?"

The voice was faint. But it was definitely a voice.

She grabbed the walkie-talkie.

"Matt! Matt! It's Nyah. Are you okay?"

"Nyah, thank god. I passed out. No idea how long, and then when I woke I couldn't reach you."

"How are you? How's the pain?"

"Pain's not too bad. Not great, but it's the cold. I'm sure I've got frostbite. I can't feel my legs, but I think I could make it. If we can just get out of here."

She was so overjoyed to hear his voice she forgot about everything else.

"Matt, it's so great to hear you. We'll get out. I promise."

"The bomb. How's it going with the bomb?"

And suddenly she was very much back in the present.

She very much had something to live for.

She dropped the walkie-talkie and ran over to the drum. She peered at the timer and nearly screamed.

20… 19…18…

She looked around desperately. In the tool box at the base of the drum was a pair of wire cutters. She grabbed them.

10... 9... 8...

She reached into the drum and found the red and blue wires connecting the timer to the bomb, but they were hard up against the side. She couldn't get the cutters between the wires and the side of the drum.

5... 4... 3...

And then she could.

She snipped them in quick succession, not giving a damn about the color.

She slumped down onto the ice and pulled her knees up close to her chest, as if the added protection would do any good against a nuclear explosion.

And she waited...

And waited...

And nothing happened.

After a minute she released herself from her fetal position and slowly stood up.

She peered into the drum.

The timer was at one second.

All the indicator lights for the other bombs were off. Cutting the wires had broken the connection and there was now nothing to trigger them.

She looked at the rest of the components. The noise had stopped. All was silent and quiet. She leaned back against the side of the drum and laughed.

Then she whooped for joy.

She jumped out of the pit and ran to grab the walkie-talkie.

"Matt, Matt, it's okay. We're going to be okay! We'll come for you soon. I promise. Then we have a lot to talk about. I promise that too." She then heard a groan coming from above. In the rush she'd completely forgotten about Murphy. "Look, I have to go."

She clicked off the walkie-talkie.

She scrambled up the side of the pit and crawled outside. It was still blowing strongly, but some of the viciousness of the storm was abating. She saw a crumpled form on the ice. Snow was piling up around it. She rushed over and rolled Murphy onto his back. He had a nasty gash on his head.

He looked up at her, his eyes blurry and confused.

"We lost the dish," he said, his voice full of despair. "There's no feed. We're on our own. How are we going to stop it now?"

She smiled down at him.

"Don't worry. I'll think of something."

Chapter Sixty-One

McCready had finally made it home in the middle of the afternoon. The weather was rainy and blowy but he didn't mind. After he'd put on the lights and dumped his things on the floor, he grabbed a beer from the fridge and walked through into the living room.

It was a far different homecoming from before.

Then, he had been in delayed shock about what Carlita had done. Now, he was just trying to come to terms with what had happened.

The whirlwind of events had moved so fast he had been left physically and emotionally drained. Over the previous weeks his feelings for Carlita had traveled the full gamut, from love and friendship, through shock and hate, to a now sad realization of what her life had been like, and what circumstances had done to her. Couple that with the revelation and death of Fernando, and the whole episode had been a tragic culmination of factors that had been set in motion many years before.

McCready had been stunned when he'd realized who

Juliano Mendes was—the small boy he'd helped all those years ago and who had brought Carlita into his life. The fact he had chosen a name with his initials was something he would never forget.

It had also been confirmed that the sub had been lost in the depths. The bodies of Solano, Fernando and Carlita would never be recovered.

It would take him a long time to process it all, to be able to fully move on.

And before he could start, there was one thing he had to do.

He walked through into the hallway and pulled on a thick jacket from a hook by the door. He then made his way outside. The rain had stopped but there was a stiff breeze blowing in off the sea. He walked down to the back of the house and opened the garage door. Inside, he found some old packing cases he stored items in from his past. At the bottom of one of them he found a small wooden box. There were intricately carved images of birds on the lid and trees and plants around the side. He had picked it up when he had been backpacking in Peru all those years ago.

He pulled it out and dusted it off.

He then walked down into the garden.

The incinerator was standing toward the end. It still held the ashes of the poncho Carlita had made for him. But he now saw them in an entirely different light to before. He now wanted the feelings, emotions and history attached to them to stay close to him.

It was all he had left of her.

He slid the metal tray out of the bottom, opened up the small wooden box, and poured the ashes inside.

He then returned to the house and placed the box on a

shelf in the center of the wall where the poncho had hung for all those years.

As he did so, all the thoughts of Carlita, from the time they had first met, came flooding back. It was strange and sometimes cruel how life worked out. But the world kept turning and you had to go on. He felt his eyes moisten as he looked at the box. It was like a page had been turned in his life.

After a few minutes, he needed some air. He made his way down to the beach and let the wind blow away the past. The waves were rolling in, in their never-ending cycle. Some rippled calmly up onto the sand, while others broke fifty feet out with spray and surf crashing onto the beach.

He had a whole exciting new future to look forward to, and he knew, deep down, it was going to be different from his past, and in the best possible way.

He also realized he didn't want to waste a single second of it.

With a final look out to sea, he headed back to the house. He hung up his coat, walked through into the living room, took a deep breath, and picked up the phone. There were a couple of calls he had to make, the first of which was making him feel extremely nervous.

He checked the time.

He didn't want to disturb the person in question due to the time-zone differences. He then checked through his contacts to find a number he had never dialed before. He keyed in the digits and waited while it rang. There were eight rings before being answered. The voice on the other end sounded elderly, but there was also a strength to it.

"Hello," said the voice.

McCready took a deep breath.

"Hello, Mr. Kowalski?"

"Speaking. Who's this?"

McCready took another breath.

"My name's John McCready. We've never met, but your daughter may have mentioned me to you."

This time McCready *held* his breath.

There was a pause and then the voice continued, but there was a curious and intrigued tone to it.

"Yes, she has mentioned you a few times. You seem like an interesting man, Mr. McCready."

McCready didn't quite know how to take that.

"Thank you, sir." He paused. "If I may, there's something I'd like to ask you."

Clare watched as Max ran around the small area of garden to the side of the pool at the rear of the house. He was actually growing up fast into a fully-fledged dog, but mentally he was still a puppy and still had a determined, independent mind to do things his way, which to him was clearly the best way to do things.

She looked up as her lifelong friend Jade Mancini walked out through the glass sliding doors at the rear of the house and onto the pool surround carrying two glasses of wine. It was sunny and Jade had come over to stay for a couple of days and chill out. Clare had not heard from McCready since he'd said he wouldn't be long and he'd get back to her. That had been days ago. On the one hand she was starting to worry—she knew if he hadn't called he could be in some kind of trouble—but on the other, she was getting a crawling feeling in the pit of her stomach. The last time he hadn't called for a while he'd ended up becoming far too close to a Japanese girl on the other side of the world.

She took the wine from Jade, smiled her thanks, and looked out over the city.

"Okay, come on, what's bugging you?" said Jade in her down to earth, no-nonsense way. "And don't tell me it's nothing. I know you, girl—it's something."

Clare smiled and looked at her friend. There was no point trying to hide it. She'd get it out of her in the end.

"He's been gone for days without calling."

"And this means…?" said Jade.

"Well, you know. What happened before."

Jade sighed, looked at her and shook her head.

"He explained what happened before. You guys are over that. Why are you worried?"

"I don't know. It's stupid, but I need to know we're going somewhere."

"Going somewhere! You told me how all loved up you were before he left. You were talking about being together long term. What's changed?"

"Well, this girl for one reason. I told you what she did to him. He was so different when he spoke to me. As though a part of him was missing—gone. I can't describe it. It didn't seem like *him* anymore."

"Well, if what you said she did was the half of it, I'd be pretty pissed if someone did that to me. You just have to give him time."

Clare smiled weakly. "Yeah, maybe, but it would be great if he showed me how much he cared."

Jade had been taking a sip of her wine. She spluttered the drink all over herself.

"Will you listen to yourself. The guy flew halfway round the world. Risked his life to go into the center of one of the worst terrorist incidents ever to strike America—to save your ass! All while you guys were 'on a break!' Yeah, I guess

I had a girlfriend like that, I'd say she showed a lack of commitment!"

Clare stared at her for a second and then looked guilty.

"Yeah, I suppose that was pretty awesome…"

"You think?" said Jade, her eyebrows raised as high as they could go.

"But I still don't know where he is, what he's been doing."

Clare was still staring pointedly at Jade when the phone rang. She lifted her iPhone from the small table next to the recliner and looked at the caller ID.

"Shit, it's John!" She looked at Jade. "Here, you answer it. I can't talk to him right now."

"No way! He's your guy, you sort him out."

But she let it ring. Jade was looking at her and becoming more and more exasperated. Finally, she grabbed the phone, glared at Clare, and hit CALL ANSWER. She spoke with a wide smile on her face.

"Hi, John, it's Jade. Clare won't be a minute, she's just on her way."

Clare shook her head vigorously and glared back at her friend.

"Not now!" she hissed.

"What was that?" said Jade into the phone. "No, no, she was just telling Max off for something. You know how he gets. She's just here. I'll hand you over."

She passed the phone to Clare, who looked daggers at her. She took it and then took a deep breath.

"Hi, John, it's been a while. How are you?"

There was a pause on the line.

"Hey, you okay?" said McCready. "I was tied up with some stuff. Had to sort a few things out. I'll tell you when I see you. I've missed you so much."

Clare felt she was folding but tried to remain firm.

"I'm good thanks."

Again, there was a pause on the line.

"You sure you're okay, you sound a little distant?"

Clare couldn't pretend anymore.

"Well, you said you were going to call right back. It's been ages. I had no idea where you'd gone or who you're with. What am I supposed to think?"

"Clare, listen to me. Think about what we said before I left LA. All that's still true. In fact, I've had a lot of time to think about this and to me it's more true than ever."

Clare took a deep breath.

"Well, it's something we can talk about when I see you."

"No," said McCready firmly, "we need to talk about it now."

"Look, John, there's nothing you could say or do that'll change anything right now. Let's just leave it at that and then we can talk when everything calms down and we can be quietly together."

The pause was longer this time.

"No... I know that's not how you feel." He paused again. "Okay, let me ask you one question and then you can leave things till we meet up if you like."

"Okay," she said cautiously. "What is it?"

"You need to go and fetch something first."

"What?"

"Just humor me."

Clare sighed. Jade looked at her with a questioning expression but Clare just rolled her eyes.

"Okay, what do you want me to do?"

"Go to the bedroom."

"Go to the bedroom? Really?"

"Just do it." His voice was firmer now. She felt slightly taken aback.

"Okay, I'm going."

She gave Jade a look and then stood up and walked into the house. Max stopped what he was doing, looked at Clare, then Jade, then back at Clare, and then woofed to himself and trotted off round the side of the pool.

Clare walked into the cool of the house. She made her way through the main living area, out into the airy white-walled corridor, and on to the main bedroom at the end with a view across LA.

"Okay, I'm here."

"Right, go to the set of drawers with my clothes in it."

She walked over to it.

"Okay."

"Now open the top draw and tell me what you see."

"John, is this really necessary?"

"You can tell me in a minute. What's inside?"

She pulled open the drawer. There were a few of pairs of boxers, which made her smile, and a pile of black socks. She shrugged.

"Just some boxers and a load of socks."

"No, there's something else, at the back."

"What?"

"The rest of your life."

Clare was totally confused and leaned in to feel behind the socks. She pushed them aside and then her fingers felt something solid at the rear of the drawer. As they wrapped around the small velvet box her heart knew something before her brain knew.

It started beating faster.

She pulled the box out from the pile of socks and stared at it. She dropped the phone as she clutched the box in her hands and slowly opened up the top. She looked in at the beautiful diamond-encrusted ring. It sparkled in the sunlight streaming in through the windows. A tear flowed down her cheek, and then another and another.

"Hello," came from the phone on the floor.

She glanced down in a daze and slowly picked up the phone. She was sobbing hard now.

"There was only this old box—nothing much," she said through the tears.

There was a longer pause this time.

"And by the sounds of things you opened it. And I'm only going to ask this once."

Jade had been glad McCready had called. She had known Clare a long time and loved her to bits. Clare was incredibly passionate, but she sometimes maybe overthought things a little, which made her get the wrong end of the stick or think something was one way when, in fact, it was the other. She hoped that was the case this time. Clare and McCready were made for each other. She hadn't spent much time with the man, but when she'd called him to tell him Clare was in trouble, even though they were technically apart, he'd come to help her against impossible odds, and he'd won through. Clare would be crazy to give up this guy.

Five minutes later she saw Clare walking slowly back through the house as though in a daze. It looked like she'd been crying.

Oh shit! What's happened?

She sat up straighter on the recliner, ready for the worst. Clare walked out into the sun and sat down opposite Jade. The tears were still rolling down her cheeks. She could barely look at Jade.

Jade moved forward to wrap an arm around her shoulder.

"It's okay, girl. Men—I've told you before, you don't need 'em. Whatever he said, it's not true. I always knew he was a waste of space... What did I say? What's he done to you?"

Clare looked up, and as she did, she raised her left hand between them and the broadest of smiles spread across her face. Jade's eyes went wide. She could hardly believe it as she looked down at the ring on Clare's finger.

No words were needed.

She flung her arms around her friend and they cried together.

When McCready got off the phone he found he was sweating and his heart was thumping. He left the half-finished beer on the table in the living room and walked up to the bar and poured a whiskey. He gulped the small glassful down in one go and then poured another. He took it back into the living room and leaned into the deep sofa and took another swig.

"Holy shit, I'm getting married!"

He threw his head back and laughed. He felt a buzz that had been missing for far too long. Everything was falling into place. Maybe now he could finally get his life in order —he realized it was what he had been searching for, for so long—and now was the time.

There was a lot to plan, though. So he thought he'd make a start.

He crossed over to a bureau in the corner of the room. In the second drawer down he pulled out a newspaper cutting. It was from just over a year ago. He placed it on the desk and looked closely at the picture on the front page. It was taken at night and showed a woman diving off one of the capsules on the London Eye, into the Thames. The woman was Clare, and it had become an iconic photograph. It was also the photo that had brought Clare and her father back together after a particularly difficult time of tension between them. He looked down beneath the picture at the photographer's credit—Fergus Beasley.

He did a quick Google search and then found and dialed a number. It was answered on the second ring.

"Hello, Beasley Photography, how can I help?"

"Mr. Beasley, you do shoot weddings, don't you?"

There was a pause. "Sure, mate. I'll shoot whatever you like, so long as you pay the bill."

"Great, how would you like a trip to Africa?"

Chapter Sixty-Two

Two weeks later

John McCready stared out from the first-floor balcony of the hotel dining room onto another world.

He was sitting at the breakfast table and gazed in wonder as the head of a giraffe eased its way over from a tree at the side of the building and moved toward him. It was like the scene in *Jurassic Park* when Dr. Grant and the kids were in the tree and the head of a dinosaur came right up to them. He watched as the nose of the giraffe moved to within a few feet of him and then a long slithery tongue protruded, looking for food.

"Back there on the tree," said McCready with a grin. "This is mine."

"Who are you talking to?" said Clare, as she arrived carrying a buffet breakfast consisting of a bowl of fruit, a croissant and a coffee. She wore a simple light blue halter-neck top and a white sarong and looked amazing.

"Just one of the locals," said McCready.

Clare let out a cry of delight when she saw the giraffe.

"No, over here!" she said hopefully, but the elegant animal had moved back to the branches and was enjoying a mid-morning snack.

Clare put the food down on the table and crossed behind McCready to put her arms around his neck and hug him tightly. She kissed him on the head and smiled. There was no pretense. No doubt. She was happier than she had ever been in her entire life.

The previous two weeks had been a whirlwind.

After it had really sunk in that they were actually going to do this, McCready had thrown all his energy and enthusiasm into putting it together as fast as he could. He had spoken with Clare at length and they had both agreed it should be a simple wedding with just close friends and family attending. She had also loved the idea of Africa as she had never traveled there. She said she was happy for McCready to sort out the location and logistics, but she was going to talk to the hotel about flowers, food and entertainment. McCready had been fine with that. She had also been at a loss as to how quickly she could find a dress, but McCready said he knew someone who might be able to help with that. She just shouldn't ask for any signed albums from the woman's dad. McCready had made the introductions and Clare had been overwhelmed that she had been happy to make something for her, even given the time constraints.

The location was important to McCready.

Many years previously he had saved the daughter of a Maasai Mara tribal chief when he had been working out in Kenya. He had been made an honorary member of the tribe and he'd always had the dream of being married there. Clare had thought it was a lovely idea, and so he had contacted the chief, who had been surprised and honored. He said he would give them a day to remember. McCready had moved the spear the chief had given him to a more prominent position in the center of his wall at home to celebrate.

The next task was who would attend.

From McCready's point of view, obviously Craig, Porter and Charlie would be there. Logan would be sorely missed, but everyone had agreed that he would have wanted the big day to go ahead and would have been so happy for John and Clare.

Also, McCready wasn't sure he should ask, but to his surprise, Prince Khalid Yassin said he wouldn't miss it for the world. He was most upset, though, that he hadn't had more notice, as he could have converted a small palace in Saudi Arabia for the event. The fact that McCready had been banned from Saudi soil didn't seem to factor into the process. He had seemed somewhat put out when McCready had said it was going to be in Africa. McCready had also added that he didn't want any extravagant gifts. With a gleeful smile, Yassin had replied with shock, "Me, extravagant?" McCready dreaded to think what was going to turn up.

He had also assumed Sarah would be there. She was one of his oldest friends as well as being his sister-in-law. He'd been saddened then to hear that Shauna had been ill recently and she didn't think she could get away.

On Clare's side, her father would obviously make the trip. They'd had a long conversation following McCready receiving his permission to marry his daughter. It was something Clare had been thrilled with when she'd heard he had asked him.

Jade would, of course, be coming, and McCready knew that would be fun. He really liked her no BS attitude and they got on like a house on fire. There had been an issue as to where Max would go for the duration. Clare had hated the thought of putting him in a kennel. In the end they'd found a friend of Jade's who would look after him for the week Jade would be away, and then Jade would take him while Clare and McCready were on their honeymoon, which would be an extended tour of some of the countries in Africa. Clare also had a couple of old school friends coming out.

And that was it.

One big argument had ensued when Porter's eyes had lit up at the prospect of a firework display. McCready had said they were in Africa and he didn't want entire rainforests burning down. Porter had looked at him aghast and promised it would be a night people would never forget. That's what worried McCready. Porter had then added that, after all, you couldn't have a wedding night without a massive bang! McCready had shuddered, but it was easier to let him get on with it rather than to try to stop an unstoppable force.

And so it was that everyone had gathered at the Wild View resort in Kenya in one of the most beautiful parts of the world. The resort had rooms in the trees, which was where McCready and Clare's wedding night would be spent. They were both staying separately until then—Charlie and Jade had insisted on it. The two had met up on the ride from the airport and nothing could pry them apart. In fact, Jade had taken quite a shine to her, which had confused Porter no end, though people still weren't sure what Porter and Charlie's relationship actually was, even though they were sharing a room.

After McCready and Clare had watched the giraffe for another ten minutes, he gave her a kiss and then left to see how the arrangements were coming along. There was going to be a sort of bachelor/bachelorette party that evening, though as they'd both be in the same resort they would clearly see what the other was up to.

McCready walked past the large oval pool that filled the area at the back of the two-story hotel. The building curved round in a semicircle, enclosing an outside eating area and space for sunbeds and recliners. The buildings were constructed in a rustic style out of local timber to fit in with the eco-friendly vibe of the resort, which was located at the edge of the rainforest, close to a watering hole, where animals would congregate. In fact, the main event each day was when the sun went down, dusk arrived, and the animals came out from the forest to drink.

McCready was just heading off to find Craig when he heard an approaching roar from the sky. It was coming from the far side of the main building. He couldn't think what it might be and so walked through the entrance lobby to emerge at the front where the cabs pulled up. Beyond the main entrance was open scrubland as far as the eye could see.

A minute later he knew exactly what the noise was.

An Airbus ACH130 helicopter sped toward the resort. At the last minute it banked steeply round to circle the buildings below. It then hovered about a hundred feet away and slowly lowered itself to the ground. As it did, the rotor wash hurled dust and loose debris into the air causing McCready to shield his eyes and cover his nose.

When the rotors had stopped turning, he watched and

smiled as Prince Khalid Yassin stepped down from the cockpit. When he spotted McCready, he threw his hands in the air and strode toward him. He gestured back at the helicopter.

"You like my new toy, John. It's very nice!"

McCready walked slowly forward to greet the prince. They hadn't seen each other since the incident in the Pacific where Yassin had saved his life. The guy was larger than life, but he had honor and he had integrity and he loved him like a brother.

When they met, Yassin threw his arms around McCready, who returned the greeting, though with maybe not quite so much fervor.

Yassin gripped McCready's shoulders and looked at him seriously.

"Now, this woman you are marrying, is she good to you?"

"Yes, Khalid, she's very good to me."

Yassin looked at him seriously. "Let me meet her. I will decide. I cannot have little John marrying someone who is not appropriate. I can always arrange a harem for you if you get bored."

McCready smiled. "I will not get bored, Khalid. I could never be bored with her."

Yassin frowned. "Hmmm, it seems you are truly smitten. Well, we will see. Come, let me buy you a drink."

And with that, Yassin led McCready back inside the main building.

Two hours later, as the sun was starting to go down, everyone met to watch the animals come out to play. McCready had made all the introductions and everyone was getting along famously. It was a fantastic feeling as they crowded on the high wooden viewing terrace overlooking the waterhole.

The first to arrive were a couple of warthogs, followed by some hyenas. A lion made its presence felt, which caused a bit of a ruckus among the smaller animals, and then the highlight of the evening was when a family of elephants came down to drink. Clare grabbed McCready's arm when she saw a baby playing in the shallow lake. It sucked up some water with its trunk and sprayed its mother. She pulled him close.

"It's like the *Jungle Book*," she said with a dreamy gleam in her eyes. "I love you so much!"

He held her tight and whispered back, "I love you too."

They watched for another half hour.

McCready noticed that Beasley seemed to be enjoying the assignment. As well as snapping photos of the guests, he'd brought a small drone he flew over the waterhole to catch an aerial view of the animals in their natural habitat. After he'd covered the wildlife, he flew it along the line of watching guests as they gave a verbal verdict on McCready and Clare's coming big day. Needless to say, the video would require extensive editing.

After the waterhole, you couldn't really top that, so they all made their way down to a sumptuous buffet that had been laid out around the pool. The food was delicious and the alcohol flowed. Everyone was having a great time.

After the meal, the guys and the girls seemed to drift off into their respective groups, and while they were doing their own thing, McCready would occasionally glance over at Clare and their eyes would meet. They were having a fantastic time with their friends, but it was clear they only had eyes for each other.

The evening turned into night.

As things started to wind down, many of the guests drifted off to their rooms. McCready found himself sitting on a recliner by the pool with Richards. He took a swig of port and watched the reflection of lights in the water.

"I'm so happy for you, John," said Richards. "You two are so right for each other."

McCready looked up through a haze of alcohol. His sleepy eyes broke into a smile.

"Yeah, she is kind of great."

He looked away into the distance for a moment, and then took a deep breath.

"I wish Sean could have been here."

Richards was quiet for a moment, thinking about McCready's brother.

"I'm sure he's looking down and toasting the two of you. He would have really loved Clare. Been so happy for you."

McCready took another drink.

"Yes, yes he would."

He then leaned back on the recliner and raised his glass to the amazing sky that was filled with stars.

Tomorrow was a whole new day.

It was the beginning of the rest of his life.

Chapter Sixty-Three

When McCready awoke on his wedding day, for a moment, he wondered why he was alone in the bed, but then he smiled. A second later, though, he groaned as the excesses of the previous evening made their presence felt. He gazed at the ceiling for a minute, but no amount of hangover could destroy the warm, fuzzy feeling he had inside.

He had never felt like this—ever.

Period.

And it felt so right.

He eased himself slowly out of bed, grabbed a glass of water from the bathroom and swallowed a couple of Advil. Next, he walked into the shower and let the jets pummel his body.

An hour later, having grabbed a quick breakfast, he was standing in the room, with Craig, his best man, putting the finishing touches to his apparel for the ceremony. They had decided that while they wanted to be smart, there would be a certain informality to the day. Suits were required and McCready had not even grumbled at the application of a tie. But after the ceremony they would all change into lighter, more casual attire.

After Richards had told him all the usual best man things and dutifully tried to talk him out of it—a complete waste of breath—they had gathered at the front of the hotel to wait for the transport out to the tribal village where the ceremony would be held.

As was befitting the location, most of them were traveling in Land Rovers, but Yassin had insisted he escort Clare and her father in the helicopter. McCready was pretty sure this had nothing to do with treating the bride like royalty and more to do with protecting the royal derrière from the ruts and bumps of the track that led to the village, but McCready didn't begrudge him that. It also meant Clare and her father would arrive in style and her father would get his first ride in a helicopter.

At one o'clock precisely the ceremony began.

It was taking place in a large covered area at one end of the village. The women of the tribe had decked out the wooden structure with flowers and garlands and it looked beautiful in the hot African sun.

Everyone was ready, standing in the small covered structure, when the howling roar of the helicopter approached. Yassin respectfully landed behind some trees a few hundred yards away, so as not to blow everyone's clothes off.

A few minutes later there were gasps from the assembled group as Clare walked up to the end of the aisle on her father's arm. McCready couldn't help but take a breath when he saw her. The dress was perfect. It was a light cream color, and simple, shaped to flow elegantly as she walked, but not so long that it scraped on the dirt of the ground below. Clare was beaming behind a chic veil. Her hair was done up with ringlets tumbling down either side of her face.

Local tribal music played and singers from the tribe sang as she walked up the short aisle to where McCready was waiting. There was a hush from the guests as they took in the dress and how beautiful Clare looked.

When she reached the end of the aisle, she let go of her father's arm and walked the final few steps to McCready. They gazed into each other's eyes for a moment and then turned to face the holy man from the village. It was a mix of two ceremonies—traditional and African.

The rings were exchanged.

They both agreed to honor and respect one another.

And then they kissed to unite their love.

There was barely a dry eye in the house. Charlie even had to pass Porter a tissue, though afterwards he claimed some dirt had been blown into his eye by a slight breeze that had sprung up.

Following the nuptials, everyone was on a high, not least the two newlyweds.

They spent several hours in the village, having changed from their formal clothes.

McCready introduced Clare to the chief and his daughter, who now had a little girl of her own. They teased Clare relentlessly as to when she and McCready might start a family. Clare had laughed it off, but looked at McCready with eager eyes. He had loved the look.

The whole proceedings were finished off with a firework display to end all firework displays. Porter was in his element. Mercifully no trees or buildings were set alight. The finale consisted of a series of banks of rockets that shot into the sky to spell out the name of the happy couple in a myriad of colorful explosions. Everyone had cheered and Porter had never looked so pleased with himself.

Eventually it was time to head back to the hotel.

Clare said she would travel in the Land Rover with McCready and her father, while her two school friends jumped at the chance of a helicopter ride with a real-life prince. McCready had told Yassin to behave himself. He had vowed to do so, but it was something McCready had not been entirely convinced by, having seen the wink that accompanied the statement.

Half an hour later they were back at the resort.

After changing again, McCready was making his way down to the pool when he saw a train of cases being wheeled through the hotel foyer. He followed them. When he arrived at the front he saw Yassin directing the porters with the luggage.

"You're leaving, Khalid?" said McCready.

"I have to get back," said Yassin. "There is work to do in the kingdom. But thank you, John, for inviting me. And you were right, you have a very good woman with Clare. In fact, if you were not…"

McCready thumped him playfully but was then distracted by a noise in the sky. It sounded like another helicopter approaching. They walked across the dirt track outside the hotel to where Yassin's chopper was parked. They watched the new one come in to land. When it did, Yassin shouted at the porters. They scurried around carrying his bags to the new arrival. The pilot shut down the rotors and walked toward them.

McCready looked on, confused.

"What, your new toy break down?"

Yassin turned to him with a massive grin.

"Hold out your hand."

McCready did so, not sure where this was going.

"Not my new toy… your new toy!" He dropped a set of

keys into McCready's palm. The pilot had arrived and stood patiently behind Yassin.

McCready stared at him incredulously.

"My wedding gift to you and Clare." Yassin beamed.

"Jesus, Khalid! What am I going to do with it? I can't fly a helicopter."

But Yassin was not deterred. He stepped to one side to reveal the pilot from the second helicopter.

"It comes with Hassan, here. He will take you wherever you wish to go." Hassan bowed slightly.

"What, like Scotland?"

"If you wish, John, but I think that is a very long way. There is a transport plane waiting at Mara Serena Airport to take it back for you. You don't like it?" he said, looking unhappy.

"It's wonderful. But you can't go around giving people helicopters."

"It would appear now, that I can, wouldn't it?" said Yassin with a grin.

He then stepped forward and hugged McCready. McCready smiled and looked at him with appreciation.

"Thank you, my friend. I'm sure we'll meet again sometime."

Yassin grinned. "You know we will... And may the adventure be greater when we do," he said with a flourish. And with that he strode off to the second helicopter and climbed aboard.

When it had taken off and the noise had finally died down, McCready turned to Hassan.

"Hi... John McCready."

"Very nice to meet you, sir," said Hassan.

Ten minutes later, McCready still hadn't got over the shock of owning a helicopter. He had grabbed a beer from the bar and was just wandering through the main building, when his phone rang. He answered it.

"John, it's Martin Steel."

McCready hesitated.

"Yes," he said cautiously.

"Just wanted to send you many congratulations."

McCready paused.

"How the hell did you know?"

He could hear Steel sigh over the phone. "John, you should know by now... In fact, I have a drone two thousand feet above you. Looks like a great party."

McCready ran outside and looked up at the sky, shocked by the revelation.

"You, son of a..."

"Just kidding!"

McCready relaxed and smiled.

"Had me going there... Anything else?"

"No, just have a great day and I wish you every happiness."

"Thanks." And McCready hung up.

He was about to head off to the pool to find Clare when he heard shouting coming from the TV room.

He wandered inside.

The TV was on. It was showing the end of the Brazilian Grand Prix. A few of the hotel staff were there relaxing, as well as Charlie. She grinned when she saw him.

"Come and sit down, John. It's a great race."

He joined her on the wide sofa. McCready felt somewhat guilty, but sat down to watch what was left of the race. A few minutes later Richards walked in. He saw McCready and Charlie and plonked himself down next to them.

"Jade and two of Clare's friends turned up and started

talking dresses," he said by way of explanation. "Thought it was time to leave."

McCready grinned and took a swig of beer. They then all turned their attention to the race.

Out by the pool, Porter wandered in from the carpark. He'd been packing up the display equipment and made it back later than everyone else. On the far side, Clare and her friends were chatting by the water. He crossed over to them.

"Hey, any of you guys seen Charlie?"

Clare looked up and smiled.

"That was an amazing show, Eugene. Thank you so much."

The other girls also looked up at him and smiled. He blushed somewhat.

"Not sure where Charlie is," said Clare, "but she did say something about watching a race."

Porter rolled his eyes.

"Thanks."

"By the way, if you see John, can you tell him I'm looking for him."

"Will do," said Porter.

He headed up toward the main building and followed the noise to the TV room.

He saw Charlie and then McCready and Richards. He walked up to stand directly behind the sofa. He stared at the screen, shaking his head.

The race had ended and the commentator was replaying the final moments, saying it was yet another convincing win for the silver arrows as a silver and black car shot across the finish line. The image then changed to the podium, where two drivers walked up and waved at the crowd. Then, as he watched, he saw a fit-looking black guy climb up onto the top step.

He moved closer.

"'Ere, that's that geezer who gave me a lift in Monaco."

McCready, Richards and Charlie all turned to stare up at him.

"What?" said Richards.

"Yeah," said Porter, looking closer, "the one who picked me off the road when those muppets threw me in the boot."

McCready looked at him like he'd walked in from Mars.

"That's one of the greatest racing drivers who ever lived," said McCready.

"Well," continued Porter, "whoever he is, I gave him some pointers on gear changes. His were a bit rough if you ask me. Looks like it paid off."

McCready shook his head.

Porter was about to leave when he remembered something.

"Oh yeah, Clare's looking for you, guv. I wouldn't get caught watching this on your wedding night if I was you."

McCready looked guilty and stood up.

"Yeah, you're right. Thought she was busy with Jade and her friends."

"Yeah, but when the missus calls… and all that. Whole new world now. Of course, that would never happen to me," said Porter confidently.

Charlie looked up with a scowl.

"Hey, Eugene, can you get me a beer?"

"Yes, luv," said Porter quickly. He noticed McCready looking at him as he stood up.

"Not a word, guv! Not a word!"

McCready found Clare sitting on her own by the pool. The others had gone to bed and she was dangling her feet in the water. When she heard him approach she looked up and broke into a smile. He sat down next to her.

"Thank you, John. Thank you for an amazing day."

She nuzzled into his neck. He held her and kissed her hair.

"I love you so much," he said. She didn't reply, but the contented sigh told him all he needed to know.

They stayed like that for a couple of minutes, then McCready looked up.

"Hey, you want to go for a walk by the waterhole?"

Clare looked at him.

"You think it'll be safe?"

"Sure, we can check if there are any animals and stay back if anything turns up."

Clare looked at him and stood eagerly.

They walked arm in arm down to the water. There was very little activity. A few smaller animals had taken advantage of the lack of large predators and were lapping at the water. They raised their heads with concern when they saw McCready and Clare approaching, but quickly realized they were no threat and went back to drinking and washing themselves.

The two of them stood in the darkness for several minutes, soaking up the experience and relishing each other's company.

"John," said Clare eventually, "I've never been happier."

"Me neither," said McCready. "This is the beginning of the rest of our lives. Everything is going to be different from now. I promise."

"I love you."

They walked further along the edge of the water and

then stood with the sounds of nature all around and a carpet of stars above their heads.

It was good to be alive.

And in that moment, McCready found himself thinking back over the tumultuous events of the previous few weeks and the impact they'd had on him.

No one could know for sure what the future held.

Solano had tried to change that, force his version of it onto the world, but in the end, who was he to say what would happen? Things certainly looked as though they would be challenging going forward, but the human race had always risen to challenges.

McCready was hopeful, in the final analysis, they would do so again now.

Epilogue

Molly Seager stacked the rest of the packets and letters onto the mail trolley and set off to do her rounds. She had always been told that if you started in the mail room you could go on to do great things in an organization by applying yourself and working hard, and that was exactly what she intended to do.

She walked down the short corridor to the entrance hall of the main admin block at Pinewood Studios. She then headed out into the fresh Buckinghamshire air.

Situated just under twenty miles to the west of London, Pinewood was where some of the world's most iconic films had been made, as well as installments of many of the modern blockbuster franchises, such as, Marvel, Star Wars, Superman, Mission Impossible, and the most iconic of them all—the Bond films. The studios were the spiritual and indeed physical home for Bond. The largest stage was called the 007 Stage and there was a Roger Moore Stage and a John Barry Theatre.

Molly loved the history that seeped from the walls as she

made her way around the corridors of the buildings and alleyways between the stages. And while she was merely dropping off the mail today, one day she dreamed of working in the movies for real.

Forty-five minutes later she was coming to the end of her round. Her second-to-last call was to the Garden Suite, a single-story building set behind the admin block that was the studio base of Eon Productions, the makers of the Bond films.

She pushed through the glass swing door and checked the mail to leave behind. There were ten normal-sized letters and a few packages.

She said *hi* to Jane, the PA at the desk at the entrance, and handed her the mail.

Then she left.

Jane flicked through the items. She selected some to open later, and those she wasn't sure about to prioritize in case they were important. There were a number of bills, some fan mail, and then one that, when she opened it, she looked at curiously. All there was inside was a photograph with a series of numbers written across it. She checked the postmark—Oban, Scotland.

She stared at the photograph again. It was a publicity shot of a silver Aston Martin DB5 taken way back in the day. She then looked more closely at the numbers.

They looked a lot like coordinates.

John McCready put the finishing touches to two ham-and-cheese omelets. He served them up onto plates and then carried them through to the dining area of his house in Scotland.

Clare looked up as he approached.

"And he can cook," she said with a smile.

McCready gave her a hug from behind and sat down at the table. She brought up the ring on her finger and smiled even more broadly.

The honeymoon had been a wonderful two weeks in Africa, much of which had been seen from the air in their shiny new helicopter. They had come back refreshed and alive like never before. They would be heading back to the States in a few days as Clare had to go and pick up Max and they had a lot to talk about with regards to the future, but there was time for that. There was no hurry.

A TV had the news on in the background. There was something about a plane crash in Australia but then the picture flicked to a lake in Switzerland. McCready thought he recognized the place and turned up the volume.

On the screen was a shot of a salvage barge sitting on the glass-smooth water. A tall crane was winching something up through the surface, disturbing the pristine reflection of the mountains. When McCready saw what it was he glanced at Clare. The presenter was explaining what was going on.

"Work has been underway to recover what is thought to be the original Aston Martin DB5 that was made famous in the James Bond film *Goldfinger*. It was stolen from a hanger in Florida in 1997 and not seen since. There has been no word as to how it was located, or any confirmation if this is the original car. From what can be seen so far, the front has sustained considerable damage and the passenger seat is missing."

Clare had started to listen to the report.

"All that fuss over a car! And the movies are a bit daft. I mean... a car with an ejector seat... come on!"

She shook her head and gave McCready a hopeless expression.

"Oh, I don't know. You never know when they might come in handy. I was thinking of getting one for the Range Rover."

She looked at him incredulously.

"You are kidding, right?"

"Yeah, maybe," said McCready with a smile.

Clare shook her head again before tucking back into her omelet.

"You know, this isn't half bad. I could get used to this!"

McCready raised his eyebrows.

"In your dreams. Honeymoon period's over, you know!" he said with a grin.

It was Clare's turn to raise her eyebrows.

They both stared at each other and burst out laughing.

The future was going to be a whole new adventure.

More by Mike Seares

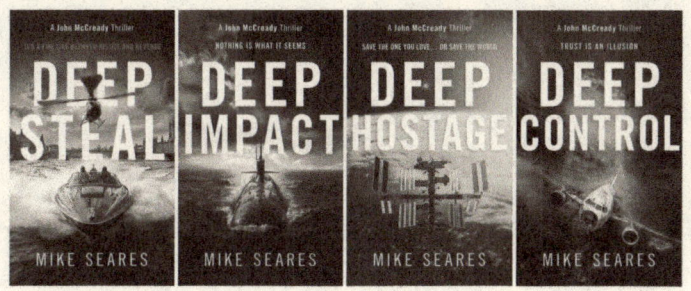

vinci-books.com/JohnMcCready

Follow the link to stay up to date with Mike Seares' new releases

About the Author

Throughout my life I have always tried to seek out adventure, whether real or imaginary. Much of this has taken place in, on, or under the water.

My love of diving has allowed me to explore the oceans of the world and also work extensively in the film and TV industry.

This spirit has filtered through to my creative writing, which includes the John McCready thrillers - a smart, fast paced action/adventure series with twists and turns right up to the end.

In the real world, **LIGHTS! CAMERA! SUB ACTION!** takes you behind the scenes of underwater projects in the film and TV industry.

But the one thing all the books have in common, is a sense of excitement and the unknown; whether journeying with a hero battling the odds on thrilling and dangerous adventures, or diving sunken shipwrecks and coral reefs in the company of sharks, manta rays and other creatures of the deep.

Lights! Camera! Sub Action!

A behind-the-scenes look at working on underwater projects in the film and TV industry.

Available in all good bookstores online